WINTER ON THE BAYOU

A Stone Cold Adventure

Robert Knox

Robert Knox

Thanks to those of you who read the first book and continued following the series despite my lack of an Editor. I I want to especially thank those of you who took the time to leave a review. I can't tell you how helpful your feedback is.

I have to also thank my amazing wife, whose love and support carry me through my self doubt and childish fears.

CONTENTS

Look for more adventures with JC coming soon.

CHAPTER 1

TRAVELING WITH THE KING

Leaving Waco with King was an experience, the man cut a wide path no matter where he went. I had to admit it made the trail easy, the entire trip was so peaceful I wondered if the Bar C just had bad luck. No one with any sense wanted to cross him or his men. The reputation they had cultivated cleared all roadblocks long before we encountered them. The land rolled by under our horses like a great sea, its waves were rolling hills and arroyos. The trail changed from a dusty path created by thousands of cattle to a road carved out by wagons, settlers and teamsters all contributing to its creation. I knew it was nothing new to the men I traveled with but to me it was an all-new experience.

Slowly the land transformed from the dry scrub that fought the harsh environment into a lush green place full of life. The air changed as we traveled too becoming heavier, thankfully not as oppressive as the summer would be but still humid. The moisture in the air lent itself to the plant life that sprung up with a vigor all around us. Trees grew to cover the trail creating a deep tunnel of shadows that held hidden secrets.

The further we traveled the more it changed. The wildlife transformed with it, life creating life in a never-ending cycle. Insect life was the first to appear. Beetles of every color crawled across the ground, every shape and type of flying creature hummed in the air. This also birthed an increase in flying pests, it was slow at first but the more we traveled to worse it got. By the time we crossed into Louisiana you couldn't take a step without something buzzing in your face.

The reptiles changed with the landscape, growing larger and more diverse. The rattlers were still around but their coloration changed, their scales darkening, allowing them to blend in easier. Black snakes, copperheads and a multitude of others I couldn't name slithered through the brush. Some of the mounts shied away from them, Danu's response to them was different. She didn't shy or try and balk, instead she stomped them one after another. By the time we reached the outskirts of Lisbon she had racked up a fair number of kills. More than once I had to check and make sure they hadn't managed to bite her.

Much like the world around us the people living there changed too. More travelers passed us, going in one direction or the other, all giving us a wide berth. Settled areas became more frequent along the road as well, the population expanding to match the natural resources. The language gradually changed with them. The slow southern twang invading, mixed with a heavy French influence replacing the heavy drawl of Texas. I knew that Louisiana had a strong history with the French, so it was no surprise to start hearing the language mixed with English. I had studied the Louisiana purchase while I was in school and understood that the population had mixed opinions on it.

With the ease of water the ranches gradually changed to farms, smaller and more densely packed. Sharecroppers and independent men trying to wrestle a living out of the land just like people I had seen on the trail. Small towns slowly grew around old trading posts. The tide of civilization ever growing, consuming more and more of the natural world with it.

Everyone was more wary, you could see it in their reactions toward us. Cowboys and outlaws shared the same look often enough that anyone this close to the nations learned to be careful around them. They were polite but not overly friendly, the few houses we stopped at for easy water kept their women out of sight. Shotgun barrels stuck out of windows and barns, not threatening but watchful.

The nights were easier the camp sites, obviously used repeatedly by travelers, were more comfortable. This wasn't by accident it was by natural design since each one held a spring or seep that constantly filled with fresh water. It struck me that even as we conquered nature to build our safe homes, we were following its lead. Creatures of all sorts depended on the life-giving water that it offered. The animals and plants that fed us also depended on it. I had learned long ago that you didn't find water when you were out in the wilds, you found life. That life would lead you to water if you knew how to follow the signs. The camp sites were markers of that story, used over and over again all because of that one resource.

The evidence of this was painted on the rocks. The art was weather worn speaking to its age, it was obvious the native people had created most of them. Which tribe and how long ago they had been made was a mystery I would never solve. Those tribes had been pushed off their land long before the current tribes existed. These were stories left by people that were here long before any of our ancestors ever came to this country. There was no way for me to know who they were meant for but the very idea that they existed fascinated me.

Simple handprints or stick figure animals and hunters.

Some were more obvious, at least I thought so. Simple waving lines that I presumed meant water or shapes that you could tell represented game of some kind being stalked by men. The most interesting of them was the repeated large four-legged creatures.

To give perspective in size the creator had added men surrounding it as they attacked. Whatever animal this represented must have been larger than the elephants I had seen in circuses. The drawings had the tusks like those great creatures, that much I could see for sure. The mystery left me stumped, there were no creature I knew of that could match that image. What really got my mind working was when one of the older hands traveling with us told me he had seen the same thing painted on caves in the Dakota territory.

What great beast could face that many men and from every indication prevail over them? A vague memory of an article tickled at the back of my mind. It was written by a scientist from France who was exploring the new country. He had proven that several large animals had existed long ago in this country. The remains of one were similar to elephants from India and Africa but much larger. I racked my mind for half of a day before the name came to me, the natural sciences had never been a strong interest.

That Frenchman had called them Woolly Mammoths, proving through remains the differences between the species.

Even documenting evidence that they were covered in fur. It was published back in 1790 or there about and brought a whole new type study to light when it was accepted. This couldn't represent that same animal though, if I remembered the article right he postulated that the mammoth he spoke of had died out millions of years ago.

Things like this sent my mind racing with questions, most of which I would never answer. It helped keep me occupied along the road. Who were the people that had been here before? What creatures had they hunted or hunted them? To further disprove the ignorant cow puncher theory many had wonder about this. I discovered I wasn't alone in this fascination one night sitting around the fire.

When the topic came up it turned out several of the hands had an interest in the fossils and paintings that could be found across the country. Some like me knew the native people spoke of legends that went back further than any history we knew. After offering the ones I knew to the conversation, a few more chimed in with theirs. One had spent some time with the Crow and talked about the stories he had heard. A few others had stories from various other tribes. It was obvious that oral traditions often dated back further than any written word ever could.

We were all keenly aware of Christendom firmly believing that our planet was 6000 years old, despite all evidence to the contrary. Condemning any scientist who attempted to put forward evidence regarding this with cries of heresy and threats of excommunication. Most recently Darwin's theory of evolution. It was groundbreaking and had caused quite a large disturbance. The catholic church had quickly condemned the work of course. I had read the study he based it on and found it compelling. His study of animals on an isolated island seemed to prove it true. I wasn't the only one who had studied Darwin's work and thought it interesting.

Several of the hands had gotten a copy, there had been some serious debates in the bunkhouses about it. A few even coming to blows between them and the more religious punchers. Finally that part had been settled by a puncher named Left. His solution was brilliant in its simplicity. He said that the lords day were likely a lot longer then twenty four hours. So those first seven days could have been millions of years. There was still some arguments but most accepted the idea as a pretty good middle ground.

This was what kept my mind occupied as we traveled. My thoughts wandering across time, trying to understand the people who had walked these paths before me. Picturing the animals that once stalked these lands was another way to fill the hours. Good mysteries with no answer, but my curiosity wouldn't let them rest. It started me on a personal quest of sorts.

I replayed my own thin knowledge of the legends I knew and began writing them down. I also wrote down the ones the other hands told me. Trying to piece them together and apply them to the paintings when I could. From now on I would pay more attention to the stories, using them to try and unravel this mystery. The paintings from rocks and cave walls were sketched with them, starting my own odd collection in a notebook. I would transfer them into a better one eventually. I also noted the time and place I found them.

That's why I was almost surprised when we rode into Lisbon that afternoon. At the edge of town the trail hands split off to find their own place to stay. King led myself and Smokey to a place that looked like the most luxurious in town, not my preference but for now I would follow the man's lead.

It was a massive three-story building in the center of town. It felt older and had an ominous air about it. Nice enough but it felt off, more than my own discomfort at its luxury. It wasn't the obvious wealth and finery it represented, there was something darker in its history. The front desk had a placard hanging below the counter, telling the story of what I felt. The building had originally been a working plantation, it even noted the number of slave it once had. It had survived the late unpleasantness simply because it was far enough away that no troops had bothered taking the area.

The comfort it now represented contrasted starkly with

the slavery that had built it. In some odd karmic twist a carpetbagger from Maine now owned it. If I believed the talk from the stable hands, he had taken it in the distasteful way a lot of southern places had been. Working with the new local judge, appointed during reunification, he had forced the original owners out using taxes. To me it seemed like a cloud of bad air hung about the place no matter how nice it looked.

After months on the trail, I had started getting used to sleeping outdoors. It would have been more comfortable for me sleeping in the loft above the stables. I would admit part of that was the history of the place. That first night did make me laugh,16 years of sleeping in a big comfy house suddenly the mattress was too soft for comfort. Sleep was slow in coming because my mind wandered over the walls in my room painting pictures of the horrors that had made this place.

CHAPTER 2

KINGS OFFER

I was a bit surprised to receive an invite to dinner from King. We had talked briefly on the road, but the big man was notoriously picky about sharing meals with working hands. Thankfully I had gotten most of my laundry back already, so I was dressed in clean clothes when I joined him for dinner. Even than I was underdressed for the formal dining room but all I had was trail clothes. Most would write it off as the inexperience of youth and ignore me anyway. The man who seated me managed not to look too far down his nose at least, especially once he heard I was joining King.

He waved me over to his private table, evidently it would be just the two of us. I hoped Smokey would join us, I liked and understood him. King, on the other hand, was a mystery. His aloof nature after having built his place from nothing but dust confused me. This was a man who had damn near killed himself building his ranch. From the stories I heard the man fought, scrabbled and dug it out of nothing. Now he separated himself from the men and it wasn't by accident. He wouldn't even share the same fire on the trail, only Smokey was allowed at at his fire and then only for business. I wasn't sure it made sense to me. It was so different from the example Max set.

"Mr. King." I shook the big man's hand before sitting down and pouring myself a cup of coffee. That got me a glare from the waiter, who was standing beside the table. He eyed me for a second before reaching for my hat, which I had hung on the seat beside me. I stopped him cold before he touched it. "That's fine where it's at."

"It's my pleasure, I don't often take meals with my hands but I do enjoy the company of well-read individuals. Though I had another reason to request your company this evening." The man's deep soft tone didn't ever ask a question. It was one of the things about him that bothered me. "I wanted the chance to talk to you before Mr. Thornton sweeps in. I sent a message to him this morning, he wants you at the ranch tomorrow if possible."

"Figured he was anxious about getting Danu back." I tried not to grimace when I said it.

"Seems so." His eyes locked on mine. They didn't look soft but there was a hint of understanding in them. "I know what it's like to have to give up a partner like Danu. You being willing to do so speaks well of your character Mr. Stone."

"Please, call me JC." I offered. Not at all expecting the man to return the favor but I still felt too young to be called mister. "Like doesn't have much to do with it, right is right. She isn't mine to keep, not really."

"I prefer to keep things more formal if you don't mind." He smiled apologetically. It made me wonder even more about the man's habits. "Something being right doesn't make it pleasant. You are of course correct, it's still what men must do."

"That has been my experience, short though it may be." I admitted with a laugh.

"I wanted to have dinner because I heard several things in Waco that, well frankly, I find hard to believe." He held up his hand to stop me before I could ask what he was referring too. "I believe them because of the men who told me. They just don't seem to match the young man sitting across from me."

"Ask anything you like sir. I don't think I have any secrets. If it's something I prefer not to discuss I'll speak up."

"That fair enough, how old are you JC?" As always the man was direct.

"Sixteen, headed toward 17 now."

"And you studied law in New York?" To my surprise the man didn't react the way most people did, no look of surprise or denial about my age.

"Yes sir. Mother insisted on it, father paid for it." I hesitated before adding. "The man is my father, but he and my mom never married. He was or is a duke back in the old country, mother is common stock, despite their love that just isn't done."

"It doesn't seem to bother you?" His eyebrows had arched up at my response, showing shock for the first time.

"He's a good man, the situation with my mother was beyond his control. I can either be pissed about something neither could control or accept it and move on. He always took care of us, even telling his wife about us. She was the one who started my education." I smiled fondly, remembering them both.

"So, no tragedy to drive you out here as a puncher? You wanted this life? Mr. Connors spoke about that education as well." I didn't mind his questions but wondered where he was going with them.

"Of sorts, the stable man where I grew up had a friend. An old mountain man who retired to a family farm. He and some of Iroquois taught me what they could. It kept me dreaming and helped prepare me." The chuckle in my voice was apparent, remembering their favorite description of me. "They all figured I was too fiddle-footed to stay away from the shining mountains."

"There's a term I hadn't heard in years. Max thought highly of the way you handled things. Not just the violence but how hard you worked to keep your name clear. He said you were very determined to avoid a reputation?"

"Just did what I could, tried not to be too clever about it. As far as the name goes, it's something no sane man wants."

"I don't know if I agree with that." He smiled, and I knew he was thinking of his own reputation. "There is a point when a name makes a difference. My reputation, for example, makes most of those on the hoot owl trail step aside."

"That's true, but you have a reputation for hard justice not as a gun hawk. As far as I know none of your hands carry that moniker either. As a group their name is a warning but not a man among them does. Its about the same for the Bar C riders, your's is a bit bigger admittedly."

"That's true, never could abide trouble hunters." It was all the man said before continuing his questioning. "That being said Max and Smythe both had high opinions of your ability to handle yourself. More importantly they thought your mind was your strongest tool."

"Appreciate their words. Mostly I have just been dealing things as they come while trying to stay above ground."

"Fair but you have an intelligent and thoughtful mind without letting your pride trip you up. That's not a common thing in someone your age. Which brings me to the topic at hand." Of all things I expected, Richard King looking embarrassed wasn't one of them. "I have a troublesome situation that I need some help with. I called in a favor from Max to hire you until spring. He was adamant about having you back at the Bar C for the gather. I would like to employ you until then."

"Well…"

"Please let me lay it all out, if you're not interested I'll rely on your discretion and we can part company." The look he gave me was clear, this was personal, and I should keep my trap shut while he explained it. "Many years ago, I invested some money into a small business in New Orleans. This particular business was one of my early investments and done as a favor. It's not what you would call a church going business, to be direct it's a bordello. The lady who runs it, my partner in the business, needs some help. With my reputation I'm a very silent partner and am limited in how I can aid her."

"That's understandable." I wasn't shocked, it made sense for him to have diverse investments. Having some that might not be viewed well in the upper crust of society wasn't too surprising.

"It seems a new group has come into the area and are doing their best to force her out. They have no idea I exist, much less that I am her partner. My name would probably back them off, but the truth is it would cost me more then the business is worth." He took a slow deep breath before continuing.

"I have stayed invested because Cherie saved my life, that is actually why I got involved at all. When I was younger someone tried to kill me one night." His tone was serious but I could see this was all hard for him to admit. "To be fair, I was a bit rough around the edges back then and put myself in the situation. The specifics don't matter so I won't go into them. They left me bleeding in an alley and she found me there."

I watched his face as he told me the story, it was an interesting mix of emotions that played out there. First it was cold, just a story but as the memories took life in his mind I could see through the cracks. The pain of the attack, relief at not dying and finally the gratitude he felt toward the girl.

"Instead of walking away, like most would have back then, she took care of me. That was 1850 or so, I was still working the river boats. The men who stabbed me were dealt with after I recovered but I felt indebted to the young whore who saved me. In 1866 after the late unpleasantness, I bought a building and refurbished it as my part of the investment. She has run it successfully ever since and has been an honest business partner, so far as I know."

"Damn." Was all I could say, it was one hell of a story. It also spoke well of the man sitting across from me. A lot of men would have just thrown her some money if anything and been down with it. King had gone further, giving the woman some power over her own life. Things like that were hard to come by for most people, powerful men very rarely gave away such things. He paused to study me carefully while the waiter put our steaks on the table with a fresh pot of coffee.

"Please eat while I talk." He waved me toward my steak. "The short of it is she's raised enough money to buy me out. We were about to finalize the sale when the trouble started. I am still unclear about what happened, but it seems some businessman wants not only the business but her as well. It appears he has some designs on marrying her, taking the business that way rather then buying it out right. According to her the man is a toad but one with money to hire guns and lawyers."

"They haven't hurt her or the girls, but they chase off her clients. The local law is either paid off or uninterested in the seedy businesses, so they won't help. Reaching out to me was her last resort. I had considered hiring the Pinkerton's, but they could be easily traced back to me." He paused to take a bite of his steak before it got cold. "You see where this is headed I hope?"

"I am unaffiliated and from what you have been told capable. Basically I seem like a cleaner option?" I answered him after swallowing. Doing my best to not let this conversation ruin a damn fine steak, it was nicely seasoned and cooked perfectly.

"Exactly so, it's worth a thousand dollars plus expenses to me if you can solve it without my name coming up." He locked eyes with me when he said the last, hammering his point home. "I have a house in the city you can use while you're there. It's buried in business names so no one will know I own it expect my lawyer. Tillman is aware of everything going on and if you agree I'll wire him so he can arrange everything."

We paused the conversation while I considered the idea and we finished off our dinner. It was a meal worth eating, more then that I really needed to consider all this before answering.

"Let me be clear on what you're asking before I agree." Sipping my coffee to wash down the last bite of green beans.

"You're not asking me to simply go kill this man?"

"Absolutely not!" He sounded as offended as I expected at the idea.

"I thought not, but this is business and it's best to be clear. I meant no offense."

"Of course." His lips were a tight line when he responded. I could tell he was still unhappy about that question but understood why I asked.

"You want me to sort it out, you don't care how as long as I protect her and the business while keeping your name out of it?"

"I don't want Assassinations but outside of that yes."

"If there is violence I will handle it as I see fit, there won't be a limit Mr. King." My tone had gone cold, and he noticed the change.

"No there won't be. I merely wanted to make it clear that was not my goal." He was stiff in his chair, not afraid but aware that there was a side of me to be wary of. One that the polite young man who first sat down kept hidden most of the time. I could see him beginning to believe the stories Max had told him.

"Last thing. If I go there and the story doesn't line up with what you've been told. I will walk away."

"If that's the case you come and tell me, I'll pay the full amount and handle it through other means. If I am being played the fool, I would very much like to know." His tone was gruff, not quite dismissive but close.

"I understand and we have an agreement. I make no promises though, I won't throw my life away." I said sticking out my hand.

"I'll wire Mr. Tillman tomorrow, he's the attorney that will be your contact in the city. As well as your attorney should you need him." He said after we shook hands. He was visibly more relaxed now, this must have been weighing on him. "Do you mind if I ask why?"

"Why do it? Several reasons Mr. King." I grinned and took another sip of my coffee. "First it gives me an excuse to go to

New Orleans rather than line ride for the winter. Second it's for you, that's not a small thing in the cattle business. Not that you'll owe me but simply being able to speak to you in some instances will open doors for me. I do have plans past punching cattle."

"That's fair, you'll have my appreciation for handling this Mr. Stone." He looked me in eyes as he spoke.

"It's appreciated but that's not the biggest reason. The simple truth is I can't abide a man using any woman like that Mr. King." I would take the money, but that wasn't what made the decision. "Whore or lady, it doesn't matter to me, it just isn't something I can sit back and ignore. I can't stand a bully."

"Please call me Richard or just King, either is fine. I feel I was abrupt earlier when I spoke about formality."

"Think I'll stick with King if that's okay, was the first name I heard, so it's stuck now. That's my reason, if the information you have is accurate."

"On that we agree, I have never tolerated a bully and worked hard to not be seen as one. I do appreciate you looking into this though, despite the payment I will feel in your debt. If you ever need my help, you'll have it."

"Once I get Danu out to Thortons I'll head to New Orleans. Mind doing me a favor?"

"Of course not." He agreed but his curiosity was piqued.

"If I get a good cow pony from him can you take it back with you? I'll pick up a riding mount from the livery if I need too. I don't want to take a working horse to New Orleans." My mind was already planning. "I'll probably take a boat across the gulf to Corpus Christi when it's done."

"Max didn't over estimate your mind, you think quick. Plan for things most would miss." King smiled admirably. "If you get a good horse I'll take it, if not there'll be a good horse ready for you when you reach Corpus Christi as a bonus."

"Works." I nodded my agreement.

"Tillman will have all the information when you get to the city, and the key for the house. It's a small place, shouldn't make you stand out much. There's a small stable with it, just enough for two horses." As he spoke he slid an envelope across the table to me. "Here's $200 for expenses, if you need more just ask Tillman."

"Tell me about Cherie, if you don't mind."

"Not much I know that'll be current. I haven't seen her in person for a lot of years. She's smart, started young as a madame and has a reputation for treating her girls well. Her place is upscale, more business owners and government types then sailors. Runs it clean and above board, always respecting the privacy of her clients and staff."

"How will she know me? I'd prefer she didn't get it in a telegraph, folks might be paying attention." Then another thought hit me. "Are you sure you can trust the lawyer?"

"Tillman is safe, very few people know I deal with him and Kennedy deals with most of that. He is my partner in the shipping business. Mostly it's his now, once my ranch got up and running I sold him the majority shares. I'm mostly out of it now a days."

"Thought most of that was down on the Rio?"

"It is but we started in New Orleans, it was the bastion of civilization back then. We could get across the gulf if we needed to and hit most ports in the area. Most of it is out of Galveston now but we both have interests in Louisiana. We don't need to cross the gulf anymore and the business has changed because of it. Steamers carry the freight across faster and safer then we ever could without significant investment."

"Any clue who this toad is?"

"Tillman will have the details. I've had him collect some information quietly. All I know is he's from money, French they say, and his family might be nobility."

"Make sense why he's in Louisiana."

"That's the extent of my knowledge. I'd ultimately like out of the situation but I want Cherie safe after she buys me out. I owe her that much."

"I'll leave as soon as this business with Danu is done." I

started unfolding from my chair. I was going to sit out front and smoke a pipe before bed. "When it's done I'll see you in Corpus Christi. How should I get in touch with you?"

"Just get in touch with a Mr. Heinlein, my attorney in Texas." Kings rich voice had a real sincerity to it. "Thank you JC, I know this isn't what you want to be doing out here and I appreciate it."

"See what I can do, can't make any promises." I nodded to the man before walking out toward the porch. "Appreciate the fine meal, next time its on me."

Rather than sitting on the bench I leaned back on the wall packing my pipe. On the trip here it had been made clear to me that King wasn't a fan of tobacco smoke, which is why I had come out here. I also needed time to think about what was ahead of me.

It was a challenging bit of work, but it had caught my interest. My curiosity and love of puzzles had me hooked, there was no way I could pass this up. There was a part of me yelling that it wasn't what I was out here to do, but my curiosity drown out the argument.

The story from King had my attention. He believed what he told me, I knew that much. He didn't tell me everything, but what he did was the truth. More importantly he told me everything he believed I needed to know. The idea that someone was bullying a woman bothered me, not one part of me cared that she was a fallen dove.

Meeting with the lawyer would give me actual information if nothing else, then I would figure it out. The simple truth was I wanted to see New Orleans and it did beat line riding for the winter.

CHAPTER 3

A BLUE DAY

The night passed uncomfortably while my mind picked at the few pieces of information I had. There wasn't much that could be planned right now, maybe after I met the lawyer. I had gone to bed still puzzling out what I did know, trying to find some sort of pattern. In the end I just didn't have enough information to figure out much.

Slowly climbing out of bed as the light started to crack the horizon my mind went back to Danu. She was going back to her proper owner today, there wasn't anything that could change that. It wasn't going to be a good day. Even trying to do a short version of my work out failed to bring me any peace. The truth hung around my neck weighing down my heart, giving up my horse was going to hurt.

I took my time over breakfast, trying to delay the inevitable, knowing it wouldn't do any good. Walking over to the livery to saddle her, my mind settled on what was going to happen. The livery man knew the story and had let two of Kings men stay in the hay loft guarding her. Five thousand dollars was a big temptation, big enough that men would risk being labeled a horse thief.

I was halfway through saddling her when four men road up outside. They were a mixed bunch but had the look of gun hawks. Just as I was cinching the saddle down their lead rider stepped out of his stirrups heading my way. If he planned on giving me grief he was going to have a rough morning. Nothing would suit me better than having an outlet for my displeasure.

"Hey boy, whatcha think ya doin?" He was a big man with a shaved head, mustache, and close-cut goatee. His tone said he was used to ordering tough men around but had just a touch too much bluster. "Get tha hell away from 'at horse or get dead boy."

"Mister this ain't none of your business, just move off." Was my simple cold response. My hand naturally flipped the thong off my colt, he must have noticed because he stopped moving instantly.

"Boy you don wanta try 'at." His hand fell to his Smith and Wesson. It looked like a well-used Russian. "I'll tak'em colts offa your dead body."

"Call me boy one more time, it'll be the last." I was done with this. The cold comfort spread through me as his three partners stepped down from their horses. They were all smiling, thinking they had the numbers to take care of this lone kid. That was until they heard the Winchesters lever in a round from the hay loft.

"We'll keep 'is between 'em." It was Keith's voice calling down from the loft. The three men stopped in place, frozen in shock. None of them had even managed to remove their thongs. The big man looked around carefully before he spoke again, trying to salvage the situation.

"Look Bo….." I cut him off before he could finish.

"I warned ya, now shut up and make your play."

I knew my temper was getting the better of me, him

pushing wasn't helping. With having to turn Danu over I was in already in a mood. This man was either going to crawl or face me. I was pushing and knew it, but this wasn't the morning for someone to test me.

"JC 'ats Big Mike, works for Thornton. He's kilt a half dozen or more in gunfights." The livery man's voice was soft, but in the deadly silence it carried easily to all of us.

"Better listen to him boy." The big man sneered out at me.

"I said make you play unless you're yellow." Now I was mad. I knew my temper was getting away from me but just didn't care.

"You son of a..." His big shoulders twitched. It gave me plenty of warning when his hand flashed to the Smith and Wesson. He was fast, his barrel came up level with me just as my colt spoke. Smoke trailing the flash of fire out the end of the barrel preceded by speeding lead.

His eyes met mine with a look of shock when a crimson stain appeared an inch to the left of his third button. Then they rolled back in his head showing nothing but the white. His gun fired into the ground as his body toppled back falling like a tree. Small clouds of dust washed out beside him from the impact, the soft sound of his last wheezing breath filled the silence.

His three shocked friends just started at me, none of them moved. I opened the gate and dropped the two spent cartridges, slipping two fresh rounds in automatically before putting it back into my holster. When that was done I met the eyes of the other men one at a time. The cold filled me as I stared at them.

"Anyone else want to call me boy?" My voice was harsh and biting, they all shook their heads. "Drop those pistol belts to the ground an take four steps back. Do it slow."

They did as I instructed, no one spoke up in disagreement. The livery man picked up their gun belts after I told him to. He laid them at my feet then I asked him to fetch their Winchesters and bring those to me as well.

Keith and Davey climbed down from the loft, shaking their

heads. King and the rest had heard the shots, arriving in time to see what was going on. Before King could take charge I stepped into the role.

"Does he or the ranch own that gelding?" I had noticed his horse, it looked like a fine animal.

"It's his." A tall skinny man who had ridden in with him answered. His voice was shrill, and it matched his skinny appearance.

"Then it's mine now, figure the law should be here in a minute, we'll wait."

"Ain't no wait'n, I'm here." A bull of a man rounded the corner, looking annoyed at this being the start of his day. "It's too damn early for a shoot'n. What the hell....is 'at Big Mike?"

"Yes sir, at kid shot 'im dead." The skinny one must be in charge because the other two stayed silent.

"Fill in the rest of that story, damnit!" The Sheriff snapped, annoyed with the pace of information coming his way.

"He pushed JC, and it turned out to be fatal." Keith sounded amused as he explained. "JC warned him, the big man drew first."

"At true?" The Sheriff looked at Skinny expecting an answer.

"Ya know how Mike was." The man shrugged, knowing he couldn't lie but I could tell he wanted to. "That damn kid says he's keeping Mikes horse too!"

"Son?" The sheriff looked at me expectantly.

"I warned him about pushing me, he wasn't as fast as he thought. I'm keeping his horse and rig." My voice still had the cold cutting edge to it. "Don't know why he pushed, don't much care. You push a man an draw on him it's what you get."

"Reckon so, he's been push'n folks since his first kill'n. It was only a matter of time afor he got kilt." The sheriff said grimly. "Carl you here yet?"

"Yes sheriff." A tall skinny man dressed in black stepped forward.

"Get'em buried an' send the bill to Thornton, he pays for his own. What about those three?" He looked meaningfully at the other three men.

"I'm guessing their boss sent them here to escort me to the ranch, figure that's what they'll do. Just riding in front of me and unarmed." My tone held no room for debate.

"What about it Skinny?" The sheriff looked questioningly at the man.

"Ats what we got sent for, don't know why Mike pushed 'im. The boss just said ride with 'im out ta the ranch."

"My men will be riding with JC." King added. "You know who I am, if any of them come back with a scratch it'll be me you answer to."

"Yes sir." All three men answered almost in unison. They all knew that threat had weight and the words impacted them hard. Everyone knew the stories about the King ranch and their capability to dispense justice, so did the sheriff.

"Ya idiots kick off 'at ruckus an I'll hang everyone of ya that they don kill!" He snapped, not wanting any part of the King hands riding into his town hell bent.

I turned ignoring the rest of the conversation. While I unsaddled Danu, Keith walked the big blue dun that had been Mikes over and I swapped my saddle for his. After hanging his saddle in the tack room, I mounted up. The dun was a beautiful blue gelding and seemed smart enough, maybe too smart. More importantly I had noticed he didn't even twitch when the guns fired. That was what drew my attention but once we started riding my evaluation went up another notch.

This was a damn fine animal, sadly not a cow pony but a well-trained riding horse none the less. He would work to get to New Orleans and back to Texas. The three chagrinned punchers lead us out the ranch in silence. Danu was on a trail rope, she nipped at the dun a couple of times just to express her displeasure.

About an hour later we rode slowly down the access road toward the Circle T main house. The three sullen men from the ranch had finally given me the name. The house was a large sprawling place, a single story shaped like a big horseshoe with two wings flaring out from the main entrance. Other hands noticed the three leading us and their lack of weapons, most looked amused more than anything. Thankfully none of them had any interest in getting involved, a few pointed at me mounted on the dun leading the mare. When we got to the front hitching rail Skinny called out to the house.

"Hello the house, Boss we got some problems." He just sat sulking in his saddle afterwards, knowing we wouldn't let him wander off just yet. The three of us sitting with our Winchesters laying across our legs made it clear there was a serious problem.

"Skinny what do you mean…." The man who walked out the front door wasn't what I expected. He was short with a round belly, dressed in a clean white shirt and vest he stood out compared to the rough looking men mounted in front of him. His balding pate shinned in the early morning sun as he surveyed the scene before him. He just sighed heavily before continuing. "What happened?"

"Mike's dead, pushed the kid and got kilt." Skinny's explanation lacked a lot but the look on the boss's face said it was enough for him.

"Names JC not kid." My tone was annoyed, I knew I was young, but it was getting old. "I was saddling Danu getting ready to bring her out here.."

"My mare!" The man immediately started down the steps toward us but I turned the dun to block him before he got close.

"Hold up, we'll get to that. We need to get this straightened out first."

"Mike got what he asked for, enough said. It's been coming for a while. You three get to the bunk house I'll sort you out later." The man seemed more annoyed about me stopping him than with his man's death. "Please Mr. Stone let me inspect her?"

"What bout our guns?" Skinny was obviously not paying attention to the mood.

"Get!" Thornton snarled. "You'll get them back when this is

done!"

The three riders turned as one heading toward the barn, presumably to unsaddle their horses. Three young boys ran out to collect the horses leaving the three to walk sullenly toward the bunk house. The boys lead their mounts into the barn to care for them, I could see them in the deep shadows as the worked. That settled it for Thornton, who looked up at me expectantly.

CHAPTER 4

THE CIRCLE T

"She's killed two men, let me introduce you." I had prepared for this and had a small bunch of apples in my saddle bags. Leading Danu to the rail she eyed me curiously. Something in her eyes recognized this place, she seemed to almost prance with nervous energy. When Thornton stepped toward her she shied away, I was prepared for it and grabbed the trail rope to hold her in place. "Easy girl, easy it's alright."

I handed an apple to Thornton while speaking softly to her. The man knew his horses, recognizing the danger for what it was. He leaned forward talking softly with the apple, she stared at him for a minute before slowly leaning to take it. I could see the moment she recognized his scent, her whole body relaxed in one breath. She stepped forward taking the apple before head butting the man.

"That settles any question I had." I chuckled at her reaction. "She knows you."

"Since the minute of her birth!" Thornton laughed with me,

scratching her neck. "JC right? Call me Vick, welcome the Circle T. Thank you for bringing her back home, I can't tell you what it means to me."

The joy in the man's eyes was obvious, he didn't just value her as stock. This man loved his horses, knew each one of them personally. If I had to place a bet he made it a point to be there anytime one of his mares dropped a foal. My respect for him went up several notches right then. Watching him and Danu told me everything I needed to know about the man.

"Walk to the stables with me?" Vick asked heading that way.

"Sure, give me a minute to square things with my escorts." I nodded toward Keith and the other hands. "Figure I'm good if y'all want to head back?"

"Mr. Thornton, the boss said if anything happens to JC he'd take it personally just so ya know." Keith looked at Vick, passing on Kings not so subtle warning.

"There won't be any problems, please tell Mr. King I look forward to seeing him tomorrow." Vick spoke over his shoulder walking toward the stables.

"JC?" Keith checked one more time, knowing his boss would want him to be certain.

"Appreciate the help this morning, pretty certain the trouble is done. I'll see y'all this evening an buy the first round at the Pearl." I tipped my hat to the men before falling in beside Vick.

"Done!" Keith said as they wheeled their mounts heading back toward town.

"She's been taken care of properly. I can't tell you what this means to me!" Vick repeated, talking over his shoulder as he led Danu. "She'll have a life of luxury from now on, probably never see a saddle again."

"That's a shame, according to Max she's one of the best cow ponies he's ever seen."

"That's the goal you understand. A smart well-built cow pony that's almost born with the knowledge. I knew she had it as just a yearling. This little filly was herding the other horses almost as soon as she could run. It was instinct not training, you understand the difference?"

"I do."

The man was speaking with passion now. Everything I had been told was right. This was his mission in life, he talked about it like a hell fire and brimstone preacher on Sunday morning.

"Her mother was a lucky find, she was the same way. Natural herding instincts like no other animal I had ever seen, before or after. Built light and agile but big enough to enforce her will. Have you ever worked with herd dogs? Like border collies?"

"No sir." He didn't really wait for my answer before he continued.

"They're almost born with the knowledge of how to herd, some of the litter at any rate. It's one of the hardest things about the breeding process, dealing with those that don't have it. If you ever go to a dog breeder it's easy to tell the good ones, they have a lot of pets. They're the ones without the instinct, but the man can't stand to put them down." He almost seemed to grimace at the thought, but I knew what he meant. It was easy to see how he made a living while building his vision. Selling those that didn't met the standard but were still good horse flesh.

"The ones with the instinct though, even as puppies they know what works. All you have to do is teach them commands that match their instincts. Her mother was like that. She knew how to herd naturally, all she needed was a rider that understood her. I was lucky enough to be that rider." I was starting to wonder if the man needed to breath. His passion was driving this impromptu lesson.

"At the time I was raising carriage horses and a few for the stage lines but I knew the trains would eventually kill that business. When I watched her mother work it hit me, cow ponies would always be needed. If I could capture that instinct in a breed? That was something to leave for my children. It's become an obsession if you ask the people around me." He laughed softly at the thought. "Especially if you ask my wife, she swears I love them more than her. It's a good thing she is a tolerant woman, rare as dog feathers she is."

I could see the smile split his face. It was the same smile my father wore when looking at his wife. If anyone ever thought this man loved the horses more then her, they were blind. This was a man who loved his wife and family they were his drive. Over the course of the day he would become another example to me of what happiness looked like. A driving passion for his path supported and balanced by a loving family.

It wasn't just that smile, it was the way his entire ranch felt. The hands worked hard sure, but even from here I could hear them japing one another. It wasn't just a happy man or family it was a well-run ranch with good hands, well there might be a few exceptions.

"What did you call her? Danu, was it? I think that's what the telegram said, a good name. Danu was my first success, but she has a younger brother with the same traits. Now you see why I needed her back don't you?"

"Yes sir, she's half the solution." It made sense, with a mare and a stallion he could start crossing in other breeds. Slowly building that instinct into a breed. With only the two it would be difficult to avoid inbreeding but with some patience he might get there. It would take time, maybe decades, but from the gleam in his eyes none of that mattered to him. What did matter was the goal and what he would leave behind for his family.

"I have some fine stock but these two are the future. My legacy if you will, they will let my children's children live in comfort." One of the boys from the barn was running toward us but Vick waved him toward my new horse.

"Bug fetch Blue, see that he is taken care of."

"If you're talking about Mikes horse, they told he owned the gelding. I plan on keeping him." I didn't put any heat in it but wanted it known.

"That's true, he bought him a year back. Blue is yours, no

question and a damn fine animal too. I'll give you the bill of sale when we get to the house along with the reward money."

"Appreciate the bill of sale, I may have some other ideas about the reward. If you're a gambling man that is."

"Oh?" That got the man's attention. I had just a second to glimpse the horse trader come to life in his eyes, then it was gone. This might be a harder trade then I thought. A big grin split his face again before he replied. "I'm always interested in keeping my money."

He got Danu situated in a big stall and left instructions that no one was to go into that stall without him. I was glad he had heard me when I said she was a killer. The boys nodded, understanding the boss was serious about it. I spotted the three-year-old stallion prancing in a stall not far away. He had the same markings as Danu but was at least a hand or so taller.

"That's Prince, her brother." Vick explained leading me toward the stall.

"You got a good start on your dream, he's a beautiful animal."

"He is a beautiful horse, and now that I have them both I can truly start to develop a breed. Come on let's head to the house, you've piqued my interest about this reward idea of yours." His grin told me I was in for a long morning and probably afternoon of dickering. I wanted horses not money, but I wanted them in ten years. He might not go for it but everything about this man said he was a gambler.

Dickering with him was far easier than I feared, in short order we agreed on a deal. Vick not only liked the idea but thought it was better for both of us. He was perfectly comfortable betting on my life, even admired my audacity.

"Have to admit JC, this idea of yours might be the first time I am hoping to lose a bet." He spoke with admiration in his voice.

Instead of five thousand now, if I lived to start my ranch he would give me ten thousand dollars in stock. I would have to pay for freight to have them transported. We both assumed by then it would be by rail when it happened. Both of us sure that the railroads would reach whatever area I was in by then. Driving that many horses across the country would be a challenge to say the least. Maybe the railroad was more of a hope?

He promised they would all be good stock that could take the harsh winters up north. There would be one stallion and 20 good mares for every hundred head. It did mean that most of a hundred would be geldings but half of those would be under three and none of them would be over six. That meant they would at best be green broke, most would be unbroken.

I had already decided on raising horses. Cattle wouldn't be a bad start, it would all depend on the market. The Hereford cattle that survived the harsh winters up north were a different animal than the notorious longhorns. Not that I knew anything except stories about either of them yet. Horses I at least had some knowledge about them. Having an agreement in place for that many horses was a good start either way.

We drew up a formal contract, laying out all the details, before noon. He invited me to stay for lunch before I rode back to town, which I gladly accepted. I liked this man, he was driven but still made time for his family. He also spoke to his hands like they were friends rather than employees. Even his household staff used their Christian names when addressing them.

The meal was a great opportunity to meet his son and daughter, I also had the privilege of meeting his wife. The children were nine and eleven respectively and he doted on them despite what I had been told. His wife was a perfect match to him, balancing out his driven nature with a soft touch and kind words. Dotty had a quick wit and knew her man through and through. The chemistry between them made me laugh several times during the meal. She had no issue shutting down his constant chatter and redirecting the conversation away from the horses.

"JC, now that you helped complete my husband's life goal, what will be your next adventure?" He light playful tone made

Vick grin broadly.

"Going to see New Orleans for the winter, sounds better than line riding anyway. Figure at some point I'll get enough line riding, right now my only commitment is to be at the Bar C in the spring."

"That city is a dangerous place, mind yourself there." She warned with a motherly tone.

"Papa won't let his hands go there." Chrissy, her daughter who was every bit her mother's child, offered helpfully.

"While I'm unsure how my precocious daughter knows such things, she isn't wrong." Vick admitted smiling at his daughter when she cringed. "The city has its finery, it also has quarters that good christian folks avoid."

"Having grown up running the streets in New York, I know how to recognize those particular neighborhoods." I grinned. "But I'll keep it in mind."

"I have a good friend in the city, Peter Durand. He's a solid man stop by and introduce yourself to him. Might be able to guide you around town for a bit."

"Appreciate it, I'll look him up." Knowing I wouldn't reach out to anyone while I was there that wasn't connected to King. I wouldn't want anything linked back to another man.

"That man's a perfect scoundrel, he'll see you enjoy the city." Dotty offered laughing.

"Uncle Pete's not a subdral!" Chance's young voice protested. "He's fun!"

"And that's why he is a scoundrel Chance." His mother laughed.

It was a thoroughly enjoyable lunch with a family that was obviously happy with their place in the world. I was almost sad when it ended with Vick and I stepping out onto the porch to smoke. Dotty had a hard and fast rule regarding smoking in her home, neither of us had any interest in challenging her about it.

Vick sent one of the boys to fetch Blue while we smoked. I would head back to the hotel to get ready to leave in the morning. My plan was to leave for New Orleans at first light, I was ready to be on my own again. In short order Blue was tied loosely to the rial, ready to go. I downed the last of my coffee and tapped out my pipe before rising from my chair.

"JC I truly hope to hear from you about those horses." Vick stuck his hand out to shake before I stepped off the porch.

"You will Vick. I have to thank you for your time today. Your family is wonderful, reminds me of being home." I shook his hand, genuinely having enjoyed the lunch. "Might have needed it more than I knew. Reminds me there is a life away from the trail."

"Thank you for bringing Danu back, do me one more favor?"

"Sure, what did you need?"

"Rename that damn horse, Blue is just..."

"To on the nose?" I laughed agreeing with him.

CHAPTER 5

THE BIG EASY

Blue was a good saddle horse, but he liked to cause some chaos if he got a chance. One of the stable boys told me a story about him escaping his stall and raising hell with the local geese. They had to add a real lock to the door because of it. Halfway back to town he spit his bit ignoring my commands, proving the story true. The boy back at the Circle T hadn't tightened it enough and the tricky horse got his tongue under it. It made me start thinking about Vick's request to rename the animal.

The next morning while I packed up to leave he showed his nature again. My brain was still running through names when he tried an old trick. I caught him taking a deep breath just as I started to cinch it his girth. It was a good trick if you weren't paying attention. If you didn't catch it the girth would be loose enough to dump rider and saddle.

Tricky didn't seem to fit so I fell on old knowledge, myths and legends. I started going through the ones I could remember. The look of annoyance he gave me when I waited him out brought the right name to mind. Smart, tricky, and a little vicious left only a few of the trickster gods, Loki seemed to fit him well enough.

"Alright Loki I got the message." I laughed digging an apple out for him. He happily took the bribe, bumping me with his head in approval. He would never be a cow pony, but he was a smart animal. "You don't leave me in a bad way, and I'll make sure the treats keep coming."

We set off following the main road, Vick had recommended sticking to it. He had warned me about the swamps and upper bayous, making it clear why I should stick to the roads. Chance had warned me about the dragons, which Vick helpfully clarified were alligators. He assured me Loki wouldn't be bothered, if anything he would warn me about them. Mike had made the trip to New Orleans several times, the man was one of the few he had trusted to go into the city.

That tidbit of information made me think a bit more about horses and the locality. If this gelding had grown up here did that make him less likely to spook from the local critters? How many generations did it take for them to learn that knowledge? I would have to send a letter to Vick about it. Maybe it was something he knew, or he would be interested in studying.

He had also given me a list of inns to stay at on the way, assuring me they were clean and safe. He made the trip twice a year for various business interests, but preferred Baton Rouge if he could. Not only did New Orleans have the normal crime of a big city, but it was also a major port. That meant sailors from across the world as well as the various businesses that cater to them brought their own perils. He had repeated the warnings several times, reminding me twice to avoid the docks unless I wanted to get shanghaied.

Louisiana was full a good people, but reconstruction hadn't been kind to them. Hard times made hard people, the slight Irish lilt I still had would help hide the New York tones, but he warned about revealing myself as a yankee. He said my best bet was being just another young man coming to see the famous New Orleans. My plan was to play stupid, being young helped people believe that when needed. It was simple, having learned from hard experience that the more complex something was the more likely it would be to fail.

Both King and Vick had warned me about the French quarter and the gangs, Cherie's place was on the edge of it luckily. Not as dangerous, but still bad enough that the rich clientele were always escorted by armed guards. That bit of information made me wonder how they were being threatened away? King said he wasn't sure but thought it might be blackmail combined with physical threats.

That didn't sit right in my mind, there had to be more to it. True it made more sense than straight forward violence, wealthy men usually responded to direct threats poorly. The elites I had seen get threatened usually didn't let it go, they hired someone to deal with it for them. The high-end clientele was the prize for both sides, risking that just didn't make sense though. Once a reputation was lost it wouldn't be easy to get back. Not from the people they were dealing with, it really made me wonder what was going on.

More and more just wasn't adding up in the story King was being told. Sadly, no matter how I looked at it the answer continued to elude me. There was some bit of information I was missing. What was more unsettling was King didn't know it, I was sure the man hadn't held anything back. That meant he was being lied to somewhere in this mess. After some arguing he had finally agreed that if something was fishy on Cherie's side I was authorized to separate him from the business no matter the loss.

It took some talking but eventually he realized that he wasn't getting the whole story. The man was fiercely loyal to those he felt earned it. Shaking that in the slightest had been a feat of verbal sparring that brought all my law school education to bear. Finally I got him to realize that losing money was better than getting caught in a fight where the fix was in. The man had his pride but was smart enough to know it wouldn't be on familiar ground and that made the price far too high.

The road to the city was easy to follow. I didn't rush, taking the time to learn what I could about Louisiana along the way. The further south I went the more obvious the differences became. Trees hung heavy with kudzu swayed over dark murky water. Its surface broken repeatedly by unknown creatures. The humid air barely moved and when it did the scent of life and rot mixed could be overwhelming.

The first time I got a good look at an alligator, Chance calling them dragons made more sense. A huge mouth full of teeth, long armored bodies moving rapidly on short legs. Watching it cover thirty feet to slip into the water and disappear before I could do more than blink was a shock. I could see the muscles that lay under that armored hide propelled it easily. Nothing about the animal said anything pleasant, I wanted nothing to do with them. My inner child pictured it breathing a long tongue of flame at me before it disappeared into the murky depths. When one hissed at me before galloping off into the water, I almost believed they could.

As threats go though they were nothing compared to the haze of bugs. They were the real torture of the trip. Even this late in the year every step was full of buzzing creatures. Loki didn't seem bothered by them, but I was suffering the death of a thousand cuts. Some part of me truly feared dying in my sleep from blood lose. The ravenous swarms never relented, night or day didn't seem to matter. Luckily a friendly Caddo shared a trick with me over the fire one night, my payment for the lesson was a can of peaches.

He taught me to make a sweet grass ointment that helped repel the vile creatures, it didn't smell to bad either. Fresh mint leaves worked to keep most of the other creatures out of my pack and bedroll too. I worried about smelling like a plant when I reached New Orleans but that concern wasn't enough to make me stop using it. Nothing would have made me give up that defense.

When I reached the outskirts of New Orleans I realized it wasn't a real concern. Several vendors were selling the same thing with various perfumes mixed in. Turns out the vile creatures didn't respect city limits or closed doors. The perfume was added, I guessed, to help ease the heavy scent of sweat. The humidity and heat still felt like a weight on your shoulders. The densely populated city didn't make that any better, if anything it aggravated the sensation.

Moving into the city, slowly riding Loki down a main street, I studied its diversity with amazement. Louisiana had elected a black lieutenant governor in 1870, the response had been the creation of a white political party lead by the democrats. That was politics, those had been easy to learn by reading a couple of newspapers and talking to a few people on the road. The city itself seemed to be moving in the same direction of New York, people of every race walked its streets.

Expensive carriages carried the wealthy down the street while a large black man drove his wagon behind them loaded with vegetables. The sidewalks weren't packed like New York but again the diversity was reflected there as well. The difference was a palpable tension that flowed under all of it. Like some building force was threatening the fragile peace. It was still a city divided by old hate and new anger, it gave me the impression of a city on the edge. It would only take a few triggers for the peaceful facade to fall into violent chaos.

Some people walked casually, unconcerned about who shared the sidewalk with them. Others though, would sneer at anyone of a different skin tone, still holding firm to their belief in white superiority. I took all this in while tracking the cross streets looking for the one I needed. Thankfully finding Tillmans office didn't take long, the streets were well marked, and the numbers easy to spot.

"Good day sir, how may I help you?" A pleasant looking young lady greeted me with a winning smile when I entered.

"JC Stone to see Mr. Tillman, I believe he is expecting me."

"Yes sir, please have a seat. I'll let him know you've arrived." She rose gracefully, walking toward a large door at the back of the office. Her neat appearance carried an air of confidence that didn't really match her nervous look. She was back in a minute, holding the door open. "Mr. Stone please come this way. Mr. Tillman will see you now."

The large office that came into view housed a bookish looking man who stood to greet me. He was short, a couple inches over five feet, gray hair lined his head with a respectable amount of exposed scalp up top. His mustache was neatly trimmed and lightly waxed, other than that he was clean shaven. The spectacles perched on his nose completed the look that was obviously intentional. My guess was he cultivated it, non-threatening but intelligent. I couldn't blame him, being a lawyer, it worked for him professionally.

"Welcome young man!" His voice was deeper than expected, what surprised me more was the accent. This man was no southerner. If I had to guess maybe Illinois or Iowa. "I received a telegram just last week regarding your arrival."

"Glad to hear it." I shook his hand noting he didn't say who the telegram was from. The door closed behind me, making me wonder if the secretary was the reason he hadn't mentioned any names.

"Now that the door is closed we can speak plainly." He grinned. "Miss Bonavia is a good woman but a bit curious when she shouldn't be. Now Mr. King explained to me what was going on. Unfortunately, I'm not sure I have any more information than he does."

"Tell me what you can, I'll figure the rest from there."

"Coffee first? Feel free to smoke while we talk." He stood and walked to door, asking for a pot of coffee to be brought in.

After closing the door he dug out a cigar from the box on his desk and offered me one. The large balcony doors behind him were open letting the air flow through, keeping it cool and venting the smoke. I declined the cigar with a wave. Taking out my pipe while we waited for the coffee to arrive, it helped me collect my thoughts. After the coffee was served and the door closed again he began telling me what he knew.

"I don't mean to be rude but," he studied me carefully before continuing, "you seem a bit young for this type of work."

"I finished my law degree in New York, passed the bar before I headed west." I smiled, understanding why he had asked. "My youth also makes people more likely to ignore me."

"There is some truth in that, I certainly am surprised by it. No matter, let me tell you what I can. The trouble started about six months back as far I can discern. A new investor came into town, immediately jumping on the coat tails of the White League. Are you aware of them?" He paused for my answer.

"Assume I know nothing of the area or it's politics." A small lie but it would be worth it to have a locals view of the situation.

"Very well, the league was formed by the Democrats in response to the Republican victory. It seems the idea of a colored lieutenant governor bothers some folks." He chuckled at that, but something about it seemed off to me. It was a bit too forced, I couldn't say for sure but it reminded me that I didn't know this man. "As a proud Republican you can imagine my opinion of the foolishness. When Oscar Dunn was elected by a large margin it started a mess that has further divided the state."

"Not to mention that many folks feel the reconstruction has forced its way into local government. Wordsmouth having served in the union during the late unpleasantness is the bigger mystery. How someone who fought for the North has risen so quickly in the area baffles me." He pulled deeply on his cigar before continuing, waving off my interruptions. "Patience please, this is all related in its way, you must understand your enemy after all."

"Now this particular gentleman showed up not long ago. He immediately got involved with the White League and has endeavored to take over a fair bit of the French quarter. Mostly the illicit trade but several more respectable businesses too. I have heard a few rumors of his involvement in some of the darker trades, opium dens and such. Coleman Wordsmouth is the name he uses, though I know it's not his given name. That's where it starts to get interesting. I can find no record of the man prior to his arrival. I did however find an interesting connection between him and a man named Cole Ward." The grin that split his face bordered on maniacal. "This I think is the twist in the game, you see Cole Ward was a lieutenant in the 7th Kansas. Worse for him, I believe he was the link between them and the Red Legs.

"Now should that prove true; our problem is easily solved. Simply revealing his past would hasten his departure from the city, if not causing him to disappear completely." His laughter was too enthusiastic, this man was lying about something.

"The desire to take Cherie's comes from his need for a legitimate tie to the area. That and the power that she seems to wield over her clients, probably blackmail. It's my belief that's why he wants to marry her to acquire the business. It's also why their conflict hasn't escalated to violence. I think Cherie knows his background, which might be part of it. If that's the case he must have as much on her. I know she helped the Lincolnites when they took the city. I can only theorize that he is aware of this connection thus creating a balance of sorts, neither can afford their secrets being revealed."

This was making more sense now, Wordsmouth was afraid of having his real past revealed but held cards over Cherie with the same threat. It raised several questions though, first was how would she know? It's possible she knew him in association with the Red Legs but that seemed thin. The Red Legs hadn't operated around here and if I remembered right neither had the 7th.

My next question was how had a Red Leg association gone undiscovered? The southerners hated them more than any other group. The chaos and destruction they had caused was as well-known as the men who rode with them. The most important question was how could I reveal this to the people here without sparking a larger problem? A part of me was tempted to just reveal both of their secrets and let the chips fall as they may. Sadly, that wouldn't serve Kings request so until I knew for sure Cherie had betrayed him that wasn't an option.

"Now let me tell you a bit about Madame Cherie, it may help you understand it all a bit more." He offered, mistakenly assuming my look as one of confusion.

"During the war she was a spy for the Union. Offering safe harbor to those who needed it and passing information when she could. A woman in her profession could collect and pass on information easily, pillow talk can work both ways after all. I think this is how she knows the good Lt. Ward." He chuckled softly before continuing. "Louisiana was a major hub during the early part of the war, but men tend to dismiss the women who share their beds."

"She's a smart lady, make no mistake about it. If you deal with her personally be wary of it, she knows how to read people. Having been born a slave, I think when the opportunity came for her to help the north she took it readily. There have been rumors that she helped some slaves escaping to Canada before the war. Some connection with the underground or some such I'm not sure. They're just rumors and have never been verified you understand." He sighed heavily before continuing. "I believe them because it would have been one avenue for the north to recruit her to their cause."

"Not long after the war she opened the business, with our friend's assistance of course but that doesn't explain her easy access to large sums of money. That actually supports her working with the North during the war. Especially because she was one of the few with ready access to greenbacks. Mr. King has tried to disentangle himself for several years, but a roadblock always seems to appear." The look of frustration on his face was intentional, but I couldn't tell if it was simple greed or something more treacherous. Either way he continued.

"At this point I am certain she doesn't want him to remove himself. It gives her more backing than a lone colored woman would have normally. Folks don't know who her partner is of course, but they know it's a powerful man. The way her problems seem to solve themselves reinforces this belief."

"So, he had stepped in before?" I asked. This had my curiosity going. Was I just another person he sent to help her?

"Yes, but this is different. This time he wants out for good and won't be put off. I'm not as sure he is concerned about helping her. He seems to have decided to end the association no matter what this time." Tillman had no clue how wrong he was. It had been a tap dance to get King to agree with me about leaving this mess behind.

"I figure you're right but appreciate the information anyway." What I was actually thinking was different. There was something about his whole story that had me on edge. Something not quite right about it, that feeling included the little man sitting across from me. "I'm going to need to get more into this than I first thought. For now, let me get the key to the house and settle in. I'll be in touch if I need anything, hopefully I can find a way to sort this all without involving you too much."

"Good because this is certainly not my area of expertise, well the business is but intrigue is not my forte." His laugh was meant to be deprecating but it sounded false. This man knew how to play every angle all while hedging his bets on both sides. It told me that I couldn't count on him picking a side until it served his interest. He reached into a desk drawer to retrieve a key before handing it to me. "One of the many reasons I stick to contract law. I had it cleaned and stocked for you, did you need a live in? I can arrange it if so."

"Maybe a cleaning lady once a day, preferably in the morning to make coffee? Laundry if possible, the stable I can take care of so don't worry about that. I would prefer not to have a live in, I like my privacy."

"Consider it done, her name is Minnie. She does my

housekeeping and I trust her. She will come by every morning, make you breakfast and tidy up. If that works for you?"

"That'll be fine." I took the key, waiting for him to tell me where it was.

"From here go down the road out front for six blocks, then a left. Three more blocks from there is Gravier St, turn left. The house is 118, the key will unlock all the doors so you can enter through the alley to stable your horse. It's not far from Cherie's place, walking distance but mind your back down there. New Orleans is a great city, that doesn't mean it's safe for the uninitiated."

"Appreciate it. I'll be in touch if need be." I stood and we shook hands one more time before I left his office. After politely tipping my hat to his secretary I made my way out to the street.

CHAPTER 6

DINNER WITH
AN EDUCATION

I found the address easily enough and after Loki was stabled I walked into the small house. The windows were opened letting the breeze flow through, it helped keep the house cool. It was a nicely appointed single story, a straight narrow house with a small yard and a nice porch on both ends. The furnishings were comfortable, spread evenly throughout. The whole place had a comfortable feel to it, a place to hang your hat. I was surprised at first but then thought about King wanting to stay low key in town. After that the house made sense, nice enough to be well thought of but not draw attention.

It felt cut off from the world to me, separated from the song by walls and roads. Again, the realization hit me that in such a short time I had become uncomfortable in houses. After making my facsimile of coffee I sat on the back porch watching the sun start to sink in the sky. Despite the offers no one had bothered to teach me to make decent coffee yet, I was once again paying the price for that lack of education.

I had spotted a cafe down the street on my way in and would wander down there to get some dinner soon. Choking down my own cooking was too much to ask, I did it on the trail but that didn't make it a good choice. Maybe I should have accepted the offer of a live in, if only for the coffee. I dumped the bitter water out over the railing before putting my cup back inside.

The slow transition from day to dusk was amazing to watch. The haze of humidity sprayed colors across the sky in bold hues. The slow-moving clouds reflected them, creating more vibrant shades accenting the growing shadows. The display was enough to make me forgive the oppressive humidity, this was worth the price.

I made it to the cafe with the last traces of sunlight fading into dark. The city was cooling off by degrees as the city workers lite the street lamps. A cooling breeze blew in from the gulf carrying the scent of spices from faraway lands. My mouth watered as the kitchens across the city started serving dinner. It was only a guess but the heat of the day must force dinner to be a later than what was elsewhere.

The cafe was simple structure that stood on a triangle corner where the road split. There was a wood facade that enclosed the small dining area from a serving counter. The kitchen was open to the outside in the back with just a rough plank ceiling over it. This kept it cooler and let the tempting scents float away on the breeze. Smells of coffee and heavy spices drifted to me, teasing my nose. It added to the pleasing mix that was carried on the wind from around the city.

The cafe sign out front announced the place to be Creole owned and operated. I wasn't real sure what Creole meant but knew the food was indigenous to the area. The friendly girl who took my order recommended gumbo, served with fresh bread. I took her word on it and ordered a cold beer with it.

When the food arrived, I was pleasantly surprised by

it. The heat was different, making my lip sweat without overpowering the flavor of the food. The taste was complex with a different spice from the peppery heat used in Texas. The cold beer went well with it and after dinner a decent coffee was another pleasant discovery. It wasn't trail coffee, but still far better then mine.

I had found my meals for the duration as far as I was concerned. I did notice a few looks from the other clients, but they were more curious then angry. I was beginning to guess what Creole meant from the clientele around me. The waitress was friendly enough and fished for information casually.

"Where ya from Cher? Not 'ere that's for certain."

"No ma'am just come in from Kansas, wandered down to see the famous city."

"Ya in da right place Cher, Nawlins got everythang ya kin want." She smiled, obviously proud of the city she called home.

"Mind if I ask what might be a rude question?"

"Naw Cher, ask us anyting."

"What's Creole?"

"Oh, Cher ya is truly new den, Creole is us. Bayou folks who grow'd up here." She smiled warmly and I was glad I hadn't offended her. "Da simple way ta think is dis, white folks is Cajuns, the rest is Creole. You keep coming here, we learn ya good."

"Will do, y'all open all day?"

"Ya, we always cook'n the right way."

"I'm staying up the road so I'll be in a couple times a day. My cooking is bad an my coffee is worse." I admitted honestly.

"Cher, no dat can't be! Come for breakfast, we getcha ta makin' coffee right." She laughed at my admission before offering to teach me. "Call it a welcome ta Nawlins, Cher."

"Don't be surprised if I wander in before you're open, its happened before."

"Open.. closed...no matter. Y'all come by an we fix ya up. Come too early an we put ya ta work, be warned." She laughed walking away after I paid. I would be back in the morning to test her words.

Strolling back toward the house I took in the deepening night around me. More people were out, taking advantage of the cool night air. Not far off I could hear the music from the French quarter mixing with the sounds of life. That chaotic mixture was different from the normal saloon music, more diverse than the tinny pianos that dominated most of them. Reminding me once again I was in a different place, different and dangerous.

Shadows slunk by in alleyways, cut throats waiting for a lone fool to drunkenly wander into their clutches. I could just see them moving from one dark pool to another, brief flashes of light on steel announcing their intentions. Urban hunters tracking their prey, the natural order of things twisted by civilization.

The weak would find themselves robbed at best, dead at worst. I knew these men, recognized their ilk from New York. Never taking any more risk than absolutely necessary, picking the weakest of prey from the fringes of the herd. Predators existed everywhere, the urban environment just created a different hunting ground.

The city was alive at night, you could feel it in the air. On a whim I turned toward the music, despite knowing I was probably walking into trouble. My guns and blade hung comfortably around my waist, the stiletto was tucked into my collar. My trail clothes were caked with dust and sweat from the road. It was an armor of sorts, a blatant warning to the predators. Look elsewhere this one isn't prey.

There were some punchers wandering the quarter, but the local wardrobe varied like any big city. The wealthier wore more formal suits, some tailored but most store bought. The working class dressed in the same heavy durable clothes that were a standard across the world. Most wore slouch hats or bowlers, there was a few top hats, and one old boy still wore a coon skin cap. I did see a few calvary hats and some Stetson's so my hat didn't stand out. The seafaring men walked in the odd sway all sailors had. Most of them wore a bright sash of some kind or another making them easy to spot.

Everyone carried guns, either under their coats or tucked into belts. There were a few wearing the open holsters favored by punchers and gun hands. Knives hung from the belts of various types of tough looking men, others were tucked into boots. The few rich had canes, but I could hear the hollow ring of hidden blades when the tapped the ground.

This city was predatory at every step, there as money to be had and everyone was pursuing it in some way. From the men waiting in shadows to the businessman in his fine coat and hat. Hunting or defending created an atmosphere that was a mixture of tension and excess. It reminded me of the breeze in the swamp, life and rot blending together. Each had different tools of the trade but the trail they left in their wake was the same. Blood-soaked corpses hidden under bushes or trash piles.

The city at first glance was civilized, police patrolled casually along the streets. Easily creating the illusion of safety, but it was just that an illusion. The wary never ventured into the darkened alleys, knowing the fate of that foolish act. Men and women of means strolled the boardwalks, adding to the facade of civility. It was all a lie built to make everyone feel like it could never happen to them. The entire city was filled with violence draped under a veneer of peace.

This all changed radically when I turned the corner onto Bourbon Street. The crowd here was loud and bawdy, the alleys darker even more threatening. The police disappeared, replaced by men who looked like they were stalking prey rather than protecting. Thugs and bully boys keeping the fronts of saloons and bawdy houses clear of free loaders. The saloons, bawdy houses, and gamblings dens were divided by harsh lines of black and white, literally. I could feel the tension between the opposing sides when their glares met.

Human waste, stale beer, tobacco, and sweat dominated the night air now. Only the faintest trace of salty air blew in from the nearby gulf. Men ruled here, the fine ladies evaporated as soon as I turned the corner. The only ones present here were fallen doves strolling in front of various establishments. Never wandering near the dark alleys while putting their wares on display. The glimpses of soft flesh luring in young and old alike.

Between the constantly swinging batwing doors men entered and exited the boardwalk. Some drunk ,staggering toward a hotel or den of ill repute, others obviously waiting to enact their nefarious plots. Predators and prey acting out a play that had existed longer than mankind. This wasn't new by any means, it was the same story in every major city.

I was walking by an alley when I made the mistake of looking down it, more out of self-preservation than curiosity. My eyes caught the glint of steel reflecting off a distant light. Silhouettes displayed the violence taking place in the shadows, telling its own bloody story. Three men stood over a lone figure. He was half crouched against the wall trying to fend them off. Something drew me down the alley, despite my disinterest. The breeze carried their words to me as I moved silently toward them.

"Turpo we warned ya! Ya kind ain't welcome round here no more, now your black ass is gonna die." The man speaking was stretched out, lean and tall.

Even in the shadows I could see the color difference, three white men against one brown or red. The thin beams of light escaping a nearby window reflected off the small pins they each wore. Tillman had showed me one earlier, they were membership pins for the white league.

"Bugger off! Y'all don't own shit no more. Kin't even manage to get elected." Turpo the man on the ground, spat at the tall mans feet. I could tell he was injured, stabbed probably, but was getting ready to lunge at the one talking.

"Ya gonna die now ni...."

Before the man could finish Turpo launched up from the ground, pushing off the wall. He managed to wrap his arms around the taller mans waist and tackle him into the muck. I had seconds to decide what to do, not that it took that long. The cold familiar feeling flooded through me as I moved forward. Ghosting from shadow to shadow in quick short steps. The closest man was reaching down to pull off Turpo when I got there.

My right hand wrapped comfortably around the familiar hilt of my Bowie as time seemed to slow. No one heard the whisper of sound pulling the blade caused. The first man never saw me step behind him, I kept my blade down hidden in my shadow. Before he could reach the two figures rolling on the ground my knife slid into his back. My aim was true, the big blade punched easily through his kidney. A quick twist of my wrist made the man's body locked up in pain, cutting off the scream that tried to escape his mouth. His death was fast but not pain free.

The last man froze in fear when his partner started to fall lifelessly into the muck. By the time his mind recognized there was another player joining the game, it was too late. I let his partners body fall to the side and stepped over it before he could react. My Bowie drove up through his lower jaw into his brain, killing him instantly. He was dead before his partners body had hit the ground and quickly followed him to hell. When I turned to look at the two on the ground the tall lean man lay in the muck unmoving, his throat cleanly cut.

The third man, Turpo, tried to get to his feet but staggered back against the wall and started to fall. His knife fell from his hand as his consciousness fled. Glancing around to be sure no one had noticed the fight, I quickly cleaned my blade on one of their shirts while searching them. I found 64 dollars and two derringers, all of it went into my pocket. Their knives had long disappeared into the mire and I had no interest in searching for them. I did pick up the stiletto Turpo had dropped, it went into my boot. Even in the dark I could tell it was a quality piece of work. When I leaned down to collect it I heard his ragged breath wheezing out.

He was still alive, but wouldn't be for long without

bandaging that wound. I wasn't sure where to find a doc, especially one that would treat a black man with a knife wound. The best I could do was get him home and do what I could. I wouldn't have wanted to bet on his chances, but they beat the ones he had laying here. Finding my way through the alleys back to Gravier Street wouldn't be too tricky. After that I would do what I could but without a doctor he probably wouldn't ever wake up.

He groaned when I picked him up but never came fully came back to consciousness. Thankfully he wasn't a big man, allowing me to move easily with him over my shoulder. Quickly cutting through the alleys to get away from the scene, I started winding my way back to the house, every step set my nerves off. It would take just one witness to doom everything.

Once I noticed the streetlights had spaced out, leaving deeper shadows I staggered out onto the street. Better to risk someone seeing the blood over getting lost or attacked in the maze of alleyways. Slurring my speech as I staggered across the boardwalk, talking gibberish to the man over my shoulder. Either by sheer luck or because someone carrying their drunk friend wasn't that uncommon we made it back to the house without being stopped.

I knew we had been followed but the man had stuck to the shadows doing an admirable job of tailing us. I'd only caught glimpses of him moving twice but it was enough to mark him long before we reached the house. He didn't make a move to attack or stop us, so I ignored his presence for now. Better to deal with him after I set down the guy over my shoulder.

I went in through the back door, doing my best to lay Turpo down gently on the table. In the faint light of a lone lamp I could see the spreading blood on the front of his shirt. He needed a doctor, but I had no clue how to find one. That's when I thought about the shadow following us, it hadn't closed the distance but kept us in sight. Playing a hunch, I eased open the back door before speaking softly into the shadows.

"If you're with Turpo come out, I need help."

"He still breath'n?" The voice came from the shadows of the small barn.

"Not for long if he don't get a doc."

"You ain't da law?" The man who stepped out of the shadows was short and stocky, one of those people built like a square. Dressed in simple cloths I noticed his dark eyes studying me carefully as he came forward. He was young, about my age with short cut hair, his skin was almost yellow. "Names Yella Henry, I kin fetch a doc that won't say nuthin."

"Names JC, I'll leave the back door open just come in. Make it quick, I don't know how bad he's stuck but it ain't good." He took one more look at me before bolting into the shadows.

Watching him disappear all I could do was hope. Back inside I found a pillow and sheet, I put the pillow under his head and started tearing the sheet into strips for bandages. I had laid him on the table in the kitchen, by sheer luck not breaking anything. I cleared the table of the various dishes after tying a makeshift bandage around him to keep pressure on the wound. He never stirred and all I could do was hope Henry made it back in time.

CHAPTER 7

MEETING THE GANG

Henry was back in under twenty minutes, but it felt like hours. I did what little I could, removed his shirt and kept a bandage on it. He never woke up and was still bleeding, that could be both good and bad. Good because it meant he was still alive, bad because he was losing a lot of blood. All I could do was wait and hope the man made it.

Hurried footsteps sounded outside, they were coming up the path and got my attention before the door opened. Henry froze staring at the colt in my hand. His two companions stopped cold behind him. All three stared at me expectantly, unsure of what to do next.

The light let me get a better look at Henry. He would have been called handsome but the weathered look in his eyes spoke of a rough life. The second of the three was a tough looking man, maybe early twenties. Strong muscles rippled underneath the thin material of his simple cotton shirt. This man had been in fights, vicious fights from the look of the scars that sliced across his face. The last of them was an older man, dressed in clean clothes that looked to have been thrown on hurriedly.

"This is Doc, he'll fix up Turpo." Henry pointed at the gentleman. The Doc wasted no time pushing me out of the way once he gathered his thoughts, completely ignoring my colt. "This 'ere is Prussian Charley, he's wit us."

"JC." The colt slipped back into my holster, and I stuck out my hand to Henry. He looked shocked at first but took it soon enough. "Glad you got the Doc, he's still breathing but has lost a lot of blood."

"He wa'nt far off, just a few streets over. Ran inta Charley on the way, figured might need'em if anyone saw ya." Henry explained but I knew better. Charley was there to help with me if I was a problem.

"Charley." I stuck out my hand, he too hesitated before taking it. When he did my hand almost disappeared into the mans grip.

"I need some water and I might need another sheet to rip up." The doc spoke for the first time. Indicating the sheet I had already started to shred.

"Buckets at the back door, there's a pump in the sink." Charley looked at me for one more moment before moving to get the bucket. "The sheets ruined anyway, go ahead. I'll get another one ready if you need it."

"He's lucky, the blade didn't hit anything vital." The doc explained over his shoulder while digging in his bag. "I'm going to stitch it closed. It's all I can do for him, that and pray it doesn't get infected. He won't be able to be moved for a couple of days, like as not he'd start bleeding again if he moves any sooner. Two days at least, three would be best."

"He can stay here that's fine, should we move him to a bed before you stitch him up?" I could see Henry tense. Turning toward him, I added. "You can stay with him if you need too."

"Ought to." Was all he said but he visibly relaxed. Charley started to hand the bucket off when the doc spoke up again.

"Be better to move him after I stitch and bind this wound. No need ruining the bed with blood if we can avoid it. Bring that water over here." When Charley went to put the water down and help position Turpo for the Doc I struck a match to light another lamp.

The man was quick, ten minutes later he was wrapping a clean bandage around the wound. He had cleaned and stitched the wound on both sides. He put a thick poultice on either side of the wound under the bandage. When he was done the Doc looked over his shoulder at me expectantly.

"There's a bedroom right there off the kitchen, it's small but should work." I indicated the doorway. "Henry will you help me get it set up?"

"Why ya help'n us?" He asked following me into the room. It was small probably meant as maids quarters, but the bed was clean and looked comfortable.

"Not sure why I shouldn't."

"Ya don't know?" Henry looked at me from across the bed as we folded back the sheets.

"Just got into the city today." I admitted.

"Turpo's the boss of an association in the ward, police prolly call us a gang." Henry laughed lightly as he spoke.

"None of my business. I saw three men attacking one, couldn't abide it."

"You ain't one of 'em do gooders, at much I know." His grin said he was joking but it made me wonder what he knew. "Cause do gooders don't kill two men slick as bird shit."

"Seemed like the thing to do." Now it was time to fish for information. "Sides those three are part of something I might have an interest in."

"You got something to do wit' da league?" He was wary again.

"Might. More with a man named Coleman Wordsmouth and his business practices." Henry studied me for a minute before speaking again.

"Dis 'bout at Gilded Dove?" He studied me for a reaction that wouldn't come. Until that very moment I didn't know the name of Cherie's place.

"Might be." I answered. "If a woman named Cherie owns it."

"Y'all ready for this boy in there?" The Doc asked and we both stepped back from the bed to make room for him and Charley to move.

"You can bring him in Doc." I answered.

They came in a minute later, carrying a still unconscious Turpo. Laying him gently on the bed, the doctor got to work as soon as he had room. Quickly checking the wound and bandage before speaking.

"I gave him a good dose of laudanum for the pain. He'll be out until tomorrow morning sometime. If he's still out in the afternoon come find me. Needs to stay in bed for another two or three days, if not he'll rip those stitches out." He turned to face Henry. "If he does that I'll put 'em back while he's awake."

"The bandage has a poultice in it, so just leave it on for a week. He can come see me to get those stitches out about then." The doc spoke as he packed up his case. "He can settle the bill with me when he's up an about. I'm leaving a small bottle of laudanum in case he needs it. I know he won't use it but it's better to have and not need. Let him eat and drink all he wants, no liquor though."

"We got'm Doc." Henry nodded his thanks. "Charley see he gets home an let the boys know where we at. 'Ave a little one come by tomorrow an he kin run orders."

Charley just nodded before following the doc out of the back door. Once they were gone I locked the door and poured some of the still warm coffee for me and Henry. This was not what I had planned but knowing how the gangs operated should work out for me. They usually knew everything going on in their city.

"You want to stay with him?" I asked while handing him a cup.

"Fair warning my coffee's horrible.

"Nope but I will, when he wakes up 'ell need me. Fool'd try ta get outta bed otherwise."

"I need to get some sleep." I yawned, the days travel and evenings excitement suddenly catching up with me. "I get up early so don't worry about it. I'll bring you something for breakfast when I get back from the cafe. If you need anything else help yourself, the pantry's stocked."

"You ain't tol me why yet?"

"Tomorrow when he's awake, it'll save me time repeating it."

"I'm trus'n you too much but at'll do for now."

"This is his, figure he'll want it back." I pulled the stiletto out of my boot, handing it to Henry hilt first. It wasn't that I cared about the knife but knew it would help him trust me a bit more.

"He'll be happy ta see it, loves at damn blade." He laughed.

Before heading to my room, I checked out my clothes. By pure luck they seemed to have come away unmarred. The little bit of blood was on my vest, but it washed off easily enough using the pump in the kitchen. I spent a few minutes checking over my knife, making sure it was undamaged and clean. The hilt needed a bit more attention but that was a easily done. After I was sure all evidence of the nights adventure was gone I finally headed to bed.

It was still dark when I woke up, but false dawn was lighting up the horizon. I left my boots off and padded to the backyard on silent feet. After going through my morning stretches I followed it up with a vigorous work out. It had been a few days since I had the time, and I enjoyed the brief moment of peace that it gave me. The cool air sent chills across my bare chest as I went through various forms, cooling done from the work out. Just as the sky was starting to lighten I walked back into the kitchen to get a bucket of water. Henry was leaning on the door frame, watching me curiously.

"What's all 'at?" He asked curiously. "Looked like what them china men do."

"Morning exercises, might have been exactly that. They're the ones who taught me." I laughed at the scowl on his face before walking back out with the bucket to clean myself up.

"Ya do it every morn'n?"

"When I can, it's a challenge on the trail."

"Puncher?"

"Yeah but I got sidetracked with some horse trouble."

"Stole a horse huh?" He grinned, assuming I was on the dodge.

"Nope." I grinned. "Returning one that was stolen."

"Yup, some do gooder." He laughed right back at me.

"I got paid for returning it."

"Makes more sense at least." He was still smiling as he followed me back to the kitchen.

"I am headed to a cafe to learn how to make decent coffee an have some breakfast, I'll bring some back. It's the creole place down the street."

"Tante Vels?" He asked quizzically.

"Yeah that's the place, waitress offered to show me how to make coffee."

"They will, tell'em the is food for me an Turpo, they'll take care of ya good."

"Will do." I agreed before heading to get dressed.

CHAPTER 8

MAKING COFFEE

It was just starting to become light when I made it to the cafe. The front was open and when I walked in the waitress from the previous day stuck her head out and smiled at me.

"Cher! Ya did come 'fore we open! Must need 'at coffee lesson." She laughed, smiling at me.

"Been catching a bit of hell over my coffee so yes ma'am."

"Come den lets get ya taught right." She led me back to the kitchen. "First ting is boil da water, you manage at right? Or ya one o'dem that burns de water?"

"No ma'am, I manage that part with a fair amount of success." I laughed. Not mentioning the two coffee pots I had melted, there was a definite risk of further teasing if I admitted that.

"Stop all'at ma'am nonsense, ya call me Binda, Cher."

"Whose names on the sign?"

"Tante of course, who else silly boy?"

"Tante?" I puzzled over the word.

"Ahh you would say it wit an A, auntie I tink."

"Oh, your aunt owns this place."

"Close enough for now. The water bin warmed, don't never add no grounds ta col' water."

"Warm the water first, got it." Yeah, I had always made this mistake.

"Dats what I say Cher, now hush an listen. Let da grounds boil wit da water. Maybe tree or four minutes see, longer is stronger but don' never go past five. Too bitter."

"Got it."

"I know'd ya was smart Cher!" Her laughter rang out again and an older woman came in through the back door.

"Why ya got dis white boy in da kitchen girl?" She demanded without any preamble.

"Aye Tante dis da boy from last night. Learn'n him ta make coffee da right way." She looked a bit embarrassed but didn't back off.

"Morning ma'am." I tipped my hat toward the older woman.

"Don' be start'n wit ma'am 'n me boy! In my kitchen ya call me Tante like da rest." Her scowl had just a bit of upturn at one corner, giving away her amusement. "Everyone got ta make cafe. Use dem ears under at long hair boy and learn right from Binda."

"Yes Tante." I smiled back. Some part of me warmed at the word coming from my mouth. There was an acceptance that went with it, one I didn't understand yet.

"Pay mind now Cher." Binda spoke up getting my attention back on the task. "It been on da boil enough now, dis part is important. When ya pull it off da heat, add col' water thru da spout. It'll settle da grounds right to da bottom. "

"That's it?" I was confused, everyone made this sound like a magic trick. I admit the cold water was new and I had been boiling it way too long, which explained the bitterness.

"Da boy look more confused now din 'e did afore Cher." Tante laughed as she walked back through the door. When she did the scent of spices and cooking food wafted into the small kitchen.

"Cher dats it, no tricks." Binda smiled.

"Thanks, you saved me from myself." I sheepishly admitted. "Now how about some breakfast?"

"Get out ta kitchen then Cher, take some cafe wit ya. I'll bring da food to ya in a bit."

"I need two meals to take back. Henry said to tell you it's for him and Turpo."

"How ya know dem two boys?" Binda studied me carefully.

"Long story." I didn't really want to get into it all.

"Them two? I betcha. T'aint nothin but trouble wit'em." Her smile told me she liked them despite her words. "I'll fix ya up some to take, don ya worry none. Now get out da way boy, got cookin' ta do."

"Yes ma'am" I said over my shoulder as I fled the kitchen with my coffee, followed by her yelling about me calling her ma'am.

The coffee was pretty good, it oddly made me feel like another piece of my cowboy education was done. At the sometime I had to wonder why no one had shown me this before? Tom had plenty of chances and Smythe could have shown me any morning. So why the big secret?

Breakfast was eggs with a spicy sausage called andouille, potatoes and perdu which was like French toast. Tante left a basket full of food on the table when she picked up my money.

"Cher, you watch dem two boys. They got a way about 'em at some folks worry 'bout. Oh, They got a sense o' honor, but ya be careful Cher." Her warning followed me as I walked out to door.

"Yes Tante."

Walking back into the house I found myself facing the twin barrels of a derringer held by Henry. He was glaring at me over the barrel with a mix of anger and curiosity. It took everything I had not to smile after I took a second to study the situation. It probably wouldn't be very helpful if I outright laughed in his face.

"Put that down before you do something stupid and make

me kill you." The cold had spread through me as soon as I saw the gun but it was already easing back.

"What are you going to do? Gotcha dead ta rights." He snapped. The confidence in his voice was shaky though, this wasn't someone used to guns.

"Last time, put it down or this'll be the last morning you wake up and Tante will be really pissed I dropped this food."

When his eyes shifted down to the basket, it was the moment I needed. My right hand swung up and knocked the derringer out of his grip. My body followed the motion through, using the movement to bring my elbow up sharply under his chin. There was an audible click when his jaw was forcefully snapped shut. His eyes rolled up in his head and he fell straight back.

I caught the derringer as it bounced off the ceiling before it hit the floor. After tucking it into my vest pocket, my right hand filled with my Colt. The click of the hammer coming back must have stirred something in his brain because he was staring up at me from the floor.

"Don't kill'em." The voice from the bedroom was weak and dry, it must be Turpo. "I told'em to find out the story."

"Take this and get in there." I held the basket of food out and waved my colt motioning Henry into the room with Turpo. He managed to regain his feet but was definitely not stable on them. The hammer was still locked back, life or death hung in the air.

"Ya got ta know this don't make no sense. What's da game?" Turpo was still calm as he spoke. He'd managed to get the glass of water from the bed side table and took a slow drink after speaking.

"It does and it doesn't. For now, just figure that I don't like three to one odds in a fight. There's more, but right now I need a reason not to kill both of you."

"Ha! You kin't. What would da police say?" Henry sounded confident for someone who didn't know me.

"When they get here it'll be my story of two dangerous men

holding me hostage while the wounded one healed up. I got lucky, grabbed one of my colts and killed them both. Who will they believe the one alive or the dead men that can't disagree?" Henry's face went pale. He suddenly realized I could get away with it and already had a story. The cold look in my eyes told him I wouldn't even miss lunch over their deaths.

"You've got two things going for you right now. First Binda and Tante will be pissed if that food goes to waste. Second Coleman Wordsmouth, I need to know what's going on with him and the Gilded Dove. Now I might be wrong but I'm betting y'all know a bit about what's going on in this city. That information is worth me helping you."

"Open 'at food Henry, he's right Binda 'll kill all of us if'n that food is wasted." Tupor was smiling now that he understood the stakes. "Far as da Gilded Dove, dats cause Cherie gonna be Mrs.Wordsmouth. Jus' one thing I gotta know, can ya explain 'at hat?"

"It do get looks an 'at feather ain't help'n." Henry laughed as he started laying out the food. He was still a bit unsteady on his feet but seemed to be recovering quickly.

I holstered my colt and turned to put some coffee on, this might take a minute. When I walked in with the coffee pot the two were eating a similar breakfast to mine. I grabbed a couple of the sausages while I filled their coffee cups. Then moved a chair around from the kitchen to sit in the door waiting for them.

"It's my hat, let's leave it at that. She marrying him by choice or trying to save her place?" I finally spoke when they slowed down eating.

"If ya say so. Don' know if they in love but she's plenty will'n. She got her claws in'ta him when he was see'n another girl." Henry laughed.

"Right, just don't make sense why they been wait'n, ain't nothin stop'n 'em."

"Well, I'd say there's a few reasons." I laughed. "He's in with the white league and she, if what I been told is accurate, ain't white."

"Na she ain't, dat girl pure creole from long back. Her people come from the original peoples back on da swamps." Turpo laughed. "Prolly escaped slave an Choctaw."

"Them white boys won't like 'at." Henry laughed with him.

"One of the other problems is Mr.Wordsmouth is actually Mr. Cole Ward. Late of the Union Army and has strong associations with the Red Legs. I doubt his southern brothers would take kindly to a Red Leg in their midst."

"Oh, he'd be dead if they know'd that." Henry's face split into a wicked grin at the thought.

"Their biggest problem is why I'm here. Cherie doesn't own the building the Gilded Dove is in, my employer does. She sent him a message asking for help but he's a man with a name and doesn't want to be associated with her business. My guess is they hoped he would come here in person so they could blackmail him. Cheaper than having to buy it."

"More like ta kill 'im." Turpo offered his thoughts.

"I don't think so, the wrath that would come down from his murder would be considerable." The certainty in my voice must have struck a chord with them.

"That big of a man?" Henry looked surprised.

"Yes, he most assuredly is. The funny thing is he wants out of the whole mess. He only bought the place to help her, he'd sell it cheap just to be done with it."

"Ain't neither o dem 'as money. He got a few other places but his white friends chased out da workers so they was cheap, no?" Turpo said laughing. That tidbit did fill in some more information for me.

"Dats da trut', that man couldn't find a dime in a bank." Henry added.

"Won't they do the same to the Dove?"

"No, all of 'em go to da Dove." Turpo laughed so hard he winced in pain. Henry picked up the explanation while he got settled back into bed.

"Aye, dem boys talk bout white purity but on a cool night they

find'em a nice creole girl at da Dove. They never close 'at place."
He paused thinking for a minute before continuing. "Thats
why he want da Dove. Power over 'em, blackmail an all."

"That's it! They all know'd 'ats how Cherie gets by!" Turpo
almost yelled. "Cherie have all them stories, she kin hold all
dem boys up."

"A power play than." It made a lot more sense now. "Who's
on the other side from Wordsmouth?"

"Who ya mean?" Henry looked at me questioningly.

"Who's he in a fight with for power? Who opposes him in
the white league or whatever? If he's going through all this to
get power it means someone is a threat." Not really expecting
an answer from either man, but there had to be one.

"Has ta be Nash, that man's bad but it has ta be 'im" Turpo
added after thinking for a few minutes.

CHAPTER 9

GETTING TO WORK

"If he learn'd 'bout at Red Leg stuff 'ed kill da man for certain! He spent da war at a prison camp." Henry agreed with the assessment. "Bad place I hear."

"Y'all know where he lives?" I asked. The mischievous look the two shared said they knew it intimately.

"Maybe so, might a been there a time or two." The smile on Henry's face explained it all.

"Can you get me in there?" I was grinning at the idea that was forming in my head.

"Kin ya sneak?" Turpo asked bluntly.

"I can manage." I grinned back.

"Three days, Nash got a game that night. We kin do it easy wit him gone." Henry said.

"You think'n ta work with 'at man?" Turpo didn't seem happy about this idea.

"More wanting to use him. If I can get him to buy the building it solves all my problems, probably some of yours." I was smiling now. "Or at least it'll cause some chaos in the white league, maybe fracture it."

"True, 'at would be good." Henry laughed.

"Three days should work. I'll have to see if my boss is okay with the plan." My brain was spinning now. "Gives you some time to heal up too. That is unless y'all try a kill me again?"

"Na, we done with'at, just had ta know the story." Turpo laughed, Henry looked a bit embarrassed but just shrugged. "Sides it didn't work out so well."

"Worked out better for you than the last man who tried." I smiled back but it never reached my eyes. They both studied me for a minute before Henry spoke again.

"I ain't try'n again, them eyes cold like death."

"I wouldn't try it again until you learn more about guns. When you stick a derringer in a man's face he can see the bullet." I cracked a big grin. "Or lack thereof."

"What?!" Henry sputtered. Turpo just started laughing. "Ya mean it wan't even loaded?"

"Nope." I laughed, opening the breech, and showing him the empty chambers.

"Putain!" I had no clue what Henry said but I was pretty certain it wasn't meant for polite company. Turpo and I just kept laughing. When we stopped and Henry didn't look like he was going to be sick anymore I got back on topic.

"So, three days? You can get me in to see Nash?"

"Be three, he out da house that night. Won't be back til late." Henry smiled knowingly.

"Works, gives me time to look into some other options. If I can avoid giving them anything I'd like to know how."

I would go see Tillman tomorrow, I knew King was willing to sell the building but for what price. He might have more solid information on Cole that could be passed on to this Nash too. I didn't like the idea of working with those people but if it got the job done and could hurt them it was worth it.

I already had some plans today, shopping mostly. I needed

some less obvious clothes. There were other punchers walking around but most people dressed in city clothes. The trail clothes and guns made me stand out too much. I'd have to buy another shoulder rig, a waste since I had a good one stored in Dodge but there was nothing I could do about it.

Maybe I could just have a shoulder rig made for the Greener? That thing would be a nasty surprise if I needed it. A bit bulky, but if I wore a longer coat it would work. Luckily, despite the humidity, most men still wore suit coats.

"Hey one of y'all know a good leather worker?" I asked. The two were focused on their food again and hadn't noticed my woolgathering.

"Ole Toby 'ill be da best, don't ask nothin or tell nothin either." Henry answered through a mouthful of eggs.

Before he could continue the back door opened without warning. I spun to face it, a Colt quickly filling my hand. To her credit the old woman standing in the door didn't scream, if anything she looked annoyed. The glare she gave me could wilt flowers in the spring.

"Boy less'n ya wanna be whooped point 'at somewars else!" She snapped. Her tone was so sharp I automatically holstered my gun while starting to stammer out an apology.

I took a second to study her before anything else happened. A lean frame, slightly bent from age and hard work, but still quick and sure of each movement. She never gave me a chance to finish.

"Mista Tillman tol' me ta come clean an make ya some coffee, if ya JC that is?"

"Yes ma'am, Minnie if I remember right?"

"That's me, who in der wit ya?"

"Jus' us." Turpo answered from the other room.

"Lordy what I do ta deserve dis, bet that wicked yella boy wit ya?"

"Yes ma'am" Henry stepped into the doorway and grinned. "Sorry 'bout da mess. Turpo got hisself stuck again, da white boy saved 'im."

"True?" She eyed me up and down carefully before asking. "Ya save dat damn fool boy? Ain't no one learn ya better?"

"Seemed like the thing to do at the time ma'am."

"Minnie, ya save my boy it's Minnie for certain."

"Momma don't…" Turpo started but she cut him off abruptly.

"Boy ya damn lucky Doc tol me ya was alive or I'da kilt ya. You quit fuss'n an lay there." She snapped. "Y'all 'et?"

"Yes ma'am, I got breakfast from Binda and Tante."

"Minnie boy, stop 'at ma'am nonsense or 'll box yer ears. Then ya ate right, got sum gumbo cook'n at da house. Bring it by for ya dis even'n'." She had stepped into the small room and despite her harsh words there was a look of concern when she inspected Turpo. "I get dis mess cleaned, y'all two stay hid for a few. Not that y'all had a ting to do with it but da law found three white boys dead. Been ask'n bout who made'em 'at ways."

"Doc fix'd me up good, gonna stay 'ere for a bit." Turpo smiled at his mother.

"Boss was right bout you Cher, a good man. My tanks for help'n at fool boy of mine." Before I could reply she turned to the front of the house to start cleaning, not interested in further conversation.

"JC, 'ats how she is."

"I had forgot someone was coming, lucky it's her." I looked at Turpo before asking. "Mother?"

"What you tink us colored folks just rise up outa the earth?" He grinned back at me. I just shook my head, as he continued. "Bout every maid in da city friend's wit us. They hear everyting an pass it along. Rich folks ignore 'em an jus' keep talk'n."

"Damn, guess somethings don't change." I laughed.

"Whatcha mean?" Henry asked.

"The gangs in New York do the same. All the maids or most of them sold or gave information to the crews workin' the city."

"All da same, don't matter da place, rich folks never mind da help." Turpo laughed. I even heard Minnie laughing from the front of the house.

CHAPTER 10

SURPRISE FINDS

Henry gave me directions to find the leather worker. His place was on the outskirts of town so I could go by Tillmans easily. There were a few shops along the way so finding some clothes would be easy enough, I really didn't need much. A dress coat, couple of white shirts, some pants and a hat that matched. I didn't like giving up my denims or my hat but blending in was more important.

On my walk to Tillmans I stopped at a few shops, managing to get everything I needed. Including a pair of boots that blended in better with the locals. I changed at the cobblers before arriving at Tillmans, dressed much more suitably. For a few extra coins the apprentice cobbler ran my purchases and old clothes back to the house with instructions to leave them in the stables.

I didn't look rich but not poor either, it was the middle class look of someone who could afford some luxury but wasn't worth noticing. I still wore my colts, but the coat kept them mostly out of sight. I had picked a longer style coat that hung to mid-thigh. The vest and bowler hat completed the look. It was enough like my clothes from school that I wasn't bothered, except for the tie. I had gotten used to just wearing a loose bandanna around my throat, so the snug tie annoyed me.

"Is Mr. Tillman in ma'am?" I asked the secretary. She was taking a far more serious look at me now that I was dressed according to fashion.

"Who may I say is calling sir?" She asked but I knew she recognized me. I gave her the same answer I had the other day.

"JC Stone."

"Very well Mr. Stone." She rose from her seat and stepped into the other room. Much like the other day in a minute she was back and waved me into the office.

"Mr. Stone, a pleasure to see you again sir." Tillman greeted me while taking in my new appearance. "Looking rather more like someone who belongs now I see."

"Mr. Tillman, I had some further questions regarding our business from the other day." I stuck to the formal conversation until the door closed.

"What can I help with JC?"

"What's the number King wants for the property?" I got straight to the point.

"Current value is two thousand four hundred, but he would take less I'm sure." Tillman sat back in his chair considering for a minute. "If he could get fifteen hundred he would call it a win I believe."

"That's all I needed right now. I did learn that Cherie is lying to him. She intends to marry Wordsmouth and take the business and property."

"How did you learn that? You haven't been here a day!" Tillman was surprised but not as surprised as I expected. He already knew, which was a problem. He was either part of it or willfully ignoring it. Suddenly I lost ally, I couldn't trust which side he would be on.

"Cities are all full of rumors if you know where to ask." I had to play this cool, not letting on that I had caught him. Lawyer or not a cornered man would do anything to protect himself. If he thought I would tell King he was playing both sides? I'd be a dead man before making it out of town, probably before I could make it Wells Fargo.

"Do you think offering it to someone who opposed them would be worthwhile?" If he knew that meant he was already involved. Now I just needed to figure out how far he was involved.

It seemed like an innocent thought, something that I was toying with but hadn't really planned out yet. His answer would hopefully give me more information. He sat there studying me for long seconds before answering, probably trying to assess if I knew something he needed to worry about. When he finally answered it revealed his mistake. He believed there was no way I could know anything.

"No, the man is unopposed. I can't think of anyone who would challenge him for it." He tapped his chin, thinking as he spoke. "And I doubt he would be willing to buy something he plans on getting for free."

"Well damn. I'm outta ideas." I put as much disappointment as I could in my response. It gave him the option of advice, hopefully revealing his hand. He could point me at someone else if he opposed them or tell me to do nothing if he was working with Cole and Cherie.

"Maybe just tell King to let it go?" There it was, he was working with one or both.

"Might be the only way, but I still don't want to line ride." I grinned mischievously. "Maybe I'll delay a bit, enjoy the winter here. I'll have to leave before spring no matter what, but if I left now I would end up working a line shack. If I could stretch out my stay here maybe I can just tramp out the last of winter at his ranch."

"Well as far as I know Mr. King won't need that house anytime soon." Give a crook some rope and they'll hang themselves every time. He was willing to let me stay if I didn't ask questions or cause problems. "Money wise I didn't really have a limit, but I wouldn't feel right giving you too much for expenses if you're not doing anything."

"Maybe just a few weeks." He wanted me to go along, and taking a bit more cash would sooth any concerns he had. "After the clothes I'll need another two hundred for pocket money if that's alright Mr. Tillman?"

"Of course!" He grinned making the assumption I wanted him to. I could be bought. He pulled a cash box out of his drawer before counting out two hundred dollars. When he handed it to me with a simple receipt to sign. "Just let me know if you run out and of course, if you find anything else out."

"Thanks sir, I doubt I will."

We shared the grin all crooked men shared. Internally thanking my time in five points for letting me recognize a man who was on the take. While saying farewell, we shook hands. I waved casually at his secretary before strolling down the street toward the leather workers. I had a bad feeling I was going to need that greener sooner rather than later.

On a hunch when I crossed the street I stepped into an alley and waited. Five minutes later Tillman came out of his office. After looking up and down the street he started walking toward the center of town. I wanted to follow the man but knew he would spot me. I was still too easy to spot no matter how I dressed. Even if he believed me it would still take time to become comfortable with it.

My luck held in the oddest way, a light step behind me gave me just enough warning. My Colt leapt into my hand as I spun to face a boy, maybe ten years old. He froze, his eyes opened big enough to show the whites. The hand reaching toward my pockets stopped in midair. It was funny since my money was tucked safety in the inside pocket of my new coat. I spoke before he could say anything.

"You want to make some money kid?"

"Sure mister." The boy nodded vigorously, still staring down the barrel of my colt.

"See that man?" I pointed at Tillmans retreating back.

"Yup!"

"Follow him all day, then come to 118 Gravier tonight, use the backdoor. Tell me where he went an I'll pay you two dollars." I flashed him the money. "If ya don't do it I'll know and won't pay you. Turbo might even take an interest."

"Yes sir!" The last bit had his attention, he knew who Turpo was for sure. I still couldn't be sure he would do it, but doubted he would get caught so the risk was low enough to be worth it.

"Go, might be more work like this if you do it right."

The boy shot off into the street then slowed when he got within easy sight of Tillman. I waited a few more minutes then stepped out into the street and walked toward Toby's. It didn't take long to find it, located exactly where they had said.

The exterior of the building was a simple wood shack, maybe a bit bigger then normal but otherwise it wasn't anything that stood out. Only a small sign hung above the door told me I was in the right place. The area had the smell and look of a leather shop. That meant both good and bad. Tanning hides is never a pleasant smell, but the scent of finished leather always made me smile.

Walking in the door it was almost overwhelming in the heat. I staggered back for a second letting my senses settle down. A large man was seated working a piece of leather on a bench behind the counter. His grey hair and beard gave away his age, but his big, gnarled hands still worked the leather deftly.

"Y'all get used ta it, give it a bit." His deep slow voice had a reassuring tone.

"It's a mix of good and bad ain't it." I laughed already having adjusted to it.

"Reckon, it's all jus' normal ta me. What kin I do ya fer?" The man looked up, setting aside his work. "Names Toby."

"JC," I offered my hand stepping forward, "need a custom shoulder holster for this."

I set the saddlebag down on the counter and pulled out the shotgun. Toby stepped forward and looked at me for permission before picking up the shotgun. He studied it than me carefully, measuring me with his eyes.

"Reckon 'ats an interestin thang." He set it back down before turning to sort through some leather hanging from a peg. "Might have sumtin at'll work here wit some fitt'n."

He turned back toward me holding a worked piece of leather. It was more ornate than I normally liked, hand tooled with a poker cards. It was beautifully done, the royal flush falling down the leather holster that looked custom made for a shotgun. I couldn't believe what I was seeing.

"You just had this around?" I asked surprised, taking the holster to study it.

It would hang down my left side, a loop hung from the bottom meant to hook over a belt. There was a simple strap that went across the back connecting the two broad pieces that went around each arm. Another piece of tooled leather hung down the right side. This one decorated with falling coins weaving between ten loops. Each one meant to hold shells for the shotgun.

"Some fancy gambla ordered it, then got his self kilt a'for pick'n it up." Toby explained. "Been hang'n there 'bout a year now, jus wait'n for some other fool want'n ta carry a scattergun."

"Mind if I try it out?"

"Figure ya ought ta."

The man obviously wasn't interested in talking about his artistic ability. The masterful way the work had been done spoke louder than any words. I pulled off my coat and slung the rig across my shoulders. It was a bit snug but without saying a word Toby stepped behind me and adjusted the center strap. Loosening it enough that it was still snug but comfortable and let me move freely. The loops on either side for the belt had simple adjustments that took me a minute to work out.

Once it was situated I put the scattergun into the holster and looped the thongs over the hammers. That's when I noticed they had a hard piece of leather turned toward the hammers.

The harder leather was built to slid off the hammers when I needed to pull the gun. It wouldn't be a fast draw but should work with some practice. It would make for a nasty surprise to someone who thought I was unarmed.

The weight pulled to one side but a quick glance gave me the answer to that problem. The loops on the other side would balance it nicely, this was obviously by design. That meant the man had figured in how many shells it would take to balance the weight correctly. I looked back at Toby with a new admiration, every detail had been considered. Each loop was angled down at about 45 degrees and would fit snuggly over the shells.

"It's perfect, did he order it with the loops or was that your addition?" I thought I already knew the answer but wanted to ask.

"Figure it to balance da weight, jus' made sense."

"It's done beautifully, not my normal taste," I indicated my plain rig sitting on the counter, "but I kinda wish it was."

"Fella were a gambler, wanted 'em purty even though they want aposed ta be seen." He explained then pointed at my plain holsters. "Them you gots is better than I kin do, perfect work."

"I ain't sure of that but thank you. How much do ya want for this?"

"Figure it's worth twenty dollars but ain't gonna sell it no time soon, call 'er fifteen?"

"I'll pay the twenty." I said pulling out a double eagle and setting it on the counter.

I put my colts back on for now. The combined weight was a bit much, but I would leave the colts at the house from now on. Maybe tucked into my saddle bags with some trail clothes in the stables. It was never a bad idea to have a cache ready to go.

"Fair, happy ta see 'em go. Things like that ain't right ta be used but I made em, reckon it's good someone 'ill have 'em." Toby spoke in his slow drawl as he sat back down and went back to work.

I took his dismissal in stride and walked back out into the

midday sun. It was a cool enough day that the walk didn't bother me, I rather enjoyed it actually. There is no way to really see a city other than walking it, learning the feel of its streets.

CHAPTER 11

LEARNING THE CITY

General stores, dry goods, clothiers, several haberdashery's and more than one bookstore filled the streets. I thought about stopping in a bookstore but remembered the library at the house and decided to wait. I did stop at a small restaurant and ate lunch while sitting in a window watching the people walk by. The act made me think about how many times I had sat and watched people just going through their day.

The streets were filled with carriages, carts, and horses traveling both directions. Some carried single men or woman, but more than one large carriage was packed with kids. All walks of life passed wealthy business owners in fancy carriages next to struggling sharecroppers on ramshackle buck boards. Trail dirty punchers rode by on cow pony's while other men almost seemed to strut down the street dressed in fancy suits.

There were even a couple of vaqueros, decked out in black clothes with silver embroidery on display. Hats, gun belts, and saddles hand tooled, accented with silver conchs. Wide sombreros shading their neatly shaved faces. Their horses almost seemed to prance down the road, animal and rider enjoying the looks people gave them.

The impressive display of humanity was a reflection of New Orleans. Native people walked by carrying furs and packs, while a doctor strolled past with his medical case. Two bow legged old Punchers waddled down one side, always politely tipping their hats to ladies. It happened so often they almost didn't move at times, but their manners never faltered. The unwritten law carved so deeply into their souls it left no alternative.

Kids of every age and color wove in and out of the crowds. Playing with one another, no matter their station in society. I took a few minutes to watch them, admiring their naiveté about the prejudice of adulthood. They were soldiers versus Indians, cowboys at shoot outs, cops chasing robbers all at the same time. They pointed fingers or rifles made of sticks at one another, dying loudly falling to the stones in the throes of death. A smile crossed my face, those days were not that far gone.

I had been so serious about my education that I sometimes forgot about those days. Seven years old chasing other boys through the parks or alleys. Both sides falling to the ground as imaginary bullets or swords punctured hearts. Maybe I had been too driven and should have enjoyed that more. I could see myself reflected in some of the older boys who trailed behind or beside their parents. Working so hard to appear adult, imitating their fathers in walk and dress.

The girls were no different. They seemed to hit an age and suddenly they were walking beside their mothers. Learning to be proper young ladies in society or how to care for a hearth and husband. Occasionally there would be one following her father, pestering them about the changing world and how they should be allowed to learn some craft or trade.

One girl declaring loudly to her father "that plenty of girls went into medicine!" To which her father tried to explain that she should be happy as a wife, there was no need for her to be a nurse. This did not win him any points as she explained loudly that she would be a doctor not a nurse. I chuckled quietly under my breath as they passed, just enjoying it all.

The afternoon passed far too fast, the shadows slowly growing across the ground like fingers reaching toward the coming night. I had been sitting at the cafe most of the afternoon just watching the city. Getting a feel for it and its people, at least on the surface. I could still feel the tension that flared occasionally as one parent, or another pulled a child away from their playmate. Not wanting them associating with people like 'them'. It was an undercurrent that swam through the city, like some venomous serpent poisoning the minds of the innocent.

As for me, my accent would stand out a bit but not as much as I feared. I had heard Spanish, French, several native languages, and that was just the recognized languages. Accents went from English to the more common heavy southern drawl. The Creole people had their own language. Some of it I recognized as French but mixed with a sprinkling of other languages I didn't recognize. I later learned it was a mix of languages from around the globe.

The Creole were their own thing, just like their language. To a person, from the young girl refilling my coffee to the old man riding down the road they looked proud and strong. They wore their heritage like a badge of honor, anyone who tried to remove it would have a very bad time of it. I had a growing respect for these people. Much like the Tejanos, they loved their home but faced prejudice and hatred on their own land. It had started with the Indians and the first Europeans to land on the east coast. The irony of a people fleeing persecution only to find themselves becoming the oppressors was the very definition of humanity.

I understood this was the way of the world, there were laws and rules to keep things civil, but they only worked within that civilization. For those outside of it? There were very few allowances made. They could be killed, enslaved, moved, pushed around, and condemned without any repercussions. Here that meant if you were a white male you had power, if not there were no promises. This one-sided way of ruling wasn't unique. Hell, even the tribes had subjugated or conquered other tribes long before we got here. It was this way throughout history, folks who had power did what they could to keep it.

Those heavy thoughts filled my head and accompanied me to the front door. Voices interrupted my reverie from the back of the house as I closed the door. It was Henry arguing with someone, I couldn't figure out who for a minute, then I recognized it. The kid from earlier, the one I had sent to follow Tillman.

CHAPTER 12

INFORMATION IS POWER

"Henry hold up!" I called out as I walked down the hallway. "I did hire him."

"Tol' ya!" The boy declared. Receiving a glare from Henry before he turned and walked back into the room where I could hear Turpo laughing. "Ya said Turpo not Henry, I ain't tell'n ya nuthin mister!"

"Boy ya tell that man everyting or ya will be answer'n ta me!" Turpos voice went from laughing to serious in a second and had the desired effect. The boy gulped loudly and started talking.

"That man went straight to da Dove, stayed 'bout half hour then went ta da Bon Cher. He stayed 'nother hour then went back to da office an lef an went home. He might a had a dawg, couldn't check on da house." It came out as one long string of words, but I got most of it.

"Here," I handed him two dollars, "follow him tomorrow and come here when he goes home."

The boy nodded enthusiastically while making the two dollars disappear before dashing out into the alley. He quickly faded from sight. Watching him disappear made me smile, not long ago I was that kid.

"Ya catch all that mess JC?" Henry asked from the bedroom. I stripped off my coat and walked in to have them explain it. Forgetting that I wore two colts and a scattergun. "Expect'n trouble from an army?"

"Better to have and not need than to need and not have." Another quote from Tom was my honest response, both of them laughed. Turpo looked a lot better, he was sitting up in bed seeming to be on the mend.

"The Bon Cher is Wordsmouths place, one o' them anyway. Who was that one follow'n for ya?"

"Lawyer that's supposed to be working for my boss." I answered honestly, seeing no reason to lie.

"Sounds like maybe not eh?" Henry chuckled."Welcome to da big easy, everyone 'ere cut ya throat for a dime."

"Seems so." I agreed.

The new information didn't do anything but confirm what I already knew. It still didn't make my path forward any clearer. If I was lucky Nash would be willing to buy the Dove just to foil a yankee, but that seemed like long odds.

I could just walk away with some certainty that King would drop it once he knew everything. The problem was I didn't like that answer. Some core part of me just bucked at the idea of walking away, especially now that someone taking Kings money was betraying him.

"Ya think'n on da next step?" Turpo asked after letting me stew on it for a few minutes.

"Can't see a way unless I can get a cats paw to deal with it, like Nash." I admitted.

"Could jus' kill'em?" Henry suggested again.

I had to admit it was an answer, not a good one though. I couldn't see Tillman drawing on me and killing Cherie was out of the question. Killing women just wasn't a thing you did, ever. It would also be contrary to what King wanted.

"Naw, not my style and I don't think my boss wants that." I managed to keep the mysterious boss at a distance.

"What then?" Turpo asked curiously.

"Not sure yet, have to think on it." I wandered into the kitchen to get some coffee without really answering. Now I knew the players but that didn't really fill in the blanks.

I took the coffee and my pipe out on the back porch to think. No matter how it flipped around in my head the best answer was this guy Nash, but I couldn't be sure he'd go for it. What if he didn't? I couldn't do anything without Tillman and that was a bigger problem. Or could I?

If he was cornered the man wouldn't be able to back out, not without being caught out by King. If I could corner him with Nash, if Nash went for it, and if Tillman didn't balk when cornered. That was far too many ifs for my comfort, there had to be another way.

The night had settled around me as I sat thinking. The last soft lights of the sun had lit up the city with every color of the rainbow. Off in the distance I could just hear the music from Bourbon Street. If I was going to play the tourist for a few days I needed to make it look right. That meant going out on the town for a bit, even if I didn't want to. It didn't matter, there wasn't an answer here and I needed to play the role.

Unfolding from the chair I strolled back into the house to find Minnie serving up food in the kitchen. She must have come in the front door while I was lost in thought.

"Done star gaz'n boy?" She asked handing me a bowl of something that smelled amazing served over rice. "Set'n eat a'for it cools, had gumbo a'for? Gotta bite to it."

"No ma'am." Was all I could get out without drooling. The food had set my stomach grumbling and the smell was too tantalizing to be ignored.

"Enjoy it boy." She patted my head as she walked by. It was comforting in a motherly way. The off handed kindness made me feel more relaxed.

The stew was a combination of spicy and savory, without the rice it would have been too hot to eat. Thankfully it knocked the heat down to a heavy sweat level. The spices were again completely different from the Mexican flavors, delicious and unique like everything about this city. I worked my way through it, enjoying every bite but needing more and more water as I ate. By the time I was done my hair was damp with sweat and my mouth felt like it was on fire. Not that it would have deterred me if she had offered another bowl.

"Damn that's…" my words were cut off by a sharp impact on the back of my head.

"Mind ya mouth boy." Minnie snapped. It was again oddly comforting, like a physical sign that this woman accepted me as part of her family.

"Yes ma'am." I smiled up at her stern face, just able to see the corners of her mouth twitch up.

"Mind her JC. She got no allowances for young folks, hers or others." Turpo said from the bedroom. "I know that sound, felt it on da back of my head more'n once."

"Same." Henry added.

"Ya might be da first white boy she adopted eh?" Turpo laughed.

"Don't make me deal wit ya two!" She snapped but her face was smiling in the way only parents do. She lowered her voice and said to me. "They tol me bout ya sav'n my boy, for that ya is family no matter da color. Least I kin do to show my 'precation for that. He's trouble, but Cher is my trouble."

"My pleasure." Meaning it, glad I had met these folks. She walked back into the bedroom with the two young men and the volume of conversation went up. Occasionally punctuated by the smacking sound when one of them swore. I wasn't sure how I had ended up here, fate or God but it didn't matter. I would just appreciate it while I could.

I took my saddlebags and packed some trail clothes and my hat in them. Out in the stables I rolled the colts up and stuffed them into the saddlebags under my buckskins. Then I loaded the rest of my ammo into them before taking them and the Winchester into the hay loft. After moving a couple of bales around I dug out a hollow and tucked the saddlebags with the Winchester into the space. It took a few minutes to arrange the hay back into place, but I was happy with the hiding spot.

That done I cleaned off any hay that hung on my pants before climbing down from the loft. I'd have to muck Loki's stall tomorrow but for right now I refilled his water and gave him a bate of oats.

"We'll go for a ride tomorrow. Let ya stretch your legs a bit." I spoke softly to the horse causing him to knicker back, or it might have been the apple I slipped him.

That done I went back inside and walked to my room. After collecting the clothes that had been delivered earlier I put them away. Hid everything except fifty dollars in a niche I had found behind the bed. Then made sure my sheath for the stiletto was secure and it could easily be reached. I felt somewhat naked without the colts but when I slung the scattergun rig on I felt a bit better. With the extra shells now loaded it balanced a lot better. I also loaded the derringer and tucked it into my pocket, just in case. Now it was time to practice.

I stood facing the mirror, drawing the empty shotgun. I repeated the motion again and again, letting my body start to memorize the movements. Noting the way the jacket could catch on the triggers if I moved wrong, how to adjust it with my left hand to make it smooth. Over and over again I practiced until it was smooth. It would never be fast, smooth was what I was trying for and after an hour I had a good handle on it.

It was time to go out and play my part. I reloaded the shells and made sure the other side was secure. Double checked the knife and derringer one more time before heading down to Bourbon Street. It was time to see what this eclectic city like this had to offer a young man on vacation.

CHAPTER 13

A NIGHT OUT

It didn't take long to make it to the French quarter. I paused in a shadow to tuck my ponytail into my hat. For the first while I just walked around like a star struck kid, which really wasn't that hard. I was still that big eyed kid on some level, one who didn't really know how to take everything in around me.

After making it about halfway down the street I spotted the sign I had been looking for. The Bon Cher, the very place I had heard about earlier. I noticed it but didn't go in, keeping with the flow of traffic I moved on a few more doors. I'd make it in there later but right now I just wanted to look around. The place I picked at random was called The Bourrée, I didn't know what it meant but they probably had beer.

When I walked into the smokey haze that filled every saloon there was a strange sense of familiarity. It struck me as funny considering how few saloons I had been in up to this point. It was crowded with men from all walks of life. The river men were easy to see, sticking together in groups. Two odd punchers sat at one of the card tables at the back of the room. I didn't recognize the game and left them alone, besides there was at least two professional gamblers at each table. I could spot them by the way they watched one another, ignoring the rest of the table.

At a second glance I realized only one of the tables was playing a strange game, the others were various games of poker. Seven card stud, five card draw there was a pharaoh table in the back corner. A delicate looking saloon girl was dealing it, that struck me as odd but after watching her sweep most of the money every hand it made sense.

Waitresses and soiled doves moved through the room, each serving men in their own way. They were every shape size and color just like the crowd. At first I didn't notice because it wasn't something that stood out to me, but after a minute I became aware of it. Most places seemed to be divided by race or color at least, but this place was a true mixed bag. Probably because of the sailors, I noticed more and more of them moving through the haze. Sea fairing men came from every land around the globe and the places that served them had to allow for that. I wove through the crowd toward the bar, amused at the contrast.

After making it to the bar I found a clear spot to lean while waiting on the bartender. When he finally appeared, I ordered a beer and left a dime on the polished wood of the bar when he asked for it. It was cool but not cold, still good though.

I managed to make it halfway through the mug before it started. The big man standing beside me finally decided to act. I had listened to his drunken whispers about robbing me in the alley for about five minutes now. It was starting to get tedious, waiting for an attack you know was coming. No fun.

There were three of them and from the look on the bartender's face this was just business as usual. It was strange to be happy about attempted robbery but once I knew what they were about there wasn't much choice..

"Eh boy why ya drink'n my bar? Ya to purty for da likes of us."

He bellowed.

His followers laughed along hoping to get a response, but I wasn't in the mood to make this easy for them. I ignored him, which usually doesn't work on bullies. It didn't work on him either, he slapped his meaty hand on my shoulder and spun me around.

"Eh did ya 'ear me boy! Maybe ya need me ta teach you…"

Whatever else he was going to say was lost in the gurgling noise that having ones throat ripped out caused. I slammed the broken handle of my beer mug into his throat when he spun me around. He had missed it when I broke the mug, too focused on picking a fight with someone he thought would be easy prey. That cold feeling filled me with icy calm, slowing everything down.

I broke the mug on the edge of the bar as he spun me around. Then it was just using his own strength when he spun me to slam the sharp edges home. After that it was just a matter of dodging any fluids, after all I had just bought this shirt.

His meaty hands went to his throat, mistakenly trying to stop the blood cascading down the front of his shirt. He slowly sank to the floor and silence filled the space around us. The bartender was trying to catch flies with his gaping mouth when I looked back at him and put thirty-five cents on the bar top.

"That's a bit for the mug and a dime for another beer." My voice had the cool calm it always had when the cold gripped me.

My words seemed to break the shock, or it was the noise of the big man's face splashing into a puddle of his own blood. Whatever cause it the man behind me took that as his sign to act. I had been waiting on him move and dove over the bar, much to the bartender's surprise. His knife slammed into the bar top and stuck fast. Since he expected it to be stuck in my back the angle threw him off balance making his chest smack into the bar.

He never saw my hand swing from where I'd grabbed my stiletto. The razors edge slashed his face open from his left eyebrow to the top of his lip on the right side. Taking his eye and some of his nose as it passed. He fell back screaming, trying to hold the skin together. The fight was kicking off across the bar now, it was time to go. I grabbed the double barrel from under the bar before diving for the back door at the end.

My shoulder hit it first, thankfully it wasn't locked. When I rolled to my feet across the alley the light from the door revealed two men crouched over a body. They bolted as soon as they saw the shotgun in my hand. Quickly scooping up my bowler, I noticed the body was close to my age and dressed similarly. I wiped my knife on his jacket and put it away before looking around. The first gun shot rang out from inside the bar telling me I was running out of time.

I fired both barrels in the air before slipping the shotgun in the dead man's hand. Cutting down the alley in the opposite direction of the other two, hopefully opening a gap between me and any pursuit. Two buildings down I stopped to check myself for blood. There was some on my hand but that came off easily in a rain barrel, thankfully my clothes looked clean.

I walked passed two more buildings in the alley before cutting back to the street. No one paid any attention to me walking out of the alley, most were watching the brawl. It had spilled out onto the street and the police were smacking anyone near the bar with their clubs, doing their best to end the melee.

I was banking on the cops here being the same as Five Points, lazy. Hopefully they would take the easy answer, assume the dead man in the alley was the one who kicked all this off. I knew no one had gotten a good look at me, besides with my hair tucked under my hat I looked about like everyone else. Well maybe not my eyes but I just had to hope no one alive noticed them. Or if they did would keep their mouths shut.

Two bars up I found a quiet high-end lounge and ducked

inside. The beer was better and cold, better still no bully was waiting for his next victim. I spent a few hours playing poker, letting things calm down outside. I got up from the poker table, with about as much money as I sat down with. The professional gambler at the table tipped his hat to me. He was the only one who knew I was sandbagging hands, he looked road worn enough to understand.

The street had calmed backdown to its normal chaos as I made my way back toward the house. I kept my ears open and caught bits of various conversations. It told me that the cops were like I hoped. They'd taken the easy answer and called it a day. That let me make it home without any problems where I was greeted by Henry. He was sitting at the kitchen table sipping coffee.

CHAPTER 14

LATE NIGHT CONVERSATION

"Ah da hero returns." He grinned over his coffee as I poured myself a cup.

"Don't know about that but it's been an educational evening." I took out my pipe and set to packing it while the coffee cooled a bit.

"Eh we heard 'bout that 'twas mor'n at, No?" Turpo carefully walked out of the room to join us at the table.

"I spotted two, how many did I miss?" I asked after puffing my pipe to life.

"Don tol' ya he'd spot 'em!" Henry laughed. "Ya saw 'em both, got an eye for it."

"Didn't think you'd catch both of 'em." Turpo smiled taking the cup of coffee I offered. "Should have know'd, ya truly is from da street. Specially handle'n Bob like at, ruined their night."

"Bob?" I figured they meant the big guy but wanted to be sure.

"Yeah, da big man in da Bourrée, he bin thump'n folks 'at way for years now." Henry explained. "Ya got da law too wit that corpse out back. They tink a sneak slit ya throat out back try'n ta escape."

"Got a quick mind for true. Scared our boys bust'n out da door like at, like ta scream they said." Turpo was grinning as he talked. "They was der ta help when ya got out back. Wan't expect'n 'at one, ya handled it for certain."

"So y'all trust me now?" Smiling over my cup, knowing they hadn't been sure about me before. I was also amused by my watcher's other activity. "Guess they were just helping that poor man out back?"

"Trust ya kin kill sure, but we know'd that. Now I know'd ya smart too, that's da hard part ta figure." Henry admitted. "Ya good wit da boys now fo'sure."

"Nice to know a night of chaos is worth more than saving you." I chuckled.

"Life's cheap no?" Turpo barked out in a laugh.

"Tante and Binda come by, they say ya should be at da cafe in da morn'n ta learn da trinity." The smile on Henry's face didn't give away much but I doubted they were talking about the holy trinity. My confused look gave away my lack of understanding which made them both laugh. "Don worry, them lady's take'n to ya, they'll learn ya right."

"Still not sure if that's a good or bad thing." I chuckled and they both joined me.

"Ya fit in wit da creole better'n mos folks, 'specially white folks." Turpo commented. "Don't much matter though, Mama adopted ya so ya family. Round 'ere that mean all o'us"

"Been meaning to ask, is the difference between Creole and Cajun really just color?" It had been on my mind because I had heard both used to refer to people. My question made both of them laugh, which told me I was missing something obvious.

"Forget how ya don't know noth'n, Creole is us, Cajun is just dem white folks was born in Louisiana." Henry explained though his laughter. "But that sure ain't da only difference. Real folks know how ta be family, you understand?"

"I do, learning more every day."

That night before I went to sleep my mind started questioning my actions again. I had killed Bob without any hesitation. The same had happened with Big Mike back at Lisbon, he had pushed and killed him. It hadn't been a year yet and there was a trail of bodies behind me deep enough to bury me.

Jose was right, I carried no weight or shame for any of them. Those men, from the first back at Caldwell's to Bob last night had pushed and I had answered. I knew it would happen again because no matter what I wanted some men just couldn't help themselves. For every one that pushed me there would be more bodies, at least until I was the one six feet under.

That wasn't my current worry though, what had my mind stuck was how quick I had acted. That was the part of the cold I needed to watch. I might not feel anything about killing but I didn't want to become killer. There was a difference, self-defense was one thing, but I had to question myself about my actions every time. It was just my internal dialogue that would hold me accountable. I know Bob was pushing me and had plans to rob me. Most likely kill me, that wasn't really a debate. I just hadn't waited and let him have a chance at it. That was the rub, did I act too fast? Was there another way out?

I couldn't say for certain but felt like killing him was the right call, I did think it was the easiest way to end the situation. Hell, I might have saved others if I had just backed him off, not that I could think of a way to make that man step back. He had made his choice, second guessing that didn't have anything to offer. Neither did this line of thought, men had pushed me, and I had answered.

CHAPTER 15

THE TRINITY

The next morning before the sun lightened the sky with more than the softest shades of dawn I was in the backyard. My mind spun through the web of lies again and again. Trying to find my way through it reminded me of the maze puzzles I had seen a few times. None of this was my forte. Using the motion of my stretches to help focus my mind usually worked, but not this morning. The game of politics and intrigue was such unfamiliar ground, and this one could carry a price in blood.

By the time I worked up a sweat I just sat down on the back steps giving up on my routine. After slowly playing through it again and having no more answers. There just wasn't one I could see. If Nash didn't go through with the purchase I'd have to walk away and tell King to drop it. Short of violence there wasn't another way to solve this mental knot.

I'd thought about selling the building to Turpo and his bunch, but they didn't have enough real power to hold it. Without a good answer I set it aside, going in to clean up before heading to the cafe. Maybe this trinity would give me the answer, if not it would distract me at least.

Turpo had finally explained that the trinity was onions, bell peppers and celery. They were the base for most local dishes, that and seasoning. The key was the spices you added to the base, but it was more complex than that. In truth I was looking forward to spending time with Binda more than anything else.

The morning was mentally relaxing, simply working in the open kitchen on the back porch helped quiet my mind. The teasing and jokes at my expense put me at ease, making me feel welcome like one of the family. There was also a simple sense of accomplishment in making food for people. I think it helped me understand Smythe and the passion for what he did.

Tante had laughed at me when I accidentally rubbed pepper in my eye, after I stopped crying there was nothing for me to do but join her in laughing. I didn't know it but things like this, being a part of something, meant more than words could express. There was something about it that kept the cold at bay, a warmth that filled me.

I spotted Turpos watchers again, one was a young boy that stayed stuck to a shadow across the street. The other took longer but on his third pass by the cafe I noticed the older boy who was doing laps around the block. I knew they were there to watch my back, not spy on me.

While I worked my mind tried to puzzle out this twisted knot again, with no more success than I had in the morning. I knew Jose would come if I called but that wasn't the answer anymore then having King ride in with his hands. Neither of those would fix this situation, it would just cause more bodies to fall.

I needed to figure this out without violence if possible. I had some help from Turpo and Henry, but this game was above their pay grade. Really it was above all three of us, but it was my snake, I just had to figure out how to stomp it. Tante noticed my distracted mind after we finished preparing the gumbo and asked about it.

"Eh boy, ya twirl'n round a problem, no?"

"Yup, and not one I'm well equipped to deal with." I admitted.

"Tell Tante 'bout it, maybe dis ol'woman know a bit." I hesitated for a few minutes, but the truth was she might know a way around it. Hell, she couldn't do any worse than I was. So, I laid out the whole situation, starting in Lisbon with King. I did omit his name, it didn't have anything to do with the problem after all. When I finished she sat back shaking her head.

"I'm good about some things, but this is beyond me." I added, finishing the tale.

"Dis man, he tell ya to get out da business no matter what no?" She asked studying me carefully.

"Yeah, he wanted to help Cherie but if he had all the facts I think he would just want out."

"The answer is simple then, don't mess wit 'at Nash, he's a bad one. Ya talk ta dis man who knows Tante. Sell 'im da build'n, he kin deal wit it after ya down ta road."

"I can't do it without involving Tillman. Since he's playing both sides it would cause trouble with the sale." I reminded her.

"Maybe so, maybe no. Ya do a deal wit dis man then ya git ta this man an have 'im deal wit that part." She smiled at me over her corncob pipe. "Ya jus' leave it ta me boy, be a day ta get ya wit dis man. He kin met ya an ya'll find a way."

"Yes ma'am." I smiled.

She was right, if she knew someone who could navigate this rat's nest, I would happily let him. It felt like something was settled, there was a way out. A way that would let me and King walk away untouched. Tante said she knew a man who understood this business and was better at playing this game. I would take her at her word and let him deal with this mess.

I left the cafe with a basket full of food again, making my way back to the house. Minnie was cleaning when I came in but quickly grabbed a pot of coffee off the stove. Turbo and Henry were already at the table, she filled our cups and joined us.

Once the food was finished Turpo spoke up.

"Been tak'n up that bed too long ya know? Dis wound is healed up 'bout as good as could be. Figure on leav'n wit Henry aft'a the dark come."

"Might be too quiet around here without you two but I'll manage." I laughed.

"Da boys still keep an eye out while ya in da city, maybe keep a blade outcha back." Henry smiled.

"Fair enough, I'd appreciate that. If everything works out I'll be out of the city in a week. Tante thinks she sees a way out of this mess that won't involve Nash."

"That be a good ting, no?" Turpo asked studying my face for a reaction.

"Very, whoever this man once make a deal, they can figure out the details. That way I can be long gone before the fireworks start."

"Cher, don ya worry none 'bout that, if she know'd 'im that man can deal wit it. Dat Traiteur knows folks more an she ever say." Minnie added as she finished her lunch. "I'll make 'at room right from da mess o those two canaille."

"Cher!" Turpo tried to protest but between all of us laughing he couldn't manage it.

Once the laughter died down I really started thinking about the next couple of days. Tonight, I would lay low, tomorrow meet with whoever this mysterious man was and make a deal. Then I would play the young man again, hang out for a few days before heading west. A few months of line riding would send me off toward the Bar C in time for round up. It was a simple plan, much better than anything else I could come up with.

I spent the rest of that day learning as much as I could from them all. They were both born in the city and knew every twist and turn, not to mention the more questionable places. I told them about New York, the years I had spent learning its streets and back alleys. It ended with me demonstrating my rusty pick pocket skills, neither of them would believe I'd ever done it. Once the show was over they still didn't believe it, turns out picking pockets is a perishable skill and I had let it perish painfully.

The next day was much quieter. Turpo and Henry had left under the cover of darkness leaving me alone in the house. They had reassured me that they would be around if I needed them. When I made it to the cafe Tante said she would bring the man, who she still wouldn't name, by after sunset. I spent the rest of the day reading, just enjoying a lazy day.

CHAPTER 16

MEETING THE MAN

That evening, I warmed up the last of the gumbo and waited. Not long after the light of day faded from the sky a light knock at the backdoor got my attention. I opened the door to find Tante, Binda and a large bald man with and impressive mustache standing in the glow from the kitchen.

"Cher may we come in?" Binda asked, but she was looking around nervously as she spoke.

I could see three shadows around the barn and guessed they were security. Stepping aside, quietly waving the three into the kitchen before closing the door behind them. Once everyone was inside she introduced the man.

"Cher dis be Lt. Governor Dunn, the man we tol ya 'bout."

"Sir." I extended my hand to the man. His grip was firm, confident without exerting the obvious strength he had. He was not a small man, the broad chest and shoulders showed a strength that didn't come from political office. The hard calluses on his hand said this man had done real work for a lot of years and earned that muscle.

"Pleasure is all mine sir. I am led to understand you may represent an opportunity to thwart some of the less savory folks in my state?" His voice was deep and cultured but there was still just a hint of a southern drawl remaining. The big man sounded like his classmates back east on the surface, it had rid him of almost all of it.

"Don't know about that, but I can arrange the purchase of a building that's currently a house off ill repute. What happens to that building after the sale won't be of interest to the gentleman I represent." I felt myself slipping back into the speech patterns of law school.

"I have been told there are some complications?" As we spoke Tante set a pot down on the stove and started warming it, the scents slowly filled the kitchen as we talked. Binda was poking around the pantry looking for some spice or another that she felt it needed.

"Yes, the attorney I was instructed to deal with has allied himself with those set against my employer. It makes handling the sale a more challenging affair."

"That could complicate things but not stop them entirely. Would your employer be willing to handle things via telegraph? If so I have a good attorney we can trust."

"He would be, the only reason I haven't taken that step is not trusting the telegraphers here in the city." I was honest about Kings concern here. Telegraphers were supposed to be bound by confidentiality but that wasn't always the case.

"I have one we can trust. I am short on time so let's not get bogged down in the minutia. When you do make contact with your employer have him message me in Baton Rouge. I'll be back there in two days. I assume it will take you longer? "

"Yes sir, I'm not sure I'd risk a telegram until I reach Lisbon and I'll need to stay here a few more days to be discreet."

"Very well sir, I'll look forward to hearing from your employer. You can also trust the telegrapher in Baton Rouge, they keep their confidence. Not out of some moral code but because they know the state capital will hold them accountable. Have them mention your name when he sends it, the ladies informed me you go by JC?"

"Yes sir, I'll have him mention JC Stone as a contact." Now that he knew I couldn't make the deal fully, he was ready to go. It made sense, the longer he stayed the higher his risk.

"It's been a pleasure sir." We shook hands again and the man swiftly departed. What threw me off was why had he come personally and not sent an intermediary?

"Cher, gonna take dis pot for 'at one on da stove. That way ya 'ave a good meal No?" Tante asked as she and Binda got ready to leave. She had taken a pot that matched the one on the stove, so it made no difference. Well other than one was full of amazing food, and one wasn't.

"Yes ma'am." I smiled at the two ladies as they disappeared into the shadows of the alley. I had no idea what she left, but it smelled divine.

Sitting at the table eating what turned out to be red beans and rice, I felt much more at peace with everything. There was also a sense of victory tinged with hesitation. I knew who Dunn was, him showing up to buy the building told me just how out of my league this was. I needed to fold this hand and get up from the table, this game was above my skill level. All I had to do was hang out a few more days then make my way back to Lisbon. Before I went to bed I did a few more things to prepare for any unplanned events.

Retrieving my saddle bags from the hay loft I repacked everything I might need. Everything had to be ready for a fast exit if something went wrong. All my clothes except the new ones got added my bedroll with my bow. I filled the saddle bags with dry goods, coffee, and most of the money.

Once it was all hidden back in the hay loft I headed to bed finally. Laying there my mind spun in circles before sleep took me. I laughed at myself for being excessively paranoid, but it was becoming a habit. There was no reason to hide that stuff but something in the back of my mind wouldn't shut up about it. That voice had quieted now that it was done, but the sense of unease didn't let up.

The night passed dreamlessly. The brisk chill of winter trickled into the house waking me before dawn. After stoking up the fire in the stove I stepped into the cool predawn air. Even with the chill a light sweat covered me when I finished. The thought of another bucket wash didn't appeal to me, it was time for a proper bath.

There was a barber just down the road that offered hot baths. I'd rather pay them to haul the hot water than do it myself. Twenty-five cents was worth not having to do it.

Some fresh bread, hot coffee, bacon, and eggs started my day off. I needed to remember to thank Tante and Binda for the bread later. Just sitting on the porch with hot coffee while smoking my pipe until mid-morning was peaceful. Even the background noise from the city didn't take away from it.

I had been enjoying a book from the small library, a newer author named Mark Twain. The book was called "The Innocents Aboard" it was a few years old now, but this was my first time seeing it. The man had a talent for turning a phrase and bringing his story to life.

I had stalled long enough, giving every indication of sleeping in after a night of carousing to anyone watching the house. It was time for that bath, then a stroll down by the water before playing some more cards. It was all the plans I needed for now and there was a sense of comfort in that too.

It was midafternoon by the time I finished at the barbers and wandered into a nice restaurant to eat. The food was…well it was much more normal? I'd been eating Creole food most of the time, the meal was good, but I missed the heat. The steak was paired with carrots, potatoes, and the ever-present coffee.

Lingering over a pipe I watched the city slide from the bright activity of the day into the more visceral activities of the night. Some people went into their homes barring doors and windows offering them what protection it could. While others strode boldly into the shadows of evening. Predators and prey assuming their given roles within this play.

That side of the city started to come alive as the shadows deepened. The sun surrendering to the purple of night and its creatures, the last streaks painted the sky in a beautiful array of colors. It caught my attention because I hadn't truly noticed the beauty that this area of the country held. My mind was so wrapped up in complicated problems, it had just slipped back into city life.

It was a different beauty than the plains, something deeper more vibrant existed here. Life teemed everywhere you looked, different from the spread-out life of open grass lands or cactus filled arroyos. It didn't have the completely civilized feel of the east either, it was somehow in-between.

It was dense, full of life that permeated every inch. It was more vibrant, almost bragging about its power. The full weight of it laid on your shoulders like the humidity, it pushed in constantly fighting for dominance. Where the great plains and north Texas had a vague soft song this area had the bouncing mad pace of a full orchestra. Not overwhelming but it would pull you deep into it if you didn't keep your senses. You could easily miss the threats it held in that trance. I let it wash over me, like a breaking wave split by a rock.

For a second it surrounded me, wrapping me with the varied life it held. The constant buzz of insects became the rhythm, croaking frogs helped create the off tempo beat. The deep hum echoing from the bull alligators blended in, holding it all together. The night birds brought in the higher tones, bringing in light notes that soared through the wind. Even the chaotic sounds of the city blended with it, somehow completing the song.

It was an amazing symphony of life that played through the setting sun. People on the boardwalk bustled too and fro, hidden all around us. Most of it unbothered by the masses of humanity who were completely unaware of their inevitable clash. It was like they knew someday this all would all be theirs again, it was just a matter of patience. I had to admit they were right, the heavy moisture hanging in the air was constantly eroding the man-made structures. Feint hints of the salty air whispered its constant threat to everything, even those made by nature.

Maybe it was my mind wandering that led my feet to the port. The call of the breeze coming in from the gulf. The sound of the tide magically harmonizing with the creaking wood of the ships. It reminded me of sailing into the harbor for the first time. The smell of sea air, human sweat, treated wood, and a multitude of trade goods packed tightly in ship holds or warehouses. The all brought back fond memories of my childhood. The momentary lapse nearly cost me my life.

CHAPTER 17

ATTACKED

A boot heel thudding on the wooden planks behind me was all the warning I got. Even as I spun the sharp bite of steel punched into my side after is skittered off something. The cold metal sent goosebumps running up my side before the burning pain erupted. I had just seconds before that pain crippled my ability to move.

My unexpected twist had granted me life for a few more minutes. Instead of steel puncturing my lung the blade cut deep into my side. I felt it being deflected out of my body by my hip bone. Its sharp edge had easily cut me from armpit to hip. The pain when it hit bone nearly dropped me, then the warm blood started falling down my leg.

Whoever was wielding the blade knew how to use it. They had twisted the knife on the way out, trying to take more organs before it left my body. I already felt weak from blood loss, it was falling down my side like a waterfall.

There were three of them, the one holding the blade looked

shocked at my movement. I could see his eyes widen when the met mine, he hadn't planned on facing me. The two larger men behind him were already starting to advance toward me. I could see death in their eyes, not any sort of anger though this was business. The soft light of a lamp shimmered off the blades they held.

Even as I started to fall back my hands worked. The shotgun came out from under my jacket with a sharp snap. Weakness was already spreading through me, but I made my hands work, locking back both triggers. Aiming didn't matter, they were close enough for this type of work. When both barrels spewed their double ought buckshot out, old man death was already reaching his cold hand for their souls. If they screamed I couldn't hear it over the pounding in my ears.

Everything was fading to black, the darkness closing in around me. Even the deafening boom of the scattergun was faint, I was dying there was no mystery there. When gravity finished pulling me down, that would be it. I would be dead. Soft voices tickled my mind as the darkness consumed me, panicked voices. Then there was nothing, just darkness.

The next thing I saw was rough cut timber which to be fair wasn't what I expected from the afterlife. My ears heard concerned voices, my body was racked with pain, and my brain couldn't get ahold of anything for long. Blinding pain so powerful it stole my voice before I could say a word than thankfully the darkness pulled me back into it. My mind drifted back into its comfortable embrace, away from the torturous existence. Faint voices tried to call out to me but I couldn't make out what they wanted. It was like trying to hear people underwater, distant and mumbled.

Then there was light and pain again. Some sort of drink being poured down my throat. My throat was happy for anything, swallowing was automatic. A vague thought crossed my mind about that, why was I so thirsty? The pain came again, raw burning pain, so hot I couldn't even define it. An oppressive heat that couldn't be cooled surrounded me.

It wasn't the humid heat of Louisiana this was an internal burning fire. My mind couldn't make sense of it. Was I in hell? Slowly I drifted out again, lost in silence.

Then there was a woman surrounded by ravens watching me. It felt like she was watching, waiting to see if I would fight or give up. I fought, fought for no other reason than to spite her. The grin that split her face revealed sharp teeth. She would take me away if I gave up but also celebrated my fight to live.

Time passed. I had no idea how long but when a light started to shine in my eyes it made me blink on reflex. At first it was like the sun piercing my eyelids, scouring my brain. It was still so hot it made everything seem much more draining. My throat was so dry I could only manage to croak out a noise.

"Easy Cher, be easy." I knew that voice. It was safe, friendly, but I couldn't remember why.

My mind cleared a bit more when some cool liquid slipped down my parched throat. It was Tante, she was holding a glass of cool water to my lips. "Slowly now, ya drink slow boy. If ya choke it'll feel like da devils come for ya."

I listened to her, not by choice but because she only let the barest trickle of water into my mouth. I wanted to grab the glass and gulp it down but didn't have the strength to move. Swallowing even that little bit felt like putting out a fire inside me but there was so much pain. Each movement felt like I was being torn apart. My body tried to choke on the cool water, making me panic. Fear gripped me but I used that strength it to force my throat to obey.

I regained control when the cold feeling filled me, calming my mind. My lizard brain knew if swallowing hurt that much, coughing would likely kill me. Everything slowed as I took control, forcing myself to accept the pain and simply swallow the slow trickle of water. It was just another fight and one I knew how to win.

"Good Cher, That's good. Ya been mos'ly dead for a week boy. Ya still ain't escape that place, jus sleep an heal. Thats all ya kin do boy, ain't even close ta eat'n 'cept broth."

My mind went in and out of the blackness for another week. Managing to drink just enough to keep me alive. If wasn't water it was broth, tasting of chicken and medicine. Sometimes it was Tante, other times Binda, once or twice I didn't know the voice but still I did as told. It was always the same, drink, don't cough, and don't move. One time it was Turpo, he was reading to me like you would a child stuck in bed. Wasn't that a change from our first meeting?

Slowly over time my mind started to clear as my body worked a very slow mending process. The pain wasn't as overwhelming and faded slightly with each passing day. I could stay conscious longer but sleep still pulled me into its depths frequently.

It was one of the days when Minnie was here. My first thought was confusion, it was the first time I thought about where I was. This wasn't the house, the ceiling was rough cut wood not worked smooth timber. The bed wasn't much more than a bedroll on top of a wood frame. The scent of herbs and medicine drifted around on the hot humid air. When my eyes fluttered open Minnie feed me some broth, when I didn't immediately pass out she smiled.

"Gonna live boy, Thats been a wonder for a bit."

"Where?" Was all I could croak out.

"Safe Cher, it's all ya need ta know. Safe an alive no?" She read my eyes for a minute before continuing. "An da minds back wit us from da dead too, that's a good thing. Jus' know dis, ya was cut bad an been near dead 'bout two weeks. Ya weak as a newborn babe for a while yet, just sleep Cher."

I did as she said, fading into slumber again. They told me later that this cycle repeated for almost a month before I stayed awake long enough to find out what had happened and where I was. It was Tante who filled in the blanks for me.

The three men on the dock were from the white league. As far as anyone had discovered, they had targeted me for helping Turpo. Someone had seen or heard about them being at the house. All three died from the scattergun. The shoulder rig had probably saved my life as much as my turning did. When the first guy stabbed me the blade had been turned slightly by the shells. That little shift is what had kept it from cutting into my organs. It would have been a slow agonizing death, and it was meant to work that way. A warning to others about helping their enemies. If that first stab had landed the best anyone could have done was end my misery.

Turpo's watchers hadn't been able to stop them. Young street kids against three armed men? There was nothing they could do but watch and help me after. They had rushed me to the Traiteurs house.

The place was far enough back in the bayou that the people looking for me would never be able to get here. They didn't dare take me to a doctor's house, besides this was better in their opinion. Turbo had eventually managed to get the same doctor who helped him to come and check on me. He had stitched my side back together, cleaned the wound and left some Laudanum. The Traiteur had cared for me with poultices and herbs since then.

The fever had come on the third night, she said it was up to the spirits after that. They would either take me or leave me, there was no way to know. I don't know if they were right but the dark woman from my vision sprang to my mind when they told me that. She had left it up to me, be taken or fight.

My few friends had been with me day and night for the first two weeks. I had been strapped to the cot, to keep my thrashing to a minimum. The biggest risk was ripping open my stitch's, loosing anymore blood would have been fatal. None of them would give up hope and after two weeks the fever finally broke. I had turned a corner and they figured I was really on the mend.

Still weak from blood lose and fever, deaths door had only just started to close at that point. Tante said it was just this week she knew for sure I would live. My color had came back, and I ate everything they offered. Today was the first day of real food, finally having recovered enough strength to chew without pain. I still looked like the undead according to the Henry, but my mind was clear. The doctor came by that evening to check on me and fill in everyone about the goings on in the city.

"You're going be in bed another week at least, even after that it will be slow going." He told me after examining my wound. "The cut is closed nicely, but the muscles are still healing. Betwixt that and the fever it'll be a solid a month before you even start to get your strength back."

"Thanks doc, once I can get up and moving I'll settle my bill."

"Don't worry about that, ain't often I see a dead man rise up." His smile was honest and genuine. "I'm not just saying that either, nine out of ten would've died from that wound."

"Still, I'll take care of it once I can get around."

The next month passed slowly, I started with walking shambling steps, helped by whoever was there. By the end of the month I was going through my stretches very carefully. Even starting my forms again, admittedly I did it so slowly it was hard to tell what they were. My strength was coming back, it was tortuous at times but steadily improved.

When the doc came back at the end of the month he was amazed at the speed of my recovery. Calling it the magic of youth, the Traiteur agreed with that assessment but credited the spirits. This started a lively debate between the two on the merits of the spirits versus modern scientific knowledge. It was a pretty good show all things considered. What truly made me smile was how she quickly maneuvered him into giving up, too many things he couldn't explain.

Another two weeks and I had put most of my weight back on. The only thing missing was the layer of baby fat that had been there my whole life. Not that there had been much, but it was the last vestiges of childhood. Now it was stripped away, leaving only a lean tough frame of sculpted muscle. The scar that arced from just below my armpit to the hip stood out on my tan skin. Its match across my shoulder, from the squabble that got me my name, stood out as well. Both permanent reminders of the price for letting my attention slip.

CHAPTER 18

DEAD AND
NOT DEAD

Even now in mid-December Louisiana was warm, the sun hung above me where I sat on the porch. I had adopted the shirtless comfort of the locals when possible. Some of that was practical, since my shirt had been destroyed. We hadn't wanted to tip our hand by bringing clothes from the house, so I only had a rough spun shirt Turpo had given me. In the humidity it was just more comfortable not to bother.

When a Houma had come by he mistook me for one of his people before he caught my eyes. I took it as a compliment, but he seemed offended by his own mistake.

"Cher he's jus thrown by not know'n ya was a white man." Binda laughed at my confusion. "Ya look'n almost Creole 'cept that long hair."

"Still ain't cutting it." I laughed, flipping my tightly braided ponytail out of her reach. This had been an ongoing joke since I found out she was the one who refused to let them cut my hair while I was unconscious.

"Ehhh shush ya." She laughed. The smile lighting up her perfect face.

"I need to go to the city, don't care if it's at night but I have to get something from the house."

"Minnie goes today, jus tell er. She kin get it Cher."

"Why shouldn't I go? She's kept the cover that I'm still there right?"

"True, but ya need ta hear what Turpo has to say. He be by tonight then ya decide, no?"

"Fair, I'll wait to talk to him." I grumped. It was a pretense, in truth the more time I spent with her the less I wanted to leave. Which made my next comment all the more painful to say. "I need to settle business here an get back to Texas."

"Boy whatcha got in Texas that ain't 'ere?" The look she gave me almost melted me on the spot. I knew she didn't want me to leave.

"You mean aside from folks tryin' to kill me?"

"Oh, an that scar on da back was?" She laughed having already having gotten that story out of me.

"Gave my word, have to be down on the Rio by spring."

It ended the debate for the hundredth time. She wanted me to stay with her. Part of me wanted to say the hell with it, build a house out here with her and just be. I had given my word though and couldn't just break it.

We both knew I had to go, and she'd never leave her home. It hadn't been easy avoiding her eyes when we talked about it. She could drink me in to those deep pools of black the moment I met her gaze. I would have given up everything just to stay in them.

I had spent so much time with her while healing that our friendship had grown into something more. It was just words to start, slowly though our hands had intertwined. Then one night sitting outside under the stars our lips had met, we both felt it. Something kept pulling us together. For the first time in my life, I had found a woman that held my full attention. She was beautiful in body, mind, and spirit. She kept me on my toes every time we talked.

Her smile could brighten my life and her anger could shatter me. I couldn't say for certain what I felt was love, but it was the closest thing I had ever known. She made my heart sing every time I saw her. One look from her fluttering eyes and my will would melt away. She was the opposite of the cold, when she was near me it felt like I was sitting to near a camp fire. She felt the same, had even been brazen enough to tell me so. Part of me wanted a future with her, strongly enough to make me think about staying. My word was the only thing calling me back to Texas. That and the reality of the world around us.

There was just too much hate left from the war, and it would be there for a long time yet. Sure, paying for sex with a Creole was acceptable so long as it was kept quiet. Truly being with one or worse marrying one? Aside from being against the law, the white league would drive you out or kill both of you if they heard about it. It had already happened more than once, a homestead burned out and a family murdered.

Most left the city if they wanted to live in peace, or kept it hidden. Far enough back on the bayou you could build a life in peace. Most of the folks living in the swamps didn't care much about the civilized rules. They had moved there to get away from it, away from the greed and hate. They lived like the mountain men of the past in their own way and by their own rules. Fighting for survival alone just so they didn't have to live by someone else's standards.

The resentment in the city was growing toward violence from what I was told. A slowly building powder keg and the fuse was getting shorter every day. More and more violent clashes were occurring in the shadows, some had spilled into the bright light of day. It was no longer a matter of months until it blew up but days. Turbo said it would be a week may be less before the violence took off past what the police could deal with. Once that happened the union troops would come in. They met violence with violence and didn't care about sides.

The white league was growing in influence, wealth was translating into power. That control was used to force people out of businesses and homes with violence. Relocating people into neighborhoods that were defined by color or race. Economic oppression was the real difficulty, more and more places wouldn't deal with people who weren't white. This had an upside, the Creole were opening their own places. Slowly they were building their own economic system.

The whole city was on the brink of destruction and there wasn't a way around it. Dunn still wanted the building, but he was in a precarious position, unsure if it would tip the balance for good or ill. He had sent word to hold off for a bit through Tante Vel the other day. I had too many Tantes now they had to have other names with the title.

The local Creole who lived back in the bayous had adopted me, taking turns teaching me about the swamps. I wasn't as good as a native, but I could move through them now. The tricks I already knew were changed to work in this new environment. It wasn't long before I could move through them easily, leaving no trace. Feed myself and live comfortably off the bountiful place. It was another level of my education that was getting added during this time of recuperation.

None of that compared to what was building between me and Binda. She had become my light through the dark weeks of healing. I enjoyed the company of everyone who helped and appreciated everything they did but she had become so much more. I found myself counting the hours until she would return. Time would drag on if I knew she would be gone for too long.

In reverse it would fly by in a heartbeat when she was with me. Everything was so much brighter when she was near. I remembered the first time I saw her framed in the sunlight while I lay in bed struggling just to sit up. My heart had fluttered making me gasp. The bright sun highlighting her lithe form through the thin cloth, it stole my breath away as much as that blade had.

She had thought it was my wound but when she looked into my eyes she had known. My heart was becoming hers, there was nothing I could do about it. I had gently cupped her face and softly kissed her for the first time that day. My entire body felt alive for the first time with that kiss, all that followed just added to the feeling.

"Cher, time for me ta go to da cafe. Turpo ought ta be about soon." Binda and I had been laying side by side, drying in the afternoon sun after swimming. I was stripped down to my pants, and she wore little more then a camisole. We had spent the day enjoying each other's company, barely managing to not cross that last line of intimacy.

"See ya tomorrow Cher?"

"In da morning, ya stay outta trouble ehh?" She said leaning down. Gently gracing my lips with a simple kiss that set my body a flame.

"No promises." I grinned watching her leave, marveling at her beauty.

Damn my word, I wanted to stay here with her. The swamps had their own magic and it spoke to me now. I could hear the land singing as I watched her walk away. It was deep thrum that spoke of ancient life. A time frozen against the tide of change. Then she was gone, taking the song with her. Slowly disappearing into the sunlight like a ghost haunting my mind. All I could do was savor the memory and wait for her to return.

Turpo showed up an hour later, he immediately started laying out the situation for me. The house was being watched now. Minnie was told today that unless I showed up she didn't need to worry about cleaning anymore. She had tried to lie, telling them that I had been there a few days ago. She thought they believed her, but it didn't change the order. They wanted information one way or the other, dead or alive they wanted to know. If I didn't show up they were taking everything including Loki. It was Turpo who offered a solution.

"We kin get in an out a there fast enough ta get ya gear. Da horse 'ats the hard bit." He admitted. "The men 'ats watch'n ain't good ones, think they mean ta kill ya. Don't know why but 'ats how it look ta me."

"How many?" I asked. The calming cold adding a chill into my tone.

"Tree, tough boys too."

"Out back?" I was still looking for pay back after all.

"Two, one watch'n a cross da road." Turpo was watching me carefully as he answered. "Ya tink'n bout taken them?"

"I want to but if I can avoid it, no. I would like to get the horse but at least I need to get into the hay loft."

"Take 'em down ya have ta leave da city, it'd tell 'em too much no?"

"You're right, how long before they go into the house do you think?"

"Not tomorrow, day after maybe, they want ya bad but dem tree dead make'n 'em careful bout ya."

"Let me think on it, can you come back tomorrow night?"

"Yeah."

"Maybe it's time." I admitted.

"Eh maybe so, Binda won't like it." He grinned at me.

"Don't you start I have….." A shout coming through the woods cut off the conversation as one of Turpos runners burst out of the surrounding gloom.

"Dey kilt'em Turpo!" The boy gasped between breaths.

"Kilt who boy?" His voice was demanding but filled with fear.

"Tante Vel and Binda!" My heart locked up in my chest at his words. Turpos voice was a hiss when he spoke again.

"Tell me 'xactly what ya mean, don be mix'n up noth'n!"

"Five men come in and they kilt'em, all wit da law watch'n. They stand'n wit Nash and Wordsmouth. Shot 'em dead an then burnt da cafe down. One of'em say this area for da whites only now." He was still panting but managed to get it all out. "Da boys wanted ta kill 'em but Henry say it want da time an got'em all back off da avenue."

"Told 'em the day would come! Damn it!" Turpo swore.

"Tante say she always bin there an always will be."

The cold had slowly filled me as the boy talked, crushing the pain that was splitting my chest. Those two hadn't hurt anyone, they just wanted their cafe and to be left alone. Binda was dead, it didn't seem real to me but there was a hollow part of me now that knew the truth. She was gone, that warmth I had felt hours ago sputtered and died with the realization. I might have just left, deciding this wasn't something I could solve, but not now. That familiar cold feeling fixed itself around my heart as I ran. Chilling my anger into a cold rage that wanted nothing but blood.

CHAPTER 19

LEAVING FOR
THE CAPITOL

Turpo led us into an alley, close enough to the cafe that we could hear and see everything while staying out of sight. Nash and Wordsmouth were still there, leaning against a wall smiling. Only Turpo's arm stopped me from walking out into street to kill them both. I wanted nothing more than to turn them in a mess of blood and guts. Since the news had reached us the cold had burned through me.

"JC we have ta be smart 'bout dis one." Turpo whispered in my ear as he held me back. "We'll get 'em but not like 'at."

"Grey Walker, JCs not meant for this." Something in my tone made him whip his head around to look at me. He had no idea what that meant but recognized something had changed.

Somewhere inside me those two people had swapped. The easy-going smooth JC had receded in my mind. The cold calculating person who could hang men, tracked and murder Apache had stepped forward. I needed my gear than my hunting would start. I would hunt until everyone of these men paid for their action, paid in blood.

"Who?" Turpo asked.

"Let's go get my gear and Loki." I didn't answer his questions but started padding my way down the alley. We were both dressed the same, having run from the swamp without thinking. Pants rolled to our knees, no shirt. My stiletto was tucked into my lower back, I hadn't grabbed the bowie or the greener in my haste. Moving toward the house my stiletto came out, blade tucked up my arm out of sight. The first bodies would be in the gutter bleeding in moments. I had let this go too long, now others had paid the price.

Some part of me knew that wasn't true, that this violence had nothing to do with me. That logic didn't apply to the primal part of me, that voice was driving my steps forward now. Later the logic would tell me that I couldn't change the way people viewed one another or the hate they carried. Not now though, now the part of me in control felt responsible for their deaths. It was tearing me apart, but every broken piece fell into a cold flame that kept growing. One that would happily burn down this entire city to make them pay for her death.

Slowing our pace, we reached the alley across from the house. I saw a shadow shift ahead of us. A big man was standing just out of sight at the entrance. Watching the comings and goings across the street. He never heard me coming, I clamped my hand over his mouth and pushed the blade into his back twisting it cruelly. My muscles tightened around him, quickly pulling his still kicking corpse back into the shadows.

When he stopped twitching I dropped his body to the filth strewn ground. Stripping off the Smith and Wesson model three and gun belt he wore, I slung it around my waist. They weren't my Colts but the 44s would do the job if need be. After tying down the holster I tested the draw, making sure nothing snagged. Once that was done we slunk across the street.

We moved up a few houses before ducking into another alley then turned toward the back of the house. Turpo pointed to the shadow on the left, I took the one on the right. They died with their blood washing down our blades, silently and in pain. I took what I wanted from their corpses, splitting the cash with Turpo. Loki never stirred, patiently standing in his stall looking annoyed and bored.

"Saddle him up for me? I need to get some things." I said before scampering up into the loft to retrieve my gear. By the time I had everything and dropped my bedroll down Turpo had Loki almost ready to go.

"Da horse?" Turpo asked. I knew the question was more asking me what the plan was.

"I'm heading to Baton Rouge before I swing from a rope. I'll leave him somewhere and come back through the swamp. It'll take me a few days, but I can make my way back. I'm going to grab the rest of my stuff while I'm here, make it look like I just left."

"Go, I kin sneak back da way we come."

"I'll be back soon, maybe a week or so. I'm going to come up with a better plan then vicious slaughter while I travel." Even over the roaring cold running through my veins I knew mass killing wouldn't be right.

"At island I showed ya, light a fire we'll know." Was all he said. I knew what island he was talking about, we had visited it just yesterday.

Without another world I went into house, quickly stuffing my clothes into the saddle bags. I grabbed the cash I had stashed, no need to leave it behind. Once everything was packed I quickly changed, throwing on my trail clothes and my own gun belt. I rolled up the 44s and tucked them in the saddlebags before I stomped into my boots. The last thing I did was fix my hat, making sure the feather ran down the side as I walked out to the stables. When I got ready to step into the stirrups Turpo stuck out his hand to shake mine.

"Ya mind the way, no need for folks ta pay ya any mind but...."

"I'll be back, y'all watch yourselves until I do. Then we'll settle the score." I looked back once watching Turpo easily move down the alley, headed toward the streets he knew so well.

I rode slowly out of New Orleans, using the shadows when I could. Thankfully the fading daylight left me plenty to choose from. They helped hide Loki's unique appearance from anyone who might have been watching. To anyone who looked I was just another puncher slowly riding out of town after losing all his money. As far as I knew they would all be happy I was gone, not worth worrying about anymore.

It took three days to reach Baton Rouge. I spent the time working out the remaining stiffness from my injury. My mind and heart were still firmly encased in the cold rage that kept me on mission, but logic was working with me now. I spent the time testing my draw, making sure it hadn't been affected. The last night I took a boar with my bow, skills were perishable, and I had been laid up far too long. Those three days let me knock the rust off stiff muscles. Between stretching and repeating the motions my confidence returned quickly.

I made it to the livery Dunn had talked about on the afternoon of the fourth day. He owned the livery so I could trust them to look after Loki. He wasn't Danu, never would be, hell there wouldn't be another one like her. I probably wouldn't be keeping him once I made it back to Texas. He was a fine riding horse though and deserved to be cared for.

The city was smaller, it also wasn't under the sway of the white league yet. There was still plenty of hate, but there were enough federal troops stationed around to keep the peace. Before riding in I had changed into the last of my city clothes. No one paid much attention to me, just another traveler riding in.

"Thats a fine look'n horse ya got thar young fella." The old man at the livery commented.

"Tricky but he's a good riding horse. Need to put him up for a week or so. I'm going to be moving around some."

"Got a big corral out back for him dur'n da day. Take fine care of 'im." The man sounded like someone who liked horses more than people. "Twenty-five cents a day."

"Two dollars should more than cover the time I need." I handed him the money as he reached for the reigns. "Know a good hotel?"

"Might." He eyed me carefully for a minute, seeming to come to some decision before he answered. "Belle of Baton its good, kinda high an mighty for my tastes. Miss Norton's boarding house 'as better beds an chow."

"Boarding house sounds good, long as she doesn't mind absent tenants."

"Long as ya pay she minds 'er own." He laughed at my concern, then offered me directions to the boarding house.

It was a well-kept blue house just a few blocks from the stables. When I stepped onto the porch a small bookish looking woman opened the door. Looking me up and down, unsure about what was standing on her porch.

"You don't look like trouble, but there is something off with you young man." He tone was brusk and she had just the slightest hint of an English accent. "I am Miss Norton."

"Might it be the Irish you see ma'am?" I asked with a grin.

"That would explain it. I do not allow drinking or drunks in my house." I couldn't blame her for the assumption.

"Mostly coffee ma'am with the occasional beer." I smiled down at the small sharp woman, having known a few like her before. "Much to the shame of my family the taste of whiskey never suited me."

"We will see." Her tone was crisp, but the slight upturn at the corners of her mouth said she got the humor. "Mind folks? That's most of my boarders."

"No, a bit ma'am." I could tell she meant non-white, which explained the livery man studying me before recommending this place. "Likely I'll be paying you more for a place to keep my things. I'll be out on business in the area most of my stay, of course I'll pay for the month."

"That's none of my concern, come in. Mind your boots, I just washed my floors." She pointed at a mat beside the door before leading me in. "Your room will be on the second floor, it's three dollars a month with two meals included. Breakfast and dinner of course."

"Yes ma'am." I liked this woman, she was direct. The fact that she welcomed anyone into her home spoke volumes about her character. The room she led me to was simply furnished a bed, dresser, small desk, and chair all perfectly clean.

"That's it." Her tone said she was expecting me to complain.

"It'll be perfect Ma'am." I handed her three silver dollars before stepping into the room, turning sideways to ease my over packed saddle bags past her.

"Coffees always on in the parlor. Breakfast is at seven, dinners at five. You're welcome to use the living room and porch, back and front. Privy's out back other then that just stay out of my kitchen."

"Yes ma'am. I'll be here tomorrow but after that I'm unsure. I might be gone for a few days, possibly longer."

"You're paid for a month, your room will be there until then. Laundry is extra but it can be done. I recommend a bath and shave before dinner. The barbershop is just down the street, Mr. Nicole does a good job, and his baths are clean." Speech and orders given she shut the door. Her light footsteps moved back down the stairs.

The boarding house wasn't ideal, but I liked it. My comings and goings would be noticed, but that was manageable. There was something more comfortable about it, they also tended to be safer from thieves. I unpacked my saddlebags and bedroll, putting my clothes away before taking her advice. I walked back out the front door to go find the barbers.

Looking in the mirror while waiting for him to finish another gentleman I realized how rough I looked. I couldn't grow an actual beard but had that scraggly bit of growth all young men grew. I had also been bathing in the swamp for a while. True it got you clean but the water, even in the springs, always had a scent to it. To be honest the man in the mirror was surprised the proper lady of the boarding house had let him in. I may have been in water every day recently, but it hadn't include soap and other such things. It might be time to add a shaving kit to my saddlebags as well.

The place was as advertised, clean and efficient. The shave and accompanying offers of a haircut were expected and pleasant enough. The man really didn't like my hair, he seemed to feel it was an affront to his craft and took my refusal as a direct challenge. The baths were hot and the water clean. I did end up paying for two after I tinted the first one, the second one got the last of the swamp scrubbed off.

There was a general store next door and I stepped in to purchase some much-needed supplies, including a shaving kit. After that I looked for a place to relax and smoke a pipe alone for the first time in several weeks. The simple answer made the most sense, I went back to Miss Norton's retrieved a cup of coffee and sat on the back porch. The afternoon sun warmed me as I sat just enjoying my pipe.

Sitting there with nothing pressing I let my mind start to open the pain that had been locked in my heart. Binda and Tante were dead, killed for nothing more than the color of their skin. My heart worked through the pain, tears streaking down my face. I remembered the laughter and teasing of Binda. Her smile tortured me when I accepted that it was now gone forever. Killed for petty differences and prejudices.

Those that had caused it would pay in blood. I knew that was a lie as soon as it crossed my mind, at best the petty men on the ground would pay. Those who truly held the power would never even notice, not the loss of good people or even their pawns. My revenge would be just that, mine. I had no hopes that it would somehow balance the scales or stop the hate.

They had attacked what I cared about, there would always be a price to pay for that. Attacking me understandable, I had begun making moves to challenge the pawns power, I was a threat. But attacking the ladies? They just wanted to run their cafe, serving good food and taking care of people. That was really the painful part of all this, good people paying the price for others greed and hate.

There was no tricking my mind, I recognized that's what this was, greed. All of this was about money and power not about race. The ones high up on the food chain didn't care about those petty motivations, if they did it was nothing more than as a bonus. Five Points was poisoned the same way, convince the masses to hate someone because they were different. Keep them fighting and distracted, all the while men in power hide in the shadows working with anyone who furthered their desires. The propaganda they sold meant nothing to them, it was just a tool they used.

The cold was still there, driving me forward but now letting me do it with a clear mind. It didn't mean the pain of loss wasn't crushing. Those two women who taught a young puncher to make coffee and so much more, they were gone from the world. A woman, possibly a woman I loved was gone. There had to be an accounting for that absence.

I made no pretense this wouldn't be driven by justice alone. Part of it would be personal, it would be done out of pain and loss but now I could do it with a clear mind. I knew this was a dangerous path but there was no choice in my mind. My belief in right and wrong wouldn't allow this to stand. It was just some core part of me that could not let this go, men would die for these crimes.

CHAPTER 20

PLOTTING VENGEANCE

What I really needed was a couple of days of normalcy to ease my heart and mind. There would be more tears, they had to be given time to come out or they could hollow a man out. Tom had taught me that, he had lost a Shoshone wife in a Blackfoot raid.

He only talked about it once and only then to teach me another lesson. He said that no matter what I did people I carried about would die. Time would be the only thing that helped and now I understood. I would never forget her smile or laugh but time would ease the pain. We both knew what we felt could never be, not peacefully in this country. That didn't ease the loss, but it added another rule to my mind. I would never tolerate that unreasoned hate around me. A man would be a man and I would take each as they came. None of this solved anything but it was my only way to start processing it.

The next two days passed with me mostly wandering around Baton Rouge. Remembering those losses, shoring up my mind once again. My heart was slowly starting to mend. It was just beginning, and I knew the scar would never truly heal but it wasn't a crippling pain anymore.

 In the meantime, I stockpiled some supplies, went for a ride late in the afternoon of the second day to create a cache. I left my buckskins, some ammo and food there. It was about halfway to New Orleans and gave me some peace of mind.

It was on a small island near a spring that would lead me back to the bayou and people I knew. The area was well off the road and tucked back in the swamp. It was a lucky find with a small, shed Loki could use for shelter if need be. The spring had good water and some graze, enough to keep one horse for a week or more. It wasn't perfectly safe, but it was as good as I was going to get for now.

That night I let Miss Norton know I'd be gone for the following day. She again reiterated that my room and things would be good for the rest of the month. My last stop for the day was the dry goods store, I picked up an extra piece of tarpaulin. It would help keep my city clothes dry and clean in the shed. I wanted my justice but didn't want to end up on a wanted poster.

The next morning, just as the pre dawn light began chasing the shadows of night across the land, I was riding Loki out of town toward my cache. Even with everything that had happened the beauty of this place still caught my attention. The colors of dawn created a light show as the night slowly gave up its grasp on the land. The road was empty except for the early morning traffic of farmers. They started the day early, bringing in their goods to sell for the day.

Once I cut off the road I was alone. After dismounting to brush out my tracks I led Loki to the shed. After unsaddling him I started a small fire. There was a lone cypress tree on this little island, I used its branches to break up the smoke. No sense in advertising my presence.

While the water boiled for coffee I changed into my buckskins. Rolling my clothes up in the new tarpaulin and tucking them into the rafters I finally relaxed a bit. I was heading back to New Orleans, there were some people to see and I was missing my scattergun. I honestly planned on this being knife work for the most part, but the colts were with me.

There were three names on my list, two for sure and the third was a maybe. Wordsmouth and Nash would die, but Tillman had some flexibility. It would depend on how he reacted when we met, not that it would be in his office. The truth was if I could get him to turn on his conspirators than maybe some of those who played in the shadows would get dragged into the light.

After I finished my breakfast, simple bacon and biscuits that I managed not to burn. I sat on my heels sipping coffee, thinking about the next steps. It would take me a solid two days through the swamp to get back in the area and hopefully meet Turpo. Then we would have to find out the best way to get at the targets. Some part of me knew I was plotting murder, but it was the only way these men would face justice. My rage was still there but that cold feeling was present constantly.

The idea of revenge had cooled, the immediate need for blood tempered by my own sense of right. What I wanted was justice, let the law hand out my revenge in the right way. The problem was the only two ways I could see it happening was either a confession or the few federal troops. I didn't have faith in the local law at all and it wasn't very likely the federalists would step over unless they had to.

I had no way to make them confess and doubted the law would get involved without cause, so that left vengeance. A thought broke through my rage as I sat there planning my hunt. Tillman, he was a coward and too used to his comfort. How much was he involved with these men? I knew he was double dealing King, that had its own risks for him. But was he in with the rest of them? If there was a weak link, he was it. Even the threat of King would make that rabbit run. Could I play that angle?

He would be my first stop, getting him to testify with enough evidence could be painted to his advantage. The man was spineless and if it suited him to turn on them he would do it. Sometimes cowards had their uses, they were always the first to turn on their friends.

My soul still howled for blood but my mind, the cold calculating rage that held my hand back, thought prison would be worse for those men. Maybe they would be hung, the union were getting frustrated with all the trouble. That much I knew from the rumors around the city. If I could do this without getting caught up in the violence it would be better for everyone left in the city. I just had to convince both Tillman and the Union that these men were a real threat.

Dousing the fire, I left some extra feed for Loki before setting off through the swamp. Every lesson the Creole had taught me came into play. Dodging snakes and gators I moved quickly through the night. When the last traces of moonlight fled I climbed high up in a tree listening to a bull gators deep hum below me.

He was the boss of all that he surveyed, proudly claiming his piece of the swamp while calling the females to him. A panthers scream broke through the deep shadows waking me late just before dawn. He wasn't far off but from the noise it sounded like he had his own problems. A loud squeal followed the scream. Whatever large boar the panther had challenged wasn't going easily. From what I could tell the cat might have picked more of a fight then it wanted.

The predawn was cool and damp when my eyes came open. Some water and jerky weren't the breakfast I wanted but it was what I had. I set off moving through the soft light of day not long after. By mid-day I knew the meeting spot was getting closer, no one would be there to meet me but that didn't matter. They would be watching and someone would come find me at dusk. It was a small island with dry land to make a fire. Far enough away that the smoke wouldn't give away my location.

I found a small stack of dry wood hung in one of the trees when I arrived. The small bundle of food wrapped with it assured me this was the right place. I hadn't brought much with me, so the small pot and few supplies were a welcomed surprise, there was even some coffee.

I tested my patience, waiting out the afternoon until that evening. Finally, I gave in, making a small fire to start some coffee. The red beans and rice that were wrapped in a leaf caused a single tear to roll down my cheek. It slowly carved a path through the dirt, the pain of loss gripped me as I stared at the food. The memory of my first time eating the dish and who made it bringing it all back again.

The want for blood welled up but it was quickly tamped down by the familiar cold. I had taken the coffee and stepped back into the shadows after dousing the fire long before dusk. Sipping the strong brew straight from the pot while I waited, crouched under a low hanging branch. I heard them approaching through the shadows not long after sunset.

"Maybe he be 'ere today?" I recognized the voice but couldn't put a name to it.

"No way to know he come back from da dead, then Thems 'at cares fo' him got kilt, might be he jus leave." I knew this one, Thomas if I remembered right.

"Henry say dis man gonna stay, pay back what he owe."

"Maybe so, maybe no."

"Still here." I said stepping out of my cover making both jump.

"Move like a damn swamp cat, too damn quiet." Thomas laughed once he recovered. "Turpo say we ta bring ya ta him, he's at da edge of da city."

"Lead on."

We set off moving at a fast pace through the swamp to meet Turpo. After an hour of silently ghosting through the shadows I could make out the city. Not long after we met Turpo in a half burned out warehouse.

CHAPTER 21

TIME TO ACT

"Made it back ta the city den!" He grinned at me as I came up.

"I did." Sitting down I started to put on my moccasins and rolling my buckskins down. "I want to get to Tillman first."

"Ta business then, he be the easy one anyway. What's the plan? Kill that one don' gain noting?" He studied me as I finished.

"True but we might not have to kill anyone, well none of the leaders." I smiled at the surprised look on his face. "I don't think Tillman's a true believer and he's a coward. Might be able to get him to go to the federal troops and rat out the other two."

"Not gonna kill'em all?" He asked quizzically.

"Which would bother you more? Death or a yankee prison?"

"True, da last ting they want is to be there." He grinned wickedly.

"Never trust a lawyer." I grinned back.

It didn't take long to find Tillmans house, the rat thought he was safe in his burrow. There was no security at the property, the ten-foot fence was no problem for us to get over. The house was empty and dark, but it was still a bit early for the man to be home. We crouched by a small shed for another hour studying the house. When nothing moved and no lights changed we moved toward it. There was no need to wait, either he was out or was already in bed.

The lower floor was locked up tight, as expected, that didn't stop either of us. With a brief flash of hand signs, we found a small window open on the second floor. The house was built from heavy wood planks, finding hand holds was easy. Silent as the night Turpo followed me through the window into a small study. Just as we got inside the noise from a room next door made both of us freeze.

After a second we recognized the distant noise of a man using a chamber pot. Both of us grinned moving to the hallway like wraiths. I waved him back outside a door where the noise was coming from. Crouched behind the door I waited while the man in the water closet finished his business. When he stepped out I grabbed him from behind before he could swing the door closed. The cold steel of my Bowie went to his throat.

"Don't fight or I'll kill you Tillman." My quiet voice hissed in his ear making him freeze. I quickly pulled him into the study and Turpo closed the door. After pushing Tillman into a chair, I stepped back but kept my knife out. Tilting it slightly so the faint light shone on the blade. "Don't make a noise or I'll take out that lying tongue."

"He look scared enough don' he?" Turpo spoke, softly laughing under his breath.

"You're going to answer my questions. Do it no louder than I am speaking now, you understand?" I asked.

"JC?" The man asked in shock, but he did keep his voice down.

"Got it in one. Now let's talk about how King is going to deal with you when he finds out you're working with Wordsmouth." I grinned at the man when he flinched. Even in the dark I could see the sweat bead on his bald pate.

"I never …" he started to lie but I cut him off.

"You are and I can prove it to him, what do you think he'll to do?" My smile wasn't pleasant.

"I ummm…. what do you want?" His mind finally caught up. I wouldn't be here just to threaten him.

"I want you to go tell the federalists everything you know about Nash and Wordsmouth. You can claim you're doing it to protect the union, take credit I don't care."

"I can't they would ruin…"

"You're ruined already, but do you want to live with it or die from it? King won't let you live, and you know it." I didn't know it but figured it was a good guess. His audible gulp was enough to confirm it though.

"They won't care about some dead black folks an you know it." Tillman was trying a different tact now.

"You're right, but them working to undermine the union? That they will care about." My accusation caught the man off guard, he hadn't known I knew about any of that. Honestly I hadn't known anything, it was another guess.

"But they…."

"They won't kill you if you move fast enough. If you do it, I'll tell King you did it to try and uncover a plot." My smile hadn't gotten any nicer, but it did offer hope. "I know a weasel like you has documents somewhere to cover your ass. Don't make me search your place for it."

"But I…" he started to deny it but the cold caress of my blade along his jaw line convinced him. "Behind the painting, a safe."

"Open it." I demanded, using the knife to point making the alternative clear.

He rose shakily and walked to the picture of an old man sitting on a horse. Maybe a family member? It took him two tries fumbling with the combination before he got it open. When he did I yanked him back to the chair as soon as the tumbler clicked, them I stepped to the safe.

There was a derringer sitting on a stack of papers, I tucked it into my belt then took the papers out. Turpo had his knife at

Tillmans throat, keeping him from moving. After closing the curtains tight I lit a lamp and set it on the floor. Keeping it low, just enough to let me read the papers.

They were a treasure trove of records and receipts for all of it. Enough to bury Nash and Wordsmouth without a problem, there was also enough separately to bury Tillman. Some of them were the evidence I needed to show King, others would get him jailed by the government. I kept all of those, tucking them into my wallet. What they revealed surprised me.

He had been steadily embezzling money from King for years. The evidence was all here laid out in black and white. It was so blatant I was actually surprised King hadn't noticed, too much trust and money I guess. The other papers showed enough purchased supplies to outfit an uprising, they named Nash and Wordsmouth as the leaders of the Crescent City White League. There was a manifesto attached that explained their goal to overthrow the union rule in Louisiana. It was enough to convict both as traitors with out question. These documents would let the federalist claim their assets and hang them both.

"You're going to take these to the Union in the morning. Before that you'll put all the money back into Kings account." I smiled coldly at the man. This wasn't what my rage wanted but it would do. "Do those things and I'll make sure King doesn't come after you. You're done as his attorney, but you'll live."

"But if I ..."

"Or you can die here, and they'll find the papers in the morning anyway?"

"You sure you can square it with King?" I had him and we both knew it.

"I can so long as the money goes back. I'm keeping these papers in case you back out or run..." I trailed off letting his imagination fill in the blanks.

"I'll go." Something shifted in his eyes, I needed to cut that off.

"You'll do exactly what I said, if you do anything else you'll see me again. Between me and King you won't make it." I let the cold tinge my voice making it an obvious threat. "They might have some power but even they can't protect you every minute. Think about it, why would they? Once they know you could doom them, why keep you alive? If they don't kill you I will."

"I'll do it, but you won't blame me if I take credit for it?" His voice was almost a whine.

"You can paint yourself as a hero. I doubt it'll do you any good once word gets out but maybe if you move east." I let the last hang as a bait. If the man fled he might be able to rebuild a life back east.

"Cher we will hear bout ya talking. Make it clear when ya talk to them, that way ya live no?" Turpos blade never moved but he stared death into Tillman as he spoke.

I felt like I should be a bit insulted, he was far more afraid of Turpo. He literally feinted at his threat. We killed the light and left the man sprawled on the floor before we slipped back out of the window. When he made it back to the waking world all he saw around him were the normal shadows. We had disappeared in front of his eyes as far as he was concerned. Turbo led me out of the city and before dawn we were back in the swamp sipping coffee. Silently watching the first rays of dawn paint the world anew.

"Tink the man 'ill do it?"

"No choice. I took the papers that would incriminate him to King and the Union. What we gave him was the only way out." My smile held no warmth when I continued. "He also knows to fear us more than the others, well definitely you anyway. He'll twist it to make himself the hero because the man's a snake, its in his nature. If he does what I told him he'll come out alright."

"Don like that none, but it's 'bout as good as we kin git." Turpo grumbled.

"Just remember men like that never last long, he thinks he's smarter than everyone else."

All we could do now was wait and hope it played out the way we wanted. Turpos boys were watching Tillman and knew to let us know what he did this morning. I was packing my scattergun and rig into saddlebags while Turpo was organizing his boys to watch the city.

The first one reported to us an hour later, Tillmans first stop was the bank. He had walked in with a heavy black bag and left an hour later empty handed. The money from the safe hopefully being returned to Kings account. He left there heading straight to the military base.

That left more waiting, we didn't hear anything new until well into the night. Sometime around ten he left the base with two full companies of blue coats, headed up by the base commander. Tillman was riding with him. That was a good indication that our plan was working.

Three hours later the final report came in on the legs of a winded ten-year-old. They arrested Nash, Wordsmouth and another five members of the white league. Quickly seizing all their holdings for treason. Each business and home were now guarded and had a seizure notice posted on the door. It looked like we'd managed to get our revenge without personally killing anyone. They were ruined and probably doomed to swing at the end of a rope.

The cold that had filled me since Binda's death didn't completely fade but it lightened its hold on my chest. We ate and got some sleep. Runners kept track of everything going on in the city. Turpo had people waiting to hear what was next, but we didn't expect to hear anything before morning.

I woke and went through my workout in the light of predawn before stirring the fire back to life. The coffee got started before I went to clean up. Turbo joined me once I made it back and was reheating some of the beans and rice. We ate in silence, both of us still thinking those two snakes would find a way out of it. Sometime after breakfast we got our answer.

They had already been tried, convicted and sentenced to be hung for treason later this morning. Their supporters made some noise but when confronted with the documents and the supplies it took the fight out of them. The testimony from Tillman sealed the deal, there was no way out for them now.

He still hadn't left the federalist compound and probably

wouldn't except to flee the area. The local population wouldn't take kindly to someone going to them and everyone knew it. I had the impression the Colonel had planned it that way when I heard he had to testify. It meant the last conspirator would be forced out of his area, making him someone else's problem.

Turpo and I both laughed when the news came in, toasting the success of a good plan. Later that morning we would be there to witness their deaths first-hand. Being hung is a bad way to go, most men feared it more than a gun fight. These two though, I could only hope the hangman made it slow.

CHAPTER 22

LEAVING THE CITY

Word spread through the city like wildfire and the gossip network was working overtime. Some folks didn't like the heavy-handed decisions of the army, mostly the city was happy with the outcome though. Both men were known for using some brutal tactics, blackmail, kidnapping, and murder. Their own decisions hadn't made them any fans in the more affluent, they preferred a softer touch in business.

Mostly people on all sides were tired of the war, they had already started to adjust to the new reality. Some not happily but even they had had enough of the violence and bloodshed, too many sons dead. It was only a small percentage of the population who wanted to keep fighting. The rest just wanted to get on with living.

There was a large crowd gathered to watch the hanging, they were always events for some gruesome reason. We sat on the roof of a building with Henry and several other boys watching the show. The rest of them were below us working the crowd, picking pockets and filching various things. Anytime there was a crowd this big it was a feeding frenzy for the underside of a city. Not just the crowd but the vacant homes and business were easy prey for the thieves.

When the officers took the stage to read off the long list of charges, the crowd fell silent listening to every word. Tillman stood off to the side looking anything but happy. There was a couple of stains from rotten fruit on his suit coat. It didn't look like he would be staying for long in the city, probably leaving via armed guard was my guess. He would find his way out of this fire, likely ending up in trouble somewhere else.

Not my concern, he had done what I wanted him to after that I didn't care what happened to him. I needed to finish what King asked than I was done with this mess and could head back to Texas. I would pass on the information to King, he could decide what to do about the man.

Twenty minutes later seven bodies danced at the end of ropes. It took no more than that to end so much evil, a simple pull and the trapdoor solved so many problems. It was done, the best vengeance I could ask for dealt to them legally. I watched their legs twitch while the life left them, it didn't help but it was a start.

The next week found another ten men dying by blade, the first were the three who started the fire. The rest were just as guilty, there was no way I would let them get away with it. If crippling the White League helped the pain in my chest I had no qualms with it. None of it helped the sense of loss I felt, the color of the city had faded in my eyes. New Orleans was now just a place to me, I still cared for some of the people here but not enough to ever return.

The vivid life that had once filled the city around me was just a dull grey to me now. It was time for me to get out of Louisiana and back to what I was supposed to be doing. Maybe somewhere along the trail back I could find an answer for the pain. That was my plan until Turpo spoke up.

"Stay'n for Christmas? Just a few days off, no?"

"I had forgotten about that." I laughed "Wasn't planning on it though, need to get back to Baton Rouge. Tie up a few things there then start making my way to Texas."

"Cher! Das no way ta spend the day, got ta be wit family." He smiled knowing he would win this. "Loki already in the stable at da house."

"Fine." Admitting my surrender without much of a fight, besides it would give me time to write home.

I hadn't sent anything home in over a month so that night I wrote my mother, filling her in on some of what had been going on. I didn't tell her everything, no mention of Binda or her loss. That was a story that would have to be told in person, if ever. I'd send it off later when I checked in at Wells Fargo before I left.

Minnie came by early to make coffee and breakfast the next morning. I was dressed in my city clothes, but still wore the colts. The streets had relaxed slightly but the tension was still there, just a bit further under the surface.

Even as I walked the streets I could feel it hanging in the air. When I thought about it, that feeling would likely hang around this city for years to come. People who had been slaves wouldn't easily let go of their freedom, while those who had lost their power would still seek to recover it. There would be violence and death still to come, I doubt there was anyway to avoid it.

Christmas Eve there was a dinner at the Gravier house. We had it there because it was a house rather than a hideout. Turpo, Henry and Minnie came with a few of the others I had gotten to know. It was a good night, food and laughter filled the house. They all talked about tomorrow, their plans both with family and one another.

I enjoyed the time, and it helped ease the cold off more than any hanging could. It also reminded me I wasn't at home for the first time. Some part of me longed to be back in New York at that moment. Not the city but with my mother and the family I had known my whole life. It helped set my decision to leave

New Orleans, it really was time to get back to Texas.

I slipped out of the city in the predawn light, Christmas morning found me on the road back to Lisbon. I had already made arrangements with Dunn, I'd have King contact him via telegram. There was no other reason for me to go to Baton Rouge once that was done. The few clothes I left at the boarding house weren't worth the trip.

After Lisbon I would make for Corpus Christi and the King ranch. I could have taken a boat but still wanted to see more of the country. Besides I still needed to waste a few months and some time alone might help me work through things.

No better way than traveling by horseback to help me think. Something about the trail made my mind wander but it helped. Sitting on Loki I looked back at the city slowly fading from sight behind me. I had found and lost so much, good people had welcomed me into their lives. Some part of me would stay there forever, buried beside the body of an amazing woman who had stolen a piece of my heart.

There were good friends too, maybe someday the pain would fade enough to come back this way. If not they would always have a place at my fire. Without any more thought about leaving I turned my head back down the road, knowing Minnie would find my note and pass the information on to Turpo. They would make their way in life and if they needed me I would come.

The road was easy, most nights I slept just off to the side when I could find dry ground. When I couldn't I stayed in stables with Loki, preferring that to the various hotels. Blending in with the other punchers drifting around the country. Most making our way slowly back toward Texas, broke from the winter in the big easy. It was an appearance I cultivated, broke and run down. Nothing of interest to anyone, even the highwaymen recognized I wasn't a decent target. Too much risk, not enough reward.

I rode into Lisbon on a Friday night. The air still held the chill of winter when the sun started to fade. I was still far enough south that it really didn't affect me or the trail, but it was winter. I had picked up a decent sheepskin coat on the way, it held off the worst of the chill. Lisbon in January was quiet, making getting a room easy. Not the one I had stayed at with King, something about that place was distasteful. When I dropped Loki off at the livery the man remembered the horse.

"That's Blue, I member ya boy. Ya kilt Big Mike right 'ere."

"His names Loki now." Was my only comment. I was cold and wanted some hot coffee and a decent meal.

"Call em whatcha like, few folks 'll care. Might be a few round that do. Ya whatch 'em that does." He took the horse before walking back into the shadows of the barn. Turning toward the hotel, a place called the Lisbon Inn, I walked across the street. After signing in and dropping off my saddlebags and bedroll I headed back downstairs to the dining room.

Dropping into a seat I ordered a steak dinner with all the fixings and hot coffee. I probably needed a bath, but the day's ride had left me hungry, wanting a hot meal more than a bath. The meal was decent, and the coffee was hot. I took a cup out on the porch to enjoy a pipe before bed. A bath could wait until tomorrow, or maybe longer.

A few people were still out and about but for the most part the streets were empty. The cold wind that blew down it drove most into the warmth of home and hearth. I was debating my pipe, because of the wind, when I heard someone striding up the board walk.

CHAPTER 23

A SIMPLE FIGHT

"Gotta be here ain't no other hotels 'cept 'at fancy one." His voice was pleasant enough but something in it got my attention.

"That old man at the livery coulda helped, damned old fool. Why didn'cha let me beat it outta 'im?" This voice was rough.

"Didn't know no more then he tol' us. He don't never ask folks business. Jus' his way, beat'n 'im wouldna done no good. Specially wouldna asked someone he know'd at kilt big Mike." Yup not a good sign for me, they were friends of the man I had killed.

"You boys want something in particular." I asked stepping into the light, flipping the thongs off my Colt.

"We ain't armed so's if'n ya shot us y'all be commit'n murder boy." The rough one grinned. "We come ta whoop ya, ain't no cowardly guns 'ere."

His grin revealed blackened teeth with more than one gap,

either rotted or knocked out in bar fights. He was a big man, a few inches shorter than me but broader across the shoulders. His knuckles said he was a brawler, I could see the scars from where I stood.

"Why?" I asked, already knowing the answer.

"Big Mike was a pard 'ats all there is ta it." This one was skinny, whip strong muscle though, he had the same collection of scars on his knuckles.

"Fine, be right back." I shrugged turning toward the door. The big man stepped forward to follow me inside and found my colt sticking under his nose. My cold tone caught both their attention. "I'm going to give the desk clerk my guns, unless you want me to keep them?"

"Ummmmmm.." It was all he got out before I walked through the doors, peeling my guns off, handing the belt to the clerk.

"Hold these please, it seems like some gentlemen want to fight."

The stunned man took the belt automatically, staring blankly when I turn to walk back outside. Some part of me was questioning my sanity as much as the clerk obviously was. Maybe some part of me still needed an outlet for my anger. A release for the rage that was still stuffed into a cage. When I walked back outside they both looked surprised to see me.

"Here?" I asked sounding uninterested.

"Mighty calm bout dis here whoop'n." The skinny one was smart enough to not like my approach to this.

"Been a long day if we're doing this lets get to it. Ain't in the mood to explain why I'm going along with this foolishness."

I had already set my feet, balanced and ready when the big man charged at me. He swung a vicious haymaker at my chin, he either thought I was a fool or that I would just stand there. If that was his expectation I sorely disappointed him.

Ducking under the swing I brought my palm up from my boots. Using my legs to drive it under his chin, the sound of breaking teeth reminded me of firecrackers going off. I came up all the way to my toes behind the blow, rocking his head back. His body played follow the leader, his boots made it about a foot off the ground before gravity reasserted its dominance with a vengeance. The back of his head made contact with the boardwalk first, a loud smack echoing across the silent street. The rest of him followed in a loud whoosh when the impact forced the air out of his lungs.

His partner looked a bit more thoughtful, suddenly reconsidering his involvement in this altercation. When I casually flicked the two pieces of teeth off my shirt his eyes got a bit bigger. He tracked their fall to the wooden planks. They danced around for a second before dropping through the cracks. Disappearing in to the lost world under the boardwalk. His eyes stayed locked on the small piece of tongue he spotted before he looked back at me.

"Well?" I asked meeting his gaze expectantly. "This is your dance."

"I'm gonna cut'cha up since ya put 'at knife inside." He grinned pulling a Bowie from the small of his back. I sighed heavily, sounding more annoyed then threatened. Simply reaching back pulling my stiletto out of my collar.

"That's not going to work out any better for you." My smile didn't promise him anything good, but his back was up against it now. He couldn't walk away, no matter how badly he might want to do.

To his credit he didn't hesitate, slashing at me much faster than I would have thought. It was meant to disarm me by cutting my arm. I didn't move more than I needed to, easily moving out of his telegraphed path. His swing was pretty good, and he would have recovered easily if it hadn't been for his partner. The oaf on the ground picked that exact moment to grab his pard for help. His hand wrapped around his buddy's ankle like a vice, throwing him off balance enough to leave me an easy opening. I took it, bringing my foot up with all the force I could right between his legs.

Several things happened at about the same time

immediately after that. Both of his hands reached for his crotch, which is a completely normal reaction. Sadly, the quick burst of pain made him forget there was a big Bowie knife in his hand.

When he grabbed between his legs another pain came to life, a much more serious one. His other hand was suddenly impaled on his own knife. I was pretty impressed with how far he managed to get, at least two inches of blade stuck out the top. It was too much for his body to deal with. His eyes rolled back in his head, and he dropped to his knees unconscious. He likely would have fallen forward face first, but his right knee fell right onto his friend's face. It threw the whole thing off kilter.

His friend groaned, just conscious enough to try to twist out of the way. That meant his buddies knee was rolled to the side which threw his unresponsive body off balance further. By luck, he managed to fall onto his side and not further impale himself. I stood there for a minute looking down at them.

Stunned by the strange course of events, then I slid my knife back into its sheath and stepped over the two of them. Casually walking back into the lobby to get my guns. The front desk clerk still had them in his hand and was staring at me with a look of awe. He had come to the window and watched the entire fight.

"Y'all got law around here right?" I knew they did but decided the question should get his brain working.

"Yes sir, I'll send for him."

"Might want a doc too, one of 'em stuck his hand pretty good." I slung my colts back into place and tied them down before walking over to get another cup of coffee. "I'll wait to make sure he doesn't have any questions."

"Yes sir." A small boy darted by me a minute later, off to fetch the appropriate people.

I walked back out to the boardwalk, lighting my pipe as I went. The sheriff made it first only slightly ahead of the doc. The two idiots had managed to make it mostly back to the real world by then but were still sprawled on the boardwalk. The lawman walked up, looked at them then at me than did a double take.

"Ain't you, JC? Rode in with King a while back."

"Yes sir. These two planned on settling with me for Big Mike. That's what they said anyway."

"They ain't shot?" He looked at them quizzically.

"Nope, said they wanted to beat me up, so I gave my colts to the front desk."

"Ya did what?" He started at me like what I said sounded foreign in some way.

"I walked back inside an gave my guns to the desk. Didn't want them getting ahold of them."

"An ya beat both of em?"

"They mostly beat themselves." I laughed before relaying the rest of the story to the sheriff. He cringed and laughed at the proper parts. The Doc had arrived half way through and was looking over the two men.

"Gonna charge'em with disturbing da peace. Want I should charge 'em for attack'n ya?"

"Shouldn't need too, think they'll leave me alone now." I grinned.

"Ain't want no part of 'at one sheriff." The skinny one groused while having his hand wrapped. The doc, who was grumbling about inconsiderate cowboys, finished with him and started examining his partner.

"Whose pay'n for this?" The Doc demanded.

The skinny one handed him a greenback and helped his pard up. A deputy had come up during the conversation and was now taking to two men back toward the jail.

"Ya gonna be in town long son?" The sheriff asked. "I ain't trying to get in ya business but figure ya been here twice now, both times I've had ta do a bunch of writing. I hate writing."

"Leaving at first light." I smiled at the grumpy old sheriff. He was shorter and had some years on him but seemed like a good sort.

"That's fine, don't get me wrong if'n ya wanna stay 'ats fine just might have a deputy hang around some. Might save some folks from themselves." He laughed.

"Be gone after breakfast." I assured him smiling.

"Fair enough, mind if I join ya for it? Usually eat at the Eatery. Allie runs it, puts on a good spread."

"I get moving early." I warned.

"She'll open at first light, I'll be in not long after."

"Works for me."

"Names Frank by the by, Frank Mills." He stuck out his hand and I took it.

"JC Stone, it's a pleasure."

"This is 'bout cleaned up. Figure I'm goin' back ta bed, the deputy can handle this mess." He nodded taking in the scene once again. "See in the morn'n."

"See ya for breakfast." I headed back into the hotel and up to my room. It was time to get some sleep.

CHAPTER 24

TARGETED

The next morning, I was up and packing before the first rays of dawn broke the horizon. Its light was just bright enough to chase the stars back into their homes when I stepped out of my room. I left my bedroll and saddlebags with the front desk before walking out into the new day. Spears of light were reaching long fingers into the town, criss crossing the road ahead of me. The deep shadows seemed to dance, trapped between the dark of night and light of day.

Faint scents blew by on the wind, the heavy musk of the swamp tainted with salt. Somewhere closer the scent of bacon wafted by, mingling with the bite of fresh coffee. It was all so normal, just another town starting another day. I had a long ride in the saddle ahead of me and the start seemed promising so far.

I turned toward the Eatery, my steps echoing in the still silent street. The unbroken frost adding a soft crunch under my boots. The sounds around me were the natural ones, they existed across the world in one way or the other. Soft bird song, insects chirping their warning while a mouse searched them out, far off the lone yip of a coyote echoed off a building.

These mixed with the sounds of civilization waking up, melding into their own unique symphony. Nickering horses in stalls, a milk cow bawling its readiness to be milked. The shutters of a window slamming against a wall when someone flung it open. The splash of a chamber pot being dumped. It was all soothing and familiar.

The Eatery's sign swung in the gentle morning breeze, squeaking on the chain. 'Allies Eatery" was scrawled in crisp white paint on the dark wood. The letters were a bit crooked and the whole thing seemed off center because of it. The doors were open, letting the lamp light spill out with the steam. Signs of the heat from the stove battling against the morning chill. A woman's voice carried through the open door onto the street.

"Frank, see yer up wit 'da sun as usual an disturb'n my morn'n." The husky female voice sounded somehow annoyed and welcoming at the same time.

"Been say'n that every mornin' Allie." The sheriff's voice was light, not trace of sleepiness from the night before.

"Ain't likely ta change anytime soon." She laughed. I caught the soft sound of metal being set down on a table. "Here's ya coffee, food 'ill be a bit."

"Got company com'n."

"Figured, heard 'bout last night's fun."

"Morning." I said, announcing myself as I turned in the open door.

"JC, figured ya wasn't kidd'n about moving early." The sheriff nodded his greeting. "That fine lady's Allie."

"JC was it? Have a seat, coffees on the table, cups there for ya." She was the same as many women running eateries, motherly and direct. She had a no-nonsense presence about her, a tall woman who looked like annoying her would have severe consequences.

"Pleasure ma'am." I tipped my hat before folding into the chair across from the sheriff and filling a chipped enamel cup.

"Allie, ain't no one calls me ma'am. Food 'ill be a bit, reckon ya heard."

"Thank you Allie." I smiled at the lady who was already disappearing into the kitchen. "Get some sleep?"

"Not enough, gett'n too old for this job." He smiled over his coffee at me. "Ya headed out this morn'n ya say?"

"Yes sir, time to get back to Texas. Had enough excitement in New Orleans for the year."

"Heard some 'bout the excitement down there, couple of folks got themselves hung."

"Happened right before I left but the whole place feels tense. Figured it was time to go." He was fishing for information, not about my involvement, probably just curious for any news.

"Folks still settl'n after the late unpleasantness." This was his only comment, giving nothing away about how he felt.

"Too young for that myself, was ten when it ended." I admitted casually. "Course I read about it, talked to folks coming home but that doesn't tell me much."

"Better 'at way son, hope ya never know that hell." The sheriff got that far away look that I had seen on so many veterans when they remembered the war. I knew better than to push, the man would talk about it or change the subject. "Where ya headed in Texas?"

"Down to the Bar C, south of Uvalde." The man must have been in some bad battles. That short remembrance had sobered him, removing the smile from his face for a minute.

"That's a ride through an some rough country, never been much south of San Antonio myself."

"Never been there." I laughed a bit at his look of surprise. "Got hired in Dodge but had to turn east because of that horse."

"That's right you 'ad that bounty horse! Not a bad payday. Hear ya bought her not knowing anything 'bout the bounty?"

"Yup, bought her in Dodge. She killed two men who tried to steal her. Damn good horse though."

"Blues a good one too." He commented.

"He is, but not a cow pony. Have to get one somewhere on my way down to the ranch. Changed his name to Loki by the way, tricky, and smart."

"Better name 'an Blue, Mike wasn't much on think'n." Frank laughed.

"Biscuits and gravy boys." Allie announced coming out of the kitchen with two big plates.

"Thank ya Allie." Frank smiled at the plate in front of him.

"Appreciate it." I scooted the plate toward me, picking up the silverware.

Conversation stopped as we both dug into our meals. It wasn't at the level of Millie's, but it was a close second. When I scooped the last bite off the plate and pushed back slightly from the table my appetite was satisfied completely. I was full but not overly so. I had learned quick that sitting a saddle with a stuffed belly was no fun at all.

"Damn good chow." I nodded toward Allie as she cleared the plates.

"Thank ya son." She gave me a big smile before turning back to the kitchen.

"Reckon your 'bout ready ta head out?" Frank asked almost casually, but he had something else on his mind. I could hear it in his voice.

"Sheriff just say it, I'll hear ya out. Have to finish this coffee anyway." I sipped my coffee, waiting for the man to collect his thoughts.

"Figure ya been here twice, left men behind both times. Maybe hop'n you're moving on?" He grinned with some humor at the statement, but I knew that wasn't what he wanted to ask. He sighed in surrender before he continued "Or maybe I got a warning for ya with an ask. Been a few folks jumped betwixt here an Texas. Ain't sure who's operating out there but someone is an they ain't the merciful types."

"Thinking there's more to it?" I asked calmly knowing he did.

"Odd thing is it started right after ya collected that bounty."

He finally admitted.

"That's been months!" I was surprised, but there had to be a connection. "Wait did they try King?"

"Funny that is, he sent a message back about them. They didn't test him but followed him ta the border. Looking for you was his guess." He hung his head slightly before admitting the last bit. "I think those two in my jail are associated with 'em but can't prove it."

"That makes more sense than them starting a random fight." I sat back thinking about what that meant. Why start the fight? When did they come into town? Too many questions and not nearly enough answers. "You think we can go have a conversation back at the jail?"

"Why?" He must have caught my smile, when he matched my grin I knew he had figured it out. "Yeah we might at that."

"Then I can tell ya the full story about that bounty." I laughed. "Doubt they're going to enjoy the tale."

Five minutes later we were at the jail. The sheriff sat behind his desk, and I sat across from him. When we came in he had gone to check on the prisoners. I could hear them grumbling about food and emptying the slop bucket when the sheriff walked back upfront. Leaving the door cracked open just enough for them to hear.

"Now tell me 'bout this bounty again, it still don't make sense ta me." The sheriff started just as we had discussed.

"Figured it wouldn't to most but it's simple. That man's got some of the best horse stock around, no question about that. I figured taking five thousand dollars didn't make sense, so we made a bet of sorts."

"A bet?" The sheriff sounded honestly surprised.

"Yeah, I inherit a ranch in ten years, good sized spread up I Montana, well closer to nine now. I bet him that I would survive, he bet I wouldn't. Double or nothing on the bounty but not in cash, we bet horses." I laughed at the sheriffs shocked look. He didn't need to act for the rest, this was all new to him.

"You bet for horses!"

"Yup, if I get my ranch he sends me ten thousand dollars' worth of quality horse flesh. I don't need money while I'm punching cattle. But horses when I get my ranch? That much stock is a good start for a horse ranch and that man knows horses."

"I'll be damned!!!" The sheriff burst out laughing. "It still ain't something most folks would ever consider but damned if you ain't right! That'll be enough horses ta give you a big start. 'Specially from him, it'll be the best stock 'round."

"You got it, and if I'm dead it won't make a difference to me. Got it all written up and legal, a lawyer back in New York is the one handling the deal." I smiled at this bit of lying. It prevented someone else trying to claim the horses, which took robbery off the table. The truth was we had just written up a simple agreement and shook hands on it. "I have to go see him in person, then he'll send out the notice to ship my horses. If I don't show up in person Thornton wins the bet, if I do he has to pay up."

We could both hear cursing from the cells out back, evidently the men could hear us well enough. The sheriff yelled at them before slamming the door shut, cutting off their noise. They wouldn't be able to hear our normal conversation now. That had been our plan after all, hopefully they would clear out of the area and move on.

"That's really the deal y'all made?" The sheriff studied me carefully from across his desk.

"Mostly, I added the lawyer bit, but the rest is true. I have to come back here, not to some lawyer." I grinned back at the now smiling sheriff. "I get the pick on a few horses."

"What now? Figure we want them ta get outta town afor ya go?"

"Yeah, I'll go to the general store and mess about, you let them light out. Either they tell them the story and they believe it, or they'll jump me. Either way it'll give me an advantage."

"Don't know how many there is though." The concern was obvious in his voice.

"I'll manage, let me worry about that."

"You're an interesting one JC. Ya look young but move like ya was born ta this life. Get outta here now an I'll cut 'em two loose." He rose walking toward the cells as I unfolded from the chair. When he cracked the door I called out as I opened the door to the boardwalk.

"Headed to the general store for supplies, then heading back to Texas Sheriff. See y'all in ten years."

"Figure I'll be dead an gone by then boy, lawman don't live 'at long." He laughed stepping into the cells. I walked down the boardwalk toward the general store.

From inside the store, I watched to two men race to the livery. They rode like the devil was chasing them out of town, heading west. Hopefully going to ruin someone's day with the information they had. That was my hope, in reality my expectations were lower. They would be waiting for me along the road no matter what they believed. Outlaws didn't give up that easily, especially not when they had been counting the money this long.

CHAPTER 25

COLLECTING A FEW
MORE DOLLARS

I wasted twenty minutes in the store, dithering over which pipe tobacco to purchase. Finally picking a pound of a local blend, a hundred rounds of 44-40 and some bacon. Stepping into the stirrups of an already saddled Loki, the sheriff had my saddlebags and bedroll brought over. Everything got balanced out and tied down. By then we had given the men a solid hour head start. Hopefully that would be enough.

I started out of town, slowing to pick up their trail. The rapid pace they left at made following it easy. Not many rode their animals that hard, it was a good way to have a horse come up lame. They stuck to the road for a few miles before cutting off the trail into the back country. Slowing Loki to follow them more carefully, the trail got trickier the deeper they went. They were still moving fast leaving clear sign of their passage, thankfully.

Ten minutes later I was in a gully listening to the men talk not too far away. Loki was a quarter mile back in a small hollow I had found, it had some fresh water and graze. That cold feeling had filled me while I stalked through the woods, letting me take in what they were talking about. My mind was working overtime, trying to get a handle on their reactions.

"Ya mean he ain't got no money?" The voice was harsh. That of a hard man who was used to ordering others around.

"Ats what dey said Butch." The man who had stabbed his hand reaffirmed.

"I ain't buy'n it, I want that story from da kids' mouth." Butch's proclamation was supported by about five other voices, all grumbling their agreement. "If it's true at boy 'ill die slow cause we been wast'n time."

That decided it for me, these men deserved what they got from here on out. My Winchester was loaded with one in the chamber, both colts were ready to go. Slipping to the top of the gully, I settle in ready for a fight. Below me were eight men, all rough and ragged. Obviously they had been living out here for a while.

"You boys just stay where you're at." I yelled down at the eight men around a campfire. Half of them were still rubbing sleep from their eyes, the rest were in various states of readiness. Knife hand and Toothless were the only ones besides Butch that looked fully awake. Butch made the mistake of reaching for his 44.

My Winchester spit flame sending the heavy 44-40 slug into his chest just to the left of center. The round exploded his heart while spinning him sideways. He hit the ground with an audible wheeze followed by a desperate gasp. His lungs fighting desperately for one last breath. Before the dust settled around him his brain had gotten the signal to give up the fight and his lifeless body lay there.

Toothless was the next, his 44 made it almost level before my next round punched into his gut. His gun fell to the ground as he doubled over screaming. He dropped back to his butt with a shocked look on his face. The slow trickle of red leaking through his hands said he was out of the fight but would be a long time in dying. The rest of them looked stunned but no one else moved. When Toothless started to moan, it took a minute for the pain break through, it broke the silence.

"All of you, move real careful and drop those gun belts one at a time. Starting with you knife boy." I waved the barrel at the wounded man. He moved his uninjured hand to his buckle and slowly dropped his gun belt to the ground.

"Now move over there." I motioned him over to the left of their camp, away from the horses and the other men.

This process was repeated with the remaining six, none of them tried me and by the time they were all separated the only noise was Toothless. Who crying about being gut shot, the pain and fear of a slow death edged his voice toward panic. All six of them were now laying on their bellies in the grass letting me walk down the hill toward their camp.

"Your gut shot and dying for sure. Did ya want to try and make it back to town?" I asked crouched on my heels beside the man.

"Ain't no good, no doc kin patch 'is up." He moaned out.

"What's your choice then, I'll do what I can for you."

"Shoot me, end it. I can't do it myself, go ta hell fer sure 'at way." His words surprised me, He was worried about hell from suicide but not from the way he lived his life?

"Want to make your peace with god first?" I asked.

"Have been." He gasped out. "Just do it."

I didn't make the man suffer anymore. Using his 44 the round punched through his brain ending his torment. The sound of the shot echoed around the small clearing, almost like it was trying to outlive the man on the ground.

I started searching around for some piggin strings through the saddlebags. Finding some in most of them, I tossed them to one of the men. He was younger than the rest, something said he hadn't been with them long. Most likely a farm boy chasing dreams of fame, now maybe finding it at the end of a short rope.

"Tie 'em up tight boy." I watched him work, making sure he didn't leave anyone obviously loose.

When he was done I took the last of the strings from him and bound his hands. After checking their bonds, I wasn't too surprised to find them all tight. I had guessed it would be the case by the cursing the others had thrown at the kid. If they were friends before they wouldn't be after this.

I then set about collecting the guns, checking each one to make sure there wasn't a round under the hammer. I rolled each set and tucked them into saddlebags I had emptied. Each filled set got stored in the panniers of a pack horse. There were three pack mules and eleven saddle horses. Like every outlaw I knew of the saddle horses were all good stock, even the pack mules were fine animals. I had to rearrange the large supply of goods they had, obviously stolen because they didn't strike me as the type to buy bolts of fabric. All of that took just shy of two hours, with thirty more minutes to saddle eight of the horses. I levered the two bodies across the worst of the saddles, no sense getting blood on good rigs.

"Sorry boys it ain't going to be a comfortable ride." The only way I could make it work was to bind them over the saddles rather than in them.

It took another hour with a lot of cussing, but I got all six of them tied across their saddles. They weren't happy about it and more than one threatened to kill me for the humiliation. The problem was there just wasn't another way I could control them and get back to Loki.

When it was done I made my way around the hill leading the string horses and mules. Three hours later I rode back into Lisbon, leading fourteen with eight men tied across saddles. All but two complaining the entire way down the short main street. The sheriff and two deputies met me about halfway.

"Sheriff think things might have worked out a bit differently than we thought." I laughed at the grinning man.

"Reckon ya might as well head ta jail, meet ya there."

"Two of 'em ready for boot hill sheriff." One of his deputies called out. "An 'is one's Billy Jacobs! What the hell ya doin wit dis bunch boy?"

"Wondered about that one." I said referring to the young man who had helped me tie the others up.

"Local boy went missing a few days back. I'll deal with him, don't think he's been wit this bunch long enough ta break any real laws. Rest of 'em will be charged with the local mess an we'll go through the posters ta see what we got. There's a bounty of a hundred each here locally." The sheriff looked down for a second before continuing. "Two of 'em pack horses belong ta local folks, or did. They been miss'n a while now."

"Sorry sheriff." Was all I could say, knowing it didn't offer much comfort.

It took the rest of the day to identify each man and get my statement written down for the sheriff. I still needed to look at the horses, then talk to the livery man about buying them. The tack and guns were another matter, hopefully either he or the general store would buy them all. I made thirteen hundred dollars in bounties from other areas. The sheriff already had my information and would deposit it in my account. The local bounty was paid in cash, I gave it back to the sheriff telling him to give it to the widows.

Billy Jacobs had been helpful throughout, telling us their names along with everything else he knew. The boy had also filled us in on how he fell in with them. He ran away from home because he didn't want to be a farmer and fell in with them. Partially by choice but mostly out of fear, by the time he knew who they were he was too afraid to leave. Butch had threatened to kill him if he left when he caught a whiff of the boys' fear. The sheriff sent the boy home that night, preferring to let the family deal with it.

The livery man told me flat out he couldn't afford all the horses and tack but would take them on consignment. When they sold, he would subtract his twenty percent and deposit the rest. Most of them were good horses but none were cow ponies. We shook on the deal, and I left the horses with him after boarding Loki overnight again. The gun smith made me a flat offer for all the guns. I didn't bother to haggle, taking the three hundred dollars and leaving without a headache. I got a room at the same hotel before gladly joining the sheriff and his deputies at Allies for dinner.

The night was decent, conversation was lite and full of laughter. It helped me further settle my heart. Time, distance and just moving on were the only things that could really help. Things like this, the normalcy of just spending time with people helped more than I thought it would. I had fled New Orleans because of that pain. Turpo talking me into staying for Christmas had started the healing. This was another step, much like traveling overland was. I needed both time alone and time with good people to heal.

The pressure the bandits had put on the town for months had finally been lifted, letting people breath again. The lawman knew they couldn't do anything about it, his responsibility was the town not the county. He had considered it of course but none of his men were scouts or trackers. They would have likely fallen into an ambush and been killed.

It did tell me he wasn't truly a sheriff but a town marshal. Most towns had that habit of misnaming their law, I had forgotten the difference until then. The county sheriff had tried to get them, but before he could catch the bunch he had been called to deal with some rustlers. It left the local law powerless and unprepared to deal with the band.

I had only succeeded by circumstance, that perfect connection of events and skills. My only concern was that it didn't reflect badly on Frank. When we told the story I made it out to be his idea. The whole thing made him uncomfortable, but he understood the need for the slight embellishment. He did need to keep his job, besides without his warning I would have walked into them blind. Late that night I finally made it back to my room, I'd try and get out of town tomorrow, again.

I managed it this time, just barely. The next morning over

breakfast Frank had asked me to help him with another problem. The man had burst out laughing when I hung my head. The humor missed me, but he found it incredibly amusing. An hour later I was riding out of Lisbon just as the sun fully broke the horizon. Its light splattered across the land in an array of colors. I didn't even bother to look back as I crested the hill, but I did take a second to admire the beauty spread out ahead of me.

I couldn't be too unhappy with the lost day. It had made me over two thousand dollars between rewards and found money. There would probably be another thousand over time from the horses and tack. Slowly my direction changed from west to south as I followed the coast. Once Loki's nose was headed mostly south I knew my next stop would be Corpus Christi.

Aside from a few outlaws it shouldn't be difficult, east Texas was more settled than the rest of the state. That didn't mean there was a lack of trouble. The Apache still hunted travelers; ex-confederate soldiers turned outlaw prowled from here to California. Texas was still a wild land where life came and went cheaply. It was changing, more and more people seeking a better life claimed their piece of land and held it.

Immigrants came into the various ports along the gulf and spread from there bringing civilization with them. The land here capable of supporting farms and small ranches. Finding unclaimed land was the only hard part. South of Corpus Christi I would find the beginning of Kings ranch. From there the lawlessness of south Texas really took hold. The harsh land was a haven for those who still sought to avoid the trappings of society.

It was the second week in January 1873 when I hit Corpus Christi. The town was sprawled in every direction along the water. Ships bustled in and out, goods traveled from around the country slowly making their way across Texas. People came with those same ships, some returning, others seeking their own dreams.

It wasn't a big city, I heard somewhere the population

was only around two thousand people. That was the actual residence though. The main business was shipping, that meant sailors and teamsters. The businesses that catered to them stood along the streets. That meant saloons, whore houses, and gambling. There was a multitude of shops that feed the growing immigrants before they ventured out of the city as well. I stuck to the outskirts of town, not wanting to get caught up in the chaos around the harbor.

On the western edge of the city, I found a small cantina that had a few rooms. It was simply called The Posadas. I got some strange looks when I checked in, but no one turned me away. When Loki was situated at the small livery attached to the place I left my saddlebags in my room and went to the bathhouse outback. An hour later when my own stink didn't make me flinch anymore I walked toward the local Wells Fargo office.

I knew there wouldn't be any mail for me, that would be sitting in San Antonio. I did have a letter for my mother to drop off with some thoughts about investments for Jacob. Money just sitting in my account didn't do me any good and I wanted him to invest some of it.

CHAPTER 26

RETURN TO THE KING

After studying a map, I knew my route needed to cut northwest from here. Since I still had time San Antonio would be my next stop, if for no other reason than checking my mail. After mailing my letters it left one more job, finding a way to contact King. After I talked to him I could plan the rest.

In truth the plan was simple, resupply and head west toward my next stop. From there it was due south to Uvalde and the Nueces Strip. The hard part of out all was finding King. I knew he had a house in town, but I doubted he was there. He had given me a lawyer to contact but the whole situation was too complicated to work through intermediaries, I needed to talk to the man himself.

Wells Fargo was what I expected, they were all basically the same. It only took a few minutes to finish my business there. Then I headed toward the general store, figuring I would restock my supplies while I was here. Scanning the street for any dangers I spotted a familiar figure leaning on a hitching rail a bit further down. Smokey was outside of a feed and grain store, Kings ramrod would know how to find the man.

"Smokey!" I called out as I got close.

"Eh?" He looked around at his name for a minute before his eyes fell on me. "JC 'at ya boy? Be damned, the boss was just wonder'n 'bout ya."

"Same here, was wondering if you knew where I could find him. Just got into town today."

"Ayup 'es over ta his place, let me finish up here. I can walk with ya atta'way."

"Sounds good." Finally, I could finish this business. It was sheer luck spotting him here, but I wasn't going to question it. Smokey finished up overseeing the order as it was loaded into the three wagons.

"That'll do 'er, the boys can manage it now, ya walk'n?" Smokey asked turning toward me.

"Yeah, left my horse at the stables where I'm staying."

"Same 'ere. I walked down ta stretch a bit, been out on the range for a week. Boss just dragged me back ta town yesterday." He laughed before continuing. "Had ta make sure I still 'membered how ta walk."

"About the same, just got in from Lisbon this morning." We turned walking down the boardwalk as we talked.

"Finish up wit all that mess?"

"Yup, pain in the ass but got it done, least wise my part in it." We tipped our hats to a couple of ladies as we passed. "Kings going to have to figure what to do with the rest."

"That's usually the way it goes, we get the leg work done an the boss figures the rest." He chuckled lightly while stepping around a group of kids.

"Be glad to get it passed off and head for San Antonio. Should be easy to make the Bar C before the round up."

"Easy travel mos'ly, be no problem from here ta there." He nodded to a puncher who passed us as he spoke. "First round up ain't it?"

"Yeah, still a greenhorn."

"Max I'll get ya straight, Bar C's a damn good bunch. They work a hard range down on the strip, popp'n' em bulls ain't no fun but they get it done."

"Looking forward to doing just that, been too much politicking and not enough real work."

"Sounds like the Big Easy wasn't easy?" He eyed me curiously.

"Not in the slightest." I shook my head trying to knock Binda's face from my memory. Smokey must have noticed something because he didn't ask any more questions.

"Ya made it out, thats more 'an most. Place 'as a reputation for mak'n folks disappear."

"It does at that." Was my cold reply, cutting off further conversation.

We finished the walk to the house in silence. Smokey could feel I didn't want to talk about it and in the usual habit of westerners, he respected my wishes.

Walking up to the front porch I took in the house. It was a big three-story thing, not quite a mansion but heading in that direction. The two lots on either side were empty, both enclosed with fences. Several horses wandered around one of them. The house was freshly painted, even the wood siding had finished look to it. It all looked out of place somehow.

The place looked like it belonged somewhere back east, it just didn't match the normal Texas style. It was built from clean cut lumber on top of a river stone foundation. Big glass windows stood out as much as the build. This place was King making a statement about his status. Even the two lots added to the presence. In some ways the man was the type that built this country, in others it felt like he wanted to be a lord or noble from across the sea.

Smokey knocked on the door rather than walking in, which reminded me again that King preferred to keep things a certain way. The attractive young Hispanic woman that answered the door greeted us with a warm smile. The scent of fresh baked bread wafted out with a mix of spices trailing it.

"Smokey, was Señor King expecting you?" She asked curiously.

"No ma'am, but I ran inta this young fella an I know he wants ta see him." Smokey removed his hat, and I followed suit. "Just let him know JC is here."

"Si, please come in while I see if Señor is available."

She stepped back allowing us into the entry way, then smiled before walking toward a door at the back of the house. She was back in a few minutes signaling us to follow her. She held open the door gesturing us through.

"Señor King will see you." She said with a smile.

"JC, come in." Kings voice carried easily in the house. "Glad to see you!"

"Yes sir, it's been trip." I offered my hand to the man as I walked to the front of a large desk.

He shook my hand motioning me toward a couch in the center of the room. It was obviously his study, bookshelves lined the walls around the large fireplace. A small bar sat to one side with a coffee pot perched on the right. His desk sat to the left with two simple chairs in front of it, two couches held the center of the room with a table between them.

"Sit down, would you like a drink?" Before I could answer he turned to Smokey. "Head back to make sure they get those wagons taken care of if you would?"

"Yes sir. JC good see'n ya back in Texas, maybe see ya in Dodge." The man nodded a farewell to me before walking out of the room.

"Thanks Smokey." I said to his retreating back and he waved me off over his shoulder. "Coffee if it's not too much trouble?"

"Some coffee if you would my dear? I think that pot is bit old."

"Si Señor." The lady turned after picking up the pot. I guessed heading to the kitchen.

"We can wait for the coffee before you tell me how things went. It's good to see you back but the look on your face says it was more than just a long trip." I could see the curiosity written on his face but appreciated him waiting.

"It was sir, but I did what I could. Mind?" I asked pulling out my pipe.

"Feel free." He opened the window behind me before sitting down across from me.

We sat in silence for a few minutes until my coffee arrived. She bought a different pot on a tray with two enamel cups and left them on the table before closing the door.

"Help yourself and please tell me how things worked out in New Orleans."

"Short version, Tillman was involved with the nest of snakes, including Cherie. He had also been embezzling from you for several years." King sat up straight and I watched the anger fill his eyes. "He put the money back and is ruined, at least in New Orleans. He'll probably just go north to start over, men like him usually do."

"No, he will not." Kings voice had the sharp edge of a blade to it. "I have friends who will deal with him should he turn up anywhere in this country."

"That's up to you, I used him to get two of them hung, one was a local businessman named Nash. The other was working with Cherie to take your building, his name with Wordsmouth. That was his alias anyway, his real name was Cole Ward a union officer who worked with the Red Legs. That's why he was using an alias. Most down there would have killed him if they knew."

"Working with Cherie? Then why try to lure me down there?"

"Blackmail. Once you were there in person they would have blackmailed you into signing over the building. Least that's my guess. A man named Oliver Dunn in Baton Rouge would like to buy it for a fair price." I pulled the business card out of my wallet and handed it to the shocked rancher. "He's the Lieutenant Governor, that's how to get in touch. Seemed like a good man from what I know."

"That will work, he can deal with the mess after that. Seems my debt to Cherie is paid in full." The anger was obvious in his voice. King was boiling mad at being betrayed.

"These will help with Tillman if he pops up." Handing him the papers I had taken from his house. They were enough to easily destroy him. I really didn't have any reason to keep them myself, lawyers like him were a plague. He took those as well, a slight smile crept to his face but didn't come near his eyes.

"These will do nicely." There was some heat in his voice, the flash of anger had fallen to a hot rage. It didn't bode well for Cherie or Tillman, but none of that was my concern. "Unless I am reading you wrong though, there is more to this tale?"

"Not that affects you sir, personal things." My response was flat, to his credit King let it drop without pushing further.

"You've gone above and beyond what I asked, did you want cash or a draft?" He moved to the business at hand.

"If you use Wells Fargo just transfer it to my account? If you'd rather a draft that's fine, I can stop by the office myself."

"Transfer is fine, just let me know the name on the account." We traded information, wrapping up our business or so I thought.

"Did you manage to get a good horse?"

"Good riding horse but he ain't worth much as a cow pony." I admitted. "Still riding that blue dun, he's a good horse just not for cattle."

"Your timings good then, if you're interested in a trade that is? I'm here selling some horses and I have one that I've held back hoping you would show up."

"Be interested long as Loki goes to a good place. Like I said he's got an easy stride and moves out well enough. Just doesn't have the temperament for working long horns."

"Don't worry about him, I happen to take a liking to his look in Lisbon. I'll be keeping him for myself if this trade works out." He smiled broadly chuckling before finishing. "If you haven't guessed I don't work cattle much anymore."

"You'll like him sir, he really does have a good gait. I did name him Loki for a reason though, he's got a troublesome streak. Spit the bit once and likes to hold his breath when you saddle him." I was glad to know Loki would go to a good owner. He would live in luxury as Kings horse. "Where this cow pony at?"

"I like a smart horse, if he can get one over on me it'll be well earned." There was a smile in his voice, so I wasn't worried about that. "Meet Smokey tomorrow morning out at the corrals west of town, he can take care of it there. Ride out there, easy enough to switch tack and handle the paperwork."

"Works, I'm about done for the day if you don't mind." There was some good food and a comfortable bed waiting for me. If we swapped in the morning I could head out then, another bit of good news.

"Thank you JC. I won't ask but I can tell this wasn't the simple job I thought it would be. You handled it for me, and I won't forget that. That makes two I owe you now."

"No sir, you hired me for a job. I did the job."

"Doesn't change it in my mind. Thornton told me about your gamble with the bounty." He smiled at me again, but there was a look of respect in his eyes. "That ranch, if it happens you reach out to me when you need stock, I'll remember this."

"Not foolish enough to turn that down." I smiled and extended my hand as I stood. "I'll do it, besides seems like we'll cross paths along the trail while I'm working for Max."

"If we see you in Dodge dinner is on me, I usually make one trip there toward the end." He shook my extended hand. "Smokey will meet you tomorrow morning, unfortunately I have a previous engagement. I wish you the best young man. I expect you're going to become something of a legend in your travels."

"Hope not, last thing I want is fame." I laughed at the idea. "I'll look for him tomorrow, it's been a pleasure Mr. King."

"JC you're always welcome on my range and if you ever need anything, please call on me."

Farewells said I made it out the door and to the general store without any problems. I restocked my supplies and arranged to pick them up tomorrow before heading back to the Pasados.

Dinner was amazing, my first real taste of Texas flavors in

months. The coolness of night settled into the small abode room making it comfortable. Laying back in my first real bed since Lisbon sleep came easy for the first night in a long time.

CHAPTER 27

SHADE

Rolling out of bed the next morning I stepped out into the small courtyard. The cool air still had a chill to it as I started moving. Just when I started to sweat the first colors of the day crack through the shadows. The breeze carried a mix of humanity and beasts, it took my mind meandering down its own path as I moved.

Today I was done with the responsibility's I had accepted from King. I would be turning toward the Bar C this morning. It was odd for a place I had never seen before to be calling to a part of me, a home I had never known. The distant pull to a place both familiar and unfamiliar, the juxtapose of it made me pause in thought. When had this happened? How had the Bar C become my home without ever laying my eyes on it?

Working through my morning workout that thought filled my mind. Home didn't seem to fit, but it was a word that had changed its meaning. It had always been someone else's house I called home. First in the old country then in New York. Now it was a faraway ranch that I had never laid eyes on.

The ranch wasn't my home, it was a place that would be home for a while but not permanently. I had grown a bond with those men in the short time I had traveled with them. I missed that camaraderie and for now that would be what made it home. Was this how the men out here felt, was it part of riding for the brand?

Most of the folks in New Orleans had reminded me of kids I knew growing up back east. City people who struggled through their lives confined to one place. Turpo and Henry would never leave that place, it was home to them. There was nothing wrong with that I understood it to a degree.

The Bar C hands were something different, maybe there was more of a kinship we all shared. All of us knowing that the open range was our home. In her own way she called to each of us, ranch's where just the places we stayed while making our way back to her. She was what we all cherished, knowing her danger but also her promise.

We all felt it, even King who had a sense of sadness in his voice when he said he didn't work cattle anymore. It wasn't the cattle that he missed it was the land. Maybe that was why he still went on one drive, trying to hear her song. Maybe I was wrong, and he heard it signing across his range. I had to hope I would find that when I eventually made it to my ranch.

The feeling you got when the land sang out in your soul, the varied songs that filled you while you were on watch. That was our home, our link to one another. I was learning to recognize that wildness in the people around me. Some it was a drive to tame their piece of it, carving it out and making it theirs.

The farmers digging out a living one rock at a time felt it too. They wanted to make a life in that one spot, something had called them there. Even they didn't want the confined life of streetlights and cobblestone roads. If that wasn't true they would never risk everything for their piece of land.

The punchers were different, they wanted the open land. The freedom to move with the wind as it blew across the country. We shared a kinship with the mountain men who came before us. Including their desire to see the elephant. The same spirit that drove them pushed us, an unquenchable desire to see what was over the next rise.

It was true that on the surface most of us were looking for a place that spoke to our souls. That one piece we all knew was out here for us. It would rise up one day and and take hold. She would set your roots deep in that place, deep enough so they would hold you fast no matter what storms came. Until that moment we would move through the land, chasing the wind just to see the next valley or mountain. For now, I was one of them, or becoming one of them I hoped, drifting until she pulled me down.

After rinsing off in my room I got dressed for the day. A breakfast of huevos con chorizo greeted me in the cantina before I took some coffee with me to saddle Loki. The stable boy said he would take the cup back for me when I stepped into the stirrups. His hands darted out to catch the nickel I flipped to him before turning toward the stock yards.

It wasn't hard to spot the corrals outside of town, the Passados hadn't been much past them. They had been part of my nighttime serenade, the bawling of cattle mixed with horses. In the cool soft light, I spotted a few hands working around the horses and called out to them as I approached.

"Smokey around?"

"That ya' JC?" One of the shadows waved, back lit against the rising sun as he hopped off the fence.

"Morning Smokey." I stepped off Loki to shake his hand.

"Want some coffee?" He offered. It was the most welcomed greeting you can get in the morning. "That the one the boss wants ta trade fer?"

"Yeah names Loki. Good riding horse but lacks the temperament for cattle, too much of a trickster." I laughed patting his neck. To prove my point Loki flicked my hand off and snuffled my hair.

"Boss liked him back in Lisbon, prefers 'em tall and heavy in the chest." Then with a smile he added, "Won't admit it but likes a sense of humor too."

"He said he had a cow pony for me?" Smokey looked at me funny before leading me toward a fire where the coffee was.

"He didn't tell ya?" He laughed a bit as he poured coffee for us.

"Tell me what?"

"Never mind, better ya see 'em. Let the sun finish climbing a bit, best ya see 'em in full light."

"Something wrong with the horse?" I was beginning to get a bit annoyed. The idea of King getting one over on me hadn't crossed my mind.

"What!? Oh no, nothing like 'at, hell I tried ta buy 'em. One of the best mounts I seen in a while." He assured me. "One of the prettiest too, even compares to 'at paloos mare ya had."

"That's a tall order, Danu was a beautiful animal."

"That she is, heard one of the best trained too?"

"Natural instinct according to Thornton." I took out my pipe, packing it as we talked.

"Had one of the boys cut Shade out last night, 'es been ready since King sent word. Course if ya don like 'em I'll make ya an offer." I could see the sun light glint off his smile as he spoke.

"Hell, you're selling him to me every time you talk!"

"Won't be no chance of it. One look an you'll be swapping saddles."

"Ya got me sold, show me this horse already." I grinned waving my coffee cup toward a random spot.

"Come on." He led me off to the left. "Reckon ya kin see enough."

In the scattered light of dawn, I could just make out a lone horse dancing in the corral. The tail and mane seemed to shimmer in shadowy tones that matched the rest of the animal. At first I thought it was a trick of the early light but as we got closer I realized it wasn't shimmering black, it was a blue roan. Different from Loki but stunning in his own way. Just as we stepped through the fence he turned to study us. I met his gaze and recognized the same glimmer of intelligence

Danu had, but there was more wildness lingering in it.

His mane and tail were a shining black, like a raven in the sun. The black spread from the mane, like a mask covering most of his face before fading to blue below his eyes. The blue roan coat seemed to shift colors as he moved until meeting the black sox on all four legs. I knew in my head the blue was a trick of the eye, subtle mixtures of black and white created the effect. None of that mattered, the animal was stunning.

He stood a little over 16 hands, only slightly shorter than Loki. He looked young enough that he might add another half over the next year. The deep chest and strong legs said he would run for days without tiring. Unlike Loki he had a good balance to his build, I recognized the same physical traits in him that Danu had, not too heavy in any one area. His even muscle structure and the graceful way he moved displayed the complete picture. It was fluid, like each hoof was placed with care, this was a cattle pony thru and thru.

"That is a Nokota blue roan, ya don't see em often down 'ere. They breed 'em up in the Dakota territory, don't mind heat or cold. This one's his own thing, too smart by far." Smokey spoke about the horse like it was a work of art and I found myself agreeing with his opinion.

"You were right, I ain't ever sell'n him." I stepped through the rails on the fence walking toward the horse in a daze. Without hesitation he stepped toward me bumping my chest with his head.

"He's got a fair disposition, well he ain't a killer like 'at mare was but there's a bit of a wild streak in 'em still. Enough so's he'll sing out at night if someone comes up on ya camp." Smokey chuckled as I scratched behind his ears. "Ain't gelded nether, so other stallions will make 'em touchy, it'll also make a mare sing out to him. Been more then one man saved by that. He's gotta tricky side to him though."

"You said his name was Shade?" I took the signed bill of sale for Loki out of my wallet, I'd signed it last night.

"Yeah, I kinda hung 'im with it, seemed ta fit." He took the paper in trade for the one he held toward me. I didn't bother checking it anymore then he did mine.

"Agreed." He did look like a soft shadow standing here in the light.

"Figured as much, seems like 'es taken ta ya as well." Smokey laughed leading Loki into the corral so we could switch my tack. Shade glared at the bigger horse but didn't otherwise react. "Nother thing, you'll find out soon enough. He's got that Indian shuffle like your mare did, it's a gait some breeds have. Jus' eats up miles."

"Yeah I noticed that with Danu, didn't seem like she had to work covering ground. Smooth and even, the land just seemed to melt under her."

"Ol' Spanish fella tol' me it was called the paso fino on their ponies. He reckoned the Indians got it from them Spanish horses they stole. Ain't sure bout it but he swore it was true."

"Paso fino, huh? It does make it sound fancier."

"Reckon it does." He shared the laugh with me before continuing. "Either way makes a damn fine trail pony an 'at one's got cow sense ta boot."

"I can see it in his eyes." I agreed switching my tack over to Shade.

"Now mind, 'es young and can get a bit ornery when ya first step up on that hurricane deck. Usually settles down after bitch'n for a minute like the rest." He warned me as I finished tying off my bedroll. He took Loki out and tied him on the fence rail.

"Guess we'll see." I smiled stepping into the stirrups. Shade nickered once, then I felt his muscles bunch.

Guess this was one of those mornings, Smokey dove back through a rail just as Shade launched himself into the air. When he landed I was getting ready for the next leap when Loki interceded. He nickered loudly once, obviously annoyed with the younger horse's antics.

Shade froze, his muscles still bunched to launch us into the air again. I swear he looked at Loki like he was waiting for more. Loki nickered loudly one more time, then locked eyes with Shade. The tension he had been holding eased off suddenly. I didn't know what to make of it, but Smokey did.

"Well damn! Ain't seen 'at in coons age."

"What?" I was clueless.

"That dun just told your horse ta knock it off." He grinned before continuing. "Can't swear to it but an injun I know'd told me once they kin talk. Fer the right rider they educate one ta other. Appears ta me Loki jus told at young fella ta go along wit ya, it's a rare thing but it happens."

"But…." I trailed off unsure about any of this.

"Horses know us JC, never doubt that. Some they know better'n others an 'ats good an bad. You gotta take it as it comes wit'em. Ya can learn from 'em more then ta other way round. Injuns know it, some 'ill judge a man based on how their ponies act round 'em."

"Well, that's something I didn't know. Thanks for adding to my education Smokey." I wasn't sure about what he said but could tell he believed it.

"Ride safe JC." He grinned swinging open the gate. "And 'member just cause at dun checked 'im this morning don't mean he won't try ya tomorrow. An watch'em round Bane, at stallion of Max's don't take ta challenges."

"I'll remember." I leaned down, shaking the older punchers hand. "You're welcome at my fire anytime Smokey."

"Same JC, an give Chet hell when ya make the Bar C." His laughter followed me down the road as the sun started warming the day.

I had planned on it taking about a week to get to San Antonio. There was a smattering of small farms and ranches peppering the land scape as I rode out of Corpus Christi. More of them than there had been around Waco, but we were closer to the coast here. More settled with a few less threats and better water. They seemed to space out more and more the further west I went. Distance from the safety of numbers thinning the crowd in a natural process. Occasionally a puncher would say howdy as the drifted by. Most letting me know I was on King range, but no one seemed bothered by me passing through.

The second night three of them called out from the darkness. Line riders for King just checking to see who was camping on their range. The third day out I was at a watering hole when a few Tonkawa appeared on the top of a rise watching me, they didn't do anything but watch me. Luckily they weren't from the confederation or at least weren't painted for war.

Shade and I got to know one another as we traveled. He kicked up a storm some mornings but didn't seem too serious about it. The days settled into a rhythm, the country moving easily below Shade's hooves. Before I knew it San Antonio grew up out of the landscape ahead of me. It as a simple town from what Jose had told me, an old Mexican fort that was absorbed into Texas.

Most of the residents were Tejanos but some of the bigger ranches around it were owned by carpet baggers. Claimed after the war, some honestly, others by trickery. It was large enough to have a Wells Fargo office, a decent local bank, a good number of shops, Inns, and enough saloons to keep it lively. The rest of the town was a mix of boarding houses and homes. I swung a wide loop around the town heading to a livery on the far side Max had told me about.

The city was more beautiful the closer I got, far more so than expected. Traditional style adobe buildings filled with elegant arches shaped the exteriors. Clean windows with crafted shutters of every color decorating the buildings. The town looked vibrant despite the drape color of adobe. They all had an obvious strength but kept the fluid beauty of their design.

The larger homes, some with two stories, showcased tile mosaics around the windows and doors. They looked comfortable, perfectly suited to the climate surrounding them. When I got a few blocks from the livery I noticed a group of horses pulling up in front of the building following a wagon. A small boy jumped off the fence, as soon as his feet hit the ground he raced forward to meet the riders. I could just hear his voice on the breeze.

"Señor Connors welcome back!"

CHAPTER 28

SAN ANTONIO

"Ah Miquel you've grown! Where is your papa?" I doubted my ears for a few minutes, it sounded like Max.

"He is coming Señor, he is just old. Jose!" Miquel jumped into my friends' arms hugging him. I watched the two, surprised by the smile on Jose's face.

I could just see them through the dust their horses stirred up but hadn't called out yet. Some part of me not believing what I was seeing. They were here? How could that be, I had planned on a lonely trail to find the ranch. Watching them as Shade slowly walked forward, disbelief written across my face. When I was a hundred yards from them Bo looked over his shoulder at me.

"Holy Shit! I'll be damned its JC!" He exclaimed making the others look at him in surprise. They all turned to look at me. I did the only thing I could think of, casually tipped my hat and smiled.

"Y'all didn't have to ride all the way here just to greet me, I would've found the ranch." I kept my tone light with laughter while trying to keep a blank face as I rode toward them.

"Figured someone as green as ya wouldna been able ta find their way." Chet shot out, quick as ever with a jibe.

"Shut your yap Chet." Max laughed as he turned Bane riding toward me. "Good ta see ya son, looks like it's been a long trail?"

"More than I want to talk about." I answered the man honestly as we clasp hands across our mounts. I could tell he wanted to ask but the unwritten rule of the west kept him from prying. Instead, he spun Bane around and we rode up to the rest of the hands. I did notice the tension in Shade under me as he matched Bane's pace.

"Damn good ta see ya!" Billy Bob greeted me cheerily.

"Good time'n, you can deal wit hire'n now." Chet smiled as he shook my hand.

"Amigo." Jose shook my hand from where he stood next to his buckskin. His words were simple but the look in his eyes said it all. I locked eyes with him and the camaraderie we shared was immediately rekindled. He would never ask where I had been but would listen if I want to talk.

"Step down an meet my ramrod JC." Max said stepping out of his stirrups and passing the reigns off to the young boy. "This is TJ."

"A pleasure." I said stepping forward after dismounting Shade. I kept a grip on him when he tried to follow Bane. TJ was tall, rangy, early 40s and looked tougher than leather. His face was trail worn with quick bright blue eyes that studied everything as they took me in.

"Same," he said taking my hand in a firm grip "heard good things 'bout you. Looks like ya got a good mount?"

"Yeah, did ya get him in Lisbon?" Max studied Shade curiously.

"Picked up a nice dun there, a good trail horse, didn't have a bit of cow pony in him." I admitted while skipping over how I had acquired Loki. "King traded me for Shade in Corpus Christi when I came back through."

"You end up working some for him?" Max asked, catching my omission but not knowing what it was exactly.

"Sorta, he had something he asked me to handle in New Orleans." I could tell Max wanted to ask but he let it go, knowing I wouldn't talk about Kings business.

"Nothin I need to worry about?" Was his only question.

"Nope, just not my story to tell." TJ studied our exchange carefully when I answered but he followed Max's lead and let it go.

"Mind that stallion 'round Bane, he's has strong ideas about the subject." Max warned noticing Bane was still glaring at Shade.

"Plan on it, hopefully they can figure it out without killing one another." I meant it too. Stallions didn't often kill each other but I knew it could happen.

That was it, I was back with the Bar C. No more questions aside from the horse. They took the rest on faith and moved on. I was home with my horse trouble settled, letting me get back to learning what I needed. Max started speaking as the young boys led the horses toward the livery. Back to business as if my arrival was nothing unexpected.

"Boys the rooms are reserved over ta the Esparanda House, ya'll have three days before we head to the Uvalde. Ya'll know how the law is around here, they'll lock you up quick if you step too far outta line. Don't make me go to your graves, keep the mess to a minimum. Jose make sure JC stays out of trouble." He just smiled at me while I did my best to look innocent, he wasn't buying it. "Don't give me that look, this is a sort of hometown to us don't subtract from the population if ya can avoid it."

"That doesn't happen by my choice." I chuckled at the accusation, knowing he meant nothing by it.

"Come Amigo." Jose motioned me to follow him when the other men started wandering off.

"Where we going?"

"Rooms, then I know a place to wash the dust off mi amigo,

good baths. The señoritas will take good care of you!"

"Bath sounds good, laundry is a must, only got one mostly clean shirt left." I laughed nervously before adding. "Senoritas I don't know…"

"Amigo, it is true you are young but know what a woman is no?" He laughed at the crimson coming into my cheeks. When he caught the hardness in my eyes his smile dropped. "Amigo?"

"Yeah I know what a woman is." I shrugged trying to stuff the pain back into its box before I continued. "Tell ya later, I ain't ready to share it yet."

"Si, es okay amigo." His was surprised, not judgmental. "I can see the pain that haunts you my friend."

"Thanks amigo, it's a rough story. One I ain't ready to tell yet." I trailed off not really wanting to explain everything that had happened, or even share my memories yet. I couldn't face that pain, especially not here in front of so many people.

"Mi Amigo we all have our stories, it is up to us to share." His laughter was good natured, trying to lighten the mood. "The place I speak of is for comfort and good conversation."

"Well, I don't know about…you know…" I knew my face was reddening more but I wanted him to know I wasn't interested in a brothel.

"Oh!" He said catching my meaning. "No! No, Amigo not that kind of place. I do not frequent those señoritas. These will take care of you in all things except those."

"So…" I studied him for a minute before I asked bluntly, "not a bordello then?"

"No amigo." He smiled a bit. "This is female companionship si, but not the other."

"Good, not that I think less of them or the punchers who spend time with them, just not for me…. well not now anyway." Again, that pain tried to find a way up, Jose must have caught it in my eyes but didn't ask.

"You will see." His grin split the dust covering his face.

We grabbed our bedrolls, saddlebags, and rifles. I took the shotgun off the saddle and put it away. We headed to check in at the hotel with the last of the other hands. It took a few minutes but eventually rooms got sorted. At the top of the stairs, we separated to drop off our gear. I took off my chaps leaving them in the room, then met Jose in the hall. He was leaning against his doorframe waiting for me.

"Bring clean clothes." Displaying the rolled-up clothes he carried. "Then we go Amigo. Leave the dirty ones outside, the hotel will clean them. Come this will be a good evening!"

After grabbing my last set of clean clothes, I followed him down the stairs. Out of habit we tipped our hats at two ladies waiting in the lobby. They seemed to be arguing with the clerk about something.

"You cannot expect us to stay in the same hotel as those ruffians!" The older of the two was complaining. She was maybe late forties, kind of round shaped with a pinched face. Her glare at Jose told me which ruffians she was complaining about.

"Ma'am with all due respect the Espranda House serves only the most reputable of people." The clerk was doing his best to calm the situation, but it didn't seem to be helping much.

"I say again, you must remove those men if you expect us to stay at your establishment!" Her voice was getting more and more shrill.

"It will be a lose Ma'am but if you feel that strongly, I understand." The clerk was done trying, I could hear it in his voice. "I hope your next accommodations will suit you better."

"We came here because there are no other accommodations!" She nearly panicked at his response. "Are you saying that you refuse to have these men removed?"

"Yes ma'am, 'at's exactly what I'm say'n." I noticed his drawl increased proportionally with his lack of interest.

"Auntie we will be fine, let's just go have dinner. This isn't like back in Iowa, this is the frontier." The girl beside her finally spoke up. She was young maybe my age, pretty but not fancy. She was that homespun beauty that kept its rough edges.

"It seems we have no choice!" Her aunt snapped glaring at

the clerk. Then she turned her small eyes on us before she turned on her heel and stomped off toward the dining room.

"So, ya'll be tak'n the room ma'am?" His grin was anything but friendly, but he didn't cross their name off the registry.

CHAPTER 29

THE HACIENDA

The hum of conversation faded as we left the building. I did hear one more shrill scream about some outlaws in the dining room before we turned the corner. I had a feeling the lady was like this no matter who or what she came across. Some people took longer to understand this wasn't wherever they came from back east, others might never figure it out. Texas was not like the civilized cities, it was still growing. I had seen her kind before though. Even in the bigger cities she wouldn't have been satisfied.

We crossed Main Street, walking a few blocks down a side street to a large adobe house set back from the road. Jose rang the bell hanging outside before explaining that this was big enough to be considered a hacienda, it just lacked the land. Before he finished an attractive older woman answered the door.

"Jose! A pleasure to see you!" She said in Spanish, thankfully I managed to catch all of it.

"Señora Cortez, always a pleasure," he answered in English "this is mi amigo, JC Stone."

"A pleasure to meet you ma'am." Taking off my hat bowing my head politely to the woman.

"My pleasure Señor," she inclined her head slightly, switching to English "please come in, be welcome in my home."

"Gracias!" Jose led the way into the lounge at the front of the house.

"First a bath I think?" She offered with a slight sniff as we passed, closing the door behind us.

"Si, we need it." Jose laughed.

"Yes ma'am, definitely." I grinned sheepishly, still not sure what the story was with this place.

"This way." She gracefully led us down a hall before pointing to two different rooms. "Jose here, and JC here."

The door opened into a luxurious space. Judging by the quality of the room hacienda was Spanish for mansion. Polished terracotta tiles in a mosaic of colors decorated the floor. The walls were covered with beautifully done paintings and tapestries. A small fireplace warmed the room, holding the chill of winter at bay. There was a table with two chairs, a comfortable looking couch, and a set of tables on either side of a large tub.

"Did Jose tell you about my hacienda?" She asked curiously.

"Not really ma'am." I admitted shyly. "He did tell me it was a respectable place."

"Si, my staff will see to many needs but not the more carnal you understand this? Jose would not have brought someone here who was not respectful, but I want to be clear." She smiled but there was a sternness to her tone I didn't miss. "I will send in Margarit. She speaks English better than most. She will wash your hair, shave you if you wish. She will talk and provide companionship through dinner, she will not do more, comprenda?"

"Yes ma'am." I visibly relaxed at her words. Thankful she

spelled it out for me.

"Bueno!" she smiled when the relaxed look appeared on my face. "The bath will be ready in a momento. Do not worry about her while you're in the bath, she is used to that. When you're ready to leave the bath, she will leave the room. Allowing you to dress, after simply ring the bell and she will escort you to the lounge before dinner."

"Thank you again ma'am. I do feel a bit out of my depth."

"Si Jose has a sense of humor." She smiled with laughter in her voice. "He doesn't bring many here, but he doesn't warn those he does."

"Sounds about right ma'am." Thinking about the grin on Jose's face when he talked about coming here.

"Please Señor, enjoy our hospitality." She smiled closing the door.

The bath was filled by a couple of boys who steadily brought in steaming water from a door in the back of the room. I stripped off my clothes when they finished. Laying a colt on the table beside the tub, before climbing carefully into the scalding water. Almost instantly the heat started to relax tired muscles, it soaked slowly in loosening stiff joints.

I managed to scrub off about two acres of Texas dust before I had to ring for the tub to be refilled. I stood uncomfortably behind a curtain while the two boys emptied and refilled the tub with clean water. Not long after I laid back in the clean hot water a light knock on the door made me open my eyes. I had almost drifted off in the tub.

"Señor may I come in?" The voice was light and soft. After struggling for a few moments to find my voice. The idea of having had a strange woman in the room while I bathed was something new. My embarrassment surged but I trusted Señora Cortez.

"Come in please." I finally managed to say without my voice cracking to bad. The door opened to reveal a beautiful young lady. She gracefully walked across the tiles, her steps were light almost silent. She moved quickly to a chair behind the tub without looking around. I saw her eyes look at the colt on the table, but she didn't mention it.

"Hola Señor Stone," her voice was musical and friendly "the Señora said you don't speak Spanish?"

"Mi espanol es mas o menos. Certainly not fluent for conversation. Jose is working on it, but I would prefer English, if that's okay?"

"Yes please, I like working on my English Señor."

"Please just JC." My voice was calmer, but I couldn't get my body to relax.

"Please call me Margarit. Would you like me to wash your hair JC?"

"Ummmmm sure?"

"Your first time at the hacienda?" I could hear the laughter in her voice, she had noticed my nervousness.

"Yes ma'am, Jose kinda sprung it on me."

"Oh! I think you will enjoy our hospitality." She gently pulled my head back to hang over the edge of the tub. "Relax you have nothing to worry about."

I did my best to do just that, laying my head back over the edge and allowing her to pull my hair out from behind me, hanging it over the edge of the tub. A bucket scraped across the tile when she moved it, followed by the sound sloshing water. Then soft delicate fingers worked through my hair as she poured warm water over it. She carefully massaged the dirt and tangles out, so gently I never felt it when the knots came loose.

"You have long hair for an Americano no?" Her question was plain. Some punchers wore their hair long, but not many wore it as long as mine.

"Just always liked it long I reckon." I smiled up at her, the upside-down view was a bit odd. Despite that I was struck again by how pretty she was.

Around twenty, a thin pleasant oval face with a pert nose. Her eyes where deep pools of black sparkling with intelligence. They perfectly matched the long black hair, neatly braided and pulled back. She needed no makeup to enhance her appearance, there was a clean pure beauty about her.

While her fingers worked to undo tangles and knots, she worked lightly scented soap into my hair. Carefully scrubbing it to the scalp. After she rinsed the soap out a light oil was worked into it, the soft scent of sandalwood filled my nostrils. More hot water removed the oil leaving just the barest trace of the scent.

"I will shave you now, please just relax and stay still." She smiled down at me before gently wrapping a hot wet towel around my face. When she removed the towel and began lathering my face with a similar lightly scented soap I did my best to lay still.

"First time being shaved?" She asked when I nervously eyed the straight razor.

"First time by a beautiful woman, most barbers aren't all that feminine."

"You haven't shaved long though?" There was a soft laugh in her voice.

"Hadn't needed too until recently."

"I have done this many times, trust my hand."

She moved the razor in smooth even motions, there was an absolute surety in them. Then she rinsed the lather off, again gently wrapping my face in a warm towel. Another few minutes and it was removed. She rubbed a pleasantly scented oil in that burned and soothed at the same time.

She started straightening my hair, gently using her fingers to get out any tangles left. Then brushing it once her fingers got them all out. When that was done she picked up a small jar that smelled lightly of sage, working a small amount of it into my hair. My guess was that this was the scented grease the vaqueros used. Relaxing at her soft touch just closing my eyes enjoying the sensation.

"This is a new experience for you?"

"Yes, very new. Not something I ever thought possible honestly."

"It is a unique thing, not many places do this without doing the other." Her face flushed red as she spoke. An awkward silence hung in the air for a minute.

"I honestly have never been to them either ma'am." I admitted.

"That is a good thing JC," she smiled down at me, the awkward silence fading away "you are a good man."

"Most still call me a boy." I laughed at myself. "Good I don't know, maybe, but not bad."

"You do a man's work. You are a man, is this not so?"

"Do you mind if I ask, how you came to be here?" I asked hesitantly, watching her face to see if I offended her.

"That is a tough thing to ask." She studied me for a minute before continuing. "I can see you mean nothing by it."

"Oh no not at all I am just curious, if it's too personal you don't have to answer Margarit."

"I can see you don't ask in a rude way. My parents were killed when I was young, it left me living on the streets. Señora Cortez found me there, she offered me a life. She is strict, demands we learn to read and write, both Spanish and English. She does all this because she wants us to have a chance at a good life."

"Sounds like a good lady." I commented watching the light from the fire play off her eyes as she talked. They so reminded of Binda's when the sun reflected off the water. Suddenly I could feel my eyes start to fill with tears, the sense of loss overwhelming me.

"JC, what have I said?" She asked almost panicking.

"Nothing, nothing at all, it was just for a second I saw someone else in your eyes. Someone I cared for very much." I couldn't tell her the whole story, but I could share enough. "She died not long ago, I am sorry I didn't men to upset you."

"Never be sorry for that, never. Each person we love, we take a piece of them with us. They will always be there, but maybe not the pain." She looked down at me before adding. "That is how it is with me Madre, all I see now is her smile but it is love."

"Thank you." I took a deep breath and gathered my emotions back under control. "You were saying about the Señora?"

"Ahhh yes. She is an amazing woman, the Señora built this from nothing." She picked up her story without hesitation. "Yes she makes money but in her heart she wants to give girls like me a chance."

"Is this a normal thing in Mexico?"

"Yes and No, it is a thing that happens for the wealthy." She admitted gently drying my hair, wringing it in a towel to avoid tangling it. When she finished she got up slowly, walking gracefully toward the door. "Please finish your bath, ring the bell when you're ready."

"Sorry if I offended Margarit." I was caught off guard by the abrupt end and spoke before the closed the door.

"You did not, it is the way of things, nothing more." She turned smiling at me as she closed the door. I finished washing the last bits of Texas dust. Even replaying the conversation in my head I couldn't understand why it ended so abruptly.

Still not understanding what I had done wrong, I put on my clean clothes deciding to just move on. Packing my dirty things in my saddlebags with my long handles, they needed a wash just as badly if not more than the rest. I could get by without them while the laundry service washed my clothes.

The last thing was putting on my guns, but when I leaned down to tie the holster around my thigh I was suddenly blinded. The tie I used for my ponytail was gone, probably fell apart when I took it out. Thankfully I always kept a piggin string in my saddle bags. Before ringing the bell, I noticed myself in the mirror. The person looking back at me caught me flat footed, I hadn't seen myself since New Orleans.

My cool grey eyes stared back at me. Skin that had once been called was tan had now darkened to match the rest of the punchers. My long straight hair was pulled back tight, the ponytail hanging halfway down my back. I was the same but different, there was a hardness that had settled into my eyes now. The last of the boyish softness had disappeared from them, buried with Binda.

It wasn't the face of a hardened man, but it wasn't the face of a boy anymore either. Standing long minutes studying my reflection I was struck by everything that had passed. I was caught between the boy I had been and the man who stood in the mirror. The boy was still learning but the hard edges won through fights and loss was showing through. Slowly I reached for the bell, softly ringing it. The soft knock on the door was followed by Margarit's soft voice.

"Are you ready Señor JC?"

"Please come in Margarit, and yes I am ready." I answered. As she opened the door I asked, "Should I take my bags and hat with me?"

"Si, there is a place to leave them near the front door." She closed the door behind me before offering her arm, taking it felt very formal in a way.

"JC please, Señor relax everything is fine. I am your companion for dinner this evening." She smiled up at me, the deep pools of shimmering darkness pulled at me. Sparking a new pain at the memory, but it was getting better. I could almost feel her smile in it now. I could see Margarit recognize it again, but knew she like everyone else would never ask. "We will have a pleasant dinner, there will be others joining us."

"I'll try." Slowly I pushed the pain back. "Just not used to having a beautiful woman on my arm."

"Gracias, see there you are learning." Her brilliant smile radiated soft humor that helped smooth over the raw edges. "Compliments are always a good option when you're unsure."

"Lucky guess, it's not that I've never been around women. It's having never been more than a servant at a formal dinner."

"Servant? You do not strike me as that Señor." We reached the lounge where she indicated a spot I could leave my gear. A long peg for the saddlebags and a shorter one for my hat.

"Not a very good one truth to tell, my mother is a maid. She works for a successful businessman back in New York, occasionally I had to help when I was young."

"New York?" She asked leading me down a hall toward the pleasant din of conversation. "This is where you are from?"

"I was born in Ireland, but we came over to this country when I was five."

"Ireland?" She said the strange word hesitantly, revealing for the first time a gap in her language.

"It's off the coast of England, they rule my old country. The man we worked for is a lord over there. He sorta moved us here, you might have heard some refer to it as the Emerald Isle?"

"I am not sure. The hacienda does not usually have Americanos."

"Lords over there are like the Dons in Mexico if that helps?"

CHAPTER 30

A GOOD MEAL

When we reached the room ahead Jose was there, cleaned, and polished. His companion she was a tall thin woman who embodied the word elegant, it was just a presence she wore around her like a shawl. Across the room was an older man, Spanish at a guess but definitely not a commoner.

He was tall with the same bearing of nobility I recognized from Jacob. The lady with him paired with that presence like she was born to it, the essence of a lady. Not specifically beautiful but attractive with an air of nobility enhancing her presence. A young man stood near them, in his late 20s very sharply dressed in black with silver conchos worked around the embroidery. His companion was a delicate looking woman, thin and graceful, her smile was demure contrasting the bold look of the man.

Señora Cortez stood overseeing the room, slowly guiding people to fill the large table with covered dishes. Finely decorated silver allowed steam to escape around lids, waiting to be used. There were four chairs on either side of the table with a single chair at the end. Matching china sat waiting for us accompanied by various crystal decanters filled with wine. Beautifully colored glass pitchers of water finished off the display of finery.

"Mi Amigo, feeling refreshed I hope?" Jose asked as we came over. The corners of his mouth quirking up in amusement. He dodged my rebuttal before I could offer it by introducing his companion. "Allow me to introduce Señorita Santiago."

"Señorita Santiago" I bowed over her hand as she offered it. "I am JC Stone a pleasure, allow me to introduce Señorita Margarit."

"A pleasure Jose." Margarit said as he gallantly bowed over her proffered hand.

"Señors and Señoritas allow me to make introductions?" Señora Cortez spoke as she stepped to the head of the table.

"Don Garcia and his son Diago are accompanied by Señorita Wuerez and Señorita Vasquez respectively. This is Jose Estata and his friend JC Stone, accompanied by Señorita Santiago and Señorita Margarit. Please be seated, dinner is ready to be served."

Everyone nodded politely, greeting one another as we sat down. I noticed Diago glowering when I was introduced but didn't bother myself with it, choosing to ignore the man's look. The table was as elegant as the rest of the house. Outdone only by the rich smell of fine food drifting around the lids.

We tucked into the table, Señora Cortez said grace followed by everyone but me crossing themselves when it was finished. The señoritas poured wine for us all as others started serving the food.

Conversation was light, mostly centered around the quality of the food and wine. Margarit taught me what each dish was and the proper way to eat it. The food was my first real taste of true Mexican dishes. The flavors where strong, building as one complimented the next. The fresh tortillas served with the meat gave a base to the seasoning, allowing the full rich flavor to come through.

The accompanying dishes created a lovely balance of taste for the pallet. The colorful display from each dish drew the eye while the smells teased the nose. It all combined to create a complete experience. It was the first time I truly understood why people sat to eat like this. This wasn't just eating, it was an experience for every sense. For me it was something I would remember for years to come.

"There will be brandy and coffee on the veranda this evening as the air is pleasant. Thankfully it is also warm enough to will allow for smoking comfortably." The plates were being cleared from the last course when Señora Cortez spoke again in her soft commanding voice.

She led the way through the double doors behind the table. Outside was a meticulously maintained garden with a covered porch. The soft fragrance of the flowers somehow still lingering on the cool night air. We found a seat under the soft lamps while the sunset painted the sky around us.

Servants offered brandy or coffee as each guest preferred. I stuck to coffee, this wasn't trail coffee it was the finely balanced rich flavor of properly made coffee. Taking out my pipe to pack it I noticed Jose doing the same, Margarit leaned forward with a match while I puffed it to a nice ember.

"Hola señors." Don Garcia greeted as he approached with the cigar he was smoking.

"Hola, Don Garcia." I nodded in greeting to the man. His voice was warm and friendly. It matched his bearing, the man walked with the air of nobility.

"Don Garcia, always a pleasure." Jose greeted the man with a familiarity I wasn't expecting. "How is the ranchero doing?"

"Sadly, Jose it is not good. The cattle market in Mexico is very bad. Too many cattle not enough buyers since the Americanos are not buying them."

"The white bastards think to strangle us." Diego spat staring at me.

"Diago!" The Don snapped at his son.

"Padre they do! This gringo here in the hacienda, he has no business around our people." He glared at me with hate brimming in his eyes.

"Diago, do NOT insult my guests!" Señora Cortez snapped before I could respond. "Or you will not be welcome here."

"May I ask Don Garcia," I started politely, "and bear in mind I am, as Jose reminds me often, a greenhorn, but why don't you sell cattle here?"

"Ahhh new to Texas then? The Texas ranchers don't let us drive across the river to your markets,. Though in all honesty we wouldn't be able to sell them in your Dodge City either. We are Mexican it is that simple."

"JC your new and think differently than most Americanos." Jose explained between puffs from his pipe. "Most would question your friendship with me. Si, Chet, and the others are friendly, but we are not amigos you understand?"

I hadn't considered it but thinking back they did act different with Jose and Juan. Less so with Jose, probably out of respect and maybe some fear. It just never occurred to me that it was because they were Mexican. I knew there was still a hatred between the Mexicans and Texans, I had seen it in the deputy at Red Station. I was starting to realize that my upbringing was blinding me to what others saw. I would have to remember to stay vigilant of that, it could cost me if I wasn't careful, New Orleans was a reminder of how that hatred could lead to violence.

"It makes no sense to me, but I do recognize it." I nodded and managed to shrug at the same time. "Maybe because in New York, I was around so many people from all over the world?"

"You're not like most JC." Jose simply stated. "If you mean to travel with me, it's something you will see."

"Si, Jose is sadly correct. There is still much anger on both sides about the war." Don Garcia continued "The cattle that you get fifteen dollars a head for, I get four in Mexico City. It is not as my son thinks, Americanos trying to force us out, but the advancing railroads that stopped the ships from coming to us. The rail is cheaper and can move more cattle, it is simple economics. Also, the Texas ranchers no longer buy from us, either from old hatred or because it is free to get them out of the brush. I believe Señor Max is one of these?"

"Si, he maintains the wild cattle on his range." Jose answered.

I froze at his words, that didn't make sense to me at first. Then thinking about it as if the Rio was physical line, I began to understand. Mexico had many rancheros so the cattle market was flooded, especially when most of its population either couldn't afford or didn't need to buy beef. Mexico was in a sense fixed, while their neighbor across the border was growing in leaps and bounds. We were struggling to get enough beef to feed the large populations in the cities. Different countries with different needs, both struggling with anger from the war and prejudice. It was a harsh reality, one with no easy answer.

The rest of the night was full of good conversation, it wound down pleasantly. Each of us politely saying good night at the end. I wished Don Garcia a good night telling him I hoped to see him again. Jose and I walked back to the hotel in silence, when we neared the hotel he finally spoke up.

"You liked the hacienda amigo?"

"Yeah I did. Thanks Jose, it did me some good." I admitted. It had, there was something about it that helped with the pain. Maybe it was just spending time around people that was pulling me back from the edge. What I did know was it helped. "Thanks amigo."

When we reached the hotel there was only one thing on my mind sleeping in a clean bed. It took the last of my energy to put my dirty clothes outside my door for the laundry service, then I was asleep.

Binda appeared in my dreams but this time it was her smile that filled them, not her death. I wasn't over it, far from it but it was getting better. More and more my mind filtered out the bad while cherishing the brief time we had together. I woke with her laughter echoing in my mind.

My eyes opened just as the suns light broke the horizon, a lone beam piercing the darkness of my room. Thankfully there was plenty of room for my morning ritual. Once that was done I washed in the basin, wetting my hair then pulling it into a ponytail. I could still smell the faint of sandalwood, the oil helped smooth my hair when I tied it back. After tying down my guns I stepped into the slowly waking world. Like most hotels there was always coffee on a stove in the lobby.

CHAPTER 31

SHOPPING AND
A BEER

Taking a cup out to the porch I folded into a rocking chair before lighting my pipe. The soft glow of dawn was slowly creeping across the buildings when Jose made it out, falling into a chair next to me. We enjoyed our usual morning smoke in silence, letting the familiar sounds fill the space around us. Just as the sky shifted toward blue Max walked out joining us with TJ.

"Señor Max, TJ." Jose said with a friendly tone. He respected TJ almost as much as Max, I could hear it in his voice. The silence held, all of us enjoying the quiet before the day. When the sun had finished painting the sky and the rest of the town slowly crawled to life Max broke the silence.

"Can't wait any longer to eat at Joan's." Max announced. "Come on."

"They'll be yell'n bout ya boss, happens every time." TJ laughed.

"Wait'n won't stop that." Max's laugher led us onto the street.

The restaurant was a few blocks down from the hotel, all four of us greeted folks as we walked. I had to chuckle at the name of the place, it was called 'Trails End.' Aside from the sign there was almost no difference from every other store front. The interior was nothing exceptional either. Simple wooden tables were scattered around the room with chairs of various descriptions around them. Its center was dominated by a single long table capable of seating fifteen people. Two ladies bustled around the room, one headed our way with a coffee pot and 4 cups as soon as we sat down.

"Saw ya try'n ta sneak by me Max." She smiled at him, "Glad ya managed to wash off some of the trail dust this time. TJ you must've warned him?"

"No ma'am, he's all grow'd did it all on his own." TJ laughed.

"Liddy, I always wash before I come in here!" Max grinned up at her.

" 'At's a bit suspect but we'll let it ride. Jose I know'd, but who's this 'er young fella?"

"Mi amigo, JC," Jose swept his hand toward me, "mostly he is trouble."

"True." Max nodded his agreement.

"Trouble? Well young man not in my place, I'll box yer ears." The women smiled but her stern tone made me believe she would do it.

"Yes ma'am." I smiled doing my best to look innocent.

"Enough blather, y'all want breakfast I am guess'n?"

"Now Liddy, I know it's early but don't bring us none of that half-cooked mess." Max grinned but quickly ducked back when she playfully swatted at him.

"Ya keep talk'n Max, I'll have Joan come outta the kitchen an dcal with you!"

"Yes ma'am, don't want that!"

We all laughed at the fun. It was easy to see that these folks were familiar with one another. In Dodge and on the trail Max was considered a small rancher, but a well-respected man. Here in San Antonio, he wasn't the big boss, but he was big enough to be respected and well liked.

" 'At 'as to be Max making a ruckus out there!" A heavy voice full of mirth came from the kitchen. The door swung open letting the tallest woman I have ever seen walked through. She looked like she could wrestle a steer for branding and do the branding at the same time. She was still obviously female, not beautiful but attractive in her way. "You giv'n Liddy a hard time again?"

"No ma'am!" Max started to smile but then Liddy spoke up.

"Nope but been talking 'bout how poorly cooked our food is." Liddy smiled wickedly. I never thought I would see Max squirm, I was wrong.

"Now holdup, that's not what I said."

There was a grin hidden behind both ladies' eyes the whole time. Staying out of it by sipping my coffee I enjoyed just watching the byplay. It was filled with familiarity. This whole place had the feeling of home, it was all down to these two ladies. They knew making the men who frequented these places sought that. They succeeded far beyond what was expected. In some ways it was one of our many homes. It hit me that for the first time I had included myself in that thought.

Places like this were scattered across the country, each one giving punchers a place to feel connected to. Missy's in Dodge, feeding men on the drift even if they were broke. Millie's familiarity with the people who came through was the same. Sanctuaries in towns and forts for everyone from soldiers to drifters, places they could feel at home for a moment. I had seen it myself, the mothering way they talked to and fed us. They did it without really knowing why, but in their way it helped keep us sane.

The food came out faster than I had expected. Steak, fresh eggs, biscuits, hashed potatoes, and more coffee. All cooked perfectly, the eggs tasted like they were fried in bacon grease, despite the lack of bacon on the table.

Once we ate all we could, and the plates had been cleared they left fresh coffee on the table. My eyes were focused outside the window watching the town do what some many others had done before. Life continued with its normal pace. Conversation had been light for most of the meal as was common. Good food didn't need talk, you filled you mouth with other business. Now we had fallen into comfortable silence while digesting the meal.

The town was busy, people going about their lives in a comfort. There was a false sense of security that held them together, safety in numbers. It helped stave off the worry about what might come blowing in next. Not for the first time I wondered why that never seemed to suit me. Fiddle footed was the answer I had been told but that only explained part of it. The truth was starting to appear, I was seeking my place in the world. My own slice of this land, a place to call home.

"Figured it's time to let JC know why we're here. Came to find four or five more hands." Max broke the comfortable silence. "See any when ya was out last night TJ?"

"Might be a couple, have ta see." TJ admitted while blowing on his coffee. "I'll wander 'round today an get the word out."

"Good, handle that. We'll met any you find tomorrow, see what we think of them." Max nodded, but he didn't look happy about it. We all knew the hands he was replacing, none of us wanted to talk about it. The gap in conversation allowed me to ask Jose about something I needed.

"Jose, who makes buckskins around here, might need a new set?"

"Si, I know a small group of Tonkawa that make good ones. Bit heavier than the plains you normally wear but they should be able to get them done."

"Need some other supplies after that. Reckon we should get moving." I said unfolding from my chair, reaching to pay for breakfast.

"Cardona's will have what ya need." Jose laughed as he stood.

"I'll take care of chow." Max said waving us off.

"Go see the Tonkawa first?" Jose asked heading out the door.

"Yeah, let's get that done. Never know how long it'll take."

They were easy enough to deal with, five dollars and two days bought me two new properly fitted sets of buckskins with moccasins. They would be dropped off at the hotel before we left. We headed toward Cordona's store after that was done. It was a neat looking clean adobe building nicely shuttered and well maintained. I picked up a couple sets of extra-long handles, some heavy wool socks, a good scarf, two heavy blankets, and a buffalo coat that was heavy as hell. It was even heavier than the one I had picked up in Baton Rouge and hung down to my calves. Two Pairs of thick buffalo hide gloves, stocked up on 5 pounds of tobacco at Jose's recommendation, as an afterthought I added a bag of cheroots I liked the smell of.

I spent a little over forty dollars total, but Jose thought I should be good for any weather. I asked about a leather shop when we finished. The heavy chaps I had picked up in Dodge where good, but I had a feeling they would be miserable in the summer. The new set was elk skin, not as durable but lighter and hopefully more comfortable in the heat. I was lucky to find a set that fit about right, the alterations would only take a day.

"We still have some time at the line shack amigo." Jose spoke as I paid the shop keeper. "You will go with me, no?"

"Thought I dodged it." I laughed through a feigned grimace, before answering. "Course I'll finish the winter with you, maybe a month more?"

"Si, then we will be riding night herd during the round up." Jose said it like I should understand. "The line shack will be our base for that. It is close to the gathering area."

"How's that work? Kind of figured we would be working on the round up?"

"Si, we will but our talent isn't so much with a rope amigo." He grinned and I understood, we were the gun hawks for the Bar C, guarding the herd would fall to us.

"Works." I finished the conversation, not overjoyed at the idea but accepting it for now.

"Do not worry amigo, you will also be doing other work." Jose said smiling.

He still had some other stops to make, and I need to go by Wells Fargo. We split up agreeing to meet back at the hotel in a couple of hours. I went by the Wells Fargo office sending off a letter and picking up two from my mother.

She was doing fine, asked me to stay safe. It was nice hearing from her and knowing she was well. Her second letter was a bit more stressed since she hadn't heard from me but all I could do was hope my letters would lessen her fear. There was also a letter from my father, nothing more than an update on our investments. He closed with best wishes and his clean neat signature as usual.

Wandering around the rest of the day, mostly walking San Antonio's sprawling streets. It was a decent sized place with about twelve thousand people living and working in and around it. After window shopping a few places I stopped in a gun smith to pick up another two hundred rounds of 44-40 and twenty more twelve gauge. I was never shy about spending money on ammunition. Having more than you need was never a bad thing.

I met back up with Jose around two outside the hotel. We walked to a saloon not far from it to grab a beer. It was a nice looking place called Iron Mikes. As it turned out the Mike in question was standing behind the bar.

"Howdy gents, what kin I do ya for?" He was a solidly built man with friendly smile and demeanor all the way down to the Irish lilt that hung in his speech.

"Beer will do us fine." I said surveying the room.

It was a simple place, a few tables scattered around with two poker tables in the back. Slow as it was neither poker table was open. The few people in the place were scattered around sipping beer or drinking whiskey.

"A dime each." Mike said setting down the mugs in front of

us, Jose handed him the money as we leaned against the bar.

I packed my pipe and struck a match on my boot to light it while studying the room. Mike slid an ashtray toward us with a smile. We relaxed just enjoying the day and the cold beer. That ended when we heard shouting in the street. Curious we walked over to see what was going on.

Out in the street three men squared off against one. To his credit he stood calmly facing the three trail worn men. The glint of a badge on his vest caught my attention when the sun reflected off it. He looked a little older than me and managed to sound confident.

"Y'all know you'll hang if ya kill me." His voice never wavered. This man wouldn't bend.

"Maybe we die, maybe we don't." The center man spoke casually. He was taller than the other two, clean shaven and neatly dressed. Something about him reminded me of a gambler. "You're the one bracing us deputy."

"Because you three robbed the Richardson's last night. We got a witness so's jus' surrender, an let the judge decide." The deputy sounded calm, but some part of him knew it was a suckers bet. To his credit it didn't show much. I doubted his opponents noticed.

"No Señor, I do not think we will." The potbellied one on the left laughed at the idea. His heavy accent giving him away as a Mexican. The closer man on the right just smiled wickedly, sweeping his coat back clearing his holster.

"Seems the odds are fixed Deputy," the middle one spoke again, "just walk away an you don't have ta die."

"Amigo." Jose said smiling as we stepped out of the bat wings onto the street, splitting to either side of the deputy. "This seems unfair no?"

"I think your right my friend. Think the deputy should face 'em one at a time?"

"Si, that seems fair."

"You two stay outta this, it ain't no concern o yours." The middleman spoke, shifting his eyes a bit nervously. He reeked of fear now, just like the others with him. Cowards one and all, none of them would stand alone. They only fought when the advantage suited them.

"I think he can go first." I offered. My hand suddenly filled with the familiar wood of my Colt, leveled at the man on the right. "You can step aside friend."

"Si, you as well." Jose's 44 guided the potbellied man off to the side. They thought about trying us, studying for just a second before they slowly raised their hands. With an apologetic smile toward the one in the middle, they moved slowly off to the side.

"What are you two do...."

"Just you an me pard, make your move or raise your hands." The deputy cut off his objections. He was completely comfortable with the situation now.

The well-dressed man stood alone in the center of the street. His earlier bravado quickly fading as his partners stepped away with their hands up. I could see his eyes shifting, trying to figure a way out of this. Just a few seconds later he slowly raised his hands.

"Take me in deputy, ain't worth dying in the street." The man backed down raising his hands above his head.

"You?" Jose spoke to his man.

"No Señor, I am good!" Keeping his hands raised.

"Same, we won't fight." The one I had covered was quick to agree. The sheriff rounded the corner at a jog carrying a shotgun just then. He slowed to a walk after quickly appraising the situation.

"I'll cover 'em Frank. You gents step forward so I can get all three with this double barrel." The sheriff spoke to the deputy. "Then ya'll can jus drop those belts to the ground an step back. Remember this thing 'ill easily kill all three if jus' one of ya gets dumb."

Jose and I holstered our guns leaning on the wall sipping our beers. When the three stepped back from the pile of gun belts the deputy collected them. The sheriff hadn't relaxed and was still watching us out of the corner of his eye.

"Gents," the sheriff said walking over toward us now that his deputy had the three men handled, "appreciate the help there. Frank moves a bit faster 'an I do now a days."

"No problem sheriff." I grinned.

"Si, many suddenly loose the urge to fight when they have to do it themselves." Jose agreed over his mug.

"Still, you boys helped out in a tough spot. I am John Banks, Sheriff here in our little town."

"JC an this is Jose. In town with the Bar C." I shook his proffered hand.

"Connors crew, 'at explains it. Ya'll always willing to pitch in. Think I met you a year back Jose, on a posse chas'n some rustlers?"

"Si, I was there."

"Tracked for us if I recollect?"

"Si, Señor Connor asked me to. It was a simple thing, tracking a hundred head was not difficult."

"Fair enough, either way thank y'all. I'll let Max know ya threw in with my deputy." He tipped his hat before heading down the street to join his deputy. He was escorting the three complaining men down the street now. We walked back into the saloon to finish our beers. Mike was grinning at us from behind the bar.

" 'Ad a feeling ya wouldna stay outta 'at."

"Like to make sure things stay fair." I admitted smiling at the bartender, he just laughed.

CHAPTER 32

HIRING

"Breakfast at Joan's?" Max asked after the sun had fully broken the horizon the following morning. It was the normal bunch of us sitting on the front porch of the hotel.

"Works." TJ said.

They took our silence as agreement, and we all climbed to our feet. The meal was hearty, and the room filled with teasing and laughter. Again, that feeling of home filled a blank spot we all carried.

Somehow the ladies made all chaos of the frontier okay. Maybe that's not the right word but they made it bearable for those who carried the weight. For those like Jose and I it helped keep our code precise, reassuring us we were still on the right side of things. They're happiness reminded us of the places we helped secure. Finishing our coffee Max coughed getting our attention again.

"Got a couple of things to talk to y'all about. Jose you think JC would work out riding the line with you the rest of the winter?"

"Si, he agreed."

"JC?" Max asked, just to verify it.

"Yeah boss if that's what needs doing. Wanted to know a bit more before I agreed is all."

"Makes my life easier," TJ spoke up, "most hate riding the line. Bunk house hands are easier to find."

"That's settled, now the next thing. Jose is an old hand at this but JC you fit the bill for it." Max nodded at Jose as he spoke.

"Hiring?" Was all Jose asked.

"Yeah, think JC can hang with you, say noon?"

"Si, no problem Jefe." He turned to explain it to me while Max and TJ got up to leave. "We sit in the saloon while they hire, the men they talk. Let them talk around us, you comprende?"

"Makes sense."

"Si, we also watch for problems. A few hombres' take being turned down poorly."

"Seems a bit much, but I can see how that would be a problem. Which saloon?"

"Señor Mikes, he and TJ know each other well." Jose grinned. "He has a good lunch to. We had crevasse's there yesterday."

"Well hell, sounds like a plan."

"Si, the trick is we do not know them."

"Right, still sounds easy enough."

"Si, most of the time."

"Well, what do we do for now my friend?"

"Da nada amigo." He grinned looking along the road in front of us. "We relax and watch the people."

We did just that, loafing around in front of the hotel drinking too much coffee most of the morning. Jose told me about Mexico, the line shack, what it was like gathering the herd. I told him about school and the big cities. I talked vaguely about New Orleans, I still wasn't ready to share that much yet. Watching him try and wrap his head around a city with so many people was amusing. Just trying to explain what a million was took a good long while. We filled the time with good conversation and laughter.

In no time we found ourselves walking toward Iron Mike's, arriving early to find a good table. Jose suggested somewhere central to the room. Still far enough away from Max and TJ to not be associated with them and where we could overhear the men talking. Waving to Mike when we walked in, he brought us a pot of coffee while we got set up at a table. After promising to bring us some lunch when it was ready he proceeded to ignore us.

There was a decent crowd hanging around, word had spread about the Bar C hiring. More than one puncher was looking for work this time of year. It was still winter, but most knew if they got picked up now it would likely be a permanent job. We relaxed, listening to the talk around us, evaluating the different men.

The table beside us was two punchers on the drift. They had been over a county when word came that the Bar C was hiring. The younger of the two looked to be early twenties while his pard was a little older. They were typical hands, usually drive hands getting cut loose at the end of the year. From their conversation they had both decided they were tired of it and wanted a home ranch to work for. When they heard the Bar C was hiring they had ridden hard for San Antonio, knowing the ranches reputation. Worth a nod, experienced and wanted it for the right reasons.

Behind us where three men, all about my age. It didn't take long to disqualify them. They wanted to be gun hands more than cow hands. Jose knew Max had no tolerance for their ilk. They're talk was more about how fast and how tough they were, hunting reputations more than work. All three were more trouble than they were worth, their inexperience and ego showed with every word. Definitely a hard pass.

The table of four off to the right was more interesting. Two different pairs of men who ended up sharing a table. Two local boys, young, inexperienced farm boys with no potential to make it on the farm. My hunch was the younger sons, wouldn't inherit and the spread wasn't large enough to hold them. Hard working but needing more education than I did. They might be worth a shot if Max wanted to invest the time. Seemed like good men, easy going and willing to do whatever they needed. Honest as the day was long and just looking for a chance.

The other two were more concerning, both in their mid-thirty's. They lectured the two would be punchers on how hard the job was and how bad it paid. Trying everything they could to talk them out of sticking around. A not unheard-of tactic but also not the most honest. If you needed to scare off competition to get hired what did that say about your qualifications? True in an underhanded way it made sense, but we wouldn't be giving them a nod.

What really had my attention was just a general read I got off them, something about them was just wrong. When I locked eyes with one of them that cold calm started to settle over me. These two where trouble, not like the kids behind us. These two would be the problem children of the day.

A couple of other hands where around but they were straight forward punchers. Different degrees of experience and backgrounds but mostly solid hands. Some older drovers looking for permeant homes, others looking to make it through the winter without riding the grub line. The only other ones that held any interest were three vaqueros at the far table in the corner. I still didn't know enough Spanish to read them one way or the other, but Jose did.

"Those three, they are good hands." He explained. "They come from an old ranchero here in Texas, the ranchero died. They would be good hands, but I am not sure if TJ will try them."

"He doesn't like vaqueros?"

"No amigo," Jose laughed, "his espanol is worse than yours. He has to rely on Chet, this makes him nervous."

"Ahh that makes much more sense, relying on Chet for something like that would be a risky proposition."

"Si he is very good for some things, others he is never serious."

It didn't take too much more time for Max and TJ to walk in. They claimed a table off beside the bar that Mike had set aside for them. Mike brought them their beers and lunch before they started talking to people. TJ asked questions while Max would glance at us. One or the other of us would give a simple nod or shake letting them know what we thought.

It all went pretty smooth until the young toughs who fancied themselves gun hands. They were mouthy when they got turned down, saying none of our hands could match them with a gun. Bragging about their abilities and claiming they would all be known men. They went back to the table still complaining about how they would teach that Bar C outfit. We mostly ignored them, it was just talk but you never knew. Both of us kept them in view.

The next tense moment came with the two that made me edgy. They took the dismissal well enough, the trouble started when the young farmers ignored their advice to leave. Mike solved the argument by laying his double barrel on the bar. It motivated them to exit the place quickly. No one wanted to face a stacked deck, especially when it wouldn't leave enough of you to bury. Marking their faces in my mind, knowing those two would be a problem, I watched them leave.

So far Max had seven men stay to talk more, the three vaqueros hadn't stepped to the table yet. To Jose's surprise TJ called them over inviting them to sit. The interview was brief, but Max told them to stay with the rest. The wanna-be gun slicks mouthed off about that, but they did so quietly enough that the vaqueros couldn't hear them. Or maybe they decided not to hear them. The three seemed levelheaded but didn't look like men you willingly picked a fight with.

Jose and I had picked over our lunch, sticking to coffee while we watched the proceedings. We knew Max wasn't looking to hire all ten but had no clue what he was thinking. Out of them he kept the farm boys and the two trail hands. The other three where hands that happened to be on the drift and looking for a winter home, all of them were King trail drovers. When Max shook their hands they headed out politely thanking Max for his time.

"Good hands." Jose explained. "They probably plan on returning to King for the drives. The pay is a high wage and Jefe wants permanent hands."

That left seven, from the look of it Max was hiring all of them, including to Jose's surprise the three vaqueros. Jose elbowed me, motioning to the door. I followed him out into the afternoon sun. After letting our eyes adjust to the change in light, he explained what was going on.

CHAPTER 33

COMPLCATIONS

"Now we have to watch their back. Sometimes people are offended when he turns them down. They don't start trouble in the saloon, Mike is not a fun man to fight."

We walked across the street to lean against the wall of an empty building, down a bit from the saloon. It gave us a clear view of the street in both directions. The two men I spotted earlier were standing down the street talking. Both looked back toward the saloon doors too often for my comfort.

"Let's move down a bit, those two ain't window shopping." I said nodding their way.

We did our best to walk down the boardwalk without drawing anyone's attention. Making it about thirty feet from them when Max and the new hands came out the batwing doors. They hadn't made it far when the young gun slicks followed them out.

"The Bar C is hiring stink'n mexs over good Texans like us

huh? Filthy bean eaters." One of them called out.

They must have had just enough liquid courage to mouth off. When Max started to turn one of the vaqueros spoke to him softly. After a few words all three of them turned back toward the young fools. They didn't say a word, just stepped into the street and spread out waiting. It seemed to unsettle the young toughs far more than any banter would have.

They wanted to be the bulls of the walk but lacked the backbone to make it stick. The vaqueros silence and comfort with the idea of death wasn't what they had planned. I could tell in one look that not one of them would step off the boardwalk to meet the vaqueros. You could read it all over them, not one of them had the sand to actually put his life on the line. With that I wrote the whole thing off and turned to watch the other two.

They were watching the unfolding drama with interest, focused on the youngsters now frozen on the boardwalk. Slowly the men who started this fracas stepped back through the bat wings into the bar. Very slowly and one at a time. No one spoke, the vaqueros waited long minutes before they dropped back into the group. Max waited another minute before moving but when Mike stuck his head out and nodded they started moving again. The two men had a quick conversation, then stepped out into the street as the group approached. Jose and I both slipped the thongs off our guns and waited.

"Hey farm boys, you owe us for the drinks." The thinner of the two yelled. Before the group could react Jose and I stepped out from the board walk.

"No, they don't." I said plainly, the cold filling my nerves making my tone icy. Jose would take the bigger man, without either of us saying a word we knew our targets.

"Who the hell are you two? And why's this any of your business?" The heavier one asked, a little taken back by our intervention.

"Amigo, we ride for the brand just like the farm boys. We say you are mistaken." Jose answered coldly.

"Why not just walk away an call it a day?" I offered locking my eyes on the thin one, waiting. These men wouldn't walk away, we all knew it. This was down to gun play.

"We ain't moving." He said.

His eyes pinched just slightly when he started to move. It was the only warning I had, his shoulder never twitched. He was fast, his gun came level just as my Colt kicked in my hand. His shot zipped past, thrown off by the impact of my lead. He had been fast, just not fast enough. Both my rounds hit just to the left of his third shining button. It glinted slightly in the sun as the red spreading across his shirt washed over it.

Jose's 44 banged a second before I shifted to the other man. Our eyes locked for a second, death slowly reached for him as he tottered. He fell straight back, kicking up a puff of dust from the street. Jose was already scanning for the other man.

I looked back at the thin man in time to see his eyes roll in shock, showing all white. Understanding hit him just in time for his legs to give out. He crumpled to the ground next to his partner, creating his own small dust cloud. In automatic motions I reloaded my Colt before looking over at Jose. There was a trace of blood on his arm.

"Hit?"

"Not bad Amigo." He grinned back at me slipping two rounds into his 44. "A graze, he was fast."

"Same, I knew they would be trouble."

"Damn can you two not leave a trail of bodies across Texas?" Max said coming up beside us. When I looked back I noticed the young toughs standing outside the bar. Their faces were white, and I swear I could hear them swallow from where I stood.

"Damn it Max, I thought your were kidding." TJ exclaimed, kneeling beside the man I shot.

"Nope." Max grinned back at him. "He don't miss."

"Why'd y'all step in?" One of the farm boys asked as they came up to us.

"Señor Connors hired you." Jose answered simply, as if it explained everything.

"Yeah?" The young man looked confused.

"At the Bar C we ride for the brand. We heard them two trying to buffalo you outta talking to the boss." I tried to explain. "Knew they were trouble before we left Mike's. The boss gets mad if he hires someone and they die before starting work."

"God damn it Connors, who'd you kill this…." The sheriff cut off his yell as he came around the corner. His eyes taking in the men laying in the street, he skidded to a stop staring at the two. "That's Buck and Gregory Martin, oh damn it all."

"They drew down on my men sheriff." Max said clearly. "Who are they?"

"Knowing them I have no doubt, got paper on both. Last I remember it's two hundred each from Wells Fargo. Hit a stage not far back up the trail, killed the driver, guard and 4 passengers, including two women."

"Good riddance then." TJ offered, spitting toward the bodies.

"Agreed, but their kin might not think so. There's 4 more of 'em round here."

"Local?" I asked.

"Family is," the sheriff nodded, "didn't know 'em two was in town."

"Where does the family live?"

"JC what are you think'n?" Max asked, already guessing my intent.

"Don't like watching my back trail, figure I'll go calling. Settle this now."

"Si amigo, I will go as well."

"You won't need too." The sheriff nodded toward 4 men walking toward the group a few blocks away. "That'll be them."

"Sheriff, let this play out, I want it settled either way." I said quietly. "The rest of y'all step out of the way, this is me and Jose's dance."

"Y'all don't shot up my town damn it! Move this mess outta town limits."

"We can do that." I agreed. The edge of town was a few blocks behind us, and we started walking that way.

When we passed Iron Mikes the pretenders were just staring at us, their faces pale and eyes wide. They thought death looked like a dime store novel. Having just witnessed how quickly death came for men in this country had forced them to look at the reality of it. We walked by them in silence. That's when I noticed the two vaqueros pacing us.

"We know what it means to ride for the brand amigos, we will stand with you. I am Manuel that is Carlos."

Studying the men as we walked, I nodded my consent. They both had that same cool calm look Jose had, they would stand.

"Welcome this is Jose, names JC."

There wasn't any more to be said as we reached the edge of town. A small burnt-out church stood on the left, the land was working hard to reclaim it. We turned to face back the way we came, spreading out slightly.

The four family members walked our way, not rushing but their strides were determined. We stood waiting, hands hanging loosely at our sides. The men coming our way ranged from later forties to one that looked about my age. There was a family resemblance, eyes and hair easily defined the blood line.

"Which two killed my brothers?" This one was late twenties maybe.

"They drew first, but for what it's worth it was me and him." I answered pointing to Jose.

"Y'all bounty hunters." Another one spat, glaring at us.

"Nope won't even claim the bounty."

"That's a damn lie." The youngest yelled, a second later the oldest backhanded him to the ground.

"Shut your mouth boy, afore you end up like 'em two idiots." He turned back to us. "Far as we're concerned this is done. I believe in family but them two skunks was woman killers. Can't stand a man 'at'll harm a woman. So, if you say it's done it's done."

"Didn't want that fight, don't want this one." I said calmly. "Ya'll take your kin an bury 'em if you like. We meant what we said, the Bar C don't claim bounties."

"Ya'll ride for the Bar C?" This one looked in his early thirties.

"Si, we all work for Señor Connors." Jose answered him evenly.

"Pa it's done, they ain't lyin'. Connors ain't ever claimed a bounty, I learnt 'at when I did 'at drive ta Dodge."

"We ain't got no problem then." The older man stated flatly. The younger man he had knocked down looked like he disagreed with that. He started to get up and open his mouth, but the older man turned to look at him. "You hear me boy? This is done, get it outta yer head."

"But Pa they...." The old man cut him off, steel resonated in his voice.

"Boy, ya think it through. You ain't nearly as good as they was wit 'at gun an they're dead." The boy flinched at the statement but didn't say anything to argue. "We lost 'em two when they kilt a women. If it hadn't been 'em it woulda been by my own hand, or did you forget why we come ta town?"

"Naw, I didn't Pa." The boy looked down ashamed. "I know'd it was to fetch them ta the law."

"And the law woulda kilt 'em" The old man had a sense of honor, you could hear it in his voice. "Those two skunks brought nuthin but shame ta the family name an' out here we can't have 'at."

"Alright Pa." The boy seemed to deflate as he spoke.

"We ain't gonna to accept their mess on our good name." The older man turned back to us. "I don't like how this ended but 'em two got the result 'ay deserved. Same as woulda been if I'da caught up with 'em. Can't have the family cast down by them two no accounts."

"Yes sir, wasn't our choice either, just happened that way." I met the man's eyes as I spoke. My cool grey locking with his strong brown. This was a man, a man who had been prepared to kill his own sons. He lived by a code and any who lived around him would honor that code or pay the price.

"Then it's done." I nodded.

At those final words all four of them turned back toward the waiting crowd. We waited while they talked to the sheriff, then the younger boy ran off down the street. He came back with a wagon in a few minutes, with no further discussion they loaded the bodies into the bed and left. We finally walked back after they turned the corner.

"Damn!" I said as we walked up. "That's a hard man."

"Surprised amigo?" Jose asked.

"I suppose not, but that man's got no back up in him."

"No amigo, it is the way out here. Kill men good or bad that is one thing, but kill a woman? No, your own family will suffer for that if they do not make it right."

"You'll learn out here son, woman don't get molested or hurt. It just ain't done, an when it does happen it don't go well for 'em at do it." TJ said flatly.

"All true an rightly so. Well, that was a full day of hiring," Max laughed while studying me and Jose for a long moment before he continued, "you boys good? Everything settled?"

"Yeah, it's settled. They had come to deal with them personally, either turn them in or…"

"Not surprised, they're good folks. Got their own way about 'em but good folks." The sheriff nodded. "The old man wouldn't have tolerated 'em two doing what they done. They might rob ya, but the rest…"

"Just aint allowed." TJ finished.

CHAPTER 34

HORSE TROUBLE AGAIN

Walking back toward the hotel, I couldn't help but wonder if this was always the way hiring went. The young toughs trying to posture when they got turned down? I understood that, but if you're wanted why would you stay in the area? It didn't make sense to me, evidently smart and criminal didn't go together often.

Maybe that's what makes certain outlaw bands stand out. They're smarter and stay alive long enough to find fame. That same fame just made them bigger targets though. Pinkerton's, bounty hunters and every young tough trying to build a reputation or collect on a bounty would come after them. All for the sake of a name that would someday lead them to an early grave.

That same afternoon we packed the two wagons with the

purchases TJ had arranged. Getting all the supplies packed away for the trip to the ranch. They would be for the last bit of winter and the first part of the spring drive. It should be enough to get the chuck to Uvalde when the drive started north.

There it would stock up with enough to make Waco and the process would keep going all the way back to Dodge City. Between then and now was a lot of hard dangerous work. Gathering a few thousand wild long horns from the brush, getting them herd broke and then starting them all north. When I laid it all out in my mind the task seemed impossible, but these men got it done. Finding a way to beat the odds year after year.

Max had already said we would stop one night in Uvalde. He bought most of his regular goods there and kept a house in town because it was convenient. The goods he bought here weren't easily available in Uvalde or would have to be shipped there from here anyway. He only came into San Antonio two or three times a year for those specific things. It was just another part of the cycle these men lived, built from dust and blood.

My new buckskins sat outside my door when I got back to my room. They were well made from soft elk hide, thicker and more durable than my other set. No fringes or bead work adornment, just as I had asked. The moccasins had heavy buffalo hide soles with soft elk sides. They all fit right and just needed to be broken in. Sweat, smoke and blood would cover that and start scenting them. That part was easier than you'd think, just hunt and wear them.

Walking down to my normal morning of coffee on the porch, I was deep in thought about my future in Texas. There were a few months of winter ahead with Jose, working the line. Then popping the wild creatures out of the brush to slowly build the herd. That would mean more time at the cabin while riding nighthawk. Again, I was amazed at what it took to get those cattle to market, all to repeat the cycle again next year.

I had to admit the trip to get here had been very different

than my childish dreams. In such a brief time there had been so many lessons, not just about this country but about myself. What struck me about it was that Max and the other hands hadn't seemed to think this year was exceptional. Maybe they didn't know the real numbers, but they all had rough guess on how many men had died and didn't think it was out of line. Was this just a normal year?

Life on the trail with and without cattle had a lot more violence than I had thought. The past few months had settled that, and I had already made peace with it. The pain from losing Binda still hurt every time I thought about her smile but getting back with the Bar C had made that bearable.

There was so much beauty in this country, but it was being bought and paid for acre by acre with lives. Families were wiped out, travelers killed for their goods but despite this they all kept coming. Sipping my coffee while thinking about all of this, Jose joined me. By now he knew how to read my moods, he sat silently let me work through things for myself.

Other thoughts trickled in, filling out the picture. True, there where bad men out here but for every one of them there were ten like Max. Men with no backup in them, who did what they had to, not just for themselves but for others.

They didn't do it for praise or rewards, they acted because it was in their power to do so. To the people out here that's just what you did. It was a simple concept, one that I hadn't seen a lot of back east in the dog-eat-dog city, but I was becoming one of those men. Someone who stood on the line between the civilized and uncivilized.

It wasn't a choice I had to make. It was something inside me that just wouldn't allow some things to stand. I wasn't some dime novel hero or story book character. I was just the same as the man sitting beside me. Separated from the others by our willingness to shed blood. Someday laws and courts would deal with things but until then men like us would have to.

The others out here were different. There was something in them, not just the men but the women carried it too.

Something that gave them a clear view of right and wrong. Clair hadn't paused to consider how adopting her niece would affect her life. There was no debate about it, she just accepted the child and continued building a life. She never had any doubt about what she should do or how she would do it. It was the right thing to do and that's what she did. Maybe that's what I respected so much about them? There was a simple rule they all followed, right was right and wrong was wrong.

Lawmen who took very little for pay, knowing they would be putting their lives on the line regularly. Men like Randy, Vance and Tucker in Dodge who hadn't set out to be lawmen. But when it was laid at their feet they took up the mantle of responsibility without thinking about it.

Sure, they joked about taking it because of a house, but that wasn't the truth. They did it because they felt like they could help. They had seen a bad example and knew they could do better. Even Red Wolf, who wasn't welcomed as an equal, didn't hesitate when asked to take on a burden that wasn't his. He had gone up against a gang of outlaws for a child he didn't know. Doing what he needed to do every time the question arose.

These were the men and women I would use as a guide to help me stay on the right path. Their ideals I understood, some core part of me knew them. Knew I wouldn't walk away when asked to throw in. I hadn't really taken time to think about what I was doing, reacting instead of choosing. Even those reactions spoke to our shared beliefs. I hadn't thought about it at all when asked, I just stepped toward the work that needed to be done.

Jose and I following the Apache into the darkness for a girl who might have already been dead. It wasn't the smart play but that was never a question either of us asked. We went because it needed doing. Sitting here sipping my coffee for the first time I started considering it all, here and now it solidified for me.

"Deep thoughts Amigo?" Jose asked breaking the silence.

"Yeah, thinking about how I fit in out here, it's different

then I thought."

"Si it is simple, no? I am not sure that is the right way to say it, but I do not know another way. Simple to me is doing what you need to do."

"That's accurate my friend, simple but not."

"In your city, you have so many people your name is lost. Here your name will not be lost amigo, it will follow you. Good or bad a man's name is all he has."

I had to stop and think about that for a few minutes. Jose didn't rush me, letting me take my time to process it. I hadn't thought about that aspect of a name. I had spent so much time worrying about getting a name but that was just one kind. There were different types of names, almost everywhere we had gone people knew Max. They knew the Bar C and the caliber of men who rode for it. King, who was a much bigger name had known Max. Treating him like an equal, not because of ranches or money but because he knew his reputation. A name meant something more out here, it held a real value in the world, it carried weight.

"You're right." I had been operating on instinct and if I am honest a sense of childish adventure.

"You will have a good name amigo. You do the hard thing because it is right. One thing I ask?"

"Ask away my friend."

"Take some of the bounties, money is a good thing to have." He laughed over his coffee.

"Agreed, when it isn't Bar C business I will."

Max and TJ joined us not to long after that, all of us enjoying the morning together. Max said we would be leaving first thing in the morning. That meant today was the last day to grab whatever we might have missed.

After breakfast Jose and I checked on the horses then wandered the town most of the day. I picked up some different pipe tobacco to try and he grabbed some of the cheap cigars. We ended up at Iron Mikes by midafternoon enjoying a cold beer and some lunch.

"You JC?" The man had come in looked around then walked toward us where we leaned on the bar. He was tall, dressed like a gambler. Wearing tailored suit and jeweled pinky ring that sparkled on his left hand, maybe thirties. His eyes had a coldness to them, like a snake watching every move I made.

"I am." I answered studying him carefully.

"The livery told me 'at blue roan's yours, I want him."

"Not for sale." I was confused, what made this man think my horse was for sale.

"He looks like one I rode years back, best horse I ever had. Until I lost him in a card game, so name your price." He had a surety to his voice, like of course I would sell him Shade without a doubt.

"Sorry he isn't for sale."

"Everything is for sale. Just needs the right price, or the right game."

"Not Shade, sorry."

"What do you mean? You'd turn down good money?"

"Got him because of his skills as a cow pony. That's a rare thing to find especially in a young horse. He's worth more to me than money."

"Look boy, I wanted this to go easy." His tone was threatening, it had a cold edge to it. "You're going to sell me 'at horse, or I'll take him."

"Oh?" I asked. The cold calm spread through me like lightning, my voice held ice in its tone. My hand moved automatically down to slip the thong off my Colt. "How do you plan to do that?"

"You don't want to be disagreeable 'bout this boy. You know who I am?"

"Nope, don't care either. You want a dance, call the tune." I said simply. Before he could respond Mike leaned on the bar between us.

"Luke, I told you I don't want any trouble in here."

"If this fool boy would just sell me the damn horse, we wouldn't have a problem!" The man whose name was evidently

Luke snapped. His frustration showed in his tone but he was trying to watch me while talking to Mike.

"Make your play." I had been pushed as far as I would be. I might have let the others go but that was his last time calling me boy.

"Luke, I'll tell you this then you decide how you want to deal with JC." Mike leveled his gaze at the man before he spoke. "I saw this man work yesterday. If you go down this road, you'll be dead. Not maybe dead, but stone cold dead laying in the street. Don't forget I've seen you draw."

When Mike finished speaking he moved off to the side, not saying another word. His words had their desired effect though, Luke stopped for a minute to really look at me before he spoke again. Some part of him suddenly realized I wasn't just some cowboy. That sixth sense someone whose been in danger more than once has was warning him. It told him in no uncertain terms this was not a fight he wanted. He studied me for a minute longer before taking a slow deep breath.

"Look maybe my temper got the better of me, I meant no disrespect an apologies for my tone."

My back was still up but I had a choice to make right here and now. It was a choice that I had to learn, this wouldn't be the last time I faced it. The answer wasn't just important here and now but every time it came up. The man was looking for a way out, I could push and play for death or I could let it pass. He hadn't actually insulted me, Mike knowing him told me enough to know I could let it go.

"No harm done, happens to the best of us." I let the ice drop out of my voice. "I understand why you want him, but he's the best horse I've seen since parting with Danu. That's life and death sometimes when you're working long horns."

"I understand," he spoke softly, relaxing as he stood there, "he looks exactly like the finest horse I ever owned. I reckon I got excited about getting another one like him. Never shoulda bet him, felt like a fool since."

"Names JC Stone, pleasure to meet you Mister?" I slipped the thong back on my Colt and stuck out my hand.

"Luke Short, pleasures all mine. Let me buy you a beer by way of apology?" He shook my hand then waved over at Mike.

"Table or bar? This is my amigo, Jose Estata."

"Jose Estata?" Luke stuttered slightly when he said it. The look that came over his face said he knew Jose's name and the reputation it carried.

"Si, we know each other?"

"No, nope never met." Luke spoke evenly as he eyed Jose, wondering if the stories were true. "Heard a few tales down in old mex about that name."

"That man is no more Señor." Jose said flatly, his tone telling everyone involved that this was not a path to go down.

"Understood, pleasure to meet you." Luke seemed to gather himself back together again and shook Jose's hand. "Let's grab a table, Mike will you send over a round for us?"

"Sure thing, y'all grab a table I'll have 'em over in a minute." Mike agreed smiling now that things seemed to have calmed down.

"I am guessing y'all are on the way back to your home range?"

"Yeah we work for the Bar C. It's been a long trail so far."

"Bar C? Damn when my mouth gets ahead of me it surely does it in a big way!" He laughed a bit before continuing, "Happens that way I reckon. I got tied up in a big game in Dallas, wandered down this way after that finished ta see Mike, mostly wasting time. Figure I'll head to Los Angeles from here, big tourney in Frisco this spring."

"Gambler?" I was curious about the life of a gambler, not knowing much about it. "Getting to be a rough trade I hear."

"Ups and downs, more gun play now a days then there was back on the river boats. Seems like gunfighter and gambler are goin' hand in hand lately."

"Sound like a hard way to make a living." I was tempted to ask him about New Orleans but there was still too much raw pain there. Jose had relaxed a little from Luke's comment but there was still a distant look in his eyes. I didn't know much about his past other than what he had shared but knew it wasn't something he was proud of.

"That's why I was surprised when Mike warned me off." He chuckled but studied me seriously for just a second before continuing. "He knows me, we crossed paths a few times over the years. I trust him. So, for him to warn me off? It's a thing at'll make ya take notice."

"More than likely because of the Bar C, Max wouldn't have let you take the horse."

"That's for Damn sure! Max ain't got no back up in'em. Mind if I offer a piece of advice though?"

"I'll take any help I can get. Jose will happily remind me.... "

"Is a greenhorn." Jose laughed, some of that distances look had faded from his eyes, letting the normal humor ease back into his voice. "Mi amigo is new to the west."

"Well, that's a twist, but the advice is simple. I think you already know it from your answer. Do everything you can to avoid 'at reputation, it follows a man. Haunts him in a way. Young fools pushing to get a name."

"Getting ready to disappear into the ranch for a year, maybe more. Who knows if Max will have me trail the herd next season."

"Oh, amigo you will certainly be on the drive!" Jose laughed out loud. "Señor Connors will be sure of that."

"Either way hopefully nobody knows me, and I can keep it that way."

"You understand perfectly JC. I really am sorry the way we started. Got a feeling your gonna make some interesting stories."

"Consider it forgotten Luke, your welcome at my table or fire anytime. It says a lot about you offering advice, you could have just left it." I wasn't sure why, but there was something I liked about the man. An ease about him that despite our rough start had won over my opinion.

"If you're ever looking for me just ask for the biggest game in town, they'll know if I am around." He smiled nodding toward the tables in the back. "Speaking of which I need to get to my job, glad I meet you both. I have a feeling we'll met again."

"Look forward to it." I nodded to the man as he rose.

"Adios amigo." Luke got up moving to a table in the back, Jose looked at me grinning like a cat.

CHAPTER 35

TO UVALDE

"What?"

"You have no idea do you amigo?"

"None, what am I missing?"

"Luke Short has name amigo, he is known."

"Known?"

"Si, a man with a name, both at cards and with his guns. A good man, from what is said, but still a known man."

"Yup had no clue." I grinned. He just laughed at my innocence.

"Amigo, I think traveling with you will never be boring."

"Likely my friend. I don't want pry but are you okay? Looked like being recognized threw you a bit."

"It is …. an uncomfortable thing to be known from then. You know I was not a good man, I am not that man now, but I still remember him. You understand?"

"I do but know this, not only have you learned from that past, but you've helped me avoid those mistakes. If you hadn't walked that road you wouldn't be able to tell me how to stay off it."

He looked down, studying his beer for a few long minutes. Taking his time to consider my words before he responded. Slowly his eyes came up to meet mine again. They still had a shade of his haunted past in them, but it was fading. I didn't look away meeting his gaze evenly.

"Gracias, mi amigo." It was all he said, but it was all he needed to say. We finished the rest of our beer before heading to find some dinner. Nodding farewell to Luke and Mike as we headed out the door.

We made it to Joan's in time for dinner, enjoyed an amazing the meal before finding our way back to the porch outside the hotel. The evening was spent just watching the town. Before the revelry got kicked into high gear I headed up to bed. The night had just enough chill in the air to make sleeping comfortable under the blankets.

The morning started the same as always, going through my routine before heading down to get some coffee. I took my saddlebags and rifle with me, wearing my new buckskins. Jose didn't comment on my attire, he knew why I was wearing them.

We had our coffee watching the day start, after Max and TJ joined us we walked to the livery. Smythe would have breakfast going this morning and I was looking forward to it. I felt like I understood the man a bit better after spending time with Tante and Binda. Three different people who shared a love for feeding others.

The vaqueros and farm boys were already there. The farm boys looked like they slept in the livery, both still wearing stray pieces of straw. The vaqueros must have been in a different hotel, they looked fresh and ready to ride.

Breakfast was a treat, I had missed Smythe's cooking. He had found some eggs to make with chops for breakfast. Had to admit he made a good version of Millic's recipe, not the same but damn good. The man really was one hell of a cook, his chops were better than hers in my opinion. He must have added some more spices to the mix, giving them a stronger kick.

The rest of the hands showed up just before he was ready to serve. The two new punchers came with them. Chris and Bo had worked a drive with them before and thought highly of them. Conversation was easy while the plates were filled, then the comfortable silence of men eating took over.

When the food was done Jose talked to the vaqueros while Smythe repacked the chuck. He got them introduced to the rest of the boys. Manuel and Caesar where brothers, Carlos had grown up with them on the ranchero. They all spoke some English and were working hard to learn more.

The farm boys where Thomas and Clint, third and fourth sons on a farm that only needed two sons. When their dad passed the eldest two brothers had made it clear they should find somewhere else to be. They had been looking for something when they heard about the jobs. Both were surprised they got hired but appreciated the chance. There was no doubt they would work hard to earn their place.

Chris introduced the last two as Pug and Tink, or Zeke and Robert respectively. Insisting that Pug and Tink were what they answered to. They had been pards for six years, drovers or temporary hands on several different spreads. Both men were skilled in most of the jobs around a ranch and seemed willing to work. Their easy attitude, going so far as to help the two farm boys learn, made them welcome additions.

"I am gonna want 'at story some time." Chet grinned.

"What story?" Pug looked at him in honest confusion. Chet just sputtered for a few minutes not knowing what to say. After a minute Pug and Tink both burst out laughing.

"Oh god damn it!" Chet swore. "Y'all take lessons from JC?!"

"They pulled that same trick when I met 'em." Chris chuckled. "Ain't got no funnier, y'all oughta come up with a new one."

"True they did." Bo laughed remembering the experience.

"Speaking of stories, young fella thar...." Pug spoke with an accent I couldn't easily place but sounded familiar.

"Might need the story 'bout 'at funny hat?" Tink pointed with a look of honest curiosity. He was pure Iowa, from toes to nose this was a cornfed farm boy turned puncher.

"Oh, don't start on his hat." Chet laughed "Of all the things bout him, that hat is noth'n. It's just some foreign thing he liked."

"That hat ain't the odd thing bout 'em? I'll leave the hat be.... for now." Pug grinned while tossing the dregs of his coffee on the fire.

"Y'all get your horses saddled up an ready to move." TJ ordered loud enough for everyone to hear. "You new hands stay clear of that big black monster. Banes got two bodies already, don't need another. Thomas, Clint, grab some better gear. Smythe threw down the best of what we have, if you want to buy it we'll work it out later. Get rid of those wooden blocks y'all call saddles."

"Yes sir." They answered almost as one, heading to the back of the chuck.

Smythe had laid out two sets of the tack, backups he always carried. They were two good saddles, not fancy ones, but good honest Texas saddles. Looking at the saddles they had I understood why. They really did look like pieces of wood covered with what might have been leather. I whistled for Shade who came over quickly enough, then did his best dodge my every move.

"Yeah, yeah, I know knock it off. We'll be on the trail soon!"

Shade managed to bump me just right. He timed it perfectly, making me lean hard on Bane to keep from falling over. The big black stallion snorted his annoyance and spun to snap at Shade. He then turned his glare on me, it felt like he was chewing me out for my ill-mannered horse.

"Señor he is a beautiful animal but seems to enjoy bothering you." Carlos laughed. Shade snapped his head up glaring at the man. He took a few steps back, watching the big horse carefully. "Apologies Señor, please excuse my interruption."

"His horse is meaner and smarter than he is." Jose laughed walking up to scratch him behind the ear.

That distracted Shade enough for me to get the saddle on him. He danced around for a minute until I mounted. Then like they knew it was coming everyone, including the horses, stepped back. He jumped off as soon as I hit the saddle and kicked his way around the corral. He wasn't really trying to throw me, more just burning some energy.

It wasn't uncommon and some of the other horses bucked around as they were mounted. This was nothing exceptional for half broke horses and most people were prepared for it. After the dust settled and everyone had calmed down, Smythe turned the chuck out of town, and we headed to Uvalde.

The trail was less visible, with few herds coming this way. It was more of a road with the ruts fading fast under the harsh Texas wind. After everyone settled down normal light conversations started up. The new hands getting to know the older ones.

Jose and I ranged out front, scouting for any problems. Occasionally one or the other of the new hands would join us. Most often it was one of the vaqueros but Tink and Pug both made appearances.

The land was a mix of hardy plants fighting to get a foothold. Arroyos moved through cutting it into different levels creating an interesting display. A few canyons cut between rock formations that jutted up from nowhere. Mesquite trees and sage brush stood out mixing with low spiny cactus. Some dotted with bright colors, tough plants showing off the first of their flowers.

It was a different beauty from the plains, more chaotic as it twisted and move ahead of us. The hum of the plains was there but the tone changed becoming more dangerous with a harsh edge. It carried the threat of death more aggressively. This land was less forgiving and wasn't ashamed to tell you.

The weather was pleasant despite the time of year, warm enough under the sun to make me sweat under my buckskins.

I could only imagine the summer, the heat would be unforgiving. Especially working amongst two thousand head of cattle. It was a beautiful open country, but even the plants had a toughness that spoke of its extreme climates.

Mule deer flourished, easily moving through the scrub. I took one the second day out with my bow. The new hands laughed when I rode out with it, that is until I came riding back with it hung across my saddle. That got me more weird looks, the new hands had never seen a white man using a bow to hunt. In my view it brought in fresh meat and helped season the buckskins. I firmly believed the old stories, you had to bloody them on a hunt before they truly became part of you. I still needed to smoke them but that would come when the fresh venison was cooking. I'd already collected some sage to toss on the fire.

The days passed with Jose and I doing a lot of out riding. He was teaching me while we traveled, I needed to know this land as a line rider. Partially we did it so I could get a feel for it, but also scouting for threats ahead of the hands. Apache and Comanche would happily take on a group as small as ours. The third day out we came across a burnt-out small ranch as a reminder. It looked to have happened a week or so ago and no one survived.

The burying wasn't a pleasant job, but everyone pitched in making it easier. Max found a name on some papers that had survived the fire so we could at least pass on the information in Uvalde. Life continued though, even as we moved along other small family ranches dotted the land. Two days later we rolled up a steep embankment to see Uvalde not far off in the distance.

The town stood on the crossroads, trails came and went in every direction. The Nueces Strip stretched out with its canyons to the south. Traveled by outlaws and the lawmen pursuing them. We would be working most of that land, the Bar C ran from the Nueces south to the Rio. Here the Leone River greeted us with its smooth rolling water. Uvalde was still a rough town, the large number of saloons and bawdy houses where surprising until Jose explained it.

"Amigo it is the only place to spend money." His smile told me he had been one of those to partake in what the town offered. We were sitting at the bank of the Leone waiting for the rest to catch up. "Aside from vaqueros and ranchers, this is the start of the Nueces Strip. Men coming out or going in enjoy what the town offers. It is a hard town amigo."

We crossed the Leone without any problems then moved down Main Street toward a livery. I could see what he meant, men walked or rode moving from one place to another. Each casting wary eyes at everyone around them. They had the wildness of the frontier wrapped around them like armor. Townsfolk moved through their day like this was all normal.

They stepped politely giving way to the men, shopped or otherwise went about their business. Nearing the livery, a scruffy old man in a beat-up straw hat stirred from the bench he was relaxing on. He adjusted his hat slowly to see who was headed his way. The grin that split his face when he spotted Max and TJ told me all I needed to know. He slowly eased up from his seat while yelling for his help, which turned out to be two young boys.

"Señor Connors!" The man called out as we approached. "Welcome back!"

"Pedro always good to see you my old friend!" Max greeted him in turn.

"Si! Si, I still live. El ninos keep trying to kill me but not yet amigo. There is no respect from the young today." He grinned down at the two boys running to help with the horses.

"They never do!" TJ smiled.

"Si! Si!" He turned speaking rapid-fire Spanish to the boys. It was far too fast for me to catch except a couple of words. My guess was half cursing and half instructing.

In a short amount of time the horses were stripped of tack and turned out into the corral. Shade pushed his way in to be scratched several times by the boys while they admired his color. He would be in good hands by the smiles on their faces.

"Alright men, we got a house here in Uvalde, just worked out easier than a hotel. Some of you will have beds, some won't, TJ 'll manage all that. Only gonna be here a night so enjoy yourself all you want, but hell or high water we leave at first light." Max yelled over the noise. There was some groaning, but it was mostly show. TJ stepped up as Max headed down the street.

"Yeah, yeah, it's a hard life boys now pay attention. Chet and Chris bunk in with me. Bo, Jose, JC, and Carlos get the bunk room on the bottom floor. Manuel, Ceaser, Tink and Pug ya'll got the bunk room on the second floor. Thomas and Clint you boys drew the short straws, bedrolls in the front room." He smiled apologetically to the two, but they didn't seem bothered.

"Chris make sure they know where the house is. For the new folks the old man meant it, we leave at first light. An I don't care if I have to tie you to your saddle." The look on the mans tanned face told me he meant what he said. "Y'all who haven't been here before pay attention, Uvalde is a frontier town. Ya pick a fight 'ere you're likely to end up dead or kill'n someone. Folks prefer to mind their own, I strongly suggest ya'll do the same."

CHAPTER 36

HOME AWAY
FROM HOME

"Amigo, come. After we drop off our things then we go to Maria's. Best tamales this side of the Rio!" Jose smiled as he grabbed his saddle bags. I took mine and slipped the shotgun in one. We cut back behind the livery to a nice adobe house. Both wagons had been parked between the buildings, the space seemed to be meant for them.

Smythe and Max where just climbing the steps as it came into view. The place had a nice sized covered porch with four rocking chairs and a bench. The porch was lined with flowers blooming even in mid-winter. They gave the house a well-loved look, cared for by someone who was proud of their home. We walked through the door and a plumb older women greeted us with a warm smile.

"Welcome señors!"

"Señora Garza." Jose bowed gracefully to the women before

introducing me. "Mi amigo es JC. Señor Connors hired him in Dodge, he helped me find the men who killed Juan."

"Welcome Señor JC. Juan was such a good boy. I pray for him still." You could see her eyes simmering with tears as she thought about Juan.

"Gracias Señora." I bowed slightly to her as she stepped to the side letting us pass by.

We stepped into the cool interior of the house, it was a welcoming place filled with life and color. Jose led me down a hallway past the front room and study to a larger room at the back of the house. It had two sets of bunks on either side of the room, there was plenty of space to put down our gear and still move around.

I took a minute to wash the dust off in the basin and change out of my buckskins. I laid them out on my bunk to dry the slowly in the shade. They had been bloodied and partially scented. They still needed a bit more smoke and sweat but that would come with time. When they dried I would wrap them in a horse blanket with a little sage to help finish scenting them.

"Come, let's go eat!" Jose grinned at me, and I had to laugh. I put on my guns back on and tied them down before grabbing my hat. I hadn't seen him this excited about any place before, so I was looking forward to this.

"Lead the way." I said after putting my hat back on, checking the feather was set right out of habit.

We headed out the house with Jose leading the way toward Main Street. It was just a touch before dinner and our stomachs were nipping at our spins. He led at a good clip down the boardwalk, tipping our hats politely to the folks we passed. Taking in the town while we walked I smiled at its familiarity.

Like most small towns it seemed everyone knew everyone, more than one person greeted Jose by name. Saloon girls and housewives spoke to one another outside of a store. Punchers drifted through or tied up at a hitching rail outside the many saloons and cat houses. The occasional wagon rolled down the street either carrying supplies or headed to get them. Hard men mixed with the normal traffic, outlaw, or lawman you couldn't tell immediately unless they wore a badge. Even these men put on the pretense of politeness while they moved through the city.

When we reached the edge of town Jose turned toward a small cantina down a side street. There was no sign out front, if Jose hadn't led us here I would have thought it was a house. The only thing that contradicted that was the small, covered porch with four small tables. Jose opened the door revealing four more tables and a bar filling the back wall.

The smell of meat cooking wafted through the room on a light breeze, spices making the scent even more tempting. A beautiful woman stood leaning on the bar eyeing us curiously as we come in. When she recognized Jose her face changed to one of joy.

"Jose!" She shouted running across the room and pulling my friend into a hug. Her voice took on a chiding tone when she continued. "Back so soon? Only a year since you wanted to visit us?"

"Si Maria, and of course I came back! How could I stay away from you?" Jose looked down at the dark-haired beauty in his arms. "Now let me go before Julio shoots me for trying to steal his woman!"

"Bah! You can have her amigo. She costs too much." A smiling man came out from what looked to be a storeroom. He was Jose's age, a little shorter and heavier, wearing a huge grin that lit up his eyes.

"No amigo." Jose struck a tragic pose as Maria stepped back from him. "I could not. She would not like the vaquero's life I think."

"Fools both of you!" She laughed at them. The sound reminded me of wind chimes blowing in a soft breeze. Something about it sang through you, there was no avoiding the happiness it carried. "You a fool for letting me go and you for thinking I would not like to be a vaquero's wife. No man underfoot? Only small hacienda to manage? How could that be bad? Now enough of your foolishness, who is this young man?"

"Ahhh Maria there is no winning with you!" Jose was smiling. His face seemed to brighten from seeing these two, the shadows that haunted him since Juan's death receded a bit more. "This is mi amigo JC. Amigo meet Julio and Maria. Two of my favorite people."

"A pleasure." I shook Julio's hand when he stepped forward but when I turned to tip my hat to Maria she swept me up in a tight hug. I stuttered for a minute before she let me go stepping back, a mischievous smile playing on her face.

"Welcome Señor, as friend of Jose you are family here. Now sit, sit I will get food! Julio stop being rude, get them something to drink!" She walked away without looking back at my stunned face. Julio and Jose both broke out in laughter at my confusion.

"She has spoken, sit. Cerveza?" Julio was still smiling as he walked to the bar.

"Si!" Jose agreed sitting at a table near the kitchen door.

"Coffee if you have it?" I asked.

"Si, no problemo." Julio brought over a beer for Jose and a cup of coffee for me and him. "Now you have been served a cup, any more an it's on the stove help yourself amigo. How has the winter been? You did not stop after the drive this year, was it a bad year?"

"Señor Conners had to hire some hands in San Antonio. That is the only reason we are here now." Jose said soberly, both of us thinking about the people we had lost. "Apologies, there was no chance to tell you earlier, it has been a hard year. Señor Max didn't stop on the way home because of it. Juan was killed, Billy Bob and Nolan also."

"Juan is dead!" Maria stood in the door to the kitchen her hand to her chest.

"Si, wc got attackcd on thc way homc."

"I will light a candle for him at the church. He was a good

boy, such a shame."

"Si, he will be remembered." Julio added.

"And the men who did this thing?" Maria asked with more than a little anger.

"Muerte." Jose said simply "We made things right."

"We?" Julio asked.

"JC and I"

"Good!" Maria said walking back into the kitchen stiffly. Julio sighed heavily as he sat in silence sipping his coffee. He shook his head as if trying to shake off the sad news.

"She will pray for him later." He said absently over his coffee. "He was so young."

"I didn't know him long, but he was a good man." I added still dealing with all the losses myself.

"Si, he was but you seem young for the type of thing Jose speaks of?" Julio studied me carefully as he spoke.

"He is like me." Jose explained, it seemed that short statement was enough.

"I see, then it is good you are friends. He will work with you now?"

"Yeah he talked me into working the line for the bit that's left." I smiled.

"Si, that is good." Julio smiled.

Maria moved out of the kitchen carrying a tray full of food, it smelled amazing. Seasoned steaks, tamales, beans, fresh tortillas, and rice. Vegetables mixed in bowls splashed bright color across the table as she placed them. It all looked and smelled amazing laid out on the table. My mouth was watering just looking at it and my stomach voiced its opinion loudly. Julio refilled our drinks and brought a glass of wine for Maria, then sat back down at the table.

Thankfully I caught Jose out the corner of my eye as he crossed himself. I ducked my head quickly realizing Maria was going to say grace. It was in rapid Spanish, I honestly didn't catch much of it except the amen at the end.

We all tucked in to a wonderful meal in good company.

Jose was right, the tamales were delicious. That is once they finished tormenting me and taught me to eat them. Julio and Maria where the type of people you just wanted to know. Good humored and caring they made you feel like family. It occurred to me as we ate that no one else had come in.

"This food is amazing, I am surprised no one else has come in?" I asked.

"Many who live here know of us, mostly the vaqueros. Not many of the Americanos," Julio laughed, "the other places have more to offer."

"Si, we enjoy our little cantina," Maria smiled, "for many of the vaqueros it reminds them of home."

"No saloon girls." Jose laughed, stating the obvious.

The idea of a quiet little place where the vaqueros and local Tejanos would feel at home made sense. For these two people especially, they wanted to live simply while enjoying the good people around them.

We chatted comfortably for the rest of the evening. Just enjoying friendly company over good food, it reminded me so much of New Orleans. Even that stab of pain was dulled by the easy laughter that flowed around me. A few more people came in, most of them locals. Tejanos who lived or worked around the town, they all spoke to us. Most greeted Jose by name, he always introduced me. One and all they greeted me happily, no one gave me a second glance. This place, like so many others, if a friend brought you here that was enough. You were accepted and welcomed.

Before it got to late we dropped some money on the table, not nearly enough for what this peaceful dinner gave us. Then it was a matter of sneaking out while Maria and Julio where busy with other people. Both of us knowing they would have refused it otherwise. The cool night air engulfed us outside the small building. Both of us let out a sigh of contentment walking in silence down the main street.

CHAPTER 37

LESSONS FROM A STRANGER

The noise of the saloons swept down the street, backed by the familiar smells of tobacco, sweat and stale beer. Laughter mixed with off key pianos and bawdy singing. Men walked from one saloon to another or stood outside enjoying to cool night air. Chris was standing outside one as we passed.

"Been at Maria's I am bett'n?" He asked laughing.

"Si, you know me. I had to tell them about the others." Jose didn't need to name them. We all knew who he meant.

"Damn good food." I added, helping to smooth over the painful memories.

"Yeah, Jose took me down 'ere once, amaz'n food jus' not lively enough for me."

"You mean not enough girls for you?" I laughed.

"You say that like it's a bad thing!" Chris grinned back at me.

"Tonight, I am with the farm boys, try'n ta keep 'em two outta of trouble."

"That could be a full-time job, those two ain't the most world wise." I smiled.

"Yeah thankfully they ain't got much money, can't do too much damage in a saloon broke."

"Si, trouble and money seem to find each other." Jose agreed, leaning against the hitching rail starting to pack his pipe. "How do they seem?"

"They're good enough, green as all get out. Ain't neither of 'em know how to work with a rope but strong and willing. I figure it ought to be enough to see 'em through." Chris started rolling a smoke as he talked. "Pug and Tink seem to have tak'n to 'em. They're both old hands, it'll work out for 'em."

"Hell, I got a lot to learn." I laughed leaning beside Jose, packing my own pipe.

"You need experience," Chris said simply, "different thing. Already got the skills an ain't clueless about folks, 'at's a different thing. How about them new vaqueros?"

"They know their business amigo, good men." Jose offered easily. "They all know what it is to ride for a brand."

"Yeah figured those three would work out no problem. Glad TJ picked 'em up, really just got the two greenhorns ta break in." As if on cue Thomas flew out the door landing in the dirt beside us. He was shortly followed by Clint, landing roughly on his brother who let out a whoop as the wind left his lungs.

"Reckon the evening is over." Chris chuckled inhaling on his smoke while looking at the two large men blocking the door. "Ralph what'd they do?"

"Tried to muscle in on a dance with no money, the other tried to stop me when I grabbed him." The big man on the left sounded bored.

"Damn kids." Chris muttered as he watched the two try and untangle themselves to get up.

"Just call it a night boys. No hard feelings." Ralph offered a hand toward the two boys. The boys looked at Chris, Jose and me casually smoking, the question was obviously written on their faces.

"Amigos, we will stop them from killing you but if you want to fight those two? That is your choice." Jose laughed as he spoke.

"Y'all gonna have to explain this ride for the brand better I think." Clint grumbled dusting off his clothes.

"It's simple, if those two set ta stomping you, why we'd step in. However, if'n you two want to have a knuckle dust up with 'em? 'at's your poor choice." Chris cheerfully explained to the two young men. "Cause I really got no interest in fighting Ralph. Tried it once, wasn't a good time."

"Fair fights a fair fight." I shrugged.

"I reckon that makes sense." Thomas admitted grinning before accepting Ralphs hand. "Sorry for the trouble."

"Call it a night boys, got an early morning anyways." Chris offered in his easy way. "Y'all got a drink an seen a saloon, let's head ta the house."

"Probably a good choice," I added, "when Mr. Connors says first light he means it."

"Yeah, ain't much fun with no money anyways." Clint agreed grudgingly as he too shook Ralph's hand. "Same, sorry ta put ya'll out."

Chris started gathering up his charges when Ralph went back inside. Jose and I continued smoking, planning on letting them get a head start. Just when they started to turn away a man walked out the door and started in on them.

"You boys tuck'n tail an run'n?" The tall lean figure was backlit by the light from the saloon. He was young wearing two pistols, his cocky grin was too obvious as he flipped the thongs off. "Figured I'd come out ta educate ya boys."

All three turn around looking at the man, none of them recognized him. I knew his ilk, different dress and place but the same type I had seen back east. A bully thinking he spotted easy prey in the farm boys. He stood proudly framed by the light, the silver conches on his black leather gun belt glinted as he moved. The same for the hatband that looked to be solid silver. Fancy clothes matched the belt. In my opinion it looked like something a kid would pick to look like a big man.

"You looking for some gun play?" I said pushing off the rail I had been leaning against. "I'll be your huckleberry."

He looked me up and down for a second as my right hand dropped down, smoothly flipping the thong off my Colt. I walked casually out into the street across from him. I watched him study me, laughing as he made his choice. My guns made him stop and think but my age convinced him I wasn't a real threat.

"Ya even old enough for 'em guns?" He cackled, trying to get a rise out of me.

"I'm wearing them. That's all you need to worry about ain't it?" My voice had gone cold.

"Si, he is old enough. Tell you this amigo, if you don't walk back into the cantina," Jose grinned from the boardwalk, "you will not grow older."

"What do you know mex, you don't even know who I am." The arrogant youth spat, anger making his voice go up an octave. This wasn't going the way he had expected, and some part of his brain was trying to warn him.

"Sonny, I do know you, don't know him." The older man who moved into the doorway of the saloon spoke up, a gambler by his dress. He bit off the tip of a cigar, struck a match letting the flare illuminated cold green eyes for just a second. "That being said, I'd bet on him every day and twice on Sundays."

"You can't be serious!" Sonny looked over at the gambler in shock. "You think this kid can take me?"

"Nope, you know me better than that. How many times you ever seen me bet on what I thought?" The gambler asked smoothly.

"You don't." He hesitated before finishing the thought. "You only bet on a sure thing."

"Ya'll mind if I use this to educate my young friend?" The gambler asked me politely.

"Not sure yet, can't stand a man who picks easy targets to convince himself how tough he is." I had my dander up. This kid had wanted to bully or kill someone just because he thought it would be easy, now the gambler was asking me to let him off.

"Amigo, let it go." Jose was calm, the warning in his voice clear. It wasn't because these men were a threat, it was a reminder. Not every fight needed to end in blood.

"We can let it go." Jose was right. I didn't want to make a show of this, it wasn't worth the cost. Stunts like this would be how I got a name, that was too much of a price to pay for a hot-headed moment.

"You remember what I told you bout that fancy rig? All show? Damn few men can draw with their left, much less shoot an you ain't one." The gambler held up his hand to forestall a protest he knew was coming. "I know you'll learn but this young man is lack'n that ego. He carries that cross draw but not for speed or show. It's for those spots where the first one empties an he still has a snake to stomp."

"Okay but that don't mean he's fast." Sonny still protested, sounding more and more like a petulant child.

"Fast ain't everything, that being said I'd say he is. Stop talk'n an let me tell you why." Grinning as he continued. Seamlessly taking on the tone of a professor lecturing his students. "You'll notice how smooth he flipped that thong off? How he didn't need to fumble to find it? That's a practiced motion, something done often enough that it's almost like breath'n to the man. You think that's a natural thing? Remember me telling you how I could shuffle without looking? What was my answer?"

"Ya said practice, years of practice but he ain't old enough for that." Sonny's protest sounded weak even to me.

I couldn't help but grin a little, the gambler really was educating his partner. Flashbacks of my professors lecturing danced through my mind as he started to pace slowly. It also made me realize this man was the more dangerous of the two by far. He was smart, aware and wouldn't be motivated by pride. He was the real predator.

"Now you came out here to pick a fight with those two, forgive me if I am wrong gentlemen, greenhorns?"

"You are not wrong Señor." Jose agreed with that easy smile on his face. He had realized the threat before me. I had noticed when he slipped his thong but now I knew why.

"Gracias," he nodded to Jose respectfully, "that being said this young man caught you off guard. You think your trapped now that you questioned his ability an age. You're not by the way, unless I miss my guess he will happily go back to smoking his pipe. I am guessing he can't or won't let you kill someone he works with. Again please correct me if I'm wrong."

"You have the right of it sir." I admitted, not having a reason to challenge the statement.

"So, Sonny what would you prefer? Dying here in Uvalde with only we five as your audience, or would you rather go back inside with Gloria? I believe she is waiting with your bottle."

 "I'll see you again somewhere." Sonny sniped childishly before turning to storm back in the saloon. I did my best not to laugh at his childish display but the slight grin that showed was shared by Jose and the gambler.

"Thank you for not pushing that. He is young an has some growing to do, but not a bad kid. Well not a bad kid for someone who rather foolishly wants a name as a gun fighter anyway." The gambler said with a smile that never reached his cold eyes. This man was a killer but not a bloodthirsty one. "My name is Duncan Foster by the by."

"A pleasure, names JC." I said walking casually back over to the board walk. I had to strike a match before puffing my pipe back to life. "Thank you, really didn't want that fight but I'm pretty sure Clint or Thomas don't even know how to draw a gun."

"Si, likely to shoot their foot." Jose chuckled at the chagrined look on the two in question.

"Thought as much," Duncan grinned, "Sonny is still young enough to think everyone is a gun slick."

"I don't rude but is he really hunting a reputation?" I had to ask because some part of me just couldn't understand the appeal.

"Oh, he is, seems to be one of those who wants to be a name of legend and myth. I have tried to dissuade him, sadly to no avail. He seems determined to die in a dusty street somewhere. Sadly, he doesn't yet grasp the cost of such a thing. Or that he'll probably die to some other young ambitious kid chasing a reputation."

"Seems to be how it works, been trying to dodge one as best as I can."

"Hard to do if you choose company that requires your intervention." He grinned with a hint of laughter in his eyes.

"Don't know that choice has much to do with it. Jose is my choice as far as company goes, he can handle his own snakes. That being said Mr. Connors would be annoyed if his two new hands got killed before they even made the ranch."

"True, Max does get touchy about those things." Chris spoke up for the first time.

"Si, hates hiring new hands." Jose laughed in agreement.

"Again, thank you gentlemen for your patience but I must return to my table. The dealers get annoyed if I am gone too long. It's been a pleasure meeting you both". We nodded to the man as he stepped back into the saloon.

"You know him?" I questioned Jose.

"His name, si. He is said to be a dangerous man to be on the wrong side of."

"Agreed, let's head to the house. Morning does come early."

"Si a good choice amigo."

The five of us walked back toward the hotel. The farm boys occasionally glancing back at me, not upset but curious. I recognized their confusion. I was another young greenhorn, but no one seemed to treat me that way. They might have heard some stories and had seen me work in San Antonio.

They were trying to figure out if it was just the gun work or something else that made me so different. Not because they questioned my place, they were just trying to find their own way.

CHAPTER 38

INTO THE NUECES

Waking up like normal, I checked my surroundings before rolling quietly out of my bunk. Jose, below me, opened one eye then went back to sleep as I moved out of the room. I padded on bare feet to the small courtyard I had seen the night before. In the soft gray of predawn I worked through my stretches. The crisp morning air nipped at me as the sheen of sweat started halfway through my routine.

My mind wandered over the past few months again as I moved. Cursing how naive I had been stepping off the train, a child dreaming of adventure like some explorer from a book. Dodge City had started to show those foolish notions false. The trail to Texas had quickly eroded the rest, they fell away with each mile. The truth slowly revealing the world I was stepping into.

Sitting in the cool air after I finished my mind played it all back. Slowly turning to the road ahead rather than the lessons of the past. Contemplating life on the ranch, the simple aspect of just working every day. The alluring scent of coffee reminded me it was time to quit my musing and focus on today.

Heading toward the basin of water I brought out with me I cleaned up and stomped into my boots. After tying down my gun I set off to find some of the aforementioned coffee. It was in the kitchen with Señora Garza and another woman, both getting breakfast ready for the punchers.

"Morning Señor," the happy woman greeted him "early one I see, café?"

"Yes ma'am please." Smiling at her while she poured the coffee, then hurrying out when she shooed me out the door. I found my way to the front porch after collecting my hat from the hall where I had hung it the night before. I got my pipe packed while watching the first light of dawn break the horizon. Jose joined me about the time I struck a match to light my pipe.

"Morning amigo"

"Morning."

He sat down joining me in our silent morning ritual. Max and TJ came out not far behind him offering quiet greetings before they sat down. Four men who preferred a silent easy start to the day, diverse but all with similar tastes.

Max, the successful ranch owner who had ridden into a hard dangerous land to carve out his piece. Jose, my friend, a councilor of sorts helping a young greenhorn learn his way. A onetime bad man, now trying to do the right thing. These two men I knew to some degree, the third was still a mystery.

TJ was still a stranger to me. Ramrod to a bunch of crazy punchers who didn't care that he was a black man. Something that would have likely stopped him from holding this position anywhere else. Out here he was respected as the boss, leading men of all races for the Bar C without question. In the brief time I had known the man he already stood out as someone to follow. There was just something about him that you respected.

These three men sat with me like I was an equal. A kid just barely old enough to be on my own, still finding my way in life. We sat together watching dawn break over the town.

"Reckon it's about time." Max finally said, rising to his feet. "I can hear the plates hitting the table."

The rest of us unfolded from our chairs before following his lead into the house. Breakfast was fresh tortillas, eggs, refried beans, and steak with plenty of coffee. All cooked and seasoned perfectly. The rest of the boys stumbled out of different rooms, in various states of wakefulness and joined us at the table. When the sun shone fully through the windows, Max pushed back from the table.

"Let's get moving, we're wasting the day." He stepped toward the door without looking back. Knowing without question the rest of us would follow him.

"Ain't even daylight yet." Chet blearily complained. He still got up with the rest, stumbling toward the livery.

What followed was the normal morning scramble of grabbing tack and saddling half wild horses. One of the farm boys got dumped off his horse but managed to land without hurting himself. When I tossed my saddle on Shades back and reached for the girth he tried to push me away. 'Damn spoiled animal,' I thought laughing to myself at his antics. When I did step up into the saddle he was all business, ready to be out on the open range.

The early birds were just stepping onto the boardwalk when everyone was mounted and ready to move. The stable boys waved goodbye, holding the new shining silver dollar between them as we filed out of town. Heading southwest, into the Nueces Strip and our home range.

I knew the ranch was near the Rio Grande, west of Laredo about halfway to Eagle Pass. Knowing this was different from understanding what that meant. Right now, they were just points on a map. Jose had said that the ranch was closer to Laredo than Uvalde, but they had lost too many hands there. Max used Uvalde because Laredo was too much of a risk. Straddling the border, it was a haven for outlaws from either side.

Max's land stretched from the Nueces River to the Rio Grande. East and West there weren't really any boundaries since it was still open range. On paper Max owned a long strip that was about five miles across. Jose had told me the maze like canyons made it impossible to set hard boundaries. When the risk outweighed the reward, they stopped. It might not have been the most accurate way to measure but it worked.

It was a land full of arroyos and deeper canyons but dotted with creeks. It was those water ways that made the land worth anything. They were lined with heavy scrub, plenty of places for the wild long horns to hide. Those wild creatures were our herd. The Bar C was a hard-won piece of land. Max had purchased it from a Don in Mexico after the war and filed a claim in Texas insuring it was his long before he started building.

They lost some cattle to outlaws running back and forth across the border at first, but Max had figure out how to avoid that. They simply didn't gather the cattle until they were getting ready for the trail. He used the laziness of hoot owls against them. They had no desire to pop ornery steers out of the thick brush that covered the strip. If it wasn't a neat herd, already trail broke to steal they moved on. Maybe killing one for food but that wasn't a big concern with the population of wild long horns, and no one begrudged a man food.

He also had a hard rule regarding anyone crossing the ranch, live and let live if it was possible. The only exceptions were Apache and anyone on foot. If you found a man afoot you had to make a judgment call about them. You would help if you could do it safely but if you couldn't? Out here, in this wild country, you cut them a wide swath. Few things are more dangerous than a desperate man and a man afoot was certainly that. If he wasn't a killer or outlaw he would be in that moment, his other choice was a slow death.

I was beginning to understand the reason the Bar C had

such a bond between the men, it was a requirement not a choice. The ranch was in rough country inhabited by hard men. Those who worked the ranch worked in teams, no one rode alone except the line riders. When Jose and Juan had done it Jose did most of the riding, Juan guarded the line shack. Jose had done it alone most of this winter but now I would ride the line and pulling my weight.

As soon as the weather broke the hands would start popping cattle out of the brush to get a herd built. Dangerous work on its own, chasing pissed off wild long horns out of heavy brush. Then sorting the calves, branding, and castrating. Separating the prime bulls from their cows while keeping them healthy wasn't easy or safe. The ones destined for Dodge were herded to start trail breaking them, all while protecting them from rustlers, Apache, and wild animals. That's not even talking about stampedes that could be cause by storms, snakes, or just a breeze.

Academically I knew what all this meant, but as usual it would be hard, probably painful lessons that really taught me. It was easy to get gored or stomped by a cow protecting her calf. That wasn't mentioning the bulls that were none too happy at the theft of their females. Horses got killed, riders got thrown into cactus or on to rocks. This place had one way for it to go right and a thousand ways for it to go wrong.

After we survived all that, we would set off to cover the ground between the ranch and Dodge, well over a thousand miles. Dealing with any number of threats while managing two thousand head of half wild cattle. The whole ranch lived with the herd when it was gathered, to prevent it from being rustled while they got trail tamed. Jose said someone tried every year, so far without much success.

Max had another twelve hands that didn't work the drive, they stayed at the ranch. Some specialized in brush work, they called it brush poppin'. The skillful art of cajoling a pissed off two-thousand-pound bull out of what he considered his turf. They gathered most of the herd and managed it the rest of the year.

Others worked with the horses, braking and training the wild mustangs into effective cow ponies. It was another dangerous job. One solid kick could cripple or kill you. It also took a natural feel for horses, something not everyone had. I liked horses but I was nowhere near that. The men who understood the language could work magic with a good horse.

They were all hard experienced men who knew cattle and horses better then guns and outlaws. Those problems fell on Jose, Chet and now me with the new vaqueros pitching in when they could. We weren't hired as gun hawks, Max hired us to work cattle. He did recognize the skills in his men and used them accordingly though. It was just a normal part of ranching in untamed country. He had some men who worked horses, some cattle and others did both. Our role tended toward protection. Nighthawks, guards, gun hands all different names for the same thing.

Jose had explained all of this to me, but it had taken me a few days to digest it. I wanted to be a cowboy not a gun hand, he had laughed when I said that. Assuring me there would still be plenty of hard work and that this was normal for a ranch that trailed cattle to market. A cowboy was never just one thing, everyone filled multiple roles. A good boss put the right men in the right role. I still had to live it, experience it firsthand before really understanding what he meant.

Talking about this with the other hands while we traveled, I was slowly building my own understanding through their experiences. It wasn't as difficult to accept as I feared. Each in their own way, the men had helped me understand my role. Max offered what he could, various others had thrown their thoughts in to help. Jose had explained it simply as usual. His council helped more than most because he understood it firsthand.

"Think of it this way amigo, some people can feel the weight of the dead. They struggle and can not bear it, like Bo. A good man, who will fight but it haunts him. Some like Chet can balance it with

laughter. He sheds the weight but still remembers and someday the laughter will not work.

Max and those like him are more common, they are pragmatic. It is the cost of living here, they accept that. Then men like us, we do not carry that weight. It is true many of us are outlaws or drifters because they never know another way. Some, like us, have a code to keep us in the right. That code can put us opposite the law, if our belief in what is right does not agree with it.

In the end we do the things other men can't, someday who knows maybe we will not be needed or wanted. That day has not yet come amigo, we are what stands between bad men and the others."

I could still hear his words in my head. I needed to hear it but was still struggling to grasp it. Now without ever thinking about it I started writing my own code, it wasn't in words or prose. It was ideals that felt right to me. All these things had been going through my head since leaving Dodge and getting my first lessons. Now approaching the ranch, they were becoming things carved into my soul.

None of it was new information, Tom, Tucker and the others had talked to me about all of it. They seemed to know or maybe recognize a kindred soul in me. Each taking time to talk to me and help me understand the world I was entering.

Tom still lived by a code. It was why he lived on the dairy farm. He couldn't get comfortable in a civilized town. The mountain men hadn't been civilized, they had their own code they lived by. They honored that above any rule of civilized men. The world they lived in was different, alone or with the tribes, it wouldn't allow a civilized man to survive. I was like those men in some way, the ideals carried in my mind were more solid than any law. They were my truth more than any social or religious morality.

Something about getting close to the ranch had brought everything back to the forefront of my mind. We wouldn't be at the ranch long before heading to the line shack. The little time there would be spent chasing horses or cattle out of scrub or helping in any of the other jobs. The wild ponies would need to be broke before the drive. Getting another remuda ready would be left to the men at the ranch but I would help. The cycle of western life was easy to track, it followed the weather.

When we crossed the Nueces we would be on Bar C range for the first time. Anyone we ran into from here would be a lawman, bounty hunter or more likely an outlaw. The Bar C attitude was simple, none of them were our concern. If Max recognized them, they got invited into camp, all others would be ignored. Most of those who made it down here knew of the Bar C. They also knew if they left us alone, we would leave them alone.

There was also the reputation the hands had. They had left enough bodies behind them to warn most about what happened if you ignored that rule. That's why we left signs, word of mouth spread faster than anything else on the owl hoot trail. The ranch also wasn't rich enough to be a worth the price you'd pay. Max knew he walked a balance out here, but he managed it every day.

The days passed as the wagons, now loaded heavy with supplies, moved slowly. They had to be nursed carefully up and down the steep arroyos. Periodically we would spook a longhorn or a small group of deer. I would barely catch sight of them before they disappeared into the dense brush. A few days out we made camp at the back of a shallow canyon, fifty-foot walls rose up on three sides leaving just the entrance open. When camp was set Smythe cooked up some fresh venison with biscuits and beans. The tantalizing smell drifted by on the soft breeze making my mouth water.

I sipped coffee watching the sun slowly sink toward the horizon. Gently splashing the land in a myriad of colors and shadows. The wish that Binda was here to see this flashed through my mind. It didn't hurt as much as it had the last time, but it was still there. Slowly my grief and pain were fading, the magic of this land ate away at it piece by piece. It mesmerized me every day with the way it changed. Small creeks birthed spots of vibrant life where color flared from the plants around the life-giving water. Twenty feet away desert sage and cactus clawed through the cracked ground, forcing life to exist despite the struggle.

"Quiet today Amigo?" Jose asked as we sipped coffee.

"Guess everything is kinda sinking in as we get close to the ranch." I studied my coffee cup while I spoke. "Knowing something is different from the reality of it."

"Si, it has been a while since I faced those thoughts, but I understand. Once I too was a greenhorn." The laughter in his tone wasn't meant to make light of my feelings. It was humor at the memory of his early days. "I think I was five then."

"Okay old man." I laughed abruptly at the thought, Jose was only a few years older than me.

"No amigo, not old. Life started for me young." His grin reflected in his coffee with the last few rays of the sun showing me that unique picture.

"We'll just call it experienced, is that it amigo?"

"Si! Experienced, I like this." We both chuckled then sank back into our comfortable silence.

Laying back on my saddle I tipped my hat over my eyes, sleep came easily like it always did on the trail. Caesar's boot scraped a rock when he came to wake me for watch. I waved him off before he got to close. After checking my boots, I stomped them on before rising to my feet and slinging my guns on.

CHAPTER 39

AMBUSH

"Señor there is a nice big mesquite tree just over there to watch from." He spoke softly, knowledgeable enough not to whisper. I nodded my thanks while pouring a cup of coffee then headed toward the opening.

The mesquite was big enough it wouldn't give me away in the soft glow of the fire. It wasn't big enough to draw attention in the dark and had a small rock shelf in front of it. Leaning my Winchester on a branch, I slowly started my routine. It not only centered me, but it also kept me warm. I didn't work hard enough to break a sweat, that was a fast way to catch a chill. When I was done I settled into the shadows sipping my coffee, letting my eyes adjust to the darkness.

My ears started picking out the song around me. Off in the distance a coyote yipped, small rodents moved in the brush searching for their dinner. Something large made its bed off in an arroyo not too far away, most likely a long horn or mustang. The sounds filled my ears, telling me the story of this place. A unique song that only existed this one night. Watch passed and when the sky started to lighten I heard Jose coming up behind me before he spoke out.

"Coffee amigo." He handed a cup to me before sliding down beside me.

"Gracias amigo." Gladly taking the offered cup. "Sleep good?"

"Si, under the stars I always sleep good."

"Same."

"Some part of us remembers. It is how we are supposed to live I think." Jose's philosopher's spirit showing again.

Nodding my agreement we both studied the slowly brightening sky, waiting for it to light up enough of the land to light a pipe. Doing so when it was too dark made you an easy target.

Behind us I could hear Smythe beginning to stir the fire to life. The scent of fresh coffee wafted on the breeze, always the first thing he made. A little further away Max and TJ were talking softly, probably kneeling by the fire. Faintly I could hear the rest of the men stirring from their bedrolls. The normal noise of camp rousting them from their sleep. Striking a match on the rock behind me I turned to light my pipe. From somewhere outside the canyon a rifle barked. The bullet whispered by my face, burning a gash across my arm.

Diving behind the rock for cover, my Winchester came up firing back at the flash. Doubtful it hit anything, but it kept someone's head down while I got solidly behind cover. The recoil jarred the burn sending a hot flash of pain down my arm when I pulled the trigger. An instant later Jose was beside me, his pistol leveled looking for a target. Behind us the camp scrambled, men ducking into cover while looking around. The shadows left by early dawn gave more cover than anything else. I knew men were hunkering down behind saddles or wagons, a lucky few ducking behind rocks.

"Y'all surrounded send out 'em horses an money, maybe we'll let ya live!" A voice sang out from the front of the canyon.

"Y'all hit?" Max's low voice reached me from where he

crouched behind a wagon.

"Just a burn, nothing to worry about."

"I am good Señor Max."

"Gonna have the men skirt back under the overhang while we got darkness. Y'all keep an eye out, if they get up top pull back with us."

"Si Jefe" Jose answered for both of us. "Amigo you got the rifle, watch to top, I can take the front with my pistol."

"Works."

My eyes immediately started scanning the ridge line above us. After a second of studying, I spotted a rock that didn't look natural. Slowly taking aim, easing tension on the trigger, the stock bucked in my shoulder again aggravating the burn on my arm. The shape jerked up and had just enough time to scream before he fell from sight. Dead or not he was hit and out of it, I started scanning the ridge line again, studying where the sun cast its early shadows. Another shape moved, I aimed and fired. There was a yelp, but I couldn't tell if I hit or just skipped rocks close by. I went back to scanning the ridge line.

"Y'all gonna die now ya sons of bitchs!" The voice from out front yelled, angry with our refusal to surrender. Jose snapped off a shot that was followed by a scream making him smile.

"Not by you Señor!" He yelled back, laughing as shots pinged off the rocks in front of us.

"Think you pissed 'em off Jose." I laughed but kept scanning the ridge while bullets whined around us.

"No Amigo, you started it." The humor in his voice was obvious.

I caught movement and sighted in just as the sun flashed off a barrel. I fired matching the flash of his muzzle with mine. He missed hitting the ground a few inches beside me. I didn't and he pitched over the canyon, dead before he hit the ground.

"How do you figure I started it?" I asked curiously.

"You killed first no?" Jose's laughter rang out over the gun fire.

"You can't blame me for their bad aim!" I chuckled while

studying the land in front of me.

With more rounds pinging off the rocks around us we needed the laughter. Jose returned fire suddenly, getting another cry of pain for his effort. I kept my eye on the top of the canyon, Jose the front.

Silence settled back over the area while the robbers plotted their next move. Up top I spotted one man raise up, before he made it a step I fired. He pitched forward disappearing from my sight without a sound. Then we heard horses in the distance, a lot of them from the sound. Thundering hooves growing louder, evidently they had decided to charge us.

"Coming from the front!" I called out, lining my rifle up.

The gunfire started then, bullets whizzed past from the front and back. The charging men firing as they rode like mad men. Max and the boys shooting at the opening without really seeing their target but knowing where they had to be. We stayed low picking our targets when we could.

Horses screamed in panic and pain. Men cried out somewhere in the middle of the pack when a horse went down, taking two more with it. Picking out silhouettes of men leaning low on horseback, I fired carefully as they closed to within thirty feet. Two more saddles emptied, and their riderless horses added to the chaos. Jose knocked two more off before we both dropped back down seconds before flashing hooves struck sparks around us.

Horses blurred by as we laid there tucked in tight behind the rock. The Bar C laid into them, dropping three more before the last two broke trying to run. Sadly, for them, they had to make it back past us. Neither of them did, each of us emptying a saddle.

Horses milled around in the dusty shadows, two dragging bodies out of the canyon at a full gallop. I stood starting to work through the mass around us. I put down two horses to end their suffering, one shot badly and another with a broken leg. Jose found two men badly wounded but alive. He stripped their weapons, leaving them where they fell for now.

"Someone get ahold of those damn horses and get this under control!' Max barked.

The men started to move, grabbing reins, talking softly to calm panicked animals. Carlos and Manuel mounted two of them, moving to gather the horses who hadn't found the exit yet. In ten minutes, everything in our canyon was captured or dead.

"Jose, JC, go find what's left an make sure 'at ridge is clear. Carlos, Manuel stay on those mounts and go with them, grab up the rest of the horses. Goddamn outlaws will end up making for an easy winter if they keep this crap up. Damn near won't need any mustangs."

"Got it boss!" I yelled back reloading my rifle.

"Si Jefe. Two wounded men up front, unless a horse killed them." Jose answered smiling at me.

We walked toward the canyon opening slowly. Moving quietly through the opening ahead of the two vaqueros. The brush was still shadowed making it tricky to pick things out and we didn't want them caught out. The deep shadows helped hide the dead and living.

We split up once we got clear of the mouth, moving through the brush. The first body was about five feet out, the blood and brains scattered across the rock said he wasn't a threat anymore. I took his Winchester and gun belt before I moved on. Slowly working my way out further I started up when I found a path leading to the ridge. I heard a single shot but nothing else.

Two more bodies were at the top, one hit in the chest. Dead before he hit the ground. The other gut shot, he was dead, but it hadn't been fast enough if I read the sign right. He hadn't waited for death, the 44 in his hand told me all I wanted to know. I took both sets of weapons and moved on. Jose and I met around the back of the canyon clearing the ridge from both sides.

"Found three, you?" I asked.

"Four, one was gut shot. I ended it." Just then a horse

nickered somewhere below us.

"Their mounts?" I raised my eyebrows in surprise.

"Maybe so, it would be better then walking back." We worked down the ridge about thirty feet and found six mounts loosely picketed.

"You're right. It beats walking back, especially with all this." I grinned motioning toward the multiple guns we each carried. Reaching for a paint on the end of the line after checking its girth. I started putting rolled up gun belts in saddle bags and finding homes for the rifles.

"Si, we agree Amigo." Jose checked the girth and cinched it tight on a nice-looking buckskin before finding homes for his collected weapons.

We lead the other four back to camp on a trail rope, running into Carlos and Manuel with another three mounts. The four of us rode into the canyon calling out before we came in. The rest of the crew busy dragging eight more bodies out of the canyon after stripping them of guns and ammo. That brought the total number of dead men to fifteen. We caught twelve horses, two where dead and one must be still running.

"Shit this keeps up we really won't need any mustangs, our remuda will be full before we even get home." TJ chuckled, the tone in his voice wasn't happy though.

"Anyone hit?" I asked.

"Just you, now get off 'at damn horse so's I kin look at it." Smythe ordered in his normal gruff tone.

"Yeah it's a bit tender." I had been ignoring the feeling of blood trickling down my arm, but it flared up when he mentioned it.

I turned the paint over to Jose before sitting down by the fire. Then carefully pulling off another ruined shirt, this one might be salvageable. That was as long as I kept Smythe away from it. The wound flared up with my movement, part of the shirt had started to dry to the blood. Smythe grumbled to himself while slowly inspecting the wound. It wasn't deep but when he cleaned it with some whiskey, making me gritted my teeth while hissing loudly.

"Son of a bitch!" I swore under my breath when he poured some corn liquor over the wound. He finished by tying a bandage around it.

"It'll heal, be sore as hell but keep 'at poultice on it til we get home."

"Thanks, Smythe." I said putting my shirt back on carefully, no sense ruining another one, trying to ignore the burning sensation.

"Bad?" Max asked walking up but he gasped when he got a look at my new scar. "Do I want to know how close that one came?"

"Just hurts, Smythe says it looks clean, especially after he doused in with some corn." I finished shrugging on my shirt before anyone else saw the scar. "Closer then I'd like to think about."

"I'll leave it alone for now, but someday I want the story. Burns like hell but seems like it stops infection. Good to ride?"

"Yeah Boss, I am good just don't have me trying rope anything yet." I grinned at him over my fresh coffee.

"Smythe let's get 'em fed. TJ can we string 'at many or should we just ride herd over 'em? Don't answer just get 'em ready to move either way." Max shouted orders after hearing my answer.

Everyone jumped to work, I started making my way over to start saddling Shade. He seemed to know I wasn't up for his foolishness this morning and stood still while I got the tack on. Breakfast was a quick affair, split biscuits with some bacon slapped in between eaten as we rode. It wasn't long before we rode out of the canyon that was meant to be our grave.

The bodies of thieves were lined against the outside wall. There was a Bar C brand scratched into the rock above them, another reminder that trying us was a bad idea. We rode away leaving them to the scavengers, a pack horse trailed behind TJ's wagon carrying their weapons and ammo.

CHAPTER 40

HOME RANGE

We crossed the Nueces River late that day, camping for the first time on Bar C range. It was a quiet night, I didn't have watch, so I relaxed around the camp sipping coffee. A cool night wind whipped through camp, making all of us huddle a bit closer to the fire. It made it easier to get to the coffee anyway.

It turned out the accent Pug had was from Boston. I finally placed it while he was spinning some yarn about Tink. He had grown up there until wandering west a decade ago. We both shared stories about big cities and life back east with the rest of the crew, most of whom had never been that far. It was amusing when we tried to explain what a million was, much like with Jose it was something most of them couldn't grasp. That was followed by both of us swearing there really were that many people living in one place.

My arm still hurt but it had settled into a dull ache now,

the river crossing had me swearing a bit, but I managed. Even got some much-needed sleep that night. Opening my eyes at first light I decided to leave off the stretches this morning. If I aggravated the wound Smythe would have my ass.

We had a decent breakfast then got moving. A broad strip of land flattened out ahead of us. If I had to guess we were riding in an ancient riverbed, long dried up. Jose told me this was the trail the used all the way to the Nueces. Most of the brush was gone, trampled down by the herd of long horns once a year. It was also carved through by the wagons often enough that moving was easy. Everyone's pace slightly faster, knowing they were almost home

"The rest of the trip will be easy amigo," Jose offered, smiling as he rode the buckskin alongside Shade, "this is Bar C range, they know it and will stay out of our way."

"Good, be nice to not ruin another shirt for a day or two."

"Si, but this area," waving his hand wide in compassing the land around us, "memorize it amigo. The cabin is a few miles west."

"How much of this do we patrol?"

"As much as weather allows."

"Always this dry?"

"No, and the Nueces is usually much deeper, drought for the last year."

"Damn, yeah kinda feels like a tinder box."

"Si, lucky no fires."

Studying the land while we rode even the sage was dry, here and there were sun bleached bones. Dust billowed up from the horses as we moved through. There were still cattle, you could glimpse them moving through the thicker brush along the narrowed water ways. Most didn't shy away like the others had. They moved casually out of our way, content to just eye us suspiciously.

"These are the herd base," TJ was saying, "we keep 'em tamed down. Mix 'em in with the wild ones to help tame 'em down a bit. Helps 'em settle faster for the trail. Closer to the ranch we'll see more of 'em, got a couple of mean bulls 'at are fairly tamed...well by Texas standards. They keep what's around safe enough, damn things could kill a griz."

"Know'd it ta happen! Crazy old man took a long horn bull up north to Dakota territory. Wanted ta cross 'em in with 'em big angus. Died in the first snow o' course, but 'at first year he was on his range when a big ol' griz wandered up after a calf." Chet pipped in, taking the opportunity to spin his yarn. He stopped there just riding along now that he had set the bait. Which, of course, one of the farmers took after a few minutes of silence.

"Well, damnit what happened?" Clint asked, swallowing it hook line and sinker.

"Well now I thought 'at'd be obvious." Chet started again in the same voice you would use to sell someone snake oil. "So 'at old griz stomped out into the pasture just sure he was the king of all 'round 'im. He jus' eyed that mossy ol' bull for a good minute. Then 'at bull starts ta pull'n clods of ground, getting ready to charge. Well,
'at griz just took one more long look, turned 'round quick like n' ran into tha woods. He jus' kept on runn'n as far an as fast as he could! Matter of fact a good friend of mine was up in the Yukon, just peaceably work'n 'es mine. Swore he seen an ol' griz running at full tilt three weeks later. Know'd it was the same bear cause of a grey streak runn'n down 'is spine."

"Ain't no bear can run like 'at!" Clint fell right into the trap just as neatly as you could want.

"Tell you what ol' son," Chet's grin stretched across his face, "when ya get one of 'em wild bulls coming at ya maybe you'll know how fast 'at griz ran!"

Everyone had a good laugh, Chet's tall tales where good for that. It had the added bonus of roping Clint in solidly. When the young farm boy did inevitably get chased out of the scrub by a bull this would come back to haunt him.

The next couple of days went smooth, the trail was easy, and I spent most of the time learning the land. Jose pointed out the landmarks and streams. I marked them in my mind while we rode, slowly creating my own internal map. The morning of the third day Jose pointed out a rise in the distance.

"That is the ranch mi amigo, just beyond that rise. Two maybe three days, then we start working."

"Nice easy days huh?" I grinned.

"Si! Of course." His grin didn't fill me with confidence about that.

We rode into the stock pens around the ranch at noon that day. It was a well thought out place, backed by the cliff walls on two sides. The front enclosed in an arcing wall of adobe around the buildings and horse corals. The main stock yards where outside the wall, they looked well maintained but not heavily used.

The wall stood twenty feet tall and about six feet wide at the top. There was a waist high knee wall around the top for defenders to use as cover. The whole place was built solid, it would stand for years no matter what you threw at it.

When we pulled into the main corral people started moving before the wagons even set the breaks. TJ snapped out a few orders making the general chaos stop. Men suddenly started moving with purpose, naturally operating into groups. It upped my respect for TJ, without much of a look he had known who suited what task and set them too it.

Horses were taken to paddocks then turned out after the tack was stripped. It was slung over fences to be sorted later. The wagons pulled up between the house and bunkhouse, supplies streamed into one or the other cellar. I realized the there was a loop behind the ranch that would allow the wagons to keep moving forward. The whole place was like that, designed for efficiency and defense.

I worked with the horses stripping off tack, Shade was identified as my mount. Jose claimed the buckskin, he called him of all things Deseirto, Spanish for desert. I told him he sucked at naming things, he just laughed agreeing with me. Once the horses were seen to we started sorting tack, emptying saddlebags and storing it all in a large barn. There was a fire going to burn the collection of dirty clothes and other odds and ends that we didn't need.

Jose's prediction was correct the rest of the day was full of work. When Smythe called us to chow, it felt I was finally working on a ranch. Heading over to chow, mixed with a crowd of tired punchers, I finally felt like I was on the path. Smythe was serving food in a covered cooking area next to the bunkhouse. There was a kitchen in the bunkhouse, but it was too warm today. Smythe preferred to be outside when he cooked as much as he could. When I stepped into line a big man with deep set eyes stepped in front of me. Glaring over his bulbous nose he looked down at me growling.

"Boy greenhorns eat last, go wait wit the rest of 'em."

Then he made a mistake, just a little too fast for anyone to warn him off. He pushed me, I didn't think just reacted. When his arms shot forward to push me back I grabbed his wrists, using his momentum to pull him with me. When we fell I buried both my boots in his stomach knocking the air out of his lungs before launching him over me. I kept ahold of his wrist to pull me on top of him, before the big man could react I dropped my elbow right between his eyes. I admit there was a childish part of me that chuckled watching his eyes cross before they rolled back in his head.

My wound had twinged when I pulled him over, Smythe would be pissed if I tore it open. Rolling to my feet like I hadn't done anything, I casually walked back to my spot in the chow line. All around me there was silence, even Smythe was just standing there watching me with a look of surprise on his face.

"Oh god damnit JC." TJ recovered first walking over to the fallen man. "You better not have killed him!"

"Don't think I did," I smiled at him innocently, "seemed like a pretty thick skull."

"Kid I don't know who you think you are, but you don't come in here and…."

"I would not push if I were you." Jose spoke softly, but it was enough to make the other man snap his jaw closed.

"Who the fuck is this kid?" Another man spoke up, he was a rat faced little man. I was done with this schoolboy bullshit. Setting my plate down I walked out to the middle of an open area.

"Let's get this settled right now." My voice had gone cold. "Names JC, I am a greenhorn, but if you think you can push me come do it now. Choose your own damn way hands, guns, or knives don't matter to me. I will not be pushed. I'll learn, I'll work, hell I'll respect you. But if you push me? I'll push back an do it right goddamn then!"

One man started to get up but paused when Max walked casually over to Smythe. Not saying anything as he stepped over the big man groaning on the ground. He took a cup of coffee from Smythe and sat down at the corner of the table where he could see everyone.

"Y'all go ahead," he said blowing to cool off his coffee, "but I'll say this, I've seen this man work. Saved my life shortly after I hired him. Ain't ever seen anyone move like 'at. Him and Red Wolf fetched 'at Chisholm boy back from kidnappers. Jose and him settled up for the boys who died in the first ambush, an that crew was more than ten men. Course that was before he and Jose took after a bunch of Apache who had taken a little girl. That little girl is alive an well in Waco with her family, those braves ain't. We don't need to talk 'bout the ambush after Uvalde, but y'all go ahead. No guns or knives though, I ain't got time to replace any of ya."

Then he just sat there sipping his coffee, the man who had started to rise sat back down studying me slowly. When no one else got up I walked over to where the big man was still laying on the ground. He had mostly recovered while TJ knelt beside him shaking his head. I stuck my hand out to the man.

"Names JC."

"Bull, an I ain't pushing ya no more." He said taking my hand. He grinned rubbing his forehead where a goose egg was starting to form. "Nope ain't push'n."

"Good," I grinned up at the big man, "cause Smythe's about

to chew me out for opening this wound again."

"You ain't getting another poultice!" Smythe almost smiled as he filled my plate before handing it to me. "But I'll look at it after chow."

Evidently that was enough, the crew at the ranch had pushed, I had pushed back. Max offered his opinion and that settled it. I started to understand the men at the ranch over the next couple of days. We worked from dark to dark, everyone. It didn't matter what your normal job was, you pitched in with getting whatever needed doing done. The only boss was TJ, everyone else just did the work.

CHAPTER 41

LEARNING AS I GO

Bull, it turned out, led a team of seven who were brush poppers and he was truly a bull of a man. Black as night, he stood at least six foot six and well over 250 pounds of heavy muscle. His voice had just a touch of southern twang buried under his Texas drawl. His crew spent most of the year chasing wild long horns out of the scrub to casterate, brand and occasionally cull them.

They were an odd bunch, who shared a certain wildness with the cattle they spent time around. All of them where scarred, missing fingers were common, three walked with pronounced limps. It took a particular breed of man to do what they did, a mix of fearlessness and an innate knowledge of longhorns. Pug and Tink were going to work in with them, they had done the job before and liked it. I liked them one and all, it was something in the way the carried themselves. They were bluntly honest to the point of offense sometimes, but all of them were good men with no back up in them.

Richard and Wayne dealt with the horses, both bronc busters. A matched set of lean hard cut men, they moved with a grace that seemed almost out of place. Each man worked through half the small herd we brought in, checking them over from nose to tail. Wayne double as the blacksmith, he checked all the shoes making sure the hooves were clean and in good shape. He had me lined up to help shoe Shade and Bane once it all calmed down.

The three vaqueros would work with them, all three had a way with horses. They had broken and trained mounts before and Richard spoke Spanish, so it made sense all the way around.

The farm boys would work with the four other general hands, that group pitched in as needed. Mostly they were there to tend the herd and remuda once it got started. They also worked branding and castrating the young animals that Bulls team brought in. It was a starting place to get their education going, letting them work in with other crews as needed. They also dealt with the other animals including couple of pigs, the few dairy cows, and the chickens.

Thomas had some smithing experience, so he helped Wayne out, enjoying the work. The young man had a real talent for working metal and Wayne appreciated the help. He also told TJ it wouldn't be too long before he would be better then him.

Jose and I floated, helping where we could. Soon enough people realized I genuinely didn't care what I did, I would happily milk cows or muck stalls. At first it took some by surprise, expecting me to argue. It helped me get accepted by the the younger men. The older hands took in everyone without question, Max hired them and that was that.

After a few days of japing me they ignored my morning routine. There were a few comments about my weird habits matching my hat but they dropped off when I didn't react. Jose took me out, just learning the land, after the first week. We rode the borders of the ranch, ran into a few small groups of men but they cut us a wide berth. At the western edge of the ranch, he pointed out a cliff line far off in the distance.

"Amigo that is Eagles Pass, we do not ever go there." He said it calmly, but something in his tone told me he was serious. "It is death to honest men."

"Outlaws?"

"Si, it is owned by them. We leave them alone, they leave us alone. Most of the time."

"Mostly?"

"Si sometimes we have killed one or two of them if they come here and make trouble."

"Like what?"

"Amigo, if you can believe it, they came here once demanding Señor Connors pay them. It did not go well. That is King Fishers place."

"King Fisher?"

"Si, he bought a rancho then started rustling more than ranching. He is a bad man. Smart and ruthless, he is not one to go against. It is said he has a sense of honor, in his way."

"But he leaves us alone?"

"In his way, he does not come after us. If his men do he leaves it to us. If you cross paths with this man do not think him weak amigo, he is deadly."

"I'll remember."

After that we finished the circuit my internal map was pretty well done, noting landmarks that denoted the boundaries. Most of it was hard country but the game was plentiful. From the hurricane deck you could see wild cattle almost every time we moved as well as mule deer.

You could tell the difference between the truly wild ones if you paid attention. They had a look they would give you. Not fear, but a wariness like they were almost studying you before disappearing into the brush.

By the time we made it back to the ranch I had a better understanding of the land around us. I had also started to understand the men who lived here. There was a rugged individual streak to them, a hardness that the south Texas life required. They had all come here for their own reasons, each seeking to live their lives their own way.

The more I knew these men the more I respected them. They're here because the freedom they want doesn't exist in towns and cities. Out here where hard work and ability defined the man? This was the life they wanted, respect was earned and your name kept it. The Bar C was a mixed lot that exemplified this part of the west. Some were half breeds from one tribe or another, hated by both sides. Half the crew were black men from back east or the south, making a life out here as free men.

The few vaqueros either from across the river or native Tejanos, they knew the life out here almost like a birth right. The white men were just as diverse, some educated on the dodge for one reason or another. Others drifted in after the war unable or unwilling to return to a civilized life. One and all for whatever reason, they decided the Bar C was their home. It promised a freedom that could only be found out here and to them it was worth the risk.

This is not to say there was no prejudices on the frontier. There were plenty of those who viewed one man or another a particular way because of his color or race. My friendship with Jose got some comments about me keeping his company. Some of the vaqueros said the same to him. It wasn't that I didn't see the differences but rather that I relished them. Cherishing each man for their unique knowledge of the world and absorbing all I could from them. I had learned this lesson years ago on the ship from Ireland.

Jose constantly taught me about the west, James had taught me about horses, mules, wagons and their care. Wayne, a freed slave from a plantation in Georgia, continued that education here on the ranch. He worked with me filling in some of the blank spots on Shades training. Helping turn him into a better cow pony and me into a better rider. The Vaqueros took that further, teaching both my horses and me in their way. Each came with their own experiences and understanding of the craft. I wanted to learn all of it.

Working with Richard and Wayne bringing in wild horses put those lessons to use. My rope work was also fine-tuned and corrected, preparing me for working around the herd. The slow grind of gentling wild horses was hours of patience followed by seconds of violence.

The first time I found myself launched into the air by a bronc was one big lesson in humility. I was definitely not a bronc rider. There was some understanding about wild horses that I lacked. Watching Richard work with them made me realize it. He truly understood the soul of those animals. Their spirit had a kinship to his. I could work in the saddle from dawn to dusk, but to stay on one of the wild mustangs? It wasn't a matter of strength but one of understanding. He instinctively knew what that horse was going to do three moves before they did it.

The vaqueros had a knack for training horses. They could stay on a bronc but their expertise was the work after that. They knew how to make a half wild horse into a cow pony, or a cutting horse. They understood the fine tuning of an animal, knowing in minutes what skills they leaned toward.

Carlos spent one afternoon teaching me to ride Shade properly. That sounds odd considering how much I'd already ridden, but he really sharpened my ability to use my horses instincts. Mostly he taught me to trust my horse. They also worked with Shade sharpening his training, he'd never be a cutting horse but they turned him into a solid cow pony. I began to understand Shade better every day. They joked about riders needing more training than horses, it was sadly accurate. Without their help I never would have been able to ride and work as effectively as I could now.

I got a new respect for the brush poppers especially. It was a job I could barely do. Pretty sure I slowed down Bulls crew trying to help. Tink and Pug integrated with them like a new parts of a well-oiled machine. Again, there was a level of understanding shared with those fierce wild animals I just didn't have. Watching man after man, as if by magic, throw a rope where the steer would be, landing it perfectly every time. It wasn't that my rope work lacked skill, it was my understanding of what that steer was going to do that was missing.

Experience and time would help of course, but in the end there was just something I lacked that they had. This is the difference between knowing something and understanding something. I knew cattle but didn't understand them. Just like with the horses I managed to be useful by sheer force of will rather than skill. I just wouldn't give up. It wasn't pride or arrogance, it was that I needed to be useful to this ranch. That stubbornness made Bull send me back to the temporary pens once because I wouldn't back off this old bull.

"Son, go back to the pens, sit for a while. 'At bulls got your number an if'n you keep at it, 'll kill ya."

"But ......" He cut off my protests quickly.

"Listen son, what your missin' is he's learning you. A couple more tries an he'll know when ya turn an catch ya. Seen it afore...my crew my rules, go set."

That same stubborn attitude kept me busy. Working with the green broke mustangs, I was beginning to understand them a little more every day. They still bucked me off when they got serious about it, but once they started working I could help train one to a point. Watching them train a cutting horse? That was a sort of magic completely beyond me.

Mostly through sheer force of will I started to land more loops over horns then I missed but still lacked the almost instinctive knowledge that the poppers had. I was still amazed at their understanding of those beasts, not just roping them but getting them to do what they wanted afterward.

At the end of the first month, I knew my place. General hand focused on dealing with the human problems, like it or not that was my skill set. I could ride and rope, do everything a normal puncher was expected to do. The more specialized skills though? I was a problem solver, a guard and hunter. While I may have recognized that it still felt wrong to me.

CHAPTER 42

STUDYING MAX

Max had a skill for recognizing where men fit, he seemed to just intuit it. That was a skill set I needed for my own place one day. He worked beside us every day, there was no ego to the man. He would just as readily help muck stalls as he would chase mustangs. I started paying attention, trying to understand what he was seeing.

He never stopped watching the men around him, studying their movements. The first lesson was his ability to stay out of the way. Max did it differently than most, he was a boss who had men around him that he trusted. He was fine just letting them do their job. Never allowing his ego to get involved, he led by letting good men do what he hired them for.

The first example came when we were poppin cattle one day with Max. A particularly tank looking bull rolled out of the brush. His horns were easily seven feet across, his body was nothing but scarred muscle. A truly wild bull whose only want was to run down anything that wasn't his. This specific old bull was known and had tallied up five horses and one man. You could almost see the notch's carved on his horns.

Why didn't they kill him? His calves, they were some of the best animals on the range and he wrangled a large herd of females. A killer he may be, but a killer worth his weight in gold. To a man like Max, it meant you just left that one alone to do his thing.

Bull called everyone back, not interested in testing the ornery animal. He didn't hesitate to snap at Max for not moving fast enough. I couldn't help but flinch, the man had a rough bite to his tone and had just let it go at the boss. Max took it, never said a word about it. He understood Bull was the man who knew this job, he either trusted that or he didn't.

My next lesson came after we started breaking the wild horses. We were watching the bronc riders when it happened. Richard was letting Clint mount up on a particularly rowdy stallion. He didn't make it two seconds before he was launched out of the saddle. The horse had taken a nasty twisted in the air and kicked at the same time. Clint landed hard and it was sheer luck he didn't break his neck.

Max hadn't said anything but when Clint got up he called the man over, ordering him to take it easy for a couple of days. The real lesson was later that night. I was relaxing outside the bunk house leaning back against the wall in a shadow. I had been lost in wonder just watching the stars when I heard Max's voice over by the corral.

"Richard you're a good man, I don't know anyone better with wild mustangs."

"Thanks boss, but I have a feeling this is about Clint?"

"Smart too, care to explain?"

"Not really boss, I flat out screwed up."

"Did you underestimate the stallion or overestimate the boy?"

"The first an was trying to teach the boy something. I had been on that stallion earlier, thought I had worn some of the bark off. Shoulda known he was sandbagging me, damn smart horse that one."

"He is that, ya can see it in his eyes. If you're not careful with him he'll kill someone. It's sheer luck he didn't get Clint a'fore we drug him out."

"Never shoulda put that boy up on that one, but he needed to learn. I still shouldn't have done it, shoulda found a different pony for the lesson. That boy needs some educating damn it." Richard was both annoyed and worried, I could hear it in his tone.

"What do you mean?"

"He's getting cocky boss. Rode a rank gelding yesterday, didn't do bad but he was the third rider. The horse was already worn out. Now he thinks he's ten feet tall an bullet proof. You an I both know 'at'll get ya killed with these animals jus' as quick as them long horns. I wanted him to remember these animals aren't ever to be taken lightly. Picked the wrong horse for it though and damn near got 'em killed."

"Well, I ain't second guess'n ya. I understand the mistake, just remember 'em two boys are as green as they come."

"Yeah boss, sorry about that."

"No need, long as you learned an think maybe Clint learned. Let's hope he did, cause he's sure as hell gonna be sore for a few days." Max chuckled as he said the last bit.

They talked a bit longer, Max ensuring the man knew he held no grudge and wasn't mad, but didn't want it to happen again. I learned what it meant to correct a man, how to do it with respect. Keep it short, if he was a good man he already knew his mistake, you didn't need to harp on about it. You had to let them know you were aware of it but that was all. It was a delicate touch managing these men, you couldn't trample their pride but still had to correct their mistakes.

Max spent his days working from one crew to another, always staying aware of the work going on. Mostly he watched, lending a hand here or there but above all he studied what was going on. There was an air about the man that said he knew everything happening on his land at every moment. More than that the men knew there was no job he wouldn't lend a hand to. He pitched in with me mucking stalls more than once, then had ridden out to help with the brush poppin.

A few hours later he was sitting on a fence rail watching a bronc spin and kick. Always respectfully letting the men work as they saw fit. Always letting the men focus on the doing, while he focused on all of it together. I wasn't learning the bookkeeping or money management end of it but that I didn't need. This part though, leading working men the right way, was something else. Max caught me of course, I shouldn't have been surprised.

"Learning some?" Max's voice asked as he stepped out from around the corner. I had been sitting out watching the stars again when he sat down next to me.

"Seems like every day something new."

"Noticed you studying me for the last while, what have you picked up from that?" He laughed when I almost chocked on my coffee.

"Should've known, first thing I learned is you notice everything." I chuckled once I recovered.

"Goes with the job."

"I expect so. Noticed you don't seem to be a boss in the ways I was taught. Your, I don't know, humble?"

"Humble is one wayta say it I reckon, think about it this way son. I don't need to have my ego stroked to be the boss, the opposite really. All I need to do is help build the new men's confidence while mak'in sure the old hands pass on what they know. Simple really, hire good men then let them do their job an stay outta the way. If you need to lord over others that you're the boss, that's your failing an it costs ya good men."

"Seen that. You're willing to do anything that needs doing, don't interfere with folks working unless you need to."

"Let me ask you this son, your pride tied up in the skill you have with those Colts?"

"No sir, the opposite actually. Never let my pride or ego get ahold of them."

"Same thing being the boss, either owner or ramrod. If you ain't a man when you start, it don't matter how much power or wealth you have...still won't be one." He slowly stood up. When he turned toward the main house he paused. "Last hard lesson I learned. If you end up hiring someone who needs constant watching? Save yourself the time an get rid of 'em right then, ain't no sense in paying someone ya don't trust ta do the job."

The next morning Max called Jose and I up to the porch after chow. It was time to head to the line cabin, Max thought there was at least one more good storm for the year. Once the bad weather ended the gather would start and we would be on nighthawk duty. The cabin would be a good place to use as a base, but we needed to get it set up better first. We would still need to ride the line, checking for any groups that crossed onto Bar C land. Especially when the gather started.

The next morning, we started sorting through gear. We had our winter kit and Max added a couple of sets of woolly chaps the ranch had. Neither of us liked the things but we packed them because the boss said to. There was food, axes, a good saw and other tools for fixing the cabin up. Extra blankets, our clothes, all of our ammo and anything else we could want or need. Once it was all laid out a serious study of the packs and mules started. We were wondering how this was going to work. TJ walked in looked at our mess and just laughed.

"Got everything?"

"Don't think I own anything else." I grinned at the laughing ramrod.

"That is true amigo." Jose offered with his own smirk.

"Well believe it or not them mules 'll carry it all fine, but kin I suggest two trips?"

"Two trips?" I asked not sure why, if like he said the mules could carry it all.

"Yup. I would head ta the cabin, get it done up with half the supplies. When at's done one of ya stay work'n on the cabin. Ta other come on back wit empty mules an fetch the rest. By the time everything is there the cabin 'll be ready ta go."

"I get that, but still why split it up if they can haul it all?" I was confused, maybe my greenhorn was showing.

"Allows the mules ta move faster, get there in two days loaded down or one wit half of it. Also allows for forgetting things."

"Si, I agree. We forgot nothing we own amigo, but who can say."

"Makes sense I was mostly curious, not questioning."

"I'll help y'all load up in the mornin, sort the first trip get it laid out an ready. I'll meet y'all here ta get it loaded."

"Thanks TJ." Appreciating the man's advice.

We got to sorting, prioritizing tools and chow over cold weather clothes and the like. We had it split fairly well down the middle when the chow bell rang. The next morning, we met TJ to load the first round. He changed a few things around then we got it loaded on the mules.

It was light enough that the mules would keep up with the horses easily. They were tacked up and waiting when we got it done. Shade and a paint mare from the remuda I liked. Jose had both of his horses, Desierto and his black mare.

"I know I'll regret this but what's the blacks name?" I asked chuckling as we rode out the gate.

"Jacinto."

"Isn't that some sorta flower?"

"Hyacinth." That was all the explanation he offered, but something in his eyes told me not to push.

CHAPTER 43

THE CABIN AND HUNTING

We headed for cabin while eating breakfast in the saddle, the land rolled out ahead of us in the early light of day. The trip was quiet, neither of us big on small talk. Travel was for once peaceful, aside from a few angry glances from longhorns we didn't see another living thing.

We got to the cabin as the sun was sinking toward the horizon. Thankfully there wasn't anything or anyone in the cabin we had to deal with. After getting the packs off and inside we got the animals into a small picket line for the night. Rather than risk the stove, we sat around a fire outside sipping coffee after a meal that would best be described as edible.

"Definitely needs some work." I said studying the ramshackle small cabin. Some of the wood was rotted in need of replacement. The roof needed a good amount repair work as well.

"Si, if Senor Max is right we will need to do much." He answered, considering the cabin with a more thoughtful look. "Amigo, what do you think if we build a new place?"

"Where? And what are you thinking?" I was curious why he was thinking about adding to our work but had a suspicion he had a plan already.

"Not far there is a cave." He motioned to the cliff wall behind the cabin. "If we build using it we can keep the horses under cover. If Jefe is right and there is a bad storm coming it might be important."

"Let's check it out tomorrow, talk it out then?"

"Si, I think you will like it, the cave will be bigger for us."

We switched watch's halfway through the night, neither of us bothered by being short on sleep. Jose woke up with the first light of dawn and made a quick breakfast. Once the sun was up we doused the fire and headed to the cave.

After chasing out a few pissed off rats we took a good look at it. From the perspective of making it livable there wouldn't be anything to difficult. It was good sized, maybe thirty by forty, and about twelve feet high. The floor was level, and the front was already cleared of brush.

The entrance was close enough to door size, making it easy to close off. A seep in the back of the cave had a natural bowl under it, about six foot long by two feet deep. It would give us plenty of fresh water, hell it was almost a natural bath. Jose thought the water came from deep spring and wouldn't freeze up if we kept the cave warm. The land out front would be easy to build a shelter and corral on.

"You're right this'll be better. Ya think we can get it done in time?"

"Si amigo, it will be some work for certain."

"You do know this is another one of those, I have studied it but only really done it a little, right?"

"I know what I am doing amigo. Mi padre was a builder of

homes, as a niño I worked with him."

"My friend, someday when you're ready I'd like to know about your family."

"Si amigo, someday but not today."

"Yeah too much work to get done, what's first." Just like that we dropped the subject, I could see it was painful for him.

Jose thought that first we should strip out the old cabin, getting all the wood from it we could. Moving the stove from the cabin into the cave would be the toughest job. Before any of that we laid branches and leaf litter across the floor of the cave. The fire got rid of any remaining rats, same for ticks and other crawling creatures. As a bonus it also cleaned the cave floor of anything else.

We moved the minimal furniture out of the cabin, two simple bunks with rawhide stretched across them to hold the bedrolls off the floor, a decent sized table with a couple of chairs. The last piece was a good-sized cupboard that held the few dishes, pots, and pans.

Then we started stripping the wood from the cabin. It took two days because we saved as much as we could but finally, we got down to the floorboards. After stripping them out we set to working the main joists. Then we started preparing them to fit the cave floor.

First we stomped the ash down, leveling the floor as much as we could. Next we laid out a rough joust system, splitting some heavy logs to make a mostly flat surface. It was more tedious then difficult, shaving boards to level an uneven surface. That took a full day to get done but Jose said it would be the slow part, the rest should come together faster. Him teaching me slowed us down a bit more but he didn't seem to mind.

We used a couple of trees to frame in the shape we wanted creating a boarder of sorts. Jose's idea to use a couple more as benches was a luxury we thought worth the time. After cutting them out and shaping rough benches along two walls it finished off the base. When they were set in place with the rough jousts down we started laying the floor.

By the end of that day, we had a solid wood floor shaped out in the cave. We had to use some of the wall boards, but it worked out in the end. Running around barefoot wouldn't be recommended but it was enough to keep us off the cold ground.

It was late that night when we managed to get the beds and the rest of the furniture inside. It wasn't a comfortable night, no stove or door to hold the cold at bay. The cave was starting to feel more comfortable, but it wasn't warm.

The next day was tedious, getting the stove in was easy. Changing the angle and extending the stove pipe was a bit more challenging. Keeping it tight against the ceiling of the cave we stopped it just outside the cave mouth. We planned on running it through the stable before turning up to vent it.

By early afternoon we were cutting and shaping a frame for the door, hauling some heavy clay from a nearby creek to fill the gaps. Making the door was another challenge, splitting wood to reinforce the existing door took the longest. In the end we managed to make a door thick enough to take a 44 round. Once it was hung we enjoyed our first comfortable night in the cave, the stove was more than enough to keep it warm. It was turning out to be a damn comfortable place.

The next morning sitting at a table sipping coffee we planned out the horse stable and corral. Jose suggested building an enclosed stable large enough to keep all four horse and the two mules inside. The benefit of being able to tack them up under cover was appealing. Attaching a simple corral so we could turn them out during the day would be the easy part. Making stables would be another matter but Jose was confident it could be done.

We used the heavy framing logs from the cabin to build the corners. Digging out the holes took more time than anything else but when we finished they were braced solidly. The roof from the cabin went up easily after that, the next day we finished the walls. Before we started the roof we extended the stove pipe to run the length of the stables, this served two purposes. First it would add some heat to the stables, not much but enough to help keep it above freezing. Second it would help keep the snow melted on the roof, hopefully making up for any failures in our construction.

The next day we laid sod over top the cedar roof. It allowed us to fill the gap from the rock face to the wood structure. It was dirty work and took two days but when it was done we had a well-built structure that should stand for years. The following day we built out rough double doors using cut logs with pegs as hinges, then we roughed in six stalls with simple cut logs. Nothing fancy but enough to keep them separate. It also gave us a clear path to exit the stables. If something was going on we didn't want to fight past scared or pissed off horses.

The corral went up fast, both of us knew how to build them. The only hard part was digging the post holes, but no one liked that job. As an afterthought we built a small smoker off to the side, I figured on doing some hunting, smoking the meat would add to our stores.

Then we started chopping wood, there was already a fair amount of seasoned wood that had been done over the last year. We had moved most of that into a covered area we had in the stables. The wood storage was built along the walls to help insulate the stables and make it easy for us to get to. We cut dead wood first adding that to our useable stores, that was until the space was filled as much as possible. The rest was stacked up on either side of the building and kept covered with tarpaulin. We had been at work a little over two weeks and felt pretty well set up. It was time for one of us to head back to get the rest of the gear.

More storage was built in above the horse stalls for miscellaneous things. There was plenty of storage for the food in the cave, so there was no need to sort that out. Jose was going to head out the next morning for the ranch. Most of the evening we just sat around enjoying coffee looking around at our hard work. We could hear the horses in the stalls, which meant we didn't need a watch. Them or the mules would let us know if anything was out of place.

"See if they can spare more coffee, maybe a bit more lamp oil?" I suggested, trying to run through anything else we might need.

"Si, I already have the extra coffee set aside but I will ask for more amigo."

"Wouldn't due to run out." I smiled puffing on my pipe. We had a good set up for the rest winter. The horses where secure and out of the weather and our cave was as comfortable.

"No riding the line until I am back Amigo."

"Agreed, might try to get some game. I'll use the bow, so it'll be quiet."

"Bueno."

The next morning, we got the animals ready to go. When he headed down the road I went back in to change into my buckskins and get my bow. It was time to add some fresh meat to our larder. It would also give me some time afoot close to the cave.

Moving through the brush north of the cave I kept my eyes focused looking for sign while dodging cattle. About a half mile out I came across some tracks, a good-sized herd of mule deer. The tracks weren't more than an hour old so if I was lucky they wouldn't be too far off. Almost two hours later I came across fresh sign and started stalking in earnest.

It took another forty-five minutes to find them and pick out a decent buck. He was a big, beautiful animal but one of four in the small herd and from the look of him not the dominate one. Taking him wouldn't hurt the population, if anything it would help. Ducking under a mesquite, using it to break up my shape and mask my scent, I waited for him to move.

My patience paid off when he crossed in front of me. Slowly drawing the bow back while sighting down the shaft I released. The arrow flew fast and accurate, it struck true. The buck jumped when the arrow hit then spun to take off into the scrub. The shot had been accurate so he wouldn't make it far.

Following the blood trail, it wasn't more than twenty feet before I found the buck bleeding out. Giving my thanks to the animal and the land like Tom had taught me before covering its eyes. I quickly drew my blade across its throat, ending its suffering.

The rustle of buckskin behind me was the only warning I got. Spinning quickly and stepping to my left, my bloody knife still in hand. I came face to face with a young Apache. He froze staring at me in surprise. His knife was in hand ready to stab me in the back. We both stared in shock for a second, then he lunged toward me, his blade flashing in the sunlight.

I moved toward him feeling the ring of metal on metal when my blade blocked his. My left hand swung in tight landing a blow on his ear, knocking off his balance. He rolled back across the ground before bouncing cat quick to his feet. Blade up and ready for me to follow up. When I didn't rush in he studied me more carefully. Nothing got you killed faster than rushing an opponent you thought might be stunned. By not doing that I had told him a bit more about myself.

Neither of us spoke, when we started moving. Circling one another, testing with feints. He worked around slow and easy, trying to get the advantage of higher ground. It wasn't much of a change, but it might be enough to give him an edge. I let him have it, knowing it would put the buck behind me.

There was no hesitation when he got the perceived higher ground, his muscles bunched giving me just enough warning before he leapt. As soon as he committed I ducked forward under his knife, burying my shoulder in his stomach. I lifted with my legs hard, flipping him over my back. His knife slid down my spine, but the burning feeling never came. It was the dull back of the blade that hit me, sliding harmlessly down my back. He had lost track of the cutting edge when I flipped him.

There was a quiet gasp when he landed behind me, but I was rolling forward. Finally coming to my feet, I spun ready to move again. The picture before me made it clear it wasn't necessary, he was impaled on the buck's antlers. The tips protruding from his chest were covered in blood and it was spreading slowly.

Even gasping for air, he was trying to reach me, the hatred burned in his eyes. His last wish was to take me with him, thankfully it wasn't to be. Lunging forward I buried my blade in his heart, my big Bowie easily punching through the bone splitting his heart in two. Then before he bled on my deer I flipped him off the buck. The squelching sound as he was yanked off the antlers hung in the air.

Tossing my rope over a tree branch I pulled the buck up. I made a few quick cuts with my skinning knife to free the hide, a few more cuts and the offal feel to the ground next to the corpse. I wrapped the liver and heart in a small piece of hide and set about quartering the animal.

Before leaving I turned to study the Apache. I recognized him as a Lipan, my age maybe a little older, lean hard muscle filled out his frame. Even in death he had a lethality to him that no civilized man could duplicate.

The Apache buried their dead in a fashion, I didn't have the man's possessions or his pony, but he had died as a warrior. It took an hour to get the grave dug and stack rocks over top to keep the scavengers out. Taking his knife and belt with me I slung the deer across my shoulder and made my way back toward the cabin.

After hanging one of the haunches in a cool area we used for cold storage I started preparing the rest. Cutting it into strips I rolled each piece in a mix of vinegar and spices before hanging them in the smokehouse. Once it had a good smoke going I went inside to cook the heart and liver for dinner. It had been a productive day, aside from the knife fight and I was looking forward to a good meal.

Chaper Forty four....riding the line

One day alone and already managed to get into a fight with an Apache, Jose's going to laugh about this. The meat finished smoking by lunch the next day and I stored it away. Took care of the daily chores around the cabin, made sure Shade and the paint got taken care of, and chopped more wood. Jose made it in by sunset. Getting the rest of the supplies stored away before the light disappeared took some quick work but we managed it.

Jose went out to stable the animals and feed them, while I started cooking some of the fresh deer. I made a quick rub for it using sage, salt, pepper and a couple of chilies I had found. The pan bread wasn't nearly as good, I had managed to learn a few things, but bread wasn't one of them. Jose came back in after I started the coffee and casually sat down watching me with a smirk.

"So, amigo, want to tell me about the new knife?" He motioned to the belt hanging from a nail.

"Went hunting like I said I would." Which made him eye the skillet sizzling on the stove warily, I laughed. "Damn you think I'm that bad?!? That's mule deer not long pig! After I shot the deer this young Apache disagreed with me about whose deer it was."

"And you won the disagreement?"

"When he realized his mistake he was so ashamed he just up an threw himself on the buck's horns, committed suicide right there. Strangest thing I ever seen, but I've heard they can be notionable." Somehow I managed to say it with a straight face. Jose's face slowly scrunched up, trying to parse out what I had said.

"Amigo I am not sure how much of that I believe. Something in your tone reminds me of Chet." I couldn't help but laugh and told him the whole story. He took it in stride, just shaking his head.

"Only you mi amigo would hunt a deer, then use the deer to

kill an Apache."

You know when he said to like that, it just didn't sound right. After diner while relaxing over coffee I looked around, taking in the place we had built. It was defendable and comfortable. We had enough supplies to get us and the animals through the rest of winter. I had felt the chill moving in earlier today, the false spring was ending. I'd bet on frost covering the ground in the morning, most likely we'd see that storm Max was talking about soon.

"Who's riding the line tomorrow?" I asked thinking it was about time we started doing what we were here for.

"You want to wander up toward the Nueces amigo?"

"Yeah sounds good, Shade needs some riding before he kicks a hole in our little barn. I'm about stir crazy myself, if I'm being honest."

"You should be able to ride the northern line, might take a day and a half amigo."

"Works, I'll head out at first light, camp up by the river then head back"

"Bueno."

I slept that night peacefully, woke before dawn going through my normal routine in the space I had left around my bunk. I finished using a bucket of water to wash up, letting the icy bite of the water cool me off. Our cave held heat just fine, the stove made it almost balmy. I filled my cup with some coffee left over from last night then started another pot to boil. When I set the bacon on to fry Jose stretched up from his bunk, I had left him a cup of the old coffee on the table.

"Fried dough and bacon, it'll be done in a bit"

"One of us needs to learn to cook Amigo." He grinned, laughing at the thought. "Cook more than meat. The venison last night was good I admit."

"Was Juan the cook?"

"No, no Juan was worse than you amigo. Your coffee is not bad."

I laughed dropping the dough in the grease as the bacon

popped. There was a quick tinge of pain about the coffee but mostly I felt gratitude. This was an old, rehashed conversation, we both knew neither would ever be worth a damn as a cook. We wouldn't starve but it wouldn't be fun for the next few weeks. While I finished cooking Jose went to turn the stock out in the corral. The temperature outside blew in the open door, it was damn cold. I swore feeling snow on the air. He came back into the cave laughing.

"Amigo I think Señor Max has a sense about this land. Take those fancy chaps. Do not stay the night, it will be very cold."

"That bad? Smelled snow on the air."

"Si, it will be Amigo. It will be a bad storm."

"Had a feeling, makes me glad we got this done the way we did."

"True, you can thank me by learning to cook!" He grinned as I sat the skillet on the table.

We picked our pieces out carefully, eating as we joked about how bad the food was. Sipping my last cup of coffee, I started throwing on my winter coat. Ignoring the wooly chaps but adding a heavy wool scarf before going to saddle up Shade. The sun was just starting to peak over the horizon when I finished. Rolling up my slicker for now, hoping the sun would keep me warm once I got moving. I loaded my saddle bags then tied my slicker across the saddle before I led him out. Ready to start my first day riding the line. When I opened the doors and stepped outside leading Shade I started to think this was a stupid Idea. The wind cut through my clothes like a knife.

I worked my way north occasionally spotting long horns moving through the frost covered scrub. The chill slowly faded as the sun rose, by ten I was tying my coat across the saddle. I stayed focused, studying the land and range, looking for sign of either human or animal. I wouldn't turn down another deer if one wandered my way. It would have to be with my rifle though since my bow was back at the cabin.

The morning was peaceful, about mid-day I stopped to put my jacket back on and make a small fire. I dug out my small coffee pot to make a few cups, warming my hands while it boiled. Sitting on my heels sipping coffee while chewing on some jerky I looked around me. Off in the distance dark grey clouds were moving in, promising snow and if I was right it would be a lot of snow. Once I finished the coffee it would be time to head back toward the cabin, that storm didn't look fun at all. I wanted no part of it after sunset, the cold and wind would be brutal.

Kneeling there I noticed movement off in the distance. I could make out a solitary figure on horseback, heading my way. I reached to untie my duster, subtly slipping the scatter gun from its holster then inside the coat as I put on. Sitting back on my heels holding my coffee with my left hand I waited. My right hand kept the shotgun hidden in the folds of my duster, but I locked both hammers back while the man was still a ways off. No sense warning them if it came to that. The man, riding a nice-looking paint, called out when he got within thirty feet.

"Howdy, mind if come into the fire?"

"Long as your peaceable your welcome, got maybe a cup left if you want it. Ain't great coffee but it's hot. That's just fair warning about the coffee." It was true, I didn't really have room in the small pot to add the cold water.

"Thanks, names John Hardin." He was a thin young man, dark hair and eyes. His voice was apprehensive, expecting some reaction from me to his name.

CHAPTER 45

INTERESTING PEOPLE

"JC Stone, pleasure."

"Drifting?" He asked pouring a cup of the coffee. His face twisted up when he tasted it. "You ain't kidding, this is horrible."

"I warned you. Pots too small to add cold water an settle the grounds." I chuckled swallowing another drink from my cup. "Nope, I work for the Bar C, line riding for the winter, you?"

"Try putting a pinch of salt in with the water, it'll help when your us'n a small pot. Drifting kinda westish, this all Bar C range?"

"I'll try that salt trick, can't make it any worse." I shrugged taking the advice as he meant it. "Yeah from the Nueces to the Rio. The boss has a live and let live attitude about folks. No one 'll bother you, least wise not from the Bar C, unless you bother them.

"Smart move ranch'n this far south, pretty much bounty hunters and outlaws." He was waiting for me to ask but I had already learned that out here a man's business was his own.

"We don't take bounties and don't interfere with folks' business, boss's rules. Don't take from us and we leave a man alone. There's enough wild stock a man can eat easy, same for deer."

"Plain enough." He agreed, visibly relaxing. "Thinking that storms coming, best get ta mov'n."

"Was thinking the same when I saw you coming, didn't want to be rude so I held up for a minute."

"Right nice of you." He studied me for a minute tensing again. "Any reason?"

"Being honest there's two, one curiosity about a man alone out here. Second and the bigger one to me, I'm about to head back to camp and didn't want someone on my back trail that close. Makes my back itch."

The man studied me for a minute, I could see him deciding what he believed and what he didn't. Finally, he must have decided I was being honest with him because he smiled chuckling to himself.

"Fair point, 'ave ta admit I wouldn't want someone 'at close on my back trail neither. You headed back south?"

"Mostly south, then a bit east."

"Works, if ya don't mind I'll drift a bit with ya until we split ways?" Again, he was watching me for some reaction, but it didn't make a difference to me.

"Makes sense." Nodding in agreement before slowly standing up. Easing the scatter gun out but keeping it pointed down. I took a risk turning my back on him to slide it back into the holster, it was calculated but I had a feel for this man. When I turned back to get the coffee pot he was watching me carefully.

" 'At's a nasty bit of work." Was all he said while I dumped the grounds on the fire then kicked dirt over it.

"Tends to help with snakes." I answered smiling. I packed the still warm pot into my saddle bag.

"Bet it does." He burst out laughing, slapping his knee as he stood to put his cup away. "JC tell ya what, I like you. Young an guess'n from the coffee a bit green, but smart and careful. Good traits out here, they'll keep ya on this side of the dirt."

"I will remember the salt trick." I grinned, accepting the ribbing about my coffee, while stepping into the saddle. "But yeah I haven't been out west long, grew up in New York."

"New York huh? How was that? Never been out that way, I grew up here in Texas, Bonham to be specific. Been some years between now and then though." His paint paced with me as we talked.

"Truth to tell, I was born in Ireland came over when I was five. New Yorks a big city, crowded an I caught the urge to come west young. The city's hard to describe I guess, over a million people all in one place."

"Damn, can't even imagine 'at. Too many people far too many. Spent my whole life with folks around, but not close." He cringed thinking about living with that many people. Like most western men the idea sharing space like that just didn't fit with his way of seeing the world.

"Don't think I knew what silence was 'til I got out here. The first couple of nights in Dodge where strange, and it ain't exactly quiet."

"Ain't been up 'at trail yet, heard it was a busy place, railroad an all."

"San Antonio was bigger, but I wasn't in Dodge at the peak of the drives. They say it's a different place when the big herds are coming in. It's still quiet by comparison, New York has this constant hum to it. That many people make a constant noise and there's always something going on."

"Easy to disappear?"

"Easier than being noticed, folks just blur together."

"Might have to make it out that way."

"It's a sight but you don't see folks wearing guns or dress'n like out here. Most folks wear suits, even the poor wear different clothes, maybe more like the miners out here."

"No guns? How's that work?"

"Got police everywhere, still a lot of crime. Wrong alley and you'll get your throat cut fast enough." I admitted evenly. "Folks wear guns, just in a shoulder holster under their coats mostly."

"Sounds like a different world."

"It is." I agreed simply.

We rode in silence for a while, just watching the miles tick by as we worked up and down arroyos, through shallow canyons. The temperature was steadily dropping as the storm got closer. The snow started in the early afternoon, after a few more hours he spoke up again, looking west.

"I turn west up here, been good riding with ya JC." We had stopped a top a gentle rise that let us have a view of the land. The sky had steadily darkened as we rode, and the snow was picking up.

"Same John, nice sharing the trail with you. Gotta ask, you sure you can make it in this storm? Got a decent place to ride it out if you'd like, just one man there."

"Think I can make it, been riding out storms like this all my life seems like." He looked back at the sky thinking for a minute.

"I ain't trying to pry but this one going to be bad, if you're not sure I'd say come ride it out with me." I liked this man, and no one deserves to die frozen.

"Appreciate the offer, I really do, but I'll manage."

"Your choice but you're welcome at my fire anytime." I stuck out my hand to the man.

"Careful what you say ta folks, some are different than others." He said shaking my hand.

"Think I'll take my lesson from Mr. Connors, take a man as he comes. The rest of his doing is his business."

"Then same to you JC." He grinned, tugging his reigns westward moving his horse off toward the setting sun. "Any fire I have you're welcome at but I'm making the coffee."

His laughter was lost in the wind as he rode off, shaking my head I turned east toward the cabin. Another thirty minutes and the snow started to fall hard, not long after the wind really started. Luckily I had spotted the creek that led to the cave, because in minutes it was a full on white out.

My heavy coat kept most of me warm enough with my slicker on top, but I would be damn glad when I saw our place. It was getting dark when a shadow loomed up in front of me. I could just make out the shape of the stables. Walking Shade in I was surprised when Jose opened the door, dressed in heavy winter clothes.

"Amigo! Was starting to think you got lost! Another few minutes I would have been out looking."

"Was a near enough thing when the weather broke. Glad I didn't stay out."

We busied ourselves taking off tack then using an old horse blanket to dry off Shade before brushing him down. Finally putting him in a stall with a good amount of feed. After a quick check just to be sure the other animals were taken care of I slung my saddlebags over my shoulder, and we walked into the warmth of the cabin.

I stripped off both coats, hanging them to dry near the stove and immediately grabbed the coffee pot to fill my cup. The hot bitter brew helped chase off the chill if nothing else. Sitting down at the table to relax I let out a sigh as the warmth slowly started to thaw me out. Jose leaned my rifle beside the table near the scattergun, knowing they needed to be cleaned once I warmed up. Jose still had some stew on and brought me a plate before joining me with his own cup of coffee.

"Anything out there?"

"Ran into a drifter around noon, shared the trail until he split off west."

"West?"

"Yeah bound for Eagle Pass, if I had to guess. Decent enough man, at least to me."

"Some men are good no matter the path they walk amigo."

"He acted like I should know him. Name was John Hardin mean anything to you?"

"Si amigo!" He laughed "He is a very bad man, wanted for several murders."

"Not surprised, he was a bit jumpy when he first came up."

"Amigo fate has set an interesting trail for you." Jose continued to laugh while I ate. The stew wasn't much better than my breakfast had been, the chili pepper he had added helped a bit though.

Snow piled up that first night and left the land buried for the next several weeks. We managed to dig our way out when it stopped blowing but kept our rides short. When the sun set temperatures dropped fast and the snow became too dangerous to ride in. The thin layer of ice that formed could injure a horse or hide a drop off.

The next few weeks passed with us just getting through the last cold snap. We rode the line as much as we could but even the long horns had bedded down. Almost nothing moved, it seemed like everything knew this was the last grasp and all they had to do was wait it out. Then one morning it all started to disappear, three days later the land started to bloom.

It was early March and spring was coming fast to Texas. The real work for the drive would start soon. Our easy time was coming to an end with the beginning of spring. I was standing outside leaning on one of the rails for the corral when Jose walked up, and a thought crossed my mind.

"Say did you think to tell them how to find us when you picked up the rest of our supplies?"

"Si, I did." He admitted smiling a bit too much. "Should be close enough to find us, eventually."

I couldn't do anything but sip my coffee and laugh. It wasn't really a problem, one of us would find the men before they ever found us.

CHAPTER 46

IT BEGINS IN SPRING

Two days later I did find them, or at least Smythe. I spotted his chuck headed toward the cabin early that morning on my patrol. The wagon was struggling to make its way up a small arroyo when I rode up on the paint. I still hadn't named the horse since it belonged to the ranch, besides its gate was rougher than a buckboard.

"Good to see ya Smythe." I greeted the cantankerous cook and got the expected response.

"I bet. Got 'nother wound ya need tend'n?"

"Nope just tired of eating my own cooking."

"An Jose's I reckon too." He did laugh at the admission.

"Yeah, we managed not to poison ourselves, but it's been a long few weeks."

"Ya'll got 'nother spot I hear?"

"Yeah, it's not far from the old cabin but I don't think there's enough flat land for the camp." I had surveyed the land around the cave and the corral took up most of the flat area.

"Jose said 'at, figure on using the regular spot. Leave much wood around it?"

"Should be plenty, we been dragging deadfalls there the last few days. Cutting them when we aren't outriding." Jose figured Smythe wouldn't want to move his camp and we had done some work to get everything ready.

"'Preciate it, make life easier when I kin start with some." I was shocked when the man smiled. "Ya'll come by tonight, I'll have dinner on, the rest of 'em won't be out til tomorrow."

"We will be there, much appreciated. Need anything before I finish my ride?"

"Naw, got everything I need an done 'is enough, figure I know how ta." He grumped as the wagon started to move again.

"See ya for dinner then."

I watched him move off before I started the paint moving again. Today I was riding the western edge of our range, it was usually quiet but was close to Eagles Pass. It paid to be alert anytime you road that near an outlaw camp. To be fair I had to do the same on the eastern border because of Laredo. The thought made me laugh because it really didn't matter which border I rode. I had run into a few men over the last week or so. It seemed like all knew the rules about Bar C range and respected it. Not one of them made a hostile move toward me, most had been friendly.

Men were men, when greed was removed from the equation they tended to be decent. That was the case when I ran into men out here, each man making their own assumptions and acting accordingly. Sometimes it was sharing a small fire and coffee, others it was just a simple nod in passing. There was one rule, aside from ours, that kept the violence at bay. You didn't ask questions, if they wanted you to know they would tell you.

Today though I didn't run across anyone. The long horns were out and about, moving around to shake off the cold. Mule deer flashed through the scrub, just out of sight and range. Life was returning, even the green was already creeping back into the plant life. Spring had come to south Texas and with it came life. Another cycle was starting with it, the hands would be out tomorrow.

Some would start building a corral for the remuda, then wranglers would be out after the mustangs we needed. Brush poppers would start too, picking cattle out of the maze of scrub. Gathering the anger monsters into a herd and slowing starting to tame them just enough to make the trip. Nightriders would take over for both when the sun set, protecting the valuable creatures from all manner of danger. Somehow I would be part of it, I would help were I could and try not to get shot, stomped, kicked, trampled, bitten, or gored.

The first few weeks were full of work and little sleep. I branded calves and helped keep the herd bunched during the day. From midnight to dawn we rode nighthawk, talking or singing to the cattle as they started to gentle down for the trail. It was hard physical work during the day and mentally taxing at night. Trying to pick out shadows moving in the dark, separate friend from enemy.

It was quiet for the first month, exhaustion had come and gone. Now we all rode half slumped in our saddles at night, awake but not as alert as we should be. I had started walking my horse just to stay awake. That was how I found them, they had been looking for a man in a saddle, not someone afoot. I heard them before I could make out their shapes.

"Tell'n ya that pony was saddled." A hushed voice carried from not too far ahead.

"Don't matter, puncher prolly fell outta the saddle asleep." This voice was deeper but still spoke softly.

These men knew what they were doing, they didn't whisper but spoke softly. I couldn't tell how many of them there were, but I knew they weren't here for any good reason.

"Let's go fetch the boys, get this done 'afore the sun shows up."

I heard them walking and slowly followed to sound. They

walked for a half mile and suddenly I spotted a small fire in an arroyo with other men silhouetted against its light. There looked to be about six of them, counting the two I was following. I wasn't sure what to do, gunshots could stampede the half tame herd, but I doubted I could take them all with my knife. I had my bow with me but unless they stayed put for a bit that wouldn't be enough either.

"Jericho, looks like its gettin ta be time." The deeper voice of the two spoke into the dark.

"Why are you here?" The man's voice was like the hiss of a snake.

"Figured it was time." The first man said, but I could hear a hint of fear in his voice.

"Figuring is my job Ed. Get back out there an watch, I'll come when its time." Jericho's voice carried a threat with it this time. "We want all them bedded down good and deep a'for we run in there. Last thing we want is any of that Bar C bunch on our tail. They all need to be kilt in the stampede."

"But how we gonna get them cows if the scattered to hell an back?" Ed sounded confused.

"Ain't need all of em, its too many for the six of us anyways. Just a few hundred be easy ta move an sell." Jericho sounded pleased with his cleverness. It was a shame I was going to throw all his grand plans off.

I listened to the two turn back toward their look out, this would make my life a bit easier. First I needed to look at the camp, maybe find out what I was up against. Slowly I moved though the brush, I had started wearing my moccasins during the night to let my boots dry. Another lucky decision, since they helped me move toward the men unheard.

I got close enough to study them, six horses stood sleeping on the far side. They were all saddled and ready to ride, probably just had the cinches loosened. Jericho was standing outside the firelight watching the two men retreat into the dark. Another man stood behind him facing the fire, knecling with a coffee cup in his hand. Two more lay just outside the circle of light, sleeping from the snores they each rumbled out.

"Swear 'em two could sleep through a tornado." The man kneeling by the fire mumbled.

"I'm going to look an make sure 'em two do what I told'em." Jericho said walking off into the night.

"Damn fools." The other man grumbled. He looked to be older, maybe mid-forties. I could just see the grey streaking his hair around his hat.

I let Jericho make it out of sight before nocking an arrow. In on smooth motion I drew back and fired, it punched through his throat in the next second. There was a soft gurgle and the faint clang of his cup hitting the ground but that was all the noise his death caused. Not nearly enough to disturb the two heavy sleepers.

I worked my way around to them. It was quick work to cut both their throats while the slept. I left them in their bedrolls, blood slowly soaking into the blankets beneath them. I was surprised the second man didn't wake up when some blood hit him in the face. Guess they were right, they could sleep through a tornado, or their own death.

In four quick steps I reached the dead man by the fire and dragged him back into the shadows. Then I scuffed any sign of his death out of the dust before easing back into them myself. It was done just in time. Jericho was tromping out of the shadows heading toward the fire.

"About 'at time." Those were his last words. My arrow zipped out of the darkness and sank to the fletching in his right eye. The point burst out of his skull splattering grey matter into the dark. The loudest part of his death was his body falling to the ground.

That just left the two still on watch. That took some patience, after finding them and waiting for ten minutes trying to decide how to do this without gunplay. In the end they presented the answer for me, one of them said he was moving off to check the other night riders. When he disappeared into the darkness I slowly crept up behind the lone man laying on the ground. My hand clamped over his mouth just before my blade slipped into his lower back. He was dead moments later, his feet kicked twice before laying still.

His partner came back a few minutes later and had no clue he was talking to a dead man. I sent him to his grave before he figured it out. His lifeless body fell across his partners corpse, and I cleaned my blade on the back of his shirt.

Now it was time for real work. Getting the horses wasn't hard but getting the men tied across the saddles took some effort. The whole thing had cost me three arrows, I had to break them off to get the men tied to their horses. I managed to get it done and string all six horses out behind me as I walked to where I left Shade.

Just as I reached Shade it all finally settled into my mind. My job wasn't being a gun hawk, true that was part of it but not all. My real job was making sure nothing happened to the others. My mind had been so hung up on the death that I hadn't been looking at it the right way. Here, now, standing beside Shade watching the sunrise it all clicked into place.

I knew the question was answered, I would never wonder down that road again. Protecting others was some core part of me, something I would do without thinking. It was some part of me, it was why I couldn't just walk away from things. A few minutes later I was riding into the camp leading a string of six horses with bodes draped over the saddles. Just as the sky started to show the first signs of daylight the men saw me. It certainly got some attention.

"Yup, gonna have plenty of good ponies for the remuda." TJ was the first to comment, as always looking at nothing but the workload.

"I'll be damned! I didn't even hear noth'n." Chet exclaimed.

Jose just laughed from where he was crouched by the fire and stood up to offer me a cup of coffee. I took the cup after stepping out of the saddle and smiled at the men around me.

"Seemed like the thing to do." Was all I said before taking a sip of the hot drink. "I'm going to need more arrows if this keeps up though."

"Amigo only you could ride alone and find six dead men." Jose laughed standing beside me, I just grinned.

The End.

LOOK FOR MORE ADVENTURES WITH JC COMING SOON.

Thanks for reading and I hope you're enjoying it so far, someday I have dreams of affording a editor. If you're looking for more by me please check out my LITRPG series. The first book is Tellus Madre. Book one of the Parental System.

I hope you enjoy this and the ones that follow. Please remeber Authors and Readers depend on reviews, if you could take the time to leave one it would be appreciated.

Robert Knox

Made in the USA
Monee, IL
24 May 2025

18098896R00194